FROZEN TIDE

GERARD FILITTI

FROZEN TIDE

Copyright © 2015 by Gerard Filitti

ISBN : 978-0-9963259-3-6

TO MAX, SEMPER FIDELIS

1

As much as he hated to admit it, Jack Reagan was out of shape. The pain in his legs told him so, and he was relieved when he stumbled across a bench atop a knoll just yards from the trail he was walking. He unslung his canvas messenger bag from his shoulder and placed it on the bench, plopping down next to it. Jack lifted the flap and reached inside his bag, searching under the sweater he had shed earlier, looking for – yes! He still had some water left, and greedily gulped it down before letting out a long sigh of relief that would have been comical had anyone heard it. Next he checked his watch; it was just after 2 p.m., and it would take him too long to walk back to the hotel, which was just as well, since he was too tired to do so in any case. Plenty of time to rest a little, enjoy the unseasonably warm and cloudless late January day, and then call a taxi to take him back for a long shower and a much needed shave of his two-month old beard. He needed to look respectable – or at least presentable – for the cocktail reception and the bachelor party that would follow. He was, after all, the best man.

Reagan stretched his legs as he slipped his iPhone out of his shirt pocket, calling up the map to check his location and figure out how far he had walked. It was a little over 6 miles, mostly down Connecticut Avenue, but he had meandered through Rock Creek Park for a bit so the total distance walked was probably closer to 7.5 miles. Maybe 8. Not too bad, considering that his daily exercise regimen was limited to walking down his half-mile long driveway to get the mail, and lately he had been using the car to get it instead. He needed to do better, and this walk had been a good start – pain and exhaustion notwithstanding. Maybe a beach holiday would help jumpstart a healthier lifestyle; he loved nothing more than walking miles and miles by the ocean. Hilton Head wasn't that far away, and the weather would be perfect for long walks. It would be something to think about after the wedding, assuming some other plans didn't materialize.

The phone went back in its pocket and Reagan leaned back on the bench, tilted his face towards the sun, and closed his eyes. Fifty-eight degrees was positively summerlike compared to the single digit temperatures he had left behind at home, up "his" mountain. The thought occasioned a smirk – he could already imagine the inevitable New York Times article claiming this was proof positive of global warming, arguing that civilization was doomed if carbon emissions weren't restricted and a carbon tax implemented. The ice caps would melt and the oceans would rise and all manner of bad things would happen – were happening, according to some – because Man had to be Man, and Man had to have industry and technology. Reversion to a primitive society sounded like a utopian paradise to those on the Left, nevermind that that primitive inhabitants of Doggerland had fared no better against the forces of nature, the only evidence of their civilization now found on the bottom of the North Sea. Somehow the proponents of global warming neglected the fact that the planet had been warming, and the oceans rising, for several millennia. Bad science and revisionist history offended Reagan, but he shook off the thought. He opened his eyes and took a closer look at the park down in front of him.

The park was new – must have been new, since it didn't appear on Google Maps. About two acres large and facing a quiet residential street, the park was bordered in the rear by the knoll on which Reagan was sitting; he figured the knoll itself was man-made, probably the result of bulldozers clearing the several hundred feet of field in front of him and pushing everything to the back. To Reagan's right, the park was bordered by a small creek, now dry in winter, beyond which was an even taller and steeper hillock full of large boulders and dense trees. To the left, the field was bordered by a dense and seemingly impenetrable thicket. A paved concrete path, not fifteen feet in front of Reagan, traced around the edges of the field, with exercise stations thoughtfully located at 100 foot intervals to enthrall the local fitness fanatics. At the right rear corner of the field, about 150 feet away from his bench, Reagan noticed a small playground by the creek, adjoining the field. Replete with a castle and swings, it was just the thing to capture the imagination of the neighborhood kids.

Reagan found himself somewhat surprised by the amount of activity in this little park on a Thursday afternoon when most people would be at work. Perhaps the warm weather had induced people to play hooky, he thought. Not fifty feet away, directly in front of him, a young couple was doing stretching exercises on the grass dressed in matching sweatpants and t-shirts, their jackets crumpled up on the ground nearby. Oddly though, they were both wearing waist packs, which Reagan supposed contained their wallets and phones. Perhaps it wasn't so odd after all, Reagan reflected, since these days people couldn't bear to be physically separated from their phones. The man was doing sit-ups, his black hair flopping about as his blond, ponytailed partner held his ankles.

Another 75 feet or so away, closer to the center of the field, two men were halfheartedly kicking a soccer ball around. They wore matching black polo shirts and shorts, and their jackets, which were resting next to a pair of large duffle bags a few feet away from them, appeared to have a similar design, probably the emblem of a local soccer team. Six more men were just entering the park, also wearing the black team uniform and each carrying a large duffle bag. Reagan supposed they were all grad students at one of the many universities in the area, their darker complexions suggesting Hispanic or perhaps Mediterranean roots.

Two pickup trucks were parked at the left edge of the field, several hundred feet away and close to the street. Four men in the uniform of what presumably was the local Parks Department were hard at work, which is to say that one man was sitting comfortably in the cab of each truck, one man was slowly offloading materials from the bed of a truck, and one solitary man was even more slowly attacking the brush with some kind of trimmer. Reagan had to smile; work crews were the same everywhere. The newest man on the crew did the work, and everyone else looked on, their seniority lending itself to a sense of superiority.

But what really made Reagan smile was the group of schoolchildren making their way down the path to his right towards the playground. Bundled up in jackets bigger than they were, with their hoods up and mittens and scarves aplenty despite the warm day, the dozen or so children were lined up and holding a thick, braided yellow rope, led by their teacher and trailed by an aide. They were singing some song Reagan had never heard before, and laughter and high-pitched giggles interspersed the lyrics. This brought back memories of Jack's own childhood, holding on to the red rope in front of Danny and Brian while Miss Brown led their kindergarten class from Little Friends School to the local park in Queens. *God, that was ages ago*, Jack reflected. Life would have been a lot more straightforward, if not easier, had he turned into the policeman or cardiothoracic surgeon he had imagined himself becoming. Everyone's path in life led somewhere different, but for now, these kids were all heading down the same one, undoubtedly looking forward to the swings and monkey bars and slides, to be followed by cookies and milk and a nap back at school before their parents picked them up.

Supervisory Special Agent Doug Cannon was getting worried. This had been laid on too quickly, and he had a nagging fear that he didn't have enough people. Although he had checked a neighborhood map before deploying, somehow he had missed that there was a preschool or daycare in the area, and so the sudden appearance of a group of children led by their teacher had come as an unpleasant surprise. Cannon checked his watch. It

4

was a good 20 minutes before their target was scheduled to show, plenty of time for the kids to reach the playground at the far end of the park and be relatively safe and out of the way should anything *else* unexpected happen. Like their target deciding to pull a weapon instead of surrendering peacefully. Cannon silently reproached himself; their target may well have been a deserter but he was still a Marine, and thus not very likely to start a firefight in the presence of children. Besides, he probably *did* have enough people, after all. Three other agents dressed as park service workers, two joggers deeper in the park, and two more as lookouts and backup in a panel van halfway down the block. That should be enough, but doubt still lingered.

Cannon discreetly brought his monocular up to his eye to take another look at the man sitting on the bench atop the knoll at the back of the park. He appeared to be in his mid to late 30s, probably around six feet tall and around 200 lbs., with dark brown hair and a beard that was somewhere between Duck Dynasty and the type favored by some soldiers deployed in the mountainous wilds of Afghanistan. The tan bush shirt, gold-rimmed aviator glasses and olive drab messenger bag all suggested a vet, or maybe a soldier on leave. Whoever he was, that man was not their target; Lance Corporal Eggerton was 28 and either 5'8" or 5'9" tall, depending on whether you went by his enlistment documents or his driver's license, and weighed 144 lbs. as of his last physical six months earlier. And of course the hair color was all wrong. The two agents masquerading as a couple doing stretching exercises had also signaled that this wasn't their target.

Cannon shifted his view to the two men playing soccer. They were closer in age and size to their target, but their complexion was all wrong. Eggerton hailed from the cornfields of Iowa, and these two were either Hispanic or...Middle Eastern? *Now why did* that *thought pop into your head*, Cannon wondered. There were a surprisingly large number of young Middle Eastern men in the Washington, D.C. area, many of them students. Some of them undoubtedly Iranian and studying nuclear physics quite openly. In any case, these two men, whatever their roots, handled their soccer ball far more skillfully than most Americans, for whom soccer still remained largely a high school sport. Cannon lingered on the two duffel bags, trying to discern their contents. One was open, and the top of a soccer ball and what looked like a blanket were visible. All things being equal, there was nothing unusual about two men playing soccer in the park. Cannon set his monocular down on the center console of his pickup truck and continued to watch as one of the soccer players knelt down by the closed duffel bag, his back towards the street as he rummaged through it. Even without field glasses, Cannon could tell he had taken out some kind of energy drink and was drinking with his left hand while his right continued to search for something in the bag.

"Heads up, boss. More people coming in," his earpiece reported. Special Agent Mike Franklin was monitoring the park entrance as he unloaded bags of gravel from the pickup truck directly behind Cannon. Cannon turned and saw six more men, wearing identical clothing and carrying duffel bags, walking into the park. One was tossing a soccer ball in the air and catching it as they walked, and Cannon could hear the group laughing even though they were too far away for him to make out what they were saying.

"Stay alert, people," Cannon commanded, his eyes scanning the group.

"Roger that, boss. Looks like a soccer team, right?" asked Ryan Pembridge, the agent sitting in the other pickup truck.

"I guess so," said Cannon, now realizing that he *did* have too few agents to cover a soccer team, a group of children and some guy on a bench if things went sideways when their target showed up.

"Maybe call for backup?" Joe Hollerman asked as he took a break from the rather admirable work he was doing cutting

6

back the thicket. *So I'm not the only one who thinks this is going too fast*, Cannon thought as he contemplated making that call.

The soccer team, if that's what they were, stopped about a quarter of the way down the field. Four of them set their bags down, and three of the four got on the ground and started doing stretching exercises by their now-open bags. The fourth looked studiously around the park and pointed at the schoolchildren two hundred feet away, and the two men who hadn't set their bags down started walking in that direction.

All six agents in the park thought that was odd, but it was Cannon who said it first. "Something's not right here, guys."

Their attention on the group of six, none of the agents was looking the right way when the kneeling man near the middle of the field dropped his energy drink, his left hand racing to extend the folding stock of the AK-74 he was pulling out of his bag.

Annie Jenkins saw it first, her eyes drawn to the standing man 75 feet away from her who suddenly lunged towards his bag. The other one who had been rummaging in his bag was now holding a – *Holy Shit!* She yelled "gun" into her mic loud enough to be heard across the open field, her hand racing inside her waist pack to her service weapon, drawing it and thumbing the safety off in one smooth motion as she started to stand to take aim. Standing proved to be a fatal mistake. It made her a larger target for the well-aimed burst from the Kalashnikov that hit her squarely in the chest. She fell to her right, dead before she hit the ground, her pistol landing a few feet away from her. Her partner had been halfway through a sit-up when he heard Jenkins yell, and he rolled to his left, trying to reach his weapon in his waist pack when he was hit by a second burst from the assault rifle. The bullets tore into his back, perforating his spleen and kidneys. Writhing in pain, he made one last conscious effort to pull his weapon but was stopped when more bullets hit his chest, ending his life instantly.

Cannon drew his weapon from its holster underneath his seat and looked forward in time to see his agents go down. *Son of a bitch!* He dropped to the floorboards just as the second shooter opened fire on his pickup truck. Glass shattering above him, Cannon yelled into his mic. "Taking fire! We need backup NOW!" The backup team on the street would call it in and race in with the heavier weapons they had in the van. Cannon crawled out the open passenger door and dropped to the ground as more intense fire started coming from the direction of the six "soccer players." He took cover behind the right front wheel-well and looked back to see Pembridge crawling out the passenger door of the other pickup, holding a shotgun. Hollerman was crouching at the rear of the second truck, returning fire, but Franklin was on the ground and writhing in pain out in the open, a few feet behind the truck. Pembridge also saw that Franklin was hit, and started crawling in his direction to pull him behind the relative safety of their trucks. They were all pinned down by fire that was too heavy to shoot back effectively. *Shit shit shit!* Cannon thought as he keyed his mic. "Agents down, agents down. We're taking heavy fire. We need backup right the fuck now!"

The ferocity of fire seemed to diminish a little, probably because some of the shooters were reloading, and Cannon risked a peek above the hood. The two men who had just gunned down Annie and her partner were now kneeling side by side, facing the pickup trucks as they reloaded. A couple of hundred feet away, four of the terrorists – they *had* to be terrorists – from the main group were laying prone on the grass, spaced at 20 foot intervals, pouring suppressive fire into the trucks. The tactical situation was lousy, but what nearly stopped Cannon's heart were the two terrorists who had broken off from the main group, as he thought of it. They were walking slowly towards the children at the back of the park. Though most of the kids were still holding that damn silly tow line, some had scattered and were running towards the playground, probably scared and running away from the unexpected and hitherto unknown sound of violence. As Cannon watched in horror, one of the terrorists lifted his AK-74 to his shoulder as he was walking and fired directly into the group of

8

schoolchildren a mere hundred feet in front of him. In what seemed like slow motion, several of the children were hit by the gunfire and dropped to the ground. *Oh my fucking God!* thought Cannon as he was forced to seek cover when a fresh volley of bullets started hitting the side of the truck.

2

Like the agents, Reagan was also looking in precisely the wrong direction when the shooting started, only in his case his eyes had been following the children as they approached the playground. He turned his head sharply when he heard the rapport of what could only be a Kalashnikov – years earlier, Reagan had fired one of those things at a range just outside of Las Vegas and the sound it made was very distinctive – and he saw the muzzle flash as one of the soccer players fired into the couple in front of him. Reagan fairly threw himself off the bench and as fast as he could crawled back behind the earthen mound of the knoll, the better to shelter him from the fire. He quickly looked behind him at the path that had earlier brought him to his bench, and was relieved to see no one on it. *Good*, he thought. *Time to run like hell.* But Reagan didn't do that. Human nature being what it is, he *had* to see what was going on. He crawled slowly forward to the top of the knoll and peeked down into the park.

It didn't take much of an imagination to guess what was happening. The soccer players were most decidedly very bad guys with very serious firepower, which they were unleashing into what had to be cops or federal agents. Reagan figured he must have stumbled across some kind of a sting that had turned into an ambush. Two cops were dead not fifty feet away from him, and now the bad guys were focusing their attention and their fire on the remaining group of cops by the pickup trucks. The two bad guys closest to him seemed to be positioning themselves to flank the cops, and Reagan wondered where the hell their backup was. He didn't hear sirens, only bursts of machine gun fire, occasional pistol shots, and...screaming children!

Reagan turned to look at where the kids had been, and was shocked to see that most were still standing there, along with their teachers, holding on to the rope. A few had run off towards the playground, but most were just standing there and...Reagan saw that two of the bad guys weren't focused on the cops at all but were walking towards the children. *Fuck!* His heart skipped a beat as he realized what the bad guys were planning, even before he saw one of the terrorists – they *had* to be terrorists – raise his weapon and shoot directly into the mass of children. *Motherfuckers!* Reagan grimaced as three kids and one of the teachers seemed to crumple to the ground before his eyes. The rest of the kids just stood there, probably frozen in place with fear.

Damn it, Jack, you've gotta do something! But what? He had a folding knife in his pocket but that was useless against machine-gun-toting bad guys 200 feet away. There was nothing he could do unless...his eyes shifted back to where the two cops lay dead, a mere fifty feet away. Yes! The woman's service weapon was clearly visible on the grass just a few feet from her body, and that wasn't really that far away, not if the bad guys weren't looking in his direction – and at the moment they weren't. *You can do this, Jack.*

Reagan crouched and eased himself forward, fully on top of the knoll, which now seemed improbably steeper than it had before the shooting started. The good news, if one could call it that, was that no one was looking his way; the two men who had shot the cops had their backs turned, and the other two seemed to be focused wholly on the children. Reagan tentatively stood taller, aware that his heart was already starting to race in anticipation. *Be fast but careful*, he told himself as he took off down the mound, his eyes locked on the pistol that now seemed so tantalizingly close.

A few feet from the gun, Jack's peripheral vision noted that one of the shooters in front of him had started to turn around. *Shit! How do I do this?* Reagan stopped practically on top of the pistol and dropped to his knees, his left side towards the shooters. He extended his left leg in their direction as he scooped up the pistol in his right hand. Keeping his weight on his right leg, he brought the gun up quickly to aim at the shooter who was now fully turned towards him and bringing his own weapon up to his shoulder. Jack's left hand quickly joined his right to steady his grip but his first shot went wild. His heart was beating too fast, he hadn't yet controlled his breathing, and this pistol felt more like a toy than the M1911A1 he was used to. His second shot fared little better, but did catch the shooter in the shoulder, knocking him temporarily off balance.

Stay cool, breathe slow, Reagan commanded himself as he shifted aim to the second shooter in front of him, who had just started turning towards him. Reagan shifted his weight forward to his left leg and forced himself to hold his breath, exhaling slowly as he gently squeezed the trigger. Seventy five feet away, his round hit the shooter squarely in the chest, but he was still turning and bringing his weapon around so Reagan fired again, this time higher, striking his target just above his right eye. The effect was like cutting the strings off a marionette; the shooter fell straight down.

Reagan quickly switched back to the first shooter, who was trying to raise and fire his Kalashnikov using just his right arm. Reagan aimed for the bridge of the shooter's nose but pulled the trigger a little too forcefully when he saw the muzzle flash from the assault rifle. His shot missed but not by much, entering his target's left eye, killing him instantly. Reagan's muscles were so tense that for a moment he wondered if he had been hit, but quickly realized that none of the now-dead terrorist's shots had come close.

Remarkably, neither of the bad guys advancing on the children had turned his way. They were so fixated on their own targets that they failed to observe their comrades go down a mere 150 feet or so to their right. For a brief moment, Reagan hesitated, thinking that perhaps he ought to try retrieving one of the

Kalashnikovs. The thought quickly faded; it was too far and he didn't want to press his luck running in an open field. Besides, he had been shooting pistols since childhood and was more confident using a weapon he knew than one he didn't. In the same vein, Jack knew he shot better standing, so he stood slowly, assuming a modified Weaver stance and taking careful aim at the head of the man who had shot into the group of children.

His heart was still beating too fast, but his breathing was well under control as Jack tracked the movement of the head, aiming slightly forward of the movement. He gently squeezed the trigger as he exhaled, sending two rounds downrange in rapid succession. His first shot was too low, catching his target in the cheek and undoubtedly causing a searing pain that lasted half a second until the second round found its mark just above and slightly in front of the right ear, shutting off brain function as it killed the murderer. Reagan adjusted his aim slightly, focusing on the second shooter who was now turning towards him. He again squeezed off two rounds, somewhat surprised by how manageable this Sig Sauer was. It wasn't anything like his .45, but his shooting was just about as good. As with the other target, Jack's first shot was too low, seeming to strike just below the nose. But as with the other target, Jack's second shot was just as deadly, hitting the terrorist squarely on the bridge of the nose.

It had been a scant minute since he joined the battle, as he now thought of it, but to Reagan it seemed like half an eternity. His mind was just starting to catch up to his actions, and again he hesitated. *Ok, now what?* The four bad guys that had been an immediate threat to him and the children were down, and he was miraculously unscathed and not taking fire. There were still four bad guys further down the field firing on the cops behind the pickup trucks, but they were too far away to engage with a pistol and sure as hell Reagan didn't want to get any closer. He could drop down and take cover behind the fallen officers behind him, or he could race back up the knoll for more substantial cover, or he could... *Damn it why aren't those kids running* away *already?* One of the kids was actually walking *towards* him!

More than anything, that made up his mind. Reagan started running towards the children, his gun hand down but his left arm waving frantically in what was the internationally-recognized signal to get back. "Go back! Run! Go go GO" he fairly screamed, gesturing towards the dried up creek. Halfway to the children, he saw the remaining teacher wake up from whatever daze she was in. She grabbed the two kids closest to her and was telling the others to run towards the creek. Reagan slowed to pick up the girl that had been coming towards him and resumed running. Half a minute later the kids, teacher and Reagan were all down in the creek bed, safe for the first time since the shooting started. A couple of children – the ones who had the good sense to run from the very beginning – were hiding in the playground, but they seemed to have solid cover between themselves and the remaining bad guys. His heart pounding, Reagan struggled to catch his breath as he stood and faced the field, his gun up, searching for targets.

On the opposite side of the field, Doug Cannon was surprised to hear the sound of small arms fire coming from where Agent Jenkins and her partner had been positioned. *One of them is still alive,* he thought as he made his way to the front end of the truck, peeking along the side, and... No, his agents were still down but so were the terrorists who had shot them. Cannon watched with no small measure of incredulity as the man who had been sitting on the bench now stood from a crouch, took aim at the bad guys advancing on the children, and stopped them cold with well-aimed double taps to the head from well over a hundred feet away. He was transfixed by the sight of the man running towards the children in an obvious attempt to get them to cover, even picking up and carrying one of them to safety. *Thank God!*

Cannon and his agents were still taking heavy fire, but their desperate tactical situation had improved substantially. They were no longer in danger of being flanked, and the children were no longer in the line of fire. He could hear sirens in the distance, getting closer. His backup agents would be arriving any second at the park entrance with their M4s, and the remaining four terrorists would be effectively trapped. They would have no choice but to surrender, unless they tried to maneuver to the rear of the park, but then they would be exposing themselves to fire from two sides *and* from the soldier – that's how Cannon now thought of the man who had been on the bench – and that guy sure as hell knew how to shoot. The engagement was over but for the shooting. Cannon took aim at the prone shooter on the far right and fired two rounds. He missed and was instantly rewarded with renewed fire in his direction, but that gave Pembridge the chance to stand by the rear of the second truck and get off a couple of rounds with his shotgun. It would go like this for a while longer, Cannon reasoned, until his two agents down the block could get in the fight.

Just then, a loud explosion echoed through the park, and Cannon could swear that he saw a fireball in the street, right by the entrance to the park. *What the hell is this?* Cannon's stomach tightened into a knot, and whatever optimism he had felt only a moment before turned into worry as he keyed his mic. "Tommy, Jay, report!" The silence from his backup team was deafening and Cannon tried again. "Tommy, Jay, do you copy?" Still no answer, and Cannon jumped to the conclusion – rightly, as it turned out – that the explosion had targeted his backup team. Still, the sirens were getting closer and there would be paramedics among them to...Cannon couldn't finish the thought, and realized he was in danger of falling into shock. He quickly forced himself to stand and fired off some more rounds across the hood, this time hitting one of the terrorists as he was struggling to stand.

15

The four remaining terrorists had been so focused on the pickup trucks that they were late to realize that their comrades were down. The explosion was meant to be the prearranged signal to leapfrog back to the street and disappear before more cops showed up, but something had gone very wrong. The shooter farthest from the park entrance stood, and even as he took a round in the leg, tried to run out of the park. He made it all of ten feet before a well-aimed blast from a shotgun knocked him down, and as he lay there, his blood turning the dry yellow grass a shade of deep purple, he wondered what had gone wrong. He would bleed out slowly, never knowing the answer.

The three terrorists still alive saw their leader gunned down and heard the approaching sirens grow louder. To a man, they felt a sense of satisfaction bordering on pride that they had killed so many of their enemy, even though they had taken far more casualties than expected. No order had been given, but each of them reached the same conclusion at roughly the same time: now was the time to withdraw. Each man rose, their collective action reinforcing their individual judgment. They ran towards the park entrance, two of them still shooting in the direction of the trucks to lay down some cover fire. Escape seemed so tantalizingly close, but they would never make it.

Special Agent Jay Tompkins was in a daze and barely able to stand. His mind told him he had been in an explosion but his body seemed numb and strangely disconnected. He couldn't feel his left arm at all, and for that matter couldn't feel his legs, even though he realized he was standing. All he could hear was a high-pitched ringing, his head felt as though it were in a vise, and he could barely see out of one eye. Yet somehow he managed to stagger forward, trying to raise the M4 assault rifle that seemed so impossibly heavy in his right hand. He saw men moving towards him firing weapons, and his mind told him that those were not *his* men. He had to do something, but now his right arm wasn't obeying his commands and he couldn't get his rifle higher than his waist, so he did his best to level his weapon and squeeze the trigger. Tompkins thought he saw his rounds hit one of the bad guys, but then he couldn't see anything at all as he lost consciousness, his finger holding down the trigger as he fell.

Tompkins' shots had actually hit two of the terrorists, and the third was felled by a shot from Pembridge's shotgun that had been more luck than skill. The sound of gunfire was replaced by the sounds of car alarms and sirens as an eerie calm fell over the park. Cannon and his agents maintained cover behind their trucks, as much from shock as from caution, waiting for the lead elements of what would undoubtedly be a massive police response. As the first police vehicle pulled into the park near the trucks, Cannon holstered his weapon and walked cautiously towards it, credentials in his left hand and his right hand visibly open. He needed a hard perimeter, he needed men to check the terrorists and make sure they were no longer a threat, but more importantly he needed medics for his men and the children. There would be plenty of time later to figure out what had gone wrong today, but for now Cannon had to secure the crime scene. His training and many years of experience helped him focus on what came next, and Cannon took command of the responding units, getting information out and directing them to check the terrorists and safeguard the children. First, and most importantly, he had to check on his agents.

Reagan watched the closing act of the firefight unfold near the street, relieved that none of the bad guys had come his way. The children were safe, he was safe, and all he had to do was wait and keep his head until the police arrived in force. The explosion in the street had been disconcerting, but then the shooting stopped, replaced by the sounds of sirens that seemed both angry and plaintive. Reagan saw uniformed police officers checking the bodies by the park entrance, and then watched as two patrol cars drove slowly onto the field. One seemed to be heading straight in his direction. *How do I do this without getting shot?* He engaged the safety on his pistol and placed the weapon on a boulder, standing slowly and raising his arms above his head. Reagan lifted himself out of the dry creek bed and walked slowly towards the patrol car, his fingers spread open so that the cops would clearly see he wasn't holding a weapon. *Hands up, don't shoot,* he thought wryly as the patrol car stopped a few feet away. Reagan stopped walking at that point and waited, his heart beating nearly out of his chest as two officers got out of the car, weapons in hand and trained on him. "Don't move! Keep your hands up!" the driver shouted as both officers started to move in.

"On your knees," commanded the other cop. Reagan started to comply but not fast enough for the driver, who shouted "Get on the fucking ground NOW!" *Jesus!* Jack was now distinctly worried by how on edge the cops seemed. He managed to lay on his stomach without getting shot, and a moment later felt a pair of hands forcefully move his arms behind his back as the cop who had been driving cuffed him and then started to frisk him expertly. Jack felt his wallet being removed from his rear pocket, followed by his pocket knife and cellphone. The officer yanked Reagan to his feet and guided him to the cruiser, frisking him again as his partner covered him. Satisfied that Reagan wasn't armed, the officer opened the rear door and simply said, "Get in." As Reagan climbed in, wondering what the hell would happen next, he heard the officer start to recite his Miranda rights. "You have the right to remain silent. Anything you say can be used against you..." Until that moment, Reagan had thought that all of his actions had been right and proper; yes, he had shot four men, but they were bad guys who had killed police officers *and children* before his eyes. For some reason, though, these cops were treating him in a manner that suggested they didn't hold the same view. *Oh God,* Reagan thought as the car door closed next to him. *What have I gotten myself into?*

3

I should have been there, damn it! Special Agent Amanda Watson gripped the steering wheel tighter as she sped her personal vehicle through the light afternoon traffic, racing towards Rock Creek Park. Today was her first day back with her parent agency after a 16 month special assignment with DEA, and she had been filling out a surprisingly large amount of paperwork when the call had come in. Her team, as she still thought of them despite her long absence, was taking fire, and she should have been there to help. There had been no time that morning for Watson to be brought up to speed on the case her team was working – for that matter, Watson wasn't even certain that she would be reassigned to her old team – but none of that mattered now. The "officers in distress" call took precedence as Watson and several other agents raced to assist. This was an attack on their family, and the "officers down" report from the backup team filled them with dread even as it steeled their determination.

For Watson more than the others, this *was* her family. An only child, she had just turned 15 when her parents were gunned down in a carjacking outside of Detroit on their way home from a date night. The next few years had been hard for her, but she managed to survive both high school and living with her grandparents before heading off to Michigan State to study criminal justice as a prelude to joining the State Police. Reading people came naturally to her, and her tenacity for digging out relevant details from seemingly trivial information brought Watson to the attention of the Naval Criminal Investigative Service during a joint investigation.

That attention had resulted in a series of interviews at Quantico, where she made a strong impression despite her youth and relative inexperience. Additional training followed, and then she had been assigned to the Washington, D.C. Field Office under Supervisory Special Agent Doug Cannon. Cannon took her under his wing and helped her develop her investigatory skills, and although she would never say it out loud, Watson thought of Cannon as a father figure as much as a boss and mentor. She could talk to him about anything, professional or personal, and he always made time for her.

Ryan Pembridge, on the other hand, was the older brother she always – and never – wanted. Every bit as supportive as Cannon, he had the tendency to yank her chain when she least expected it, often teasing her mercilessly when it came to her social life, or lack thereof. More than that, he could crack a joke no matter the circumstances or their surroundings, and humor, however inappropriate, did a lot to help balance some of the awful things that they saw. Mike Franklin, on the other hand, brought a much more focused intensity to the team. At work, he was all business. He often had little patience for Pembridge's joshing and came across as more than a little uptight. But after work, especially when a tough case was finally laid to rest, he was every bit the practical joker. It was widely rumored, but never proven, that after bacon had been removed from the new, health-conscious commissary menu, Franklin had been responsible for the greased pig seen running around their section of Joint Base Anacostia-Bolling.

Watson didn't know the other agents in the park as well, most of them having rotated in from other assignments during the last year. But they were still her family, and her family was under attack. She reached the park just behind an ambulance, and noted that the street in front was already filled with close to a dozen marked and unmarked police cars, as well as several ambulances. The scene could only be described as organized chaos; near the park entrance, medics were frantically working on someone near what looked like the site of an explosion, while farther away another set of medics was rushing a loaded stretcher to a waiting ambulance. Out on the field, she could see groups of

uniformed police officers standing in four separate areas by...
Jesus! That's at least fourteen bodies – including children!
Watson was shocked by the sheer magnitude of the carnage. She
had expected things to be bad, but somehow not *this* bad.

"My God, Amanda, this is a nightmare." Special Agent
Grady Purdue had arrived just behind her, and was now standing
next to Watson with his partner.

"Yeah, it really is." Watson didn't know what else to say.
No words could convey the range of emotions she was feeling.

Purdue put his hand on Watson's shoulder. As shocking
and grim as this scene was, it was nothing compared to what he
had seen at Ground Zero as a rookie cop with the NYPD. "Let's go
find Doug and get things figured out." The three agents headed
off towards the pickup trucks, where they could see Cannon
talking to a couple of police officers. The cops headed back
towards the street as the agents arrived.

"Looks bad, boss," Purdue told Cannon.

"Very bad," responded Cannon. "Jenkins, Barr and
Nicholson are down. Tompkins is hurt bad, doesn't look good.
Franklin took a couple of rounds to his legs but he's stable,
should be OK." Cannon had been so focused on directing the
police response that he hadn't yet had time to process that three
– maybe four – of his agents were dead. *My* agents, he thought.
My fault. He seemed to deflate a little and reached out to steady
himself against the truck.

"What happened?" asked Watson.

Cannon took a deep breath and released it slowly before
answering. "Our target never showed. Instead we got ambushed
by eight shooters posing as soccer players. We never saw it
coming... I never saw it coming." Cannon took another deep
breath before continuing.

"When we got here, those two were already in the back of
the field, playing soccer." Cannon pointed to the rear of the field.
"I sent Jenkins and Barr to check them out and cover them, just
in case. Then those kids showed up." Cannon pointed towards the

21

playground where the children had been gathered up by some officers at his direction. "And then the other six shooters showed up on the field, posing as soccer players. Two of them broke off and started heading towards the kids just as Jenkins yelled 'gun.' It all went too fast. Jenkins and Barr went down before I even saw what was happening, and then the newcomers unloaded with AKs and we got pinned down here. Franklin got shot but we got him to cover."

The agents were surprised by how shaky Cannon seemed recounting these details. Cannon had always been a rock; nothing had ever seemed to faze him before. But then nothing of this magnitude had ever happened, either.

"I radioed Tompkins and Nicholson to get the word out and back us up – they were in a van just down the street. We were completely pinned down here, Amanda. These guys sure seemed to know what they were doing. But this guy..." Cannon pointed to the bench on the knoll to the rear of the park. "There was a guy that showed up and was sitting there. Not our subject. Somehow he got hold of Jenkins' gun and took down the shooters at the far end. Then he got the kids out to safety."

Watson and Purdue silently calculated the distances and traded a look as Cannon reached into the bed of the pickup and took out a plastic bag containing the wallet, phone and pocketknife of the man who had come to their aid. He reached in and removed the wallet, flipping it open, expecting to find... But no, there were no agency credentials, no badge, no military ID card. Just a New York drivers license, credit cards, cash, a charge slip from the Hay Adams, and... an attorney ID card and bar association card? *What the hell*, Cannon wondered. *Who the hell is this guy?* Cannon looked up and he, too, calculated the distances this...lawyer...had shot from. *This doesn't make any sense.* Cannon put aside that thought and continued recounting the details of the engagement.

"Anyway, next there was an explosion at the park entrance. Nicholson was apparently killed instantly but Tompkins still somehow managed to engage and we got the last four shooters as they were trying to bug out." It suddenly dawned on Cannon that the lawyer's – if that was what he was – intervention had somehow blown the shooters' plan. If he hadn't taken out the bad guys at the far end, Cannon and his agents would have been flanked and they would all probably have been killed. Cannon grew angry with the realization of how close the terrorists had come to succeeding. Anger was good right now; it steeled his determination and helped him focus.

"OK then. Grady, Mike, sketch and photographs," Cannon commanded. "Scan and check their prints, and secure their weapons. Get forensics down to the blast zone, quick as you can. I imagine FBI, ATF and God knows who else is gonna try to muscle in, so work fast." Purdue and his partner nodded acknowledgment and headed off as Cannon turned to Watson.

"Are you OK, Doug?"

"I will be, Amanda. I have to be." Just then Cannon's phone rang, and the caller ID showed his Director's number. Cannon paused before answering. He put the wallet he was still holding back in the bag and handed it to Watson. "He's in the police cruiser by the playground. Take him back and run him. Figure out who the hell he is, but don't interview him yet. I'll do that myself when I get back." Watson took the bag and headed off, and Cannon managed to answer the call on the fifth ring, bracing himself for what was to come.

Reagan didn't know how long he had been sitting handcuffed in the back of the police car, but a lot of activity had taken place. The cops seemed less on edge – all of their weapons were now holstered – and more officers had arrived to round up the kids and try to comfort them. Reagan turned and looked towards the park entrance. A large police response seemed to be focused on several bodies, and Reagan wondered how they would get the kids out of there without subjecting them to what had to be a gruesome sight. He set aside that thought and focused instead on his own predicament. *What happens now?* The police obviously seemed to think that he was some sort of criminal, or at least that's how they were treating him. *I need a lawyer,* he realized, and *that* thought caused him to grimace. *Nick's mom is some kind of lawyer, for a lobbying group. Maybe she can refer someone. If she isn't too busy with her son's wedding. Damn it! Well... maybe I can survive a few days with a public defender.* The last thing Reagan wanted was to bother his best friend with this problem. Not two days before his wedding. *Why the hell didn't you just run away, Jack? Why did you have to get involved?*

As he continued scanning the scene behind him, Reagan focused on a woman walking towards his cruiser. Her wavy light brown hair, pinned in a ponytail, seemed almost reddish the way the afternoon sun caught it. She was tall – maybe 5'8", Jack guessed – and thin, but with very feminine features that were not well concealed by the elegant light gray pantsuit she was wearing with very sensible flats. As she got closer, Reagan noted the fine features of her face, which seemed fetchingly beautiful despite the sadness so clearly visible in her eyes. *Federal agent,* he thought. She was far too pretty for how Jack figured female cops should look, and in any other circumstance he would have pegged her for a lawyer or a junior corporate executive. He guessed her to be in her late twenties or early thirties, but Reagan had lost his ability to accurately gauge a person's age. The older he got, the more he saw people as simply either younger or older than he was; she was younger.

The female agent showed her credentials to the police officer standing near the cruiser, and they exchanged a few words that Reagan couldn't make out. The cop opened the door and told Reagan to stand, rather more politely than he had expected.

"Sir, I'm Special Agent Watson, NCIS," she spoke as she showed Reagan her credentials. "I'm going to take you back to my office to get your statement, but first can you give me your name?" Reagan did so.

"Can you please turn around, Mr. Reagan?" Her tone was soft, and her timbre pleasing. Though her smile was obviously forced, Jack figured that she was probably very good at getting suspects to talk. He complied, and the police officer uncuffed him. Reagan almost started to feel relieved, but then realized that the cuffs were coming off only so that they could be replaced by Agent Watson's. At least she was nice about it, and provided some semblance of a reasonable explanation. "This is procedure, Mr. Reagan. I have to cuff you for safety." More ominously, though, she next proceeded to recite Reagan's Miranda rights. *Great*, he thought. *Twice in fifteen minutes. This is getting serious.*

Agent Watson and the cop walked Reagan out of the park in silence, steering clear of the carnage by the entrance as much as possible. Though his view was mostly blocked by the cops working the scene, Reagan nevertheless saw the bodies, and somehow the carnage caused by automatic weapons fire seemed even more gruesome than any Hollywood depiction. The trio stopped in the middle of the street, slightly up the block from the park, and just then it started to fully sink in to Reagan how lucky he was to have survived unscathed. *Lucky is an understatement*, he thought, the vision of the bodies fresh in his mind.

Special Agent Watson stopped dead in her tracks when the trio she was leading reached her car. She realized that her car, along with all the others she could see, were effectively blocked in, and turned to the cop who was helping her. "I'm blocked in. Do you think you can find someone to give us a ride?"

"Sure thing, ma'am," the officer offered. "Where are you going, Quantico?"

"No, DC field office," she replied, and the cop took off in search of a car.

Watson's eyes followed the cop, and she studiously avoided looking back towards the park entrance, where Agent Nicholson's body still lay. Or what was left of it. The bomb blast looked horrific, and his blood was everywhere. Watson frowned, unable to shake the thought. She hadn't known Nicholson except in passing, hadn't seen him in over a year, and hadn't known him particularly well. But he was still family, and that thought occasioned a sharp physical pain as Watson was reminded of the crime scene photos from her parents' shooting. At least Nicholson probably died instantly and never saw it coming, she thought. That was something to hold on to.

The cop waved to her from the perimeter, where the street was blocked off, and pointed at a police cruiser. Watson guided Reagan to it and secured him in back before taking the passenger seat. The helpful officer, whose name Watson had somehow already forgotten, started driving as she angled the cop's laptop towards her. She used her ID to log on to the National Crime Information Center and typed in 'Jack Reagan,' not at all surprised that the search result was "no records found." They drove in silence, each of them lost in thought, trying to shake what they had seen in the park.

Although no record was found, the mere fact that someone had run an NCIC check on Jack Reagan triggered an alert to pop up on a computer screen at the Old Headquarters Building of the George Bush Center for Intelligence, more commonly known as the headquarters of the Central Intelligence Agency. The CIA routinely monitors the searches made by other agencies of names on a master list of "persons of interest." Many, but not all, employees and contractors – past and present – would be surprised to learn that their names are included on that master list, even though it makes perfect sense that the CIA would want to know about outside interest in its own people. Computers made everything easier, and a simple program ensured that any flagged names were routed to the appropriate administrator in the Directorate of Support for further action. In this particular case, the low-level alert indicated that NCIS was interested in someone who had a past affiliation with CIA, and the administrator receiving the alert would need to search a different set of records on a non-networked terminal and assess what that affiliation was before deciding what to do with the information. As it happened, the administrator had left early when his wife had gone into labor, and the assistant monitoring his workstation figured this particular alert was not important enough to merit immediate attention. She had more pressing things to do, and this could wait.

4

Osman Mansuraev pulled over to the side of the road under the watchful eyes of the neighborhood drug dealers not 100 feet away. He put the 1999 silver Toyota Camry in park but left the engine running as he walked away, knowing full well that the car would be gone in five minutes and stripped for parts in a matter of hours. The operators of the chop shop would be very happy to have less work to do, since Mansuraev had already removed every VIN and serial number from the car as soon as he bought it weeks earlier from an elderly widow moving to Florida. Within an hour, he would be at a safehouse, his bushy beard shaved and his dirty sweats incinerated along with the platform shoes that made him a full three inches taller than his lanky 5'7" frame. He would look nothing like the man who had watched the shootout in the park from down the block before using his burner phone to set off the bomb left by one of his men at the entrance. Mansuraev dropped that phone in a trash bin as he walked, pausing a moment later to drop the battery into a storm drain as he pretended to tie his shoelace. The SIM card he had already casually dropped out the car window blocks away.

Mansuraev wondered if any of his men had survived. As good as their training and tactics were, he doubted it; American federal police officers were highly skilled, and had the advantage of calling upon all manner of resources for backup. More than that, they would be enraged by such a vicious attack on them and on the children who had fortuitously arrived in their midst, and the police would show no compassion should any of his men try to surrender. Not that such a thing was likely; Mansuraev was confident that his men would fight to the death. Theirs was a cause that required such sacrifice, and it had been ingrained in them since childhood that death in martyrdom would be met with glorious reward in the afterlife. His brave men were almost certainly dead, Mansuraev thought, and by now the timer in their van would have set off another explosion, hopefully killing some more officers. The loss of eight of his men didn't bother Mansuraev in the slightest. He had many, many more he could call upon.

The church van with Metro Baptist Church of God painted on the side didn't look the least bit suspicious, but Officer Rafael Jimenez ran the plates all the same. He had been tasked to run all the tags on this side of the street, while another officer did the same for the cars on the west side. The tags came back clean, but Jimenez realized that this was the only vehicle on the street large enough to have transported the eight bad guys that had shot it out with federal agents in the park not twenty minutes earlier. All the windows were tinted – which was technically illegal – but that wasn't so unusual. The church busses at Jimenez's church had tinted windows too. He pressed his face to the glass nonetheless, trying to get a look inside, wondering what this church bus was doing here, of all places. Jimenez turned to look up and down the street, but couldn't see anything that resembled a church or community center. His next thought was to call a supervisor over, so Jimenez started scanning faces, not wanting to fill up radio traffic with this seemingly minor report.

The street was now filled with all manner of marked and unmarked police vehicles, ambulances, and even a fire truck was parked farther away by the corner. There were dozens of brother officers, plus the federal agents involved in the shootout, not to mention paramedics and even a couple of men wearing windbreakers with FBI written on their backs. Jimenez saw a sergeant from his precinct by the park entrance and started to head in his direction. He didn't make it more than four steps past the van when the timer inside reached zero, triggering a spark that activated a fertilizer compound sealed in a bottle surrounded by gasoline. Jimenez neither heard nor felt the explosion that sent parts of the van tearing through his body; the blast killed him instantly even as it injured, to varying degrees, half a dozen other officers within a fifty foot radius.

News of this second explosion rippled through the government, attracting immediate director-level attention from every agency with any responsibility for defending the homeland. For the agents in the field, the immediate task at hand was relatively simple; an investigation, even a complex one, tends to be much more straightforward than the process of determining and implementing a policy and coordinating a response. For the agency directors and executives responsible for that process, the confusion engendered by incomplete information from a still-unfolding situation made it difficult to balance a response to what *had* happened with a response to what *could* happen. The rapidly developing consensus pointed towards a terrorist attack directed at NCIS, but it was far too early to reach that conclusion with any degree of certainty. It was possible that the shooters' targets had been the schoolchildren, just as it was possible that this attack was merely one part of a larger terrorist scheme yet to play out.

Despite the uncertainty, the conference call that had just ended moments earlier had resulted in some measure of agreement. For starters, the threat level would be elevated nationwide, and more so at government facilities. Since NCIS was already involved in the investigation that seemed linked to the shooting, it would continue to lead the investigation – for now – but the FBI, whose purview extended to terrorism, would join in as well. ATF would be brought in, in a supporting role for its expertise with the weapons involved. The Metropolitan Police Department, assisted by the FBI, would look into the possibility that the children had been the targets. All of this, of course, was subject to change as more information was developed. But for now, primary responsibility rested squarely on the shoulders of NCIS and its Acting Director, Francis Xavier Smythe.

Smythe leaned back into his seat and briefly closed his eyes, contemplating his next call as his driver sped them across the Arlington Memorial Bridge. The conference call had been borne of necessity, but Smythe's experience as Deputy Director of Operations for close to a decade before his retirement the previous year made him very reluctant to discuss sensitive matters over a cellphone. Even a secure, encrypted cellphone. His time would have been better spent in his office at Quantico, but Smythe had to see the scene for himself. It was his agents who had come under fire, his agents who had lost their lives or been wounded. So he *had* to go there, not just to see the scene but to pay his respects to the fallen. More than that, he had to show his support for the men and women who now had to pick up the pieces, running the investigation while trying to set aside their devastation and grief at losing so many friends.

Smythe fought the urge to call Doug Cannon again; he would be on scene soon enough. The normally unflappable Cannon had seemed particularly shaky over the phone earlier, and Smythe understood the profound sense of responsibility that Cannon must be feeling over the loss of his men. He felt it too. But Cannon was a professional, and Smythe knew there would be no one better to spearhead this investigation. Cannon was easily one of the best investigators Smythe had ever worked with, respected as much for his leadership and development of new agents as for his fieldwork. But for his aversion to bureaucracy, Cannon would now be in his old job. Unfortunately, Cannon's approach to administration was not dissimilar to a bull in a china shop. A china shop filled with red-glazed porcelain. Smythe nearly smiled at that thought, realizing that his own approach to bureaucracy was rarely equanimous. It was just that he had 15 years on Cannon, and therefore more experience dealing with the bullshit.

The perimeter had been expanded to a quarter mile by the time Smythe arrived, and he had to wait for nearly 20 minutes before being allowed to proceed on foot. Agency director or not,

31

no one would pass through the perimeter before the dogs finished sniffing for any other explosives that might be hidden God knows where. Smythe noted the carnage and destruction as he approached Cannon. Somehow it was even worse than he had expected. Smythe waited for Cannon to wrap up the phone call he was on before extending his hand. "Glad you're OK, Doug."

Cannon took the offered hand and shook it as he responded. "Thanks, Francis. A lot of good agents down. I just got word that Jay didn't make it. He died in the ambulance just a block from the hospital."

"Damn" was all that Smythe could reply. Cannon had filled him in earlier on the preliminary details of the shootout and both men knew it very unlikely that Tompkins would survive his injuries. Smythe tried to come up with some words of comfort, but it was Cannon who spoke first.

"I'm trying to set all of that aside and focus on this first. Right now we've got nothing, Director. No IDs on the shooters. We've run their prints and none of them are in the system. Facial recognition is going to be a real bitch – some of them don't really have faces anymore, not good enough for comparisons. We're sending the prints and pictures to London and checking Interpol as well. I also want to send them to the Israelis."

"You're thinking they're from the Middle East?" asked Smythe.

"Just an assumption on our part right now. Hopefully we'll get something that firms it up one way or another. Their clothing and bags are generic stuff you can get at any big box store, so that won't help. Maybe we'll have some luck with the weapons, but that won't tell us much. Same with the bomb residue. It might point us in one direction or another, especially if it's exotic, but then anyone can follow directions they find on the internet. I don't have high expectations for leads from this crime scene," Cannon concluded with a shake of his head.

"Connections to Eggerton? I mean, the timing of this..." Smythe left the thought unfinished, but Cannon picked up the thread.

"Yeah, the timing suggests more than a mere coincidence and besides, the threat board was clear. No chatter about possible domestic attacks on soft targets. Not that I've heard, anyway." Cannon didn't have to add that there *wouldn't* necessarily be chatter about an attack; terrorists had learned with surprising alacrity to mask their communications much better ever since Edward Snowden started revealing the inner workings of American intelligence. "Eggerton never showed. Instead, we got eight guys with assault weapons who did a pretty good job ambushing us."

"That tells us something. Or at least it suggests something, that Eggerton isn't working alone."

"That it does, Director. But the question is, to what end?" Cannon pondered. "These shooters weren't just eight guys picked off the street. Their shooting and their tactics were just a little too good. Hell, if we hadn't gotten some help, we probably would have been flanked and we wouldn't be having this conversation right now." Cannon paused, again thinking about how close to disaster he and his agents had come. "Then again, there's nothing to suggest that Eggerton *is* working with anyone. We looked into his phone calls and e-mails before he went AWOL and nothing was out of the ordinary."

"So we were the targets, then? Unless someone has the resources to use so many men as throwaways, in which case we're looking at something bigger?" Smythe asked, realizing that there were too many unknowns. "For that matter, what do we really know about Eggerton?"

"Not enough, and that's one of the things we need to look into. Let's not forget that Eggerton probably expected to meet his ex-wife here, so it's very possible she was the target, not us." Cannon didn't discount that possibility.

Neither did his Director. "Yeah, I've considered that. I've sent two agents to sit on her and we're coordinating a protective detail with Metro and Capitol Police. What's next?"

"Next? Maybe the canvas will turn up something. We need to look at surveillance cameras and traffic cams. Forensics might give us some leads." Cannon was hopeful, but not particularly optimistic. "I'm going to interview the guy who helped us out. Maybe he saw or heard something. And I need to do a proper interview with the ex-wife. Maybe she knows something, maybe she doesn't, but she's probably the best person to help us build a better picture of Eggerton. He seems to be the key to all of this."

"I'll set it up with the Congresswoman," Smythe promised. "What do we know about him?" he asked, referring to the man who had come to the aid of his agents and helped rescue the children.

Cannon shrugged his shoulders. "Jack Reagan. Lawyer from New York, would you believe? Seems to be a bystander, in the wrong place at the wrong time. Or the right place at the right time, depending on how you look at it. I've got an agent checking him out."

Smythe turned to look down the field and mentally calculated the distances. Impressive shooting, he thought. "I'm going to sit it on that interview. At the very least I want to shake that guy's hand. So, what do you need from me, in terms of resources?"

"Priority and manpower, Director." Cannon paused for a moment before adding, "This case is going to be a real bitch."

"Priority you've got, "Smythe responded quickly. "Manpower will take a little time but you'll have that too." *I hope,* he didn't add. "Until then, use the FBI. There's a Special Agent Greg Capusto on his way down to coordinate. Tell him what you need."

Cannon nearly rolled his eyes at that one, and Smythe saw his shoulders slump. "Problem?"

"Oh no, Director, not at all!" Cannon responded with a tinge of sarcasm. "At best they're going to muscle in and try to take over the case, and at worst – well, you know the adage about too many cooks, right?"

"That's not going to happen," Smythe assured him. "Our agents. Our casualties. Our case," he added firmly. "I'll make sure of that. Whatever you need, tell me. I'm always available."

"Absolutely, Director." Cannon took his boss's hand for a firm shake, adding "And Francis, thanks for coming down." With that, Cannon took his leave to talk to the forensics team that had just arrived.

Smythe stood alone on the field for another minute, taking in the scene. Based upon his agent's description and the layout of the bodies, he could just about picture the firefight that had taken place. He felt a deep chill take hold with the realization that, as bad as things had gone, they could have been even worse. On his drive down, Smythe remembered the shooting at CIA nearly 22 years ago to the day. That had been carried out by one man, acting alone. But this was different. This was coordinated, he thought, and that made it not only worse, but also part of something bigger. Smythe walked slowly back to his car, not realizing how right he was.

5

Time always seems to fly, unless of course you're watching a clock waiting for something to happen. Reagan had been sitting in a windowless interrogation room watching the second hand slowly sweep around the wall clock for over two hours, ever since yet another agent had read him his rights and handcuffed him to a metal bar atop the table. By this point, he could even imagine hearing the silent clock tick. Reagan shifted his weight, first stretching his legs and then flexing his arms on the table. His initial feelings of anxiety and worry about being detained had long since morphed into frustration and even anger at the way he was being treated. The slow passage of time had allowed him to go over the events in the park several times in his head, and Reagan was satisfied he had done the right thing. More than that, he was certain that he was – should be – in the clear; he had acted in self-defense and in the defense of others, and even if some ambitiously undereducated prosecutor should file charges, they would be dismissed rapidly on motion.

All of this made his treatment by these NCIS agents all the more mystifying. *No, mystifying isn't the right word for it*, he realized. Reagan had seen the aftermath of the battle and knew that at least three agents were dead. He assumed that some were injured as well – he had seen paramedics working on at least two. Then there were the children... It made sense that the agents were still reacting to the shooting and probably hadn't given much thought yet about what to do with him. That made his treatment understandable, at least in the abstract. Reagan still wasn't very happy it was happening to him. *I should be having drinks with friends I haven't seen in ages, not be sitting handcuffed to a table, damn it!*

Just then the door opened, and the rather attractive female agent who had taken custody of Reagan in the park walked in. She stopped mid-step, her eyes narrowing as they focused on the table, and she turned and walked out the door without a word. Seconds later she was back, this time accompanied by the male agent who had cuffed Reagan to the table.

"I'm so sorry, Mr. Reagan," she started to say with what seemed like a good measure of sincerity as the male agent removed the cuffs. "I didn't realize you were still handcuffed. That shouldn't have happened and I apologize."

Reagan merely grunted an acknowledgement as the male agent left the room. The female agent – Watson, he remembered – stayed behind, standing next to Reagan. She held out her hand with what looked like his iPhone, and spoke again. "Would you please unlock your phone for us?"

At least she had phrased it as a polite request. Reagan paused a moment, searching for words to reply in kind. "I'm sorry, but I can't do that. My device contains communications and documents protected by attorney-client privilege and/or attorney work product doctrine." Reagan purposely called it a device rather than a mere phone. Anticipating Agent Watson's response, he continued, "Even if you obtain a warrant, I will continue to decline to unlock my device until the issue of privilege is resolved by a judge."

Agent Watson was taken aback. More often than not, people agreed to unlock their phones, sometimes with a little coaxing. She wasn't sure whether she expected Reagan to comply, especially after finding that he had been left handcuffed for a few hours. But she certainly didn't expect a legal objection. Then again, she had never asked to search a lawyer's phone before. *The hell of it is, he's probably right*, she thought. *Damn lawyers, always making things complicated*. She would have to run this by Cannon, or maybe call the legal office.

"I see," she responded, quickly adding "We'll take that under advisement." She almost smiled, thinking her response rather clever. "In the meantime I'll have someone bring in some water. Is there anything else that you need?"

"No, thank you." Reagan couldn't very well say he needed to use the bathroom, mostly because he didn't feel like being handcuffed again and watched by agents as he did so. "One question, though. What happens now?"

"My boss, Special Agent Cannon, is going to talk to you about the shooting when he gets back from the crime scene. I don't know when that will be. Until then, if you need something, just knock on the door." Watson took her leave, closing the door behind her. For his part, Reagan was relieved to be able to stand and stretch properly. It felt like every muscle in his body was sore, not just from the long walk but from the physical exertion that followed.

Special Agent Cannon had, in fact, been back at his desk for nearly twenty minutes when Watson spoke with Reagan, tracking down the one lead they seemed to have. The problem, he learned over the course of a phone call with the FBI agent who had just spoken with the minister at the Metro Baptist Church of God, was that the church didn't own any vans. Someone else had registered the van in the church's name, using the address of a derelict row house in a part of town that wasn't known for its cooperation with police. This wasn't a dead end yet, but Cannon thought it likely it wouldn't lead anywhere. There was a paper trail of sorts, but the papers would probably turn out to be fake. The best they could hope for was that the DMV had a video showing the person who registered the van, but even then, if that person turned out to be one of the dead shooters, they would be back to square one. Cannon was getting frustrated; the past two hours hadn't resulted in a single solid lead. He needed to switch gears, and figured now would be a good time to interview Reagan.

First, though, Cannon needed background information. He never walked into an interview without knowing as much as possible about the person he was interviewing. He set off in search of Agent Watson and found her going through her notes at one of the cubicles set aside for agents visiting from other offices. Cannon sat in the chair at the end of Watson's desk and spoke without preamble. "Tell me about Reagan."

"Jack Reagan, 37 years old, lives in upstate New York. He was born in Queens to Anthony and Allison Reagan. Double major in Economics and History at Columbia, followed by a MSc in Economics at the London School of Economics and a law degree from the University of Michigan. He went to work at one of those mega law firms in New York City and practiced commercial litigation. I found a cached copy of his profile page; his photo matches, by the way. He worked on some big cases and is mentioned in a few things I pulled up on Lexis, but he seems to have kept a low profile. About three years ago, he left the firm and moved from an apartment on Park Avenue to a small town in the middle of the Adirondack Mountains in upstate New York. There's nothing to indicate what he's been doing these last few years, but if I had to speculate I would guess he was spending time with his mom, who had the same upstate address. She passed away last year from a stroke. His dad passed when he was in college, and he doesn't appear to have any other immediate family."

Watson flipped through her notes and continued. "He's clean; doesn't have so much as a parking ticket. He's been through several background checks before, including for a New York pistol permit, which is current. His financials, at least the ones I've been able to get, seem in line with his profession, but I don't know what he's been doing the past few years. He has no social media presence whatsoever, by the way. Owns his home with no mortgage and a couple of cars with no notes. I've been going through phone records but nothing stands out. His only international calls have been to London and Munich, to phones registered to people with the surname Ryan or von Ryan, which was his mom's maiden name. Other than that... well, there's not much there, Doug. He checked into the Hay Adams yesterday and is scheduled to stay until Monday, but there's nothing to suggest why he's in town."

"No military record?" Cannon was surprised.

"None that I could find." Watson flipped to another page in her notes. "His dad went through ROTC. Army Captain, Artillery, one tour in Vietnam but that's all. Went back to trading stocks after that. Maybe his dad taught him how to shoot," Watson added, speculating on the question both agents had.

"I guess we'll find out soon enough. No government work? How about international travel?" asked Cannon.

"No government work I could find, and I haven't received his passport file from State yet. Obviously he's been to England, and I would guess he's probably travelled a bit. But that's just a guess based on a general profile of a big city lawyer. Oh, I did call the Sheriff's Office in the county Reagan lives in; he's not on their radar in any way. The deputy I spoke to said most people up there are self-sufficient and keep to themselves. He described the area as more like the West than what people think of when they hear 'New York.'"

Cannon sat in silence, weighing his thoughts. The information he had just received was very much at odds with his expectations. Reagan's actions in the park had just been too polished, and Cannon had initially pegged him as military or former military. Despite what he had heard, he was having a hard time accepting that a simple bystander could act so deliberately and decisively and shoot with such accuracy. Still, Cannon didn't doubt that Reagan was one of the good guys, and nothing he had heard contradicted that. His skill was a curiosity, but one that would soon be explained.

"I'd like you to sit in on the interview and follow up with whatever comes out of it," Cannon told Watson. "What are your thoughts, overall?"

Watson flipped through her notes one more time before speaking. "My sense is that this guy is what he seems to be, just a bystander. There aren't really any red flags, but the two things I keep coming back to are how good his shooting was, and that he has no web presence. Also, I'd like to know more about what he's been doing in upstate New York."

Cannon smiled at the remark about no web presence. He personally didn't find that odd in the least; Cannon had never bothered with Facebook or Twitter or Instagram or any of the multitude of online social media outlets. But Amanda, at only 28 years old, was part of a generation which lived at least as much online as in the real world. Cannon, stood, still smiling. "Let's go find out," he said, heading to talk to Reagan. Watson grabbed her laptop and followed. The two agents found their Director hovering by the door to the interrogation room.

"Mind if I join you for a few minutes, Doug?" More than anything, Smythe wanted to thank the man who had intervened to help his agents and save the children.

"No problem, Director. He looks clean, by the way. Seems to be just a good Samaritan, a lawyer from New York," Cannon replied.

"Military?" Smythe asked, having made his own suppositions.

"Nope. Surprising, isn't it? Caught me short, to be honest," Cannon offered.

"More than surprising," Smythe said, his bushy eyebrows raised along with his curiosity as he opened the door for his agents.

Cannon walked in first and extended his hand to Reagan as he spoke. "Mr. Reagan, I'm Special Agent Doug Cannon. We'd like to talk to you about the incident in the park this afternoon."

Reagan stood and shook the offered hand as he contemplated his response. He was partly relieved that things finally seemed to be happening after so many hours of waiting,

41

but he also dreaded what would come next. He tried to frame his reply as politely and clearly as possible. "Sir, I am invoking my right to counsel and respectfully request that I consult with an attorney at this time."

Cannon was stunned. He had been about to thank Reagan for his actions, and his mind didn't have time to catch up with the words that came out of his mouth instead. "Why? Are you guilty of something?" he said, instantly regretting his reply. It was precisely the wrong thing to say, and Cannon saw his Director flinch almost as badly as Reagan. "I'm sorry," he offered quickly. "I didn't mean to say that."

Damn it, Doug! Smythe thought, his mind racing to salvage the situation. "Mr. Reagan, my name is Francis Smythe. I'm the Acting Director of NCIS. First, let me apologize for Special Agent Cannon. As you can imagine, we are all operating under a very high level of stress. The shootout resulted in the deaths of four of our agents, and our reactions may seem a little strong in light of that. Next, I'd like to personally thank you for your help in the park. We are all grateful for your actions in saving those children and for preventing greater harm from occurring to our agents."

Reagan hesitated before answering. "I understand." He paused before continuing. "Nonetheless, I would like to consult with an attorney before proceeding."

"May I ask why, sir? For the record, we have no intention of charging you with anything. We believe your actions were fully justified, and that you acted properly." Smythe noted that Cannon deferred to him to handle this unexpected development. "We merely want to interview you as a witness to the attack."

Reagan sat back down and composed his response as carefully as he could. "With respect, your words are at odds with the events of the past few hours. I have been advised of my Miranda rights three times, and spent most of the past two hours handcuffed to a table in an interrogation room. It seems to me that I am the subject of a custodial interrogation and am exercising my rights accordingly."

"I didn't know that," Smythe admitted. The look he gave Watson bordered on hostile. "We have been responding to this as best as we can, but obviously we made a mistake. I apologize sincerely for the treatment you received, and you have my word that you will not be charged with anything. Is there anything I can do to persuade you to talk to us now?"

"I understand what you're saying," Reagan responded neutrally. "However, as far as I know, your promises are not binding on a prosecutor. I'm not a criminal defense attorney, and for that reason I would like to consult with one." He paused, thinking back to criminal procedure he hadn't studied since the bar exam many years earlier.

Smythe saw the look on Reagan's face and recognized that his wheels were spinning. He decided to prompt him gently. "And?"

Reagan hesitated, but decided to risk continuing his thought. "And... well, frankly speaking, even with representation I would be reluctant to answer any questions, absent a written guarantee from federal prosecutors that I will not be charged with anything."

Cannon nearly rolled his eyes at that; *Lawyers! Always complicating things,* he thought.

For his part, Smythe took it in stride. He hadn't expected this complication, but Reagan's request was not without precedent. For that matter, he had to admit, it was pretty reasonable. He couldn't fault his agents for their caution and adherence to their training, but then he also couldn't fault Reagan for being overly cautious. Lawyers will be lawyers. "You mean immunity?" he asked.

"Effectively, yes." Reagan responded.

"I'll see what I can do," Smythe promised, and left the room followed closely by his subordinates.

Reagan let out a deep breath as the door closed, wondering if he was handling this properly.

Several miles away, Osman Mansuraev leaned back into the plush leather of his sofa and flipped through the channels on his TV, settling on a local station that was showing a live feed from Rock Creek Park. The shooting was receiving continuous coverage on all the networks, but the cable channels were mostly running commentary. He had just watched a lively panel discussion on CNN, the gist of which was a warning to viewers about how much danger there was in everyday activities because of the unpredictable nature of terrorist attacks. Mansuraev couldn't help but smile at the irony; the government and corporate mass media were doing his job for him, ensuring that the effects of one attack would be felt by society as a whole. Fear and overreaction went hand in hand, and the panic felt by many people far removed from any realistic threat of terror would gradually lead to increasing restrictions on the free movement of people and goods. It never ceased to amaze Mansuraev how much liberty Americans seemed willing to relinquish quite eagerly for the illusion of security. Not so the Israelis, who had learned long ago that the best way to defeat "terror" was to pick up the pieces and carry on.

The live feed zoomed in on some agents, presumably forensics experts, examining the charred remains of a van. Bright and dedicated as those agents were, Mansuraev could read their faces and body language and tell they were somewhat overwhelmed by the scale of the attack. Good. So far, things were going mostly to plan. Mansuraev knew that about a dozen children had entered the park and was surprised that only three had been killed. Something must have gone wrong, but he shook off the thought. That was irrelevant; what mattered was that Washington D.C. was now on edge, and that was essential to Act I, as he thought of it. Rock Creek Park had merely been the prologue.

Mansuraev stood and walked to the bathroom. He needed another shower before heading out and he took his time with this one, resting against the marble wall as the water fell on him from multiple shower heads. The bathroom, like the rest of the apartment, was pure luxury. The lease was arranged through a prominent local law firm, and the apartment was exquisitely maintained by a management company for visiting executives from the Argentine wine exporter Mansuraev purportedly represented under another alias, Domingo Martinez Vilanova. His shower completed, Mansuraev/Vilanova headed for the bedroom and toweled off as he contemplated his attire for the evening. He selected a black Dolce & Gabbana suit paired with a cream-colored shirt, but decided to forgo a tie. He lingered in front of the mirror, primping himself just so, and satisfied that he looked the part of a successful young Latino executive, headed out.

Mansuraev walked a few blocks north to a Starbucks he had scoped out a few months earlier. He ordered a cappuccino and found a seat near some Asian students engrossed in their laptops. Mansuraev took out his Android smartphone and opened the WiFi submenu. He was relieved that there were still two unsecure connections, probably from the apartment building above the coffee shop. He established a connection to one of them, and then opened an app that provided a random IP address for anonymous browsing. Next, he opened his eBay app and began typing, listing a candy-apple red 1967 Corvette for sale. The only important part of the listing was the end date and time of the auction. The listing was a very simple message to some of his cells, requiring no cryptography or steganography. His men knew their target and knew their jobs. Now, they would know to commence their attack when the auction ended next Friday at 2:30 p.m. Congress would be in session. Mansuraev had checked, and double-checked. Satisfied that the listing was accurately posted, Mansuraev finished his coffee and hailed a cab, heading to a random Georgetown eatery for dinner.

6

Government bureaucracy can move with surprising rapidity, especially when prompted by an agency director in the aftermath of a terrorist attack. It had taken just under 90 minutes, following a conference call with the Attorney General and the Director of the FBI, for the immunity agreement to be delivered to Director Smythe from the U.S. Attorney's Office on 4th Street, NW. None of the men had any reason to suspect that Jack Reagan was anything other than a good Samaritan who happened to be in the right place at the right time, and the Attorney General had even called his actions heroic. It also helped that Reagan was a lawyer; his request didn't even raise an eyebrow, as it would have had it come from some plumber from Peoria. It was a reasonable request, approved expeditiously.

Document in hand, Smythe decided it was preferable to talk in a conference room this time around, the better to make everyone feel more at ease. He instructed Special Agent Watson to escort Reagan – nicely – to a room on the second floor overlooking a bullpen of desks, and Special Agent Cannon joined them there. Smythe handed the immunity agreement to Reagan without preamble, and Cannon set up a video recorder while Reagan reviewed it. For his part, Reagan was relieved both at the palpable change in attitude towards him and at having an acceptable agreement that he would not face criminal prosecution. After he signed the document and copies were made, coffee was brought in and the agents took seats across the table from Reagan.

"Mr. Reagan," Smythe started rather formally, "My name is Francis Smythe. I am the Acting Director of NCIS. With me are Supervisory Special Agent Doug Cannon and Special Agent Amanda Watson. We are going to interview you about the events

46

that took place in Rock Creek Park earlier today. As you can see, this interview is being recorded. Further to my representations earlier that you will not be subject to prosecution with regard to your actions in the park, an agreement to that effect has been executed by the United States Attorney's Office, and you have agreed to its terms. Is this correct?"

"Yes, it is," Reagan responded, nodding for emphasis.

"For the record, can you tell us your name and address?" Smythe asked. Reagan did so, spelling everything out without being prompted to do so.

"Mr. Reagan, first of all I would like to thank you for coming to our aid in the park. Your actions were quite remarkable and undoubtedly saved a lot of lives. On behalf of myself, my agency, and my agents, I thank you." Smythe looked at Cannon to his left and continued, "Doug, can you proceed?"

Cannon had already decided to take a softer approach to this interview, and leaned back in his chair as he spoke. "What brings you to Washington, Mr. Reagan?"

"One of my oldest friends is getting married on Saturday, and I came down for the celebrations. Actually, right about now, we should have been getting together for drinks."

"I see," Cannon replied. "Where are you staying – and, can you tell us your friend's name?"

"I drove down yesterday and checked into the Hay Adams," Reagan responded. He hesitated a little before continuing. "My friend's name is Nick Videtti. He's a naval officer."

"Can you spell that out, please?" asked Watson. Reagan did so, watching her type the name on her laptop and seeing her eyes narrow when a "Restricted Access" notation appeared on her screen. Watson angled her computer towards Cannon, who picked up the questioning.

"Your friend is Commander Nicholas Videtti?"

"Yes."

"Can you tell us what he does for the Navy?"

"He's a SEAL, but more than that I can't really say," Reagan responded.

Cannon frowned, but decided to let that go; it wasn't particularly relevant right now, anyway. "What did you do last night, and today before you went to the park?"

"Well, I got in late yesterday afternoon, just before sunset. I unpacked and sent my suits to be pressed, and then I took a short walk around the block, mostly to stretch my legs. Then I went back to my room and ordered room service, called Nick to ask him what the plan was for today, and went to sleep. This morning I woke up around nine. I saw the weather forecast and decided it would be perfect weather to take a nice, long walk, so around ten I set off towards the National Zoo. When I got to the Zoo, I figured I had it in me to walk some more, so I cut across to Rock Creek Park and sort of meandered on some trails. I figured I could always call a taxi if it got late. Anyway, around 2 p.m. I decided it was time to head back so I started looking for a way out and came across that field or whatever it is. I stopped to rest a little on a bench in the back of the park."

"Did you stop anywhere for breakfast or lunch?" Cannon asked.

"No. I don't normally eat breakfast, and I figured there will be more than enough to eat what with all the events planned this weekend," Reagan responded with a smile.

"Did you see anyone when you were walking through Rock Creek Park?"

"Yes, at one point I was passed by two women jogging together. Early twenties," Reagan guessed.

"Anyone else?"

"No. Not until I got to the park and sat down on that bench."

"What did you see when you sat down?" asked Smythe.

"Closest to me was a young couple exercising – your agents, as it turned out. A bit farther away were two men kicking around a soccer ball. I had them pegged as grad students, maybe, but obviously I was wrong. I also saw four people dressed as park employees working by two pickup trucks close to the street. Then I saw a group of children and two teachers come in to the park, holding some kind of tow rope. They were walking along the side towards a playground in the back. And then finally I saw a group of 6 men with bags come into the park. One of them was tossing around a soccer ball and I assumed they were there to meet up with the two guys already in the park." Reagan tried to remember if there was something else he might have missed, but couldn't come up with anything.

Cannon picked up the questioning. "Did you see any weapons? Anything that struck you as suspicious?"

"Weapons, no. Suspicious? Not exactly. But I did remark some things that seemed odd."

"Odd how? Cannon asked.

"Well, for starters, the couple doing exercises. They were both wearing waist packs. Seems like an odd thing to wear when you're doing sit-ups, for example. Four men trimming bushes, or whatever they – you – were doing, seemed like a bit much. Then again, that sort of inefficiency is probably typical for government employees. As for the soccer players, I guess I still have some old prejudices," Reagan mustered.

"What do you mean by that," Cannon asked, confused.

"When I was growing up, the only people out in the streets during the day were the elderly and the infirm," Reagan explained. "At least where I lived in Queens. Able-bodied men were either at work or looking for work. Yeah, I know, times have changed. A lot of people don't work nine-to-five jobs anymore, but I still kinda look twice at people and wonder. Simple curiosity, I suppose. Anyway, I assumed the soccer players were probably grad students – they seemed about the right age. Besides, the weather was certainly nice enough to play hooky."

"I see," Cannon said. "So that's what you were doing on the bench, looking at the people in the park?"

49

"Yeah. When the shooting started, I was looking at the children. I was remembering how, when I was in kindergarten, our teacher took us to the park using the same kind of tow rope. I didn't actually see the first exchange of fire, but rather heard the rapport of a Kalashnikov."

"You knew it was a Kalashnikov?" asked Smythe.

"Yeah, I fired one at a range outside of Vegas a few years back, and I remembered the distinctive sound. All the AKs I could see had folding stocks. I think they looked like -74s."

"I see," responded Smythe, his surprise not quite showing. The weapons *were* AK-74s, but that's not the sort of detail most lawyers from New York would know.

"What happened next?" inquired Cannon.

"I turned my head towards the sound of the gunfire. I saw the muzzle flash from one of the soccer players, who looked to be kneeling, and saw the two agents in front of me go down. Or rather, I should say, I saw the female agent go down. The male agent had been on the ground and I think he tried to roll away. I didn't actually see him get hit, I don't think. At around that time I got down on the ground as quickly as possible and crawled back over the berm to shelter from the fire. I checked behind me to be sure it was clear and figure out the fastest way I could get out of there." Reagan paused, taking a sip of coffee.

"Why didn't you? Get out of there, I mean," asked Cannon.

Reagan set down his coffee, contemplating his answer. "To be honest, I'm not entirely sure. I looked back over the field to make sure no one was coming towards me. I saw two men from that group of six break away and start heading towards the children, and I actually saw one of them level his weapon and shoot into them. That bothered me. A lot." Reagan paused and let out a soft sigh. "I didn't like what I saw. Those children were helpless and it seemed clear to me they were about to be slaughtered. You guys – your agents, I mean – were pinned down by the trucks. It looked like they were going to get flanked by the bad guys closest to me. And the kids were just standing there. It looked like no one was going to come to their rescue and I couldn't just let them get shot."

Silence lingered briefly until Smythe spoke softly. "So you acted," he prompted.

"I did. I saw a pistol on the ground by the female agent, and it didn't seem all that far away." Reagan paused, searching for words. "No one was looking in my direction. I took off my sunglasses and started to move forward a little, and still no one was looking in my direction. To be honest, I'm not entirely sure just *what* I was thinking, except that maybe if I got my hands on that gun, I might make a difference. At the very least maybe get the bad guys to focus on me instead of the kids. You know, buy some time for them to run or for your backup to show up."

"You knew about our backup?" Cannon was astonished.

"No, not at all. Just an assumption on my part. It didn't take much imagination on my part to figure that this was some kind of a sting or undercover operation gone bad. I just assumed there would be more agents somewhere, probably out on the street."

"Agents or cops?" Smythe asked a little sharply.

"At that point, I didn't make a distinction," Reagan answered. "Some time during the... incident? I saw that the pistol I retrieved was a Sig Sauer. P226, is it? I don't know what the local cops use but that seems to be a favorite of federal agencies and I suppose in my mind I had you pegged as feds. Another assumption on my part." Reagan paused before adding, "I also assume that you weren't expecting eight bad guys with assault rifles."

"What makes you say that?" asked Smythe.

"You were outgunned. At least that's how it sounded. You were returning fire with what sounded like pistols and shotguns, nothing heavier. I assume that if you were expecting this level of... trouble, I guess, your agents would have had better firepower. And that the kids would have been intercepted before they entered the park." Reagan had thought about this at length during his long wait in the interrogation room. He saw Smythe and Cannon trade looks before Cannon continued the questioning.

"Anyway, you decided to go for the gun you saw on the ground?"

"Yes," Reagan replied, pausing to take another sip of coffee. "I don't know if I was thinking I could even the odds, so to speak. But I'm confident in my skill with a pistol, and I did think that maybe I could buy some time for those kids and your agents. No one was looking my way, I saw a chance and I took it."

"Big chance," Watson couldn't help herself from commenting.

"I know," Reagan nodded. "Believe me, I know. But I couldn't just run away and let those kids get slaughtered. I don't think I'd be able to live with myself had I done that. I had to at least try to do something, even if it meant getting killed. Don't get me wrong, I'm no hero and I'm not suicidal either, but... Well, I'm single, no family, no one counting on me for support. It seemed like a reasonable risk, in context. Besides, I wasn't exactly thinking 'you're going to die.' I was thinking more, 'you can do this.' Anyway, I made it to the pistol without anyone seeing me, but one of the two shooters in front of me turned and saw me just as I was picking up the gun. He was bringing his weapon around to shoot at me, but I was able to shoot him first."

Reagan paused, pouring himself more coffee. "My first shot went wide. I was off balance, my heart was racing, and my breathing was too fast. But my second shot caught him in the shoulder, I think, and knocked him off balance. The second shooter was turning towards me by that time so I switched targets and found better balance half-kneeling. I'm not sure about my first shot but the second one was a clean head shot and I saw him go down, so I switched back to the first shooter and managed another shot to his head. At that point I saw that the other shooters still hadn't seen me. The two heading towards the kids were probably too focused on them, and besides this all happened very quickly. Those two were farther out, but I figured they were still in range." Reagan took another sip of coffee – he was addicted to the damn thing, many people had noted over the years.

"For a moment I thought about retrieving one of the Kalashnikovs but decided against it. I was worried about drawing fire and it seemed like it would take too much time, time those kids didn't have. Besides, I feel more comfortable with a pistol, even though this wasn't the .45 I'm used to. I decided to engage the two shooters heading for the kids with the pistol, and stood do so – I'm more used to shooting from a standing position," he added. "I started with the one that was slightly closer to me and aimed two rounds at his head, then took two more shots at the other guy. At least one of them managed to get some rounds off, but they both went down. At that point I really wanted to run back over the berm because it was closer, but those kids were just standing there still, so I ran towards them to get them in the creek and out of the line of fire. After that, it was just a matter of waiting for the cavalry. I contemplated trying to angle my way in behind the remaining shooters, but I didn't have enough ammo for that. I thought it would be better to stay in place in case they tried to run in my direction."

Smythe and Cannon traded a look in the silence that now filled the room. Both men thought the exact same thing – Reagan's actions, as he had described them, were remarkably well thought out. Both men imagined that, had they been in Reagan's shoes, they would have acted similarly. But they were well-trained and highly experienced agents, and Reagan wasn't.

"Why head shots?" Cannon asked, beating Smythe to the very same question.

"In part I was worried they might be wearing some kind of body armor," Reagan replied. "They had assault rifles, after all. Largely though, it's because that's how I'm used to shooting. At paper targets, that is. I seem to remember reading somewhere that 'chest is best, but head is dead.'"

53

"Where the hell did you learn how to shoot?" Smythe asked.

"Would you believe summer camp?" Reagan replied with a smile. He sipped some more coffee and continued. "When I was in middle school, my parents shipped me off to a summer camp somewhere in Pennsylvania. I learned to shoot a .22 rifle and kinda had a knack for it. I made sharpshooter before camp ended. This was back in the day when this sort of thing wasn't politically incorrect," he added. "I also shot a .22 pistol, but didn't get to developing my skills with it. Anyway, when camp ended I went to stay with my grandparents – mom's parents – in upstate New York. They had retired back to Germany but had a sort of gentleman's farm up there they would visit in summer. My granddad taught me how to shoot properly with his Army-issue .45, and wanted me to enter a local competition by the end of summer. The funny thing is, he misread the competition instructions, so instead of teaching me how to shoot at 50 feet, he set up targets at 50 meters. I did OK in the competition, but I was determined to get good at the longer distance so I kept up the practice during the summers when he was still alive." Reagan smiled; he had very fond memories of those summers, his days spent hiking, riding and shooting, and his evenings relaxing by a fire, hearing his grandfather's stories from the two wars he served in.

"I didn't shoot much for years after that, but picked it up again a few years ago when I bought a cabin up in the mountains. Nowadays, at home, I go through a couple of clips every few days, still with his .45. It's pretty much the only thing to do in the middle of nowhere." Reagan didn't add that more often than not, he stood on his deck and trimmed dead branches with his pistol. Surely the agents weren't interested in *that*.

"Very impressive shooting," Smythe offered, the other agents nodding agreement.

"Thanks," Reagan shrugged. "Mostly, though, I had a lot of good luck."

7

The questions continued for another half hour, with the agents trying to elicit any additional details about the shooters that Reagan may have forgotten. They also delved into his personal life, gingerly inquiring about his relationships, work and finances. They discovered that he had left his job as a lawyer to care for his ailing mother after she suffered a stroke, and now mainly supported himself by trading stocks. He lived a quiet and unassuming life in the woods, and clearly had no connection to anything that transpired in the park. Reagan was just what he seemed to be – a bystander in the right place at the right time. More than that, he was a hero, the agents thought. But for his intervention, more children would have died. Probably more agents, too.

Smythe stood, preparing to thank Reagan again and take his leave, but Reagan interrupted his speech. "Just a few things, if I may," he said.

"Sure, go ahead," Smythe replied, sitting back down.

"I dropped my bag in the park, and the police took my wallet and..."

"We'll get your things back to you right now," Cannon said before Reagan could finish.

"The other thing... I'd really like to have my name kept out of this, as much as possible. Especially with the press." Reagan had given this some thought while waiting to be interrogated.

"Why's that?" Smythe asked with a laugh. "You don't want to be fussed over, being a hero and all?"

"It's not just that," Reagan replied. "I don't know about this 'hero' stuff – I just did what I felt I *had* to do. But I like my privacy and my anonymity. More than that, these guys – these terrorists – undoubtedly have friends."

"Undoubtedly? What makes you say that?" Cannon asked with surprise.

Reagan felt uncomfortable, realizing that these agents may not have thought things all the way through. He needed to explain, and reached for his coffee while thinking through his words. "Someone had to set off that explosion by the park entrance, and I don't think it was one of those eight shooters. Did you bag whoever it was?" Reagan noticed that Smythe and Cannon traded a look, one he perceived as uncomfortable, and took that as a no. "I saw the aftermath when Agent Watson walked me out of the park. It looked to me like that bomb was set to take out your backup agents, probably to give the shooters a chance to exfiltrate. From what I saw, the timing of the explosion was just right – for the shooters, I mean. That suggests it wasn't something on a timer, but rather something that was set off by someone with a line of sight to the park entrance. You didn't catch him, did you?" he pressed, noting that Cannon deferred to Smythe to answer.

"No, we didn't. Your speculation corresponds with our assessment. We also believe that there was someone else who set off the explosions, and we're working on it."

"Wait a minute – you said explosions, plural?" Reagan asked in surprise.

"Yeah, there was another explosion after Agent Watson brought you in. A van parked on the street – we think it was the vehicle the shooters drove – detonated, killing a police officer and injuring half a dozen officers and agents," Cannon replied.

"Jesus!" exclaimed Reagan. "I'm so sorry to hear that." He leaned back in his chair and closed his eyes. "This rather changes things, doesn't it?" he added before opening his eyes again.

"How do you mean?" asked Smythe.

"I'll get to that in a moment," Reagan promised. "But first, going back to my request, can you keep my name out of this? Based upon everything I've seen and heard, I am, quite frankly, concerned for my safety."

"We can do that, at least for now," Smythe responded. "There is a lot the media doesn't have and we won't give them, and we plan to keep a lid on this. We're treating the details as classified. I have to admit, though, that it's still possible your involvement will get out eventually. There are a lot of other agencies involved, and this has all the hallmarks of eventually ending up before a Congressional committee of some sort. We'll cross that bridge when we come to it, and please rest assured that we will look after you. At the very least we owe you that much."

Reagan let out a sigh of relief. "Thank you for that," he said.

"What did you mean about the explosion changing things?" Cannon wanted to know.

"I mean there's more to this than just what happened in the park. A lot more, probably. Part of something bigger?" Reagan said softly.

"What makes you think that?" asked Smythe.

"This was just too well-organized, at least from my perspective," Reagan answered. "The attack was too clever, for lack of a better word. And a second explosion to take out first responders? That's as much psychological as anything. Let me ask you something – the two shooters that were kicking the ball around, were they already in the park when you set up?"

Cannon nodded. "They were. I sent two agents to check them out and cover them in case something happened."

"Does that tell you something?" Smythe asked Reagan.

"It suggests you were ambushed; your agents were the targets. The intel behind your sting, if that's what it was, was either faulty or intentionally misleading. Of course, it's also possible that the shooters were there for the subject of your sting. Or the children, for that matter, but I don't think it likely."

"Why not?" asked Smythe, wanting to get the measure of the man across the table from him. "It was a sting of sorts, incidentally," he added.

"It's overkill. You don't need eight shooters and two explosive devices to take out one person. Same with the children – they're helpless enough against one bad guy with a revolver. You don't need eight men with assault weapons for that, and if this was meant to be some kind of terrorist attack against soft targets, with that kind of firepower they could have done a lot more damage at a shopping center or the Mall or hell, the National Zoo." Reagan paused, feeling the need to hedge his answer. "Of course, I could be erroneously ascribing rational behavior to irrational actors, and obviously I don't have enough information to go on. But all things being equal, that's what it looks like to me."

"That's what it looks like to me as well," Smythe admitted.

"What *did* I get involved in – what were your agents doing in the park to begin with?" Reagan asked, finding the right time to finally voice the question that had been on his mind for several hours.

Smythe considered his response. The information was technically classified and certainly politically sensitive, but Reagan was an educated man who had proven to be clever both in his actions and in his analysis. More than that, as a lawyer, he was used to keeping secrets. *Besides*, Smythe thought, *we owe this man. He has a right to know – he's earned it.* "What we tell you stays in this room, and you will consider it classified. Do you understand?"

"Yes, of course," Reagan said at once.

"Your speculation is pretty much dead on," Smythe continued. "It *was* a sting of sorts. We received information early this morning that someone we were looking for would be in the park this afternoon at 2:30, and we set up an operation to take him into custody." Smythe turned to Cannon, adding, "Fill him in, Doug."

Cannon, not normally one to discuss an ongoing investigation with an outsider, was a little surprised at his Director, who generally kept things as close to the vest as he did.

It probably came naturally to the Director, he thought, since Smythe had spent a good many years at CIA early on in his career. "Marine Lance Corporal Lawrence Eggerton was stationed in Afghanistan for nearly seven weeks before he left his unit the day after Thanksgiving last year," he started. "His fellow Marines reported that he had grown more distant and isolative, but there was nothing to suggest why he disappeared. He put on civilian attire, left behind all his equipment and personal effects with a note that simply said 'bye,' and left base in the night. A subsequent search of the countryside failed to locate him, and none of the local population reported seeing him. He simply vanished, and no one has seen him or heard from him since. Until this morning, that is, when he called his ex-wife, Congresswoman Natalie Langhorn of Illinois, asking for her help. He asked her to bring two thousand dollars in cash to that park this afternoon at 2:30, saying only that he needed the money so he could buy some time to figure things out. Congresswoman Langhorn, whom we had interviewed when Eggerton disappeared, called us straight away and, as the Director said, we set up in the park to take him into custody when he showed up. Only he never did."

Reagan leaned back in his chair, contemplating what he just heard. None of this had made the news, which he read voraciously on his high speed internet connection deep in the woods. Then again, this wasn't the sort of thing to make the news. "There's a lot more to this shooting, isn't there?" he said softly.

"What do you mean?" Cannon asked.

Reagan shrugged his shoulders and half waved his right hand, as though brushing away his remark. "I'm only speculating, and I'm sure that's neither relevant nor useful to you."

"You'd be surprised," Smythe interjected. "I'd like to hear your speculation, Mr. Reagan. In my experience, sometimes it's helpful to get an outside perspective on things, to hear from someone who is more detached from a situation. Besides, so far your assessment – or your speculation, as you call it – has been pretty much right on the money."

"OK then, does Eggerton have any language skills – Pashto or Farsi?" Reagan inquired.

"None that we know of," replied Smythe, already knowing what Reagan was probably going to say next.

"Well, that suggests to me that someone is lying, either Eggerton about his language ability or the local population about not seeing him. I find it hard to believe that he could travel around with no language skills and without being seen. Without being taken prisoner or hostage, for that matter. More than that, there's the question of how he was able to get back to the United States without help; I'm assuming that he's on some kind of watchlist?"

"He is, and we have no record of him coming back to the States," Canon answered. "It's something we're looking into."

"For that matter, do you even really know that he's *in* the States?" Reagan asked.

"Huh? How do you mean?" Cannon was as perplexed as his colleagues, Reagan noted.

"I mean, did you trace the call?"

"Yeah, the number came back as registered to a VoIP provider," Cannon replied.

"Well then, unless someone saw him at the park, or somewhere else, how do you know he didn't call his ex-wife from, say, Kabul, using Skype?" Reagan pressed.

Smythe looked at Cannon, who merely looked uncomfortable. Clearly he hadn't considered that possibility yet. "We don't know, actually. But we'll look into that," Cannon promised his Director.

"What else?" Smythe asked Reagan.

"I don't know, Director. As I said, I'm just speculating here. It just seems to me there's a lot more going on here, something I'm not seeing." Reagan paused, trying to organize his thoughts. "It seems clear to me that the shooters in the park are somehow linked to Eggerton, either working with him or...maybe working against him, even. It's hard to believe that their presence was just a coincidence. Not when there are so many other targets for eight bad guys with assault rifles. Maybe the Congresswoman was the target, but as I said earlier, it strikes me as overkill. Why use eight shooters on a soft target? Unless maybe someone is sending a message. But even then, there are plenty of bigger targets other than some relatively unknown elected official." Reagan stopped, realizing that he was rambling. "Sorry guys, it's hard to organize my thoughts and I'm just rambling now."

"No, please go on, Mr. Reagan," Smythe commanded.

"It just doesn't make sense," Reagan continued, his mind trying to reconcile conflicting thoughts. "Does Eggerton have any gripes with NCIS or with his ex-wife?"

"Not that we know of," Cannon responded. "He wasn't on our radar before he disappeared, and the divorce was years ago and not contentious."

"And now, I assume, you have an APB or BOLO or whatever you call it out for him?" Reagan asked.

"Yeah, a B.O.L.O. Right after the shooting," Cannon replied.

"OK, so we have no clear motive and the shooting actually makes things tougher for Eggerton since now it isn't just NCIS looking for him but everyone. It doesn't make sense," Reagan repeated.

"You're assuming that the shooters were working with Eggerton, and that may not be the case," Smythe pointed out. "Besides, what motivates a person to do something isn't always clear or even readily explainable. Crazy doesn't need a reason."

"You're right," Reagan admitted. "So let's replace 'working with' with 'connected to' - it's hard to dismiss the shooters as coincidence. It's true that crazy doesn't need a reason, but I think that applies more to one person, acting alone. Look at the CIA shooting in...1993, I think. But when you have people acting in concert, you have a conspiracy. Conspirators have a common purpose or aim, and to some extent each individual conspirator at some point calculates that he will derive some benefit acting in concert with others instead of acting alone. So the question becomes, how did these nine individuals – I'm including the person that set off the bombs – think they would benefit from attacking federal agents, or a Congresswoman, or children. The only explanation that makes sense to me is that the benefit they derived was to prevent Eggerton's capture, and *that* suggests there's a lot more to this story than just what happened in the park."

Reagan paused to sip his coffee before continuing. "Of course, all of this is supposition built upon speculation, and I'm ascribing my own logic and biases to individuals who could very well have an entirely different thought process and different motivations. This *could* just be a terrorist attack on targets of opportunity, but it doesn't feel that way to me. As shocking and appalling as shooting children in a playground is, there are a lot of even bigger targets for eight or nine bad guys with assault rifles and explosives."

Smythe leaned back in his chair and considered Reagan's analysis. He was right; it was an awful lot of supposition, speculation and conjecture. But the analysis felt right all the same, and Smythe had been thinking along the same lines earlier. Hearing someone else reach the same conclusion, however tenuous, was helpful, but only in the abstract. They still had an investigation to run, and the facts would speak for themselves. Smythe looked at Cannon and Watson and could tell that his agents were mulling over what they had just heard.

"Assuming Mr. Reagan is right and the shooters were there to prevent us from bringing in Eggerton, how does that affect the investigation?" Smythe asked Cannon.

"It doesn't, really," Cannon replied. "It just adds a sense of urgency."

"Out of curiosity, Mr. Reagan, what would you look at to firm up your analysis?" Smythe asked next.

"I'd look at the shooters, of course, and whatever evidence can be gathered about them. But mostly I would want to know more about Eggerton. I think he's somehow at the center of all this, and if you look into him enough you'll get to the shooters and the guy that got away," Reagan responded confidently. "What else can you tell me about Eggerton?" he asked Cannon.

"Not all that much, unfortunately," Cannon answered. "I looked through the workup we did on him last year and, quite frankly, there isn't much there."

"I wouldn't mind seeing that workup," Reagan said quickly. "It's more than idle curiosity on my part, mind you. I feel like I sort of have a stake in this, if you know what I mean," he added.

"Fancy yourself an investigator, do you?" Cannon asked wryly but with some measure of humor in his voice.

"Oh, I harbor no illusion – or delusion, for that matter – that I'm any kind of special agent," Reagan replied with a laugh. "But I *am* a litigator, and what I do is argue the law as it applies to the facts of a case. I get those facts through discovery, looking at documents, interviewing people and deposing them. In a manner of speaking, part of my job entails being an investigator, just with different tools and guidelines than you have. Sorry," he added, "it was presumptuous of me to ask."

Smythe took in the exchange with a smile that faded as he swiveled his chair to look out the conference room window to his agents working in the bullpen. A good many of them appeared to be hard at work, a look of focused determination on their faces. But just as many seemed to be lost in their thoughts, distraught at the shock of losing so many friends and colleagues. His agency was reeling from the attack, Smythe realized, just when time was of the essence and everyone needed to focus. *We might not have the manpower we need*, he thought. Even though Smythe had over a thousand agents working across the globe to call on for support, the main task of running this investigation fell to the men and women he saw in front of him, and he wasn't entirely happy with what he saw. *If we can't do this, the FBI will take over and* that *will be one more devastating blow to the Agency.* He turned to look at Reagan, noting the curiosity that went hand in hand with intellect. *Why not... what do we have to lose? This guy seems sharp enough,* he thought. *Maybe he'll see something we don't. At the very least, an extra set of eyes can't hurt.*

"My son-in-law is a lawyer. Used to be, anyway. He got a real estate license and now he's flipping houses. Did you know that, Doug?" Smythe asked, turning towards Cannon. "He used to work at one of those big firms, too. He hated being a lawyer. He was always complaining that all he did was go through documents and summarize interrogatories and depositions. Never got a chance to practice 'real law,' as he called it, but he definitely learned a lot about investigations. What can it hurt?"

Cannon, for his part, was not happy at the thought of an outsider getting involved in their investigation. However smart Reagan seemed, he was likely to be more of a nuisance, or at best a hindrance, than any real help. Smythe was a good judge of character, however, and had a talent for reading people second to none. "Why not?" he replied, deferring to his boss if not quite agreeing wholeheartedly. "Just so we're clear, you can't discuss this with anyone outside this building," he told Reagan.

"Understood," Reagan responded.

"Why don't you set him up at a desk next to yours," Cannon told Watson. "Go through Eggerton's file as well; I want you fully up to speed on this."

"You got it, boss," Watson answered, very much surprised that a civilian was being allowed access to their investigation. *He seems smart enough, but still...* she let the thought linger as she stood to escort Reagan.

Smythe stood as well, reaching into his pocket for a business card, which he handed to Reagan. "If you find something, or there's anything you need, call me. My cellphone is always handy." He shook Reagan's hand warmly, adding, "Thanks again for your help. Both in the park and now."

8

Time hardly seems to move when one is engrossed in work, and Special Agent Watson was surprised to realize it was already close to midnight. Unlike most people her age, Watson actually wore a watch, although she hadn't looked at it since the interview with Reagan had ended many hours earlier. She looked across at where he was sitting and saw that he was still reading files on the computer, pausing occasionally to scribble notes. Interestingly enough, she had practically forgotten that he was still there; they hadn't spoken since she showed him how to pull up the files he wanted. It had taken Reagan all of five minutes to figure out how to use the file server, something that normally required new agents a ninety minute presentation from the IT people to figure out. She had smiled politely when he grumbled about preferring paper documents, and the extent of their interaction since then had been pointing out where the bathroom was. Defying Cannon's expectations, whispered in her ear after the interview, Reagan had been neither a nuisance nor a hindrance. In fact, his presence was oddly comforting; it somehow felt good to know that someone else was there, in this isolated corner of the office, going through the same material.

Watson needed a break, and decided to walk over to Reagan and check on him. He was angled away from her, writing some notes while listening to music. She waited until he finished writing before tapping him on his shoulder. "What are you listening to, Mr. Reagan?" she asked after he removed his earbuds.

"Mozart Horn Concertos," Reagan responded. "And the name's Jack, by the way."

"Ok Jack, my name is Amanda," she replied. "I see you're still with us. Don't you have a wedding to take part in?" she asked with a smile.

"Not until Saturday," Reagan answered, checking his watch. "Tomorrow was set aside to rest and recover from tonight, but I called earlier and made my excuses."

Watson had heard part of that conversation earlier, and had been greatly surprised at the vague and unassuming way he had described his involvement to what had to be one of his best friends. "I got caught up in an incident in Rock Creek Park," he had said. "Some federal agents and children were killed. I'm fine – I'll be down at NCIS for a while." Hardly a full and accurate description of events, Watson had thought, observing that this lawyer from New York was full of surprises and not at all what she expected. All things considered, she found Reagan to be very intriguing.

"What are you looking at – anything interesting?" she asked.

"I started with his jacket, or whatever you call his service record, and now I'm going through the transcripts of his squad's interviews with NCIS," he replied as he stretched his arms above his head. "This stuff is more interesting for what's not in it than for what is," he added.

"How do you mean?" asked Watson, pulling up a chair.

"For starters, how does a boy from Iowa farm country with no family history of military service end up in the Marine Corps? I mean, he dropped out of Iowa State with mediocre grades after a little over two years, and then stumbled around some. Farm hand, would-be rodeo rider, then moved to Chicago where he tended bar and worked as a mechanic. Met, married and then divorced a somewhat older woman who went on to successfully run for Congress," Reagan recited from memory. "Eggerton seems better suited to life as a drifter than as a Marine. His stated purpose for joining is suitably patriotic, at least as it's written in his file, but I would have expected some degree of self-reflection. I wonder what he was expecting from life as a Marine," he added.

"Whatever he was expecting, he must have been satisfied enough, since he re-upped at the end of his enlistment," Watson replied.

"Maybe," Reagan allowed. "But keep in mind that this was an Obama enlistment; that is to say, he enlisted after Obama's first election. People who enlisted after September 11 knew we were in a war, and knew we were going to war. People who enlisted after Obama heard his promises to withdraw our forces and end our involvement in wars, so expectations were different. Besides, Eggerton wasn't deployed overseas until well into his re-enlistment, so it's possible that change played a role in why he left his unit."

"Very possible, but that's just speculation," Watson pointed out.

"Agreed," Reagan nodded. "That brings me to the information that is most notably absent, namely what Eggerton was doing in Afghanistan. I haven't gotten to the interviewers' notes yet – I wanted to read the transcripts first without bias – but something changed in the period running from before his deployment to his disappearance. By all accounts, Eggerton was an 'average Marine,' an 'OK guy' who hung out with his fellow Marines on occasion but wasn't especially close with any of them. He fit in, but just barely; at least that's my sense. Yet in Afghanistan, his squad members noted that he gradually became more isolative. Even though Eggerton seems like a loner who jumps from one thing to another haphazardly, there was enough of a change in his moderate socializing that it was noted. So the question is, what exactly was he doing by himself?"

"Good question," Watson responded. "When you get to the interviewers' notes you'll see that they had the same question, but didn't come to any conclusions as to what he was doing."

"How about his personal effects? What did Eggerton have with him on deployment?" Reagan asked.

"I haven't gotten to that yet – let's check." Watson reached across Reagan's desk to his mouse and pulled up an inventory.

"His laptop, camera and phone – where are those?" Reagan asked as the two went through the list.

"They're somewhere in the building. Their contents are archived on the server and you can access them here," Watson replied, showing him how to call up the files.

"Thanks. I'll check them out in a bit," Reagan promised, hoping that those files would answer some of his questions. "The other thing that stood out in what I've read is that Eggerton was written up a few times, improper equipment and failure to keep formation, or something like that." Reagan couldn't quite remember the exact language that had been used. "What's that about?"

"I saw that too," Watson said. "It isn't very clear, actually. But I have it in my notes to check out later."

"One other thing to maybe check when you're doing that is whether anyone else was written up for the same things," Reagan offered. "I mean, that might tell us whether it's an Eggerton problem, a unit problem, or a hard-ass CO problem."

Watson smiled at the way he phrased it. "I'll do that," she promised. She hadn't thought about that – *yet*.

"Anyway, that's pretty much everything that stood out from what I've read so far, but I haven't gotten very far," Reagan said as he rose. "I need some coffee. Can I get you anything?"

"I could use a coffee too. Black please," Watson replied with a smile as she headed back to her desk. *Isn't that odd*, she thought. *Talking to Reagan is a lot more like talking to a colleague than to a civilian off the street. Definitely not what I was expecting.* She went back to work, reminding herself to stop being surprised by this guy.

Mansuraev walked back into his apartment, draping his jacket on the back of a chair as he turned on the television. Most of the channels he flipped through were running commentary on the terrorist attack in the park, with the talking heads contributing nothing more than a sense of anxiety. The fearmongering was remarkable, Mansuraev thought as he noted that MSNBC was now showing a graphic of what the effects of a nuclear blast in Rock Creek Park would be. As much as he had studied America, Mansuraev had to admit to himself that he would never fully understand Americans. He was greatly surprised at the dichotomy between the media's reporting and the reactions of ordinary citizens, many of whom got their "news" from sources that were neither accurate nor reliable. Still, watching the network news coverage, one would expect most Americans would be hiding in their basements with their loved ones, waiting for the world to end. But the streets of Georgetown had been packed with students and young professionals, and Mansuraev had nursed several drinks at the bar before a table became available at one of his favorite restaurants.

In many ways, the indifference of most young Americans was stunning – whether to terrorist attacks or to politics and policy in general. It was as though they took the pronouncements of trusted public figures as gospel, forsaking independent rational analysis in favor of an easy and unquestioning acceptance of "consensus" announced by actors, comedians, or anyone with a liberal agenda. These were the trusted public figures of American society, people who as often as not lacked the education or experience to even fully grasp the full extent of the opinions they passed off as facts. Al Gore, a marginal student who couldn't hack it as a law student or even a divinity student, was the Prophet of Global Warming, and men like Jon Stewart and Stephen Colbert – comedians – were respected purveyors of real news. This made America weaker, Mansuraev thought, and given enough time, the once-mighty nation would destroy itself. *No, that's not quite right,* he thought. For every Obama or Clinton, there was a Reagan or Bush, and America was just too unpredictable to be so easily dismissed. *Which, of course, is why I'm here – to help push it over the edge.*

Mansuraev opened a bottle of Pinot Noir as he started thinking about his future. It had taken close to twenty years of careful work to establish his aliases and bona fides – twenty years of work to set the stage for an ambitious plan initially conceived in very general terms and refined methodically to culminate in the operation that would unfold the following week. Years of hard fighting in Chechnya, Abkhazia and Georgia, gradually ingratiating himself with regional Islamist groups as he made a name for himself. Years spent rising through the ranks of global terrorist groups, always careful to avoid the infighting that resulted in so many purges and betrayals. Years spent cultivating connections and talent, organizing his own cells even as he travelled to South America and the United States to develop his legends and study the weaknesses of his enemy. His life's work would be realized in the coming days, but Mansuraev was still a young man so he sat on his sofa, drinking his expensive but rather disappointing wine, contemplating a future triumphant – albeit secretive – return home.

Across town, Special Agent Cannon was also considering going home, if only for a short nap in his own bed. He was long past the age at which all-nighters were anything but arduous and exhausting, and like most people, he simply functioned better when he was well-rested. A day that had started normally, even optimistically, with the resolution of an open case within easy reach, had turned into the worst day of Cannon's life. It was all the more frustrating that no leads had been turned during several hours of intensive labor. The coroner had identified the shooters' dental work as likely originating in the Middle East or Eastern Europe, but that wasn't particularly helpful by itself; their identities remained a mystery. Their clothes were mass-produced and had been in circulation for over 15 years, so that too was a dead end. Interestingly, though, none of the clothes – or even the shoes – appeared to have ever been worn before. Forensics had fared no better with the explosive devices; both were simple designs used by terrorists across the world. The identifying features of the Kalashnikovs had been filed away, but ATF reported they were most likely manufactured in Russia rather than in some other country under license. Practically speaking, they had nothing to go on. Little wonder, then, that Cannon felt so frustrated.

Younger agents, both NCIS and FBI, would spend the night continuing to review video from traffic cameras and the precious few buildings in the area of the park that had security cameras installed. Yet more agents were reviewing pictures taken at Customs of foreigners entering the country by air, comparing them with the pictures of the dead shooters. Around the world, investigators were also comparing the pictures of the shooters with their files in the hope of turning a name. The NSA was monitoring chatter for mention of the attack, complicated by the fact that the attack was the lead story in every news outlet across the world and, consequently, many perfectly innocent people were talking about it. The wheels of the investigative process were spinning, but so far nothing had been produced. *Hopefully tomorrow,* Cannon thought as he made his way through the office, letting his agents know that he was stepping out but always available by phone.

He was surprised to see that Reagan was still sitting there, across from Watson, jotting down the occasional note as he scrolled through files on the computer. *Interesting,* he thought. *Somehow I managed to forget all about him.* Cannon was relieved that Reagan hadn't turned into the hindrance or nuisance he thought him to be, and for a brief moment considered walking over to talk to him about what he was reading. He checked his watch and shook off the thought, remembering that most of the lawyers he knew loved the sound of their own voice, and he was too tired to get into a lengthy discussion. Instead, he took out his cellphone and called Watson.

"How's it going, Amanda?" he asked.

"Slow and steady, Doug. I'm getting through it. No earth-shattering revelations here, but it's good to get the whole picture," she responded.

"Good. How's Reagan doing?" Cannon wanted to know.

"Pretty good, actually. I talked to him earlier and he's got mostly the same questions I have." Watson spoke softly, a little uncomfortable to be talking about someone sitting within earshot. "Some things he tweaked to before I did. An extra pair of eyes helps," she added.

"OK then, keep doing what you're doing. And give him a ride back to his hotel when he's done. I'm heading out but you can call me if you need anything," Cannon said as he sought to stifle a yawn.

"Will do, Doug. See you in the morning." Watson looked at her watch, surprised it was well after one in the morning. Next she looked over to Reagan and saw that he was still engrossed in the files, apparently looking at the photos that had been on Eggerton's camera. Whatever else he was, Reagan certainly was methodical, she thought as she went back to reading about Eggerton's divorce.

For Reagan, the most challenging part of his evening had been figuring out Lance Corporal Eggerton's Marine Corps packet, or whatever his official file was called. It was pretty much unlike anything he had read before in terms of format, but it made it somewhat easier to think of it as a medical chart, and Reagan had reviewed plenty of those in his life. The rest of the documents on the computer were straightforward enough: interview transcripts, investigators' notes, e-mails and photos were all things he had reviewed before. For the most part, what he saw was interesting but not particularly informative, and the more Reagan read, the more questions he had. *Who are Eggerton's friends – who really knows him?* was one of the first things Reagan had written down on the scratchpad he found in the desk. Hours into his research, Reagan felt that he had a better picture of the defendant, as he now thought of Eggerton, but that first question remained unanswered.

Even after checking Eggerton's e-mails in his Outlook folder, Reagan had no better idea who the man's friends were. There was nothing to suggest any particularly close connection with anyone, and Reagan knew that Eggerton had no living family. *Subpoena other ISPs*, Reagan wrote, wondering if perhaps Eggerton used something other than the Yahoo! account he seemed to favor. All the personal communications he found were with other Marines – men whose interviews revealed that they knew Eggerton well, but at the same time not well enough. *That's not too surprising, actually*, Reagan thought, remembering that all of *his* friends were either work-related or former schoolmates. *My friends would certainly be evasive answering questions about me – maybe that's it; maybe Eggerton's friends were just being evasive.* He made a mental note to talk to Cannon or Smythe about that, perhaps to suggest another round of interviews.

Reagan pulled up the folder containing the photos from Eggerton's digital camera and started going through them. The financial documents could wait; Reagan saw enough financial disclosures on a daily basis and was glad for the change of pace. It felt very good, for a change, to be doing something that came close to what he used to do as a lawyer, and not for the first time, Jack realized how much he missed practicing law – the thrill of digging into the facts during discovery, the excitement of researching the law and applying it to the facts, and the exhilaration of crafting a persuasive argument. More often than not a winning argument, he remembered with satisfaction. But all of that came at a high price, Jack remembered equally well; he tended to get too engrossed in his cases, to the exclusion of everything else: family, relationships, and even friendships. Reagan had focused too much on work, and his personal life had suffered. That had all changed when his mom's health deteriorated, but he still regretted that he hadn't made more time for her when she was still in good health.

The past few years had been a blur of long days and hard nights, of profound sadness masked by a veneer of cheerful optimism that faded instantly on those rare occasions Reagan had a few minutes to himself. Time stood still up the mountain in the deep woods, with each day the same as the one that came before it. Only the changing seasons marked the progression of time, a beautiful yet silent reminder that change is inevitable as life moves along a path set forward in a plan known only to God. Reagan hadn't entirely lost his faith, but it had been shaken by the suffering his family had endured. Picking up the pieces had been hard, and was difficult still. He had just begun to finally shake the lingering depression and think about the future – albeit a future in which he would never develop his once-promising legal career into a satisfying practice at a large firm. Reagan knew well enough that once derailed, the path to partnership or even counsel was foreclosed absent connections that he simply lacked.

Trading stocks was singularly unsatisfying and even frustrating, but Reagan was trapped into doing it in order to pay his bills and eek out some semblance of a living. The economy – and the market – had changed substantially since he received his degrees, with the irrational exuberance that Alan Greenspan had warned against proceeding apace, spurred on by easy money fueled by a lax monetary policy. The lessons of the tech bubble well over a decade earlier had long since been forgotten, with money flowing into companies that had no real assets and very little promise of producing returns on those investments. Even the more recent lessons of the housing market collapse had been forgotten, with developers building anew and house prices rising precipitously even though real wages remained stagnant and more people were out of the labor force than ever in America's history. Inflation was a real concern as well, with the real level masked by the government's manipulation of the "basket of goods" that served to measure it.

The psychology of investors had changed, too. It used to be that when Acme Corporation made a substantially better widget, it was rewarded with higher valuation as investors bought its stock, raising the price of that stock. But now, pundits who didn't even understand how a widget was made expressed disappointment that the new widget wasn't as good as they had expected, so the company was punished, its valuation dropping along with its share price. Reagan found that irrational, if not distasteful, and it provided yet one more reason why he would rather be doing anything else other than trading stocks. He was grateful to Smythe for allowing him to look into Eggerton. More than satisfying his curiosity as to what he had gotten involved in earlier in the park, it felt good to be doing something he found interesting.

As Reagan clicked through the photos, he realized that both his adrenaline and the effects of caffeine had dissipated. He felt tired now, bordering on exhausted, and on checking his watch saw that it was well past two in the morning. He stretched as he stood and walked the few feet to Watson's desk. "Sorry to bother you, Amanda," he said. "I think my brain's fried – all these pictures are starting to look the same. I'm thinking of heading back to my hotel to get some sleep, and then come back and finish up in the morning."

Watson looked at her watch, surprised yet again to have lost track of time. She had been going through Eggerton's financials, which were as dull and uninformative as one might expect. "I'll drive you," she said, securing her computer and retrieving her purse from a desk drawer.

Reagan started to object but was interrupted by Watson. "It's not a problem, Jack. I need a break, too. Besides, I was ordered to," she said with a smile. "Are you going to take your stuff?" she asked, seeing that Reagan left his bag behind as they walked towards the elevator.

"No, I'll just get it tomorrow," he replied, figuring that at least this way he had one more reason to get back inside the building.

"Sure you will!" Watson laughed, having guessed the real reason from the get-go.

It took them a couple of minutes to find Watson's car, which another agent had thoughtfully brought back from Rock Creek Park. Perhaps not so thoughtfully after all, since the radio was turned on and set at full volume, blasting them as soon as Watson turned the ignition. Amanda and Jack both jabbed their hands at the power button, neither of them sure who got to it first. Then Reagan started to laugh as Watson blushed a bright red.

"Interesting choice, Special Agent Watson," Reagan said when he finally stopped laughing. "Don't worry," he added, "I bought quite a few copies of that book when it came out," referring to the book-on-CD version of President Bush's *Decision Points* that had been turned to full volume by some practical joker. "Your secret is safe with me. Although if you want to cover your ass, you might consider hanging a photo of President Obama from your rearview mirror."

Watson started laughing as she turned towards Reagan, trying but failing to adopt a stern demeanor as she playfully replied, "Shut up!"

"Yes ma'am," he said with a chuckle. "Actually, the more I think about it, don't hang that photo. The Secret Service might take issue. And if they don't, someone might point out it's racist." They both had a good laugh at that. *I needed a good laugh after today*, thought Watson, still smiling in the darkness as she put the car in gear.

The drive took no time at all thanks to the absence of traffic at that late hour, but it lasted long enough for Reagan to get Watson to open up and talk about herself a little. For her part, Watson was surprised how easily the words came to her; she was generally reluctant to talk about herself, especially to people she didn't work with. For some reason, however – probably the late hour – it was easy to talk to Reagan. "What time should I pick you up in the morning?" she asked as she drove around Lafayette Square.

"I can just catch a cab," Reagan replied. "I don't want to be a bother."

"You haven't been a bother yet," she responded with a grin. "Besides, I'm staying at the Marriott a few minutes away. I sublet my apartment the previous year when I went off on assignment with DEA and haven't figured out my living situation just yet. Today was my first day back, actually."

"Hell of a thing to come back to. I'm sorry – it can't be easy. As for the time, whatever is good for you," he said.

"How about 7:30, then?" she asked. "And thanks, by the way. Both for what you did in the park and for looking through this stuff with me," she added.

"Seven thirty it is. See you then! And...you're quite welcome," Reagan replied as he got out of the car, guessing that the day that had already started would be a long one. He stopped by the front desk to request a wakeup call and went to his room overlooking the White House, where he managed to kick off his shoes before collapsing on top of the bed, falling asleep almost as soon as his face touched the pillow.

9

A ringing phone never failed to wake Reagan, who over the years had become an expert at shutting off any kind of alarm clock in his sleep. The urgency of a ringing phone, on the other hand, could wake him from the deepest sleep. It did not, however, guarantee that he would wake up in a good mood, and Reagan fought the urge to grumble as he picked up the phone. After all, it wasn't the fault of the hotel operator that he had slept for less than four hours. His whole body ached as he got out of bed, and Reagan silently cursed himself for forgetting that his bottle of Motrin was in his bag back at NCIS. He started the coffee maker before getting into the shower, happy that the warm water was relaxing his tense muscles. After a few minutes he started to feel better, and left the shower to drink some coffee before attacking his beard with an electric trimmer, followed by a close shave with a sharp blade. As much as his sensitive skin hated shaving, he was glad to be rid of that thing on his face, and after a second shower he felt almost human again.

As he dressed, Reagan thought back over the material he read the previous night. *There's something I'm missing*, he decided. *There has to be. Something that was probably staring me right in the face and I didn't see it.* Something was odd about the photos he was looking at when exhaustion overtook him, but Reagan was hard-pressed to say what, exactly, that was. *I'll start with the photos this morning*, he thought, confident that his mind was more alert than it had been last night. Forty-five minutes after his wakeup call, Reagan was out the door, exactly on time. He was looking forward to the challenges that lay ahead even as he realized he also looked forward to seeing Amanda again. *Don't think that way, Jack*, he warned himself. *You should know better.*

Special Agent Watson was parked in front of the hotel and looking towards the entrance, but she didn't spot Reagan until he was halfway to her car, practically doing a double-take as she took in the freshly-shaved face that revealed a strong chin emphasizing an easy smile. He wore a well-tailored pinstripe suit over a white shirt and blue tie that was elegant in its simplicity, looking every bit the lawyer he was. Rather handsome too, she thought as he got in the car.

"Good morning Jack," she said with a smile. "Looking good this morning! You know, you'd do pretty well undercover," she grinned.

"Thanks," he replied with a chuckle, briefly remembering a long-distant past that he could never discuss with anyone. "You look great, by the way," he added as he took in her navy pinstripe pantsuit over a cream blouse. He couldn't tell if she was wearing makeup, but her face seemed positively radiant in the morning sun, despite a night with very little sleep.

"Thank you," she said, turning towards Reagan as she put the car in drive. "Looks like we're a matching set today," she added with a wink before pulling out into traffic. *What is it about this guy,* she wondered, realizing that she wasn't quite acting like her normal self. Watson was generally much more reserved; it took her a while to feel comfortable around someone and let her guard down. But Reagan was just different – easy to talk to, with a calm demeanor that masked the intensity she could see in his eyes. The pair drove in silence, listening to a news radio station whose anchor demanded that the government stop allowing Muslim extremists into the country to prevent more attacks like the one in Rock Creek Park.

As Watson went off to talk to Cannon, Reagan sat at his computer, scrolling through the photos from Eggerton's camera as he sipped at his coffee. There were slightly over one hundred pictures, roughly half of them nature shots of the Afghan countryside and the other half Eggerton's squad members mugging for the camera. Reagan decided to search for more pictures on the archived copy of Eggerton's laptop and was surprised to find thousands of them, neatly catalogued in subfolders. *This guy photographed everything*, he thought, scrolling through pictures of flowers, leaves, houses, cars, and lots of seemingly random people. Some of the shots were pretty good – Eggerton seemed to be a decent amateur photographer who took his hobby seriously. *Why, then, does he have so few picture of his tour in Afghanistan*, Reagan wondered, switching back to the camera roll. He switched to a detailed list of files showing the date and time of each picture, and instantly noticed that the files jumped in sequence. A lot of files were missing, he realized – several hundred, in fact, judging from the file names. Reagan went back to the laptop archive and checked the file lists. *Interesting*, he thought, observing that all of the pictures there were in sequence. Eggerton hadn't deleted any pictures from his laptop, not even the blurry, out of focus ones.

Reagan looked up and saw Watson walking towards her desk. He waved her over. "I've got something interesting here, Amanda. These are the pictures from Eggerton's camera," he said, pointing at the detailed list on his screen, "Notice how the files jump in sequence? It looks like he deleted several hundred photos. Now look at the pictures on his laptop." Reagan pulled up a detailed list of one of the folders. "He didn't delete anything. Not even the bad shots."

"I see what you mean," Watson replied, leaning over Reagan to reach the mouse and switch views.

"Can you find out if there is any way to retrieve the deleted photos from the memory card?" he asked. "I think this is very important," he emphasized.

"I'll check right now," she promised, heading to her desk to make some phone calls. *How did I miss that?* she wondered. She had gone through the photos the previous night but hadn't found them very revealing.

Reagan started writing down the dates from which they had no photos as Watson made her calls. He also counted the number of missing photos, which easily exceeded 900. It was a laborious process, and by the time he finished more than half an hour had passed. He walked over to Watson's desk, observing that she was now going through the photos, doing the exact same thing he had just done. "Here you go," he said, handing over his notes.

"Thanks," she replied with a laugh. "You just saved me a good half hour. No go on the deleted files, Jack. IT and Forensics both looked at the memory card and agree that the photos can't be retrieved. They were deleted on the camera, and there's something about the way that particular camera overwrites the files that makes the deleted ones impossible to recover."

"What now?" Reagan asked, disappointed.

"I don't know, really. But for starters, let's go brief Cannon," she replied as she stood, leading Reagan through the maze of desks. They found Cannon at his desk, updating Acting Director Smythe about the precious little progress that had been made the previous night – the van had been spotted once on a traffic camera in the northern suburbs, but it was wasn't clear where it had come from, and Mossad had a possible match to one of the shooters but had no identity to go along with it. Both men took in the change in Reagan's appearance as he approached with Watson.

"Good morning, Mr. Reagan," Smythe said, somewhat more cheerfully than he felt at the lack of discernible progress on the case. "I see you're still with us. Looking good, by the way," he added with a smile.

"Really, Director?" Cannon asked with mock surprise. "I think he looked better the other way. Now he just looks like every other suit."

"What's wrong with suits?" Smythe asked Cannon, finding a bit of levity in the moment. "What can we do for you this morning?" he continued, turning to face Reagan.

82

"Jack found something we both find interesting, something we think you should know about," Watson answered for Reagan.

"What's that?" Smythe noted his agent's use of the plural personal pronoun. She explained, pulling up the photos on Cannon's terminal as she did so. Cannon and Smythe crowded the monitor, looking at the photos and studying the file lists.

"Very interesting," Cannon admitted. "How many photos got deleted?"

"Jack counted upwards of nine hundred," she said, handing over his list.

"That's quite a lot," Smythe said in surprise. "Very interesting indeed."

"All the more so when you consider that this guy seems to have never deleted a photo before. Not even a photo I found of dog poop," Reagan added.

"So what do you make of this, Mr. Reagan?" Smythe was fairly impressed by his discovery, as much as by his persistence.

"Call me Jack," he started. "What I make of this is that these photos were deleted for a reason. Why does anyone delete a photo?" he asked hypothetically, proceeding to answer the question. "Either to make room for more photos, get rid of bad ones, or get rid of something you don't want anyone to see. Eggerton had plenty of space on his hard drive and hoarded even the worst shots. That leaves getting rid of something he didn't want anyone to see. Of course, we don't know that it was Eggerton who deleted the photos. It could have been someone else. But the question remains the same: what was in them that someone didn't want us to see?"

"Good question," Cannon offered. "Is there any way to recover those files?" he asked Watson.

"Jack asked the same question," she replied, explaining why it wasn't possible.

"Where does that leave us?" Smythe wanted to know. "This is just one more question about the mysterious Lance

Corporal for which we have no answer. Without those photos, we have no idea what he didn't want us to see."

"Maybe. But maybe not," Reagan thought aloud. "Maybe we don't need *those* photos to answer the question." He paused, seeing the look of confusion on the agents' faces. "What do you do when a witness won't talk – you try to find another witness, right? Since we don't have Eggerton's photos, maybe we can look at the photos taken in the same time period by the men he was serving with. He was with them practically all the time, as I understand it, so there's bound to be some overlap in the subject matter of the photos. Is there any way we can collect the photos on their cameras? Cellphones and computers too?"

"Absolutely," Cannon answered, surprised by how quickly Reagan had come up with the idea. "They're still deployed in Afghanistan, which makes it much simpler since they're all in one place. It will still take a few days to ship things over though," he warned.

"Maybe upload the images first," Reagan offered. "That way we can start to go through them before the physical media gets here."

"Good idea," said Smythe. "Let's get that done. Any other ideas, Jack?"

"Just one, for now. Re-interview the people in his unit. After going through his e-mails and phone records, it seems to me that they're the people who come closest to being his friends, but they didn't come across as knowing him very well in their interviews. Maybe Eggerton was as much a mystery to them as he is to us, but then again, maybe his friends were being a little cagey."

"His fellow Marines didn't seem evasive," Cannon objected.

"That may be so, but bear in mind that back then they were being questioned about a disappearance. Maybe they didn't want their friend to get in too much trouble for being AWOL. If you question them now, they're potential conspirators in a terrorist attack that resulted in the deaths of several people, including children. I suspect you might get slightly more out of them now, in any event," Reagan concluded.

"Fair enough," Cannon replied. In fact, he had already considered re-interviewing the Marines but there were other things to do first. "I don't suppose you have any ideas about tracking down the shooters, do you?" has asked with a judiciously raised eyebrow as he leaned back in his chair.

"How were the bombs set off?" Reagan asked in return.

"Cellphones," Cannon said. "How would proceed?" he pressed, wanting to get a better measure of the man.

"Cell tower logs," Reagan answered at once. "We know roughly when the explosions took place, so that will narrow down which phones were connected to the devices – they'll be the ones that don't respond when you ping them. Maybe that will get you the originating phone number as well. The numbers will give you information about the phones themselves – like who activated them. Probably aliases but it's one more piece of the puzzle. More than that, it might be possible to narrow down where the phones were sold, and that might lead to something more. Although of course if they were part of a batch re-sold to bodegas, you probably won't get anything. As for the originating phone, the one used by the guy that got away, maybe once you have that number you can see where he went before he dumped it."

"I see you've talked some with Agent Watson," Cannon remarked.

"Not about this, boss. Not at all," Watson spoke softly, yet again surprised by Reagan.

"Really? That's interesting..." Cannon, too, was surprised by Reagan. *This sort of thing isn't really in the purview of a commercial litigator*, he thought. "We've been running things along those lines," he added, not quite wanting to divulge their methods. "So far, we've come up empty but we're narrowing it down. Anyway, are you going to dig around some more, or are you off to your wedding?"

"I'd like to look into this some more, if you'll allow," Reagan answered.

"Fine by me," said Cannon, no longer bothered by Reagan's presence or his participation in the investigation.

"Me too," Smythe added, giving his seal of approval. "Good work, guys."

Cannon turned to Smythe as Reagan and Watson returned to their desks. "He's pretty sharp, isn't he?"

"That he is," Smythe replied with a nod. He had judged Reagan correctly the previous night. The eyes gave it away – the curiosity that went with intellect, the confidence that came with a strong education and multitude of achievements, and the decisiveness of a man used to doing the right thing, for the right reasons. "Pretty sharp indeed."

His index finger poised above the carriage return, Mansuraev stared at his computer and hesitated briefly before pressing the key, completing the purchase of a First Class ticket on an American Airlines flight to Miami the following Wednesday. As much as he wanted to stay in Washington to witness the aftermath of the attacks he had planned, he knew it was foolish to do so. Most, if not all, of his men would almost certainly be captured or killed, and it wouldn't take long for any one of the captured ones to break in interrogation and give him up. That was all part of the plan, of course – the world would soon come to learn that the most audacious terrorist attack in American history had been planned by a devout Muslim, a fundamentalist radicalized on the battlefield of his native Chechnya. It was just better that Mansuraev not be in America when his role came to light.

Although he was wary of the American intelligence apparatus, Mansuraev wasn't particularly worried. He had conducted his operations far too carefully and besides, none of his men knew about his other aliases. For that matter, no more than five people in the world knew his real name. The only real danger to him was if one of his men gave a description accurate enough to result in a sketch – which was why he was taking the American Airlines flight to Miami, to be followed by another flight to Rio before yet one more flight to Buenos Aires. In a matter of weeks, his appearance would be changed so as to be unrecognizable; certainly he would bear no resemblance to whatever description the Americans would have of him. Mansuraev was looking forward to spending a couple of weeks in Buenos Aires, lounging poolside at his palatial safehouse. He needed a vacation, and figured he had earned one.

First, though, he had to prepare for his meeting on Tuesday with two California congressmen. He looked over at the large stack of printouts on his desk, copies of proposed legislation advocated by California vintners as a protectionist measure to safeguard their profits, and groaned at the thought of having to read all that garbage. It was highly unlikely that the congressmen had ever read those bills – Mansuraev was amazed, yet somehow not entirely surprised, by how much legislation had been passed in recent years without ever having been read. At least that's what the papers said. But they would have aides at the meeting, and aides would be paid to read such things. Mansuraev would have to read it too, for the sake of his cover. No one could suspect that the real purpose of his trip to Capitol Hill was a final reconnoiter of his target. He closed his laptop and poured himself some Jack Daniels, the better to stomach the tripe that American legislators can come up with.

10

By early afternoon, Reagan had finished going through everything he could find pertaining to Lance Corporal Lawrence Eggerton and was disappointed to have more questions than real insight into the man. As much as he had enjoyed digging through the puzzle that was Eggerton, Reagan was frustrated that he hadn't come up with anything new. He looked through his copious notes and decided to type up a summary of his conclusions, such as they were. An hour and two coffees later, Reagan was satisfied with his meager five page report; the hardest part had been separating what he *knew* from what he *thought* he knew, but that had been a good intellectual challenge. He printed the document and walked it over to Agent Watson, who was looking through what appeared to be the records of phone sales.

"I typed up a summary of my notes," he explained. "Nothing earth-shattering, really, but it's the least I can do."

"I'll give a copy to Special Agent Cannon and Director Smythe," she replied as she flipped through the pages. "All done for the day?"

"I suppose I am," Reagan replied, "unless there's something else you can think of for me to look through. I'd really like to see his unit's photos when they come in."

"You will. We're in the process of collecting them now, and should have them uploaded sometime tonight. Definitely by tomorrow. I'll give you a call and arrange to have you picked up when they're ready," she promised.

"Thanks," Reagan said with a smile. "I'll look forward to that."

"Just so long as it doesn't interfere with the wedding," Watson laughed.

"It won't," Reagan responded with a laugh of his own. "Meanwhile I have a dinner to get to. I get to meet the bride's family."

"I'll drive you," Watson said, grabbing her purse. Reagan started to protest but she cut him off. "It's the least *I* can do. Besides, I need a break from this, and I don't think anyone will miss me too much."

The drive to Chevy Chase took longer than expected thanks to all the people leaving town early on a beautiful Friday afternoon, but eventually they pulled up to a bright yellow colonial on a quiet, tree-lined street.

"Nice house," commented Watson. "What does the bride-to-be do, anyway?"

"She's NSA – an analyst, I think. I haven't seen Brenda in years. She and Nick have been on-again, off-again for quite a while," he explained, seeing a curtain move aside before the door opened and his friend came jogging out, stopping in the middle of the driveway and standing comically at attention, a wide grin on his face. "Want to come in and meet everyone?" Reagan asked.

"Maybe next time, Jack," she offered with a smile. "In any case, I'll see you later. Thanks for your help."

"Thanks for the ride – and see you later!" he replied, getting out of the car.

Watson watched Reagan walk up to his friend, who saluted crisply before embracing him in a massive hug. She waved to the pair and drove away, thinking it interesting that Reagan's best friend was a SEAL marrying an NSA analyst. *There's got to be a story there, and I wouldn't mind hearing it when this is all over.*

"Well, well, well, *Mister* Reagan... Damn good to see you, bubba!" Despite a Bachelors Degree from UCLA, an MBA from Harvard and proficiency in half a dozen languages, Commander Nick Videtti proudly maintained his Texas drawl, at least off duty.

"Good to see you too, pal," Reagan replied as the two walked into the house.

"For a moment there we thought you wouldn't make it. You had us worried, pal. You remember Brenda of course," he paused as Jack hugged her. "These are her parents, Bob and Carol Angelo. Bob is retired Bureau," he added as Reagan shook his hand.

"I'm just a Bureau widow," Carol Angelo laughed, shaking Reagan's hand.

"Pleased to meet you both," Reagan said with a smile. "I'm Jack Reagan. Brenda, you look fantastic!"

"Thank you so much," said the beaming bride-to-be.

"We've heard a lot about you," Carol added. "Quite a few stories, really. Why don't y'all head into the front room while I put on some coffee. I suspect you guys have some things to talk over." Carol's twang suggested origins somewhere in the South. Little wonder Nick seemed to get on so well with Brenda's parents.

"Nice shooting, son. Very nicely done," said Bob as they sat in what most people would call a living room.

"You heard about that, did you?" asked Reagan.

"Yeah, kinda hard to miss, since it was all over the news last night. Nick told us you were somehow involved and I made some calls. Before I retired I was S-A-C in Denver, so I still know lots of people," Bob explained. "Even got to see some of the photos. Wish I was that good with a pistol!"

"Me too!" laughed Nick. "What the hell happened, anyway? Brenda's still NSA, in case you didn't know, and I've sort of read in her dad on some of the highlights of your previous career."

"That's right," Brenda said. "They bumped me up to Section Chief. Probably worried I might defect," she added with a chuckle. "So... spill!"

"It seems to have started with a Marine Lance Corporal named Lawrence Eggerton," Jack started to explain. He was breaking his promise to Smythe not to discuss the investigation, but everyone in the room was or had been cleared higher than Top Secret. The explanation took ten minutes, interrupted only by Carol bringing in some coffee before excusing herself; she was used to strangers discussing classified matters in her house.

"That's some story, Jack," Bob said as he shook his head. "I already heard some of it, but the way you describe it – you're right, the shooters are way too polished. That's more Nick's area though. Sounds like you played it exactly right. As far as Eggerton goes, I think you're right about him, too. He sure as hell seems to wiggle like a player."

"We've been seeing sharper operators the last few years," Nick chimed in. "The bad guys are learning better tactics, but more than that, they're showing better discipline in implementing them. I'd love to know where your shooters were trained. I know they couldn't stay dumb forever, but if we can take out some of their instructors, it would help. As far as *your* tactics, I see you remember the basics pretty well. You took a hell of a chance though, and you're lucky to be alive. A hell of a chance," he repeated, "but to be fair, Bob and I would probably have done the same thing you did. It's lucky you're such a good shot. Oh and as for your boy Eggerton, he's as dirty as a hooker's...you-know-what. Some of my boys were tasked with tracking him down when he disappeared, but we couldn't find a trace of him. I always thought he had help – the locals were just a little evasive."

"I've been thinking the same thing about local help. As for the shooting in the park, my worry is that we've seen this sort of thing before – obviously not on this scale in this country, but this kind of attack has always been a prelude to something bigger," Jack reminded Nick.

"That's true," Nick replied. "But the alert level has been raised and I haven't heard about any new threats. Not domestic ones, anyway."

"There was some chatter a few months back out of northern New Jersey, something to do with planes, but nothing came of that as far as I know," added Brenda. "You're right though – the only way it makes sense to take on federal agents and blow up first responders is if this is part of something bigger."

"What's bigger?" Jack asked hypothetically. "I mean, let's assume, based on their tactics, that these bad guys are smart enough to figure out that the attack will lead to increased security across the board. How does *that* help them? Is there anything we can infer about their ultimate objective?"

"That's the question, isn't it," mused Bob as the room fell silent.

"Here's a thought," Nick said after a while. "What if increased security is what they're after because it will give them some kind of access that they wouldn't ordinarily have?"

"That's plausible, not to mention a scary thought," Jack admitted. "But it still doesn't tell us anything about what the objective is."

"What does NCIS think?" Brenda wanted to know.

"My sense is that they're thinking along similar lines, but they're more into working the case than looking at the bigger picture. I haven't discussed this with anyone to the same extent as with you guys, though. The shooting hit them pretty hard, and it shows," Jack answered.

"They don't know your background, do they?" Nick asked with a chuckle.

"God no. I'd probably still be sitting in an interrogation room if they did," Jack replied with a laugh of his own.

"Not necessarily," objected Bob. "I've heard good things about their Acting Director, Francis Smythe. He came out of retirement for this gig – he's good people. Used to be an Operations guy, and before that he was Agency. Before your time though. If you want I can reach out and try to have him brought up to speed. I'm sure he'll take what you say seriously once he knows your pedigree."

"He seems to listen well enough as it is and besides, my experience is far enough in the past that it isn't very relevant. I'm just a has-been lawyer in town for a wedding, in the wrong place at the wrong time," Jack replied. "More to the point, as interested as I am in figuring this stuff out, it isn't, strictly speaking, my job."

"Maybe it should be," Brenda countered. "You've got the skills, obviously, and from the stories Nick tells, you were a pretty good analyst, and then some." More than anything, she wanted to know why Jack had left to pursue a career in law, but it wasn't her place to ask. Her husband-to-be told her everything, but had always evaded talking about *that*. "Besides," she added with a slightly vicious smile, "don't you want to work with that hot brunette that dropped you off?"

Jack saw an opportunity to change the topic of discussion and gladly took it. "Speaking of hot brunettes, Nick, what did you end up doing with the strippers I ordered for you last night?" he asked with a grin.

"Oh, I want to hear this!" exclaimed Brenda with a chuckle as she leaned forward on the sofa.

Her father leaned forward, too. "What strippers?" he demanded in fake outrage.

"You mean the gay male midget strippers you sent to our restaurant? Jesus, Mary and Joseph, Jack, where the *hell* did you find those people?" Nick demanded as they all burst into laughter.

"Amazing what you can order online these days," Jack replied to renewed laughter.

Special Agent Watson returned to an office teeming with activity. She noted her colleagues' new-found restless energy and read the signs for what they were: something had happened. "Hey Grady, what's going on?" she asked Special Agent Purdue after nearly colliding with him in the hallway.

"We've got a lead on Eggerton," he replied. "Cannon's briefing everyone in the bullpen."

"How solid?" Watson queried as she walked with Purdue.

"Don't know yet," he answered. "But we're about to find out." The bullpen, they both saw, was packed with agents and support personnel. Everyone in the building was interested in this development. They watched Cannon climb atop a desk and clap his hands to get everyone's attention before he spoke.

"Listen up people, we have a solid lead on Lance Corporal Eggerton. Last night we released his photo to the press. A few hours ago we received a tip that he's been staying at a low-income apartment complex in Manassas, Virginia. The tip comes from a retired deputy sheriff whose wife works for the building's management company. The deputy has a solid history and we therefore consider his tip highly reliable." Cannon was interrupted by some applause that quickly died down following a stern look. "The FBI is sitting on the building right now," he continued, "but they have not personally observed Eggerton entering or exiting the premises. We've thought the situation over and, in light of what happened yesterday, have decided to conduct a raid on the apartment sooner rather than later. FBI SWAT is going to breach, but then the scene will be ours. Eggerton, if he's there, will be taken into custody by NCIS." More enthusiastic applause filled the room as Cannon concluded his remarks. "You know your jobs, people, so let's get it done. Pembridge, Hollerman and Watson, come see me please. That's all for now."

Watson made her way to Cannon's desk as the gathering dispersed, and the three agents sat and listened as Cannon outlined what he expected from each of them at the scene. "Do you really think we'll bag him?" Pembridge asked as their meeting concluded.

"No, not really," Cannon admitted. "If I had to hazard a guess, I'd say he's long gone. By the way, Amanda, is Reagan still around? He might find the take-down interesting."

"No, I gave him a ride earlier. He has some pre-wedding dinner, whatever that's called."

"Rehearsal dinner," Pembridge and Cannon replied simultaneously.

"Oh come on, Amanda – no way you didn't know what," laughed Pembridge. "And don't tell me you haven't already planned *your* wedding right down to the seating chart," he teased.

"Sorry, Ryan," she replied with a chuckle. "I don't lay awake at night planning things that might never happen. I tried that once but you still haven't grown up."

"I still think you have a wedding gown already picked out, tucked away in your closet." Sometimes Pembridge could be relentless.

"Why's that, Ryan? Are you looking for something to wear?" Watson had missed this type of banter, but this particular subject hit a little too close to home. She hadn't had a serious relationship in years, at first thinking that her commitment to her career precluded such possibilities. It was hard meeting someone who could keep her interest, and the dating pool was shallow to begin with. Most men, their protestations to the contrary notwithstanding, couldn't accept that she was as dedicated to her career as they were to theirs. Then came the category of men who dated as many women as there were days in the week; Watson was definitely not interested in that. She had no interest in flings or casual relationships. Colleagues were out, even from other agencies – there were just too many horror stories. That didn't leave many options, nor did Watson have much free time to search out a well-educated, charming, funny, compassionate, supportive and handsome partner who would be as committed to her as she would be to him. She had a better chance at finding a pink unicorn, she thought.

"Save it for later, guys, and go get your gear," Cannon commanded, ending Watson's self-reflection. "Hold on a second, Amanda," he added, effectively dismissing Pembridge and Hollerman. "Just so you know, I'm going easy on you with respect to the apartment search for a reason. That bit about the photos that you and Reagan figured out – the Director and I kicked that around earlier and we agree that it's pretty damn important. I want you two to stay focused on that and go through the stuff that comes in very carefully. Whether or not we get Eggerton tonight, it's going to be key to figuring him out."

"Understood, boss," she replied. "Reagan has that wedding tomorrow, but otherwise he seems interested in seeing this through," she added.

"Out of curiosity, how much of this photo thing was Reagan's idea and how much was yours?" Cannon wanted to know.

"All Reagan. I'd like to think I would have come up with it independently, but in all honesty, I didn't think the pictures were all that important until he told me otherwise," she admitted.

"Interesting. You know, Reagan just might be the first lawyer I've come across that isn't totally useless," Cannon said, forming a smile. "Anyway, go grab your gear and meet me outside."

Osman Mansuraev crawled into bed with a headache, already feeling the effects of the many mojitos he had enjoyed in one of his favorite Georgetown bars. He had given up trying to read the legislative propaganda advanced by the California vintners – it was just too boring, and besides, Mansuraev felt restless after the excitement of the previous day. So he had showered, fussed with his appearance, and gone out in search of a good distraction. The pickings had been slim; for some reason, Thursday night seemed to be the preferred night for going out. Still, he had found an overexcited redhead from the Midwest who was fascinated by his dark hair, mischievous smile and expensive suit. As they headed for her hotel, she had gushed that she had never been with a Latino before, but Mansuraev didn't believe her for a moment. She seemed quite experienced in the shower, on the bed, and eventually on the floor, and he was a bit surprised she didn't ask for a "gift" at the end. Mansuraev would have gladly paid; she had been just the release that he needed.

11

The wedding had been an exquisite affair, elegant for its simplicity. Only the immediate families and closest friends of the bride and groom had been in attendance at the candle-lit ceremony in the beautiful brick church that Brenda Videtti had attended since childhood. Vows were exchanged, photos were taken, and the happy couple and their guests relaxed in their limos as they headed for a large, festive and even raucous reception at a suburban hotel with enough room for what was as much a networking event as a celebration of a marital union. The groom's friends and family, most wearing the uniforms of the United States Navy, were well and truly outnumbered by the bride's friends and families. Ironically, of the 150 people or so in attendance, the bride and groom were only really close to the handful of friends who shared their table.

Jack Reagan discreetly checked his watch. Special Agent Watson had called him about an hour earlier with news that the photos from Afghanistan were available and that there had been some new developments. She was on her way to pick him up, but the reception – which had given signs of winding down when he spoke with Watson – was now showing renewed signs of vigor as the DJ started to play dance music. Jack looked up and saw Amanda standing by the door, scanning the room. He waved her over when she looked his way, and stood as she approached.

"Hi Amanda, sorry I'm running late," he said. "NCIS Special Agent Amanda Watson, this is my friend Commander Nick Videtti and his new bride, Brenda."

"Pleased to meet you," she told Nick. "You look beautiful," she told Brenda, receiving an unexpected hug from the bride.

"These two gentlemen are Lieutenant Commander Pete Sinclair and Lieutenant Jim Mason," Jack continued. "Mister

Mason here is due to receive an extra half-stripe any day now," he added.

"Nice to meet you," Watson said as she shook their hands.

"Here, have some champagne," Brenda ordered, practically thrusting a flute into Watson's hand. "Sit and join us for a few minutes. It's nice to finally put a face to the name – we've heard a lot about you."

Watson sat next to Reagan, taking a sip to feel more at ease. "You have, have you?" she asked.

"We most certainly have," Brenda replied. "So tell me, Amanda, are you single? Jack here is a great catch," she said with a twinkle in her eye, noting that both Jack and Amanda seemed to blush a little.

"That's my wife – the matchmaker!" Nick laughed. "What's new in the investigation?" he asked.

"We're in the process of following some leads," she replied a little guardedly.

"It's ok to speak, Amanda," Nick prompted. "You're among friends. And besides, everyone at this table is cleared TS or better," he added.

"Well..." Amanda hesitated before continuing. "We had a solid lead on Eggerton and raided the apartment he had been staying in. He wasn't there; it looks like he cleared out some time ago. Forensics is going over the apartment with a fine toothcomb, and we're waiting to see what they turn up."

"Gathering actionable intel is a real bitch," Pete laughed.

"You'll get it done, won't you, Amanda? And Jack will be there to help," Brenda proclaimed, a little affected by the champagne.

"We'll do our best," Amanda replied. "Jack's been a real help," she said with a smile.

"So what do you think of this reception?" Jim wanted to know.

"A lot of people having a great time," Amanda said.

"Funny thing is, we don't know most of these people. That's weddings for you," Jim exclaimed. He tried to avoid settling down as much as he avoided the plague.

"Very patriotic too," Amanda noted. "I see a lot of men – and women – wearing flag lapel pins."

Brenda had a good laugh at that observation. "That's so the photographers know who *not* to photograph," she explained. "The *really* funny thing is that whenever I envisioned my wedding, I never imagined it would be classified."

The group continued chatting for a few minutes, with Watson feeling well at ease with these good friends she had just met. "There's something I wanted to know for a while now," she said, her curiosity getting the better of her. "How did you guys meet?"

"Nick and I ran into Jack a long time ago, in Paris of all places, and just hit it off," Pete replied. "We kinda adopted Jim here along the way. Hey Jack, I need your phone," he added, reaching into Jack's pocket and retrieving his iPhone. "I'm programming in my number. Jim and I, along with some of these other jokers, are going to be in town for another week. We're meeting our detailers. If you need anything, anything at all, give me a call and we'll be there!" he promised.

"Thanks, pal," Jack said, turning to Nick. "It's about time I..."

"Yeah go ahead, Jack, you've done your duty," Nick finished his friend's thought. "We're going to head off in a few minutes as well, so you might as well beat the mad rush out the door."

Jack rose, hugging his friends and wishing them a fun honeymoon.

"It'll be fun for sure," Brenda promised.

"See you when I see you, bubba, and stay safe," Nick grinned.

Jack held Amanda's chair as she rose, and she very nearly took his hand as they walked out together. *What is it about this guy*, she wondered, not quite ready to admit the obvious chemistry between the two of them.

Watson led Reagan to the conference room he had been interviewed in that first night, where he found Director Smythe talking to Special Agent Pembridge.

"Welcome back, Jack," Smythe said with a smile.

"How was the wedding?" Pembridge asked.

"It was fun," Reagan replied simply. "Anything new come in?"

"I imagine Agent Watson has briefed you on last night's raid?" Smythe asked. He saw Reagan nod and continued, "Forensics matched Eggerton's DNA and fingerprints so we know he's been there, but judging from the dust he hasn't been there for at least four days. That's pretty much it for now. The photos have all been uploaded to the server, but I have to warn you, Jack – there are a whole lot of them. It will take you a while to go through, if you're still willing."

"I am," Reagan replied, nodding in emphasis.

"Excellent. In that case, we'll set you up with a terminal and a phone in this room. It doesn't get much use anyway, so you can use it as an office for as long as you need. We've got other agents in to help with the investigation, so the desk you've been using is now occupied," Smythe explained.

"Thanks," Reagan said. "Just one thing, since I may be here for a while. Do you think you can get me a rate at a local hotel?"

"Not a problem. We'll set you up at the Marriott with Watson. At the very least it'll make commuting easier," Smythe replied with a laugh. He stood and handed Reagan an envelope. "There's an ID in there to get you into the building, a base pass in case you ever need to drive yourself in, and passcodes for the computer. I'm heading back to Quantico, but if there's anything you need, please feel free to call me at any time, day or night. Or talk to Doug Cannon – he'll get you what you need."

"Thanks," Reagan said again, opening the envelope to see that the ID contained his picture, taken from his driver's license. Ironically, it was a pretty good photo. "One more request, if I may. Since it's probably going to take some time to set up the computer, can I go down and see Eggerton's apartment for myself?"

"Why's that, Jack?" asked Pembridge. "The apartment was pretty much a bust – it was cleaned out."

"I would feel better seeing it for myself," Reagan replied, leaning against the wall. "Once upon a time, I was defending a real estate developer and construction company against allegations that the residential apartment building they put up had lots of construction defects. The case had been churning through the system before I inherited it. Anyway, when I got the case, I drove down to see the building, expecting it to be falling down and held together by duct tape and the plaintiffs' prayers. What I saw was a solid building that didn't match those expectations in the slightest, and within a month the case was settled. Anyway, the point I'm trying to make is that I've learned not to rely too much on the descriptions other people give. Wherever possible, I prefer to see things for myself."

"Fair point," Smythe said, finding it to be a very useful story to remember. "Grab Watson and take him to down to Manassas," he told Pembridge. "Anything else, Jack?"

"Not that I can think of. Sorry to be a nuisance," Reagan apologized.

"Hardly a nuisance, Mr. Reagan," Smythe replied. "Oh, the hotel – starting when?"

"Tomorrow night, I suppose." Reagan expected *this* night would be long indeed.

Eggerton's apartment building looked every part the roadside hotel it had once been. The rooms on the ground floor opened directly onto the parking lot, and the rooms on the second floor opened to a long open balcony with railings that ran

101

the length of the building, which itself seemed to be in admirably good repair. "Manassas Arms Residences," the sign proclaimed, leading Reagan to wonder what, precisely, those "Arms" were. Reagan also noted the unmarked police cruiser in the parking lot, towards which Pembridge now walked to show his credentials. He assumed the cops were there to question anyone who hadn't been present during the initial canvas of the residents.

"What do we know about this place?" Reagan asked, turning to Watson.

"Eggerton showed up on January 2 and signed a six month lease under the name Larry Carton, paying $3,000 in cash for the whole term in advance, plus a $250 security deposit. No one seems to have bothered to ask for an ID or references. He was seen driving a late-model blue Ford Focus, but didn't register the details with management and no one remembers the license plate numbers. There are security cameras, but none of them work. The neighbors we spoke to don't remember him, but that's not unexpected," she replied, looking through her notes.

"When did they stop working?"

"Years ago, apparently," Watson said.

"How about the money itself, did anyone copy the serial numbers?"

"In a place like this?" Watson asked with a raised eyebrow. "They're just happy to be paid, Jack."

"How about the room – did Eggerton request a specific one?"

"Not exactly. He said he preferred something on the ground floor but had to settle for one on the second floor. Corner unit, next to the stairs," Watson pointed.

"How about his neighbor, what did she have to say?" Reagan asked as Pembridge rejoined them on their way up the stairs.

"She's one of the people we didn't talk to," Pembridge responded. "The building manager said she stopped by about a week ago in tears, saying her mom was sick back home and she was going to go see her. Has two small kids, I understand."

"Her name is Latasha Johnson," Watson added as they passed her door.

Pembridge unlocked the door and Reagan entered first, turning on the lights as he did so. The apartment itself resembled a hotel room. The front portion of the room contained a medium-sized table underneath the window by the door, along with a chair and a loveseat. Further back was a full-size bed with two nightstands, all under a window on the side wall – this was a corner unit, after all. A wardrobe was squeezed against the opposite wall, with the bathroom behind it. Across from the bed, on the wall shared with Ms. Johnson, was a large dresser with a TV on top. In the rear of the so-called apartment, a kitchenette was squeezed into a space once occupied by a double sink, and next to it was a bathroom that probably hadn't been updated since the building was constructed.

Reagan walked around the apartment slowly and then sat on the bare bed, thinking the sheets had probably been removed by the forensics team. He reached for the remote on the nightstand and turned on the television. "No cable?" has asked, seeing only static as he flipped through the channels.

"No," Pembridge replied. "That costs extra. Internet too. Eggerton had neither."

"That's interesting. I wonder what the hell he was doing when he was here," Reagan thought out loud as he took out his iPhone to search for a WiFi connection. "No WiFi either, unless there's a hidden network."

"Hidden network?" asked Watson.

"Yeah, not all WiFi networks are visible. Some of them don't broadcast their IDs. You have to know how to log on to access them," Reagan explained.

"I don't know if we checked," Pembridge admitted, "but I'll find out."

Reagan turned off the TV and went to the bathroom, where he stood on the toilet and pulled down the cover from the ceiling fan. He found nothing but dust and pushed it back in place. Other than the fan, he could see no reasonable place to hide something so he checked the door, examining the hinges.

"What are you looking for, Jack?" asked Pembridge.

"Signs that the screws have been worked recently, in case there's a blind."

"We checked thoroughly – there isn't any. Wait, you know about blinds?" a surprised Pembridge asked.

"Yeah," Reagan said, walking to the table and sitting down, as though to look out the window. "What's the view like?" he asked, knowing it was too dark out to see anything.

"Strip mall with some low-end stores and a pizza place. And yes, there *is* a video camera, oriented towards their parking lot. We're checking the footage," Watson replied, anticipating his next question.

"How about that?" Reagan asked, pointing at the dresser.

"Thoroughly checked, Jack. Empty and pretty clean," Pembridge said.

Reagan walked over to the dresser all the same and looked behind it, seeing only a power strip plugged into a wall outlet. He pushed the heavy dresser to the side and walked behind it, kneeling by the outlet, where he noticed a small object that had been dislodged from somewhere under the dresser. "I've got something here. Either you have a camera?" he asked as he backed away.

"Yeah, I do," said Pembridge, removing a Nikon DSLR from his bag and placing a marker on the floor next to the object before taking a couple of pictures. He then took a latex glove from his bag and used it to pick the thing up and place it on the dresser, where the three of them crowded to examine it.

"What is that?" asked Watson.

"Don't know," Pembridge shrugged. "It feels like plastic, probably broke off something else. The wall outlet, maybe?"

Reagan maneuvered behind the dresser and again knelt by the outlet, examining it. "Nothing seems broken here," he said. "Has this thing been dusted for prints?"

"I'm pretty sure it has been," Pembridge replied, handing Reagan a glove all the same.

Reagan put the glove on his right hand before handling the outlet, noting it was loose. It seemed to be barely screwed in, and he used his fingertips to unscrew it all the way, letting it hang into the room. He used the light from his phone to check behind it, seeing only the wires at the back of the outlet from the adjoining apartment. His curiosity getting the better of him, Reagan put his finger carefully against the back of the neighbor's outlet and pushed gently, surprised that it readily gave way and fell into Ms. Johnson's apartment. "This is weird, guys" he said, explaining what he found as he made way for Pembridge to check it out. "Any other loose outlets?"

Watson went around the room checking and shook her head. "No, they're all screwed in tight. What are you thinking, Jack?"

"I'm thinking that plastic thing is the clip off the end of a phone cord or a LAN cable, and Eggerton was snaking one or the other through the outlet from his neighbor's apartment," he replied.

"That's a bit of a stretch!" Pembridge objected, even though he found that explanation very plausible.

"Remind me what we know about the neighbor," Reagan asked Watson.

"Single mother, age 32. Two kids, boys, ages 7 and 9. She's got a record for possession of narcotics a few years back, but nothing recent. Works part-time at a mini-mart down the street. She's lived here for three years – Nashville before that. The building manager says she's quiet, keeps to herself, always pays her rent on time and in full. He said she stopped by last Friday in tears and told him that her mom was sick and she would be taking the boys to go see her. That's all we have...No, wait, she drives a brown Chevy Malibu. The car isn't in the lot," Watson replied as she flipped through her notes.

"Can you track down the mother?" Reagan asked.

"We're in the process of doing just that," Pembridge said.

"Please check on the progress. Right now, please," Reagan asked, the urgency clear in his voice.

"Ok, fine," Pembridge replied, taking out his phone. Watson looked at Reagan, shaking her head in the universal expression for "what?"

"I've got a bad feeling about this. Somehow I don't think Ms. Johnson went home to visit her sick mom," Reagan offered as he walked out to knock on the neighbor's door, followed closely by Watson.

Pembridge joined them a minute later, a puzzled look on his face. "Kirk Johansen spoke with Mrs. Johnson. She hasn't heard from her daughter in almost three years."

"I think we need to get this door open, and right now," Reagan said.

"We can't just kick down the door, Jack. We don't have probable cause," Pembridge warned. "We can probably – let me emphasize, *probably* get a warrant, but it'll take a bit of time."

"How about a wellness check, then?" Reagan suggested.

"We don't do those," Pembridge responded.

"Yeah, but they do," Reagan countered, pointing at the unmarked police car. "What can it hurt to ask?" he pressed.

"Fair point," Pembridge replied, heading down the stairs. A few minutes later, having explained the situation, he was back with two detectives.

"What do you expect to find in there?" asked the older one.

"At best? An empty apartment that's been thoroughly scrubbed. At worst? Three bodies," Reagan replied grimly, surprising not only the detectives but Agents Watson and Pembridge as well.

"Ah shit," mumbled the younger detective as he sized up the door. He drew his service weapon and gave the door a good swift kick, his right heel connecting just below the doorknob as he transferred his weight to his right leg. The door crashed open, and the two detectives went in, followed closely by Watson and Pembridge. Reagan kept his distance, despite not having been told to do so. This apartment, he noted instantly, was much larger than Eggerton's. It had a proper living area and two separate bedrooms to the side, with a kitchen and bathroom towards the rear. The apartment itself smelled oddly rancid, a smell Reagan instantly associated with death.

"We've got bodies here," the older detective called from one of the bedrooms moments after the apartment had been cleared. Everyone crowded the door, but no one approached the three bodies stacked between the two beds, tightly wrapped in plastic sheets sealed with packing tape. "I suppose y'all want the scene?" asked the same detective, breaking the silence.

"We do," nodded Pembridge. "Any objections?"

"None I can think of," the older detective replied, unable to look away from the bodies of the children. "How old were they?" he asked softly, adding "Damn!" after Watson answered.

Reagan backed away to look through the rest of the apartment, careful not to touch anything. It was hard not to miss the contrast between the family photos and colorful children's drawings that lined the walls and the complete absence of any signs of normal family life; this apartment had been scrubbed as clean as Eggerton's. There was no mess, no clutter, not so much as a single piece of garbage in the trash. Jack found the LAN outlet where he expected it to be, next to the outlet he had pushed through, under a desk that was slightly discolored from the heat generated by a well-used laptop that was conspicuous for its absence. He took one last look around the room and went outside, finding a bench on the ground floor by the stairs. He sat there, lost in his thoughts, not feeling the cold night air despite having left his coat in the car.

Some time passed before Agent Watson joined him, sitting next to him, her hand on his shoulder. "Are you ok, Jack?" she asked, leaning closer, mistaking his pensiveness for something else.

"I am," he replied. "As horrible as that was, it's not what I was thinking about. I was thinking about how methodical – how calculated – all of this is, which in turn got me thinking about *what* this is. There's a lot more going on than just the shooting in the park and this homicide here, but I'm not seeing the bigger picture. I'm having a hard time figuring about how to go about figuring it out, if that makes sense."

"Just keep working the case and it will come to you. If anyone can figure this all out, it's you. Hell, you've been at least a step ahead of all of us from the get-go – and one of these days, I'll have to sit you down so you can explain to me how your mind works," Watson said with an encouraging smile.

"Hmm? It isn't working very well at the moment, I'm sorry to say," Reagan admitted sheepishly.

"That's because your brain is freezing to death. It's like twenty below out here," she exclaimed with an exaggerated shiver. "Come on, let's get you warmed up in the car, because this is going to take a while."

"It's really not *that* cold out, Amanda," he objected with a smile.

"Yes it is. And I'm glad to see you're actually wrong about something. It makes you *almost* human," she replied, almost playfully. "Now come on, let's go," she said, taking Reagan by the hand and leading him to the car.

Reagan watched from the warm comfort of the car as the parking lot slowly filled with vehicles, their red and blue flashing lights intruding upon the darkness of the moonless night. The groups of agents crowding the apartment door parted when the bodies were carried out, their heads bowed respectfully, paying silent tribute to children whose dreams and ambitions would never be fulfilled. Reagan, too, bowed his head, thinking not just of these children but the ones whose lives were cut short in the park. He continued watching the scene after the coroner left with his precious charges, but his thoughts were on the children in the park – the look of terror on their faces as he ran towards them, trying to usher them to safety. Reagan felt suddenly tired, as though he had just lived through the shooting again. His mind was wandering, he knew, and that wasn't good, so he leaned his seat back, closed his eyes and went to sleep.

12

The sun was fully above the horizon when Reagan opened his eyes to the sound of the ringing phone. He stifled a groan at the prospect of waking up this early on a Sunday morning – or any morning, for that matter. He was not at all a morning person; he was at his most productive in the afternoon and evening, and did his most creative work late at night. His colleagues had once remarked his tendency to work well into the night, rewarding his flurry of two a.m. e-mails with a vintage Navy poster depicting a submarine with the caption, "We Dive Deep While Others Sleep." That poster, like so many other things from his past, was now secured in a storage lockup in New Jersey.

Reagan felt a momentary pang of guilt at the realization that so many agents had worked the crime scene all night while he was sleeping comfortably, but there was nothing he could do about that. He had no idea how to work a crime scene, and would only have been in the way. The photos, he saw on his return to the NCIS office at three in the morning, were such a disorganized mess that without some forethought into an approach to their review, going through them would have been an unproductive waste of time. So he chose to return to his hotel to sleep, well used to processing his thoughts even while he slept.

Agent Watson was looking as pretty as ever, Reagan observed as he put his luggage in the trunk of her car, noting that her hair was up in a complicated ponytail that must have required a fair bit of effort on her part. "Good morning, Amanda – you look great this morning, as always," he said as he climbed in the car next to her. "Nice ponytail, by the way," he added with a smile.

"Why, thank you, Jack," she replied, practically beaming. She would never admit how long she had fussed to get it just so, and nor would she admit that these last few days she had been taking more time than usual to get ready in the morning, wanting her appearance to be just right for a man she had just met but whom she felt she had known for ages. "You're looking good, too," she added, observing that Reagan's idea of Sunday casual was a dark suit worn over a checkered blue shirt without a tie. Nothing had turned during the night, so the two talked about the weather as they drove quickly through the empty streets; on winter weekends, the nation's capital is as deserted as a Western ghost town. The temperature had dropped precipitously, and snow was in the forecast.

On walking into his office, such as it was, Reagan stopped short and laughed. Someone had placed a coffeemaker on the table, with a bright red ribbon on top. His fondness for coffee had been noticed by agents well-trained to observe small details. He plugged the machine in and brewed a pot, wondering whom to thank, then reached for the phone to call Director Smythe, asking for some help with software from someone in the IT Department. Next he started reading the inventory of Ms. Johnson's apartment that he found on his desk, placed on his keyboard. He looked up when he heard a knock on his open door.

"Special Agent Reagan? My name is Armando Diaz. I'm a computer forensics specialist. Director Smythe called me and told me to help you with whatever you need, sir." Diaz was a gifted programmer who could have made a fortune working in Silicon Valley, but was passionate about serving his country and chose to work at NCIS instead. His family had served in the Marine Corps, participating in just about every military action since World War I, but Diaz had lost vision in his right eye due to a childhood infection so was precluded from enlisting in the military. If he couldn't fight for his country, at least he could help those who did.

"It's just Jack Reagan – I'm not an agent, special or otherwise," he corrected. "I need to review a whole lot of pictures, but the only program I could find on this computer is the built-in image viewer. My personal laptop has a program that lets me sort through pictures in various ways, such as by date or by geotagged location. Do you have anything like that I can use?"

"Absolutely, let me set that up for you," Diaz replied, removing a USB drive from his backpack and installing the appropriate software. "Do you need me to show you how to use it?"

"That's OK, I think I can manage. Thank you very much." Reagan's first computer had been a Commodore 64, and he had learned to program at age six. Computers were easy for him to understand.

"If you need anything else, please call me at any time, sir," Diaz said, handing over his business card.

"Actually, I just thought of something. Can you set up a second monitor as well? I'd like to be able to compare photos side by side."

"I'll go get one right now," Diaz promised, turning to head out the door.

"Wait, sorry, one last thing," Reagan called out. "Can you go see Special Agent Amanda Watson – she's using a visiting agent desk. She's going through these photos too and might find this program useful."

"Will do," Diaz nodded as he walked out.

For her part, Watson wasn't so sure the program would be helpful. Despite being born in the Age of the Internet, she wasn't nearly as computer savvy as one might expect. She needed the tutorial and sat through it, trying to remember all the features and how to access them. At the end, she gave the program a try but quickly decided it would be faster for her to revert to the simple program she knew better.

Reagan organized the photos by date and started to go through them, looking at Eggerton's pictures on the additional monitor while he compared them to the new photos on the laptop. Many of the pictures his fellow Marines had taken showed the same scenery that Eggerton had snapped – a landscape that seemed every bit as desolate as some parts of the American Southwest. Then there were the pictures of the Marines mugging for the camera, much like some of the photos Eggerton had taken. What jumped out at Reagan, however, was that whereas Eggerton's camera contained very few pictures of towns or the Afghan people, his fellow Marines had taken many, many photos with those subjects.

Next Reagan noted that on the dates matching Eggerton's deleted pictures, the other Marines had predominantly taken photos of villagers going about their daily activities – a woman hanging out her washings, two men smoking in the shade, children climbing on a Humvee, young adults posing with the Marines. Eggerton himself appeared in a number of photos, which Reagan studied closely, examining the eyes and the body language, trying to understand how this man was capable of participating in the murder of children and federal agents. He tagged all the photos in which Eggerton appeared, and separately tagged the photos taken on dates for which Eggerton had deleted photos. Reagan was so engrossed in the photos that he lost track of time. Eventually, though, his eyes started to feel excessively dry, so he leaned back in his chair and closed his eyes.

"Sunday afternoon nap, Jack?" Reagan opened his eyes to see Watson standing in his door with a grin on her face. He glanced at his watch and saw it was already past three.

"Wow, where does the time go?" he asked. "Not napping, just resting my eyes. I thought they were going to catch fire."

"I figured," she laughed, handing him a small bottle of Visine.

"Very thoughtful of you," he replied, eagerly grabbing the bottle. "What have you been up to?"

"A whole lot of pictures, and a whole lot of nothing in them," she replied. "I'm not sure what I was expecting, though."

"Horns and a pitchfork, maybe?"

"Maybe," she allowed. After the gruesome scene in Ms. Johnson's apartment, Watson wouldn't have been surprised.

"Anyway, I've come to get you for a meeting. We're going to go over what we've got so far from last night."

Reagan accompanied Watson to a larger conference room packed with agents. He leaned against the back wall and listened to the presentations, pen and notepad in hand to jot down anything of interest. The meeting started with an overview of the coroner's initial findings, which for all the clinical and antiseptic language, revealed a crime of shocking brutality. Ligature marks suggested that all three victims had been restrained, the plastic cords cutting into their wrists and ankles. Bruises of various discoloration revealed beatings on multiple occasions. Ms. Johnson had likely been raped repeatedly, and even more disturbingly, the marks on her neck suggested she had been asphyxiated manually – someone had strangled her, and left an impression of his hands in the process. She had probably been killed within a day of when she told the property manager she was leaving town.

Her sons survived her by a few days before their throats were cut with such force that they had very nearly been decapitated. They had been found with gags in their mouths, and the stains on the carpet suggested they had been tied up next to the bed, forced to sit with their mother's body, perhaps even forced to watch her raped and killed before their very eyes. *Brutality against children*, Reagan wrote, wondering what horrors Eggerton had endured in his childhood to cause him to act with such viciousness. There was little doubt that Eggerton was the rapist and killer; his DNA and fingerprints were everywhere. Some other DNA and fingerprints were found as well, in the bathroom, but there was nothing to compare them to.

Johnson's apartment had been cleaned almost as thoroughly as Eggerton's. Her cellphone was missing, probably destroyed since Verizon had been unable to ping it. Her credit card records showed she owned two laptops, both of which were nowhere to be found. There was a modicum of hope that her ISP would be able to provide some minimal history of her internet use, but the packets of data reflecting her usage were mixed with the packets of data from the entire building, meaning that it would take a fair bit of time to sort through. There was good news, however. This apartment had not been cleaned nearly as well; a SIM card was found tucked into the sofa, and that was expected to generate some solid leads. *Unless it was planted there*, Reagan thought skeptically. Nevertheless, he circled *SIM* on his pad as a reminder to himself to find out more about it.

The only other thing that caught his attention was the fact that Johnson's car hadn't been found within a reasonable walking distance of her apartment. Together with the unknown DNA in the bathroom, this told Reagan that Eggerton had at least one accomplice. He had his own car, and couldn't very well drive both at the same time. More than that, the DNA didn't match any of the shooters in the park. *Conspiracy*, he wrote. It wasn't enough, of course, but it was a lot more than they had just one day earlier, and the investigation was pressing on. The meeting wrapped up and the agents trickled back to their desks, returning to whatever they had been working on with their enthusiasm somewhat reinvigorated by the apparent progress that was being made. Reagan lingered, wanting to talk to Cannon.

"Nice work, Jack," Cannon said when they were alone.

"What for?" he asked, confused.

"For pushing the issue with regard to the neighbor. We would have gotten to it in due course, but you got us there much faster, so thanks, and nice work," Cannon replied. "What can I do for you?"

"Is there anyone I can speak with in Afghanistan about the pictures and other details?" he wanted to know.

"Special Agent Tommy Cho is heading things up there. Very good agent. Anything specific you want to know?"

"Not really. Or rather, not yet. I'm sure I'll have some questions. Right now I'm still organizing my thoughts but figured it might be easier to pick up the phone and hear it directly rather than play telephone and have everything relayed. If that's OK with you," Reagan added.

"Fine by me, Jack. You seem to have a decent handle on things. Cho's got a satellite phone – I'll give you the number." Cannon read the number off his phone as Reagan wrote it down, repeating it to make sure he got it right. "Just remember there's like a 9 hour time difference," Cannon pointed out.

"Nine and a half hours, I think," Reagan corrected.

"Like I said, Jack, you seem to have a decent handle on things," Cannon chuckled.

The rest of the day flew by as Reagan continued going through the thousands of photos, paying careful attention to flag each one in which Eggerton appeared, as well as the ones showing other people with whom he had posed. It was tedious work to be sure, but Reagan thought it essential to organize them in that manner. It seemed the logical way to do it, and he had long experience keeping track of complicated fact patterns, finding the best way to make sense of the data. Coffee helped, as did the Visine, and eventually he got through all the photos. He leaned back in his chair and closed his eyes, breathing a sigh of relief, confident that he hadn't missed anything. Leaning back, though, caused him to become suddenly dizzy, and he realized that he hadn't eaten anything all day other than the Snickers bar he bought from a vending machine after the mid-afternoon meeting ended six hours earlier.

Reagan stood in front of the vending machine and contemplated his options, vaguely reminded of his college days – then, too, he had subsisted on stale coffee and junk food. Another Snickers bar would hold him over, he thought, remembering that the Marriott had 24-hour room service and a decent burger. Chocolate in hand, he walked over to Watson's desk, as much to check on her progress as for a pleasant diversion before returning to more closely analyze the photos.

"Hey, Jack!" she said, smiling as she looked up at him. "I stopped by earlier but you seemed to be so focused on your monitors that I didn't want to bother you. What're you up to?"

"Never a bother, Amanda. I decided to grab some dinner," he replied, holding up his candy. "How are you doing?"

"Going blind, of course. That's not a very healthy meal, you know." She tried to sound stern but couldn't keep a straight face.

"Really?" Reagan asked, ostentatiously looking at the empty chocolate wrappers in her trash. "Yes, I see... Very healthy!"

"Hush!" The way she said it made Reagan grin. "Yes ma'am," he replied. They spent a few minutes talking about nothing of consequence – both had simply needed a break and found one another's company enjoyable – before Jack excused himself to head back to his office, eating his dinner as he walked.

He selected only the several hundred photos that included Eggerton and sorted them by time and date, preparing to review them carefully, when suddenly he stopped, slapping the table with his hand. "Shit," he cursed, loud enough to catch the brief attention of an agent walking past his door. *You stupid idiot, how could you forget that!* Reagan cursed at himself, remembering that the timestamp on each photo would not be accurate unless the owner of each camera had set the date and time correctly. More than that, Reagan realized that he personally never adjusted the time when he travelled – all his photos, regardless of where in the world they were taken, showed Eastern Daylight Savings Time. He had no way of knowing which Marines had adjusted their settings and which ones hadn't, and instantly confirmed there was a problem when he looked at the progression of shots on his screen. Some of the photos – probably taken in very close proximity because they showed more or less the same thing – were separated on his screen by as much as a two days.

But no more than that. *Ok, I can work with this.* For now, hyper-accuracy was not as important as the overall picture, so to speak. He would ask Agent Cho to check the date on each camera – assuming the cameras weren't sent here along with their storage cards – and then have someone manually adjust the timestamps. No big deal, just lots more work. For someone else, Reagan realized, allowing himself to relax a little as he started scrolling through the pictures, spending no more than a few seconds on each. Within half an hour, it was clear to him that there was a story in the pictures, and Reagan felt a pang of excitement as he slowed down and started over, studying Eggerton's facial features and body language carefully, frame by frame, validating his initial impressions as he did so.

In the photos taken during the first two weeks of his deployment, Eggerton seemed normal, for lack of a better word. He mugged for the camera with apparent good humor, striking what he must have considered to be fun poses. He seemed to be smiling in pretty much every shot, with his eyes as much as with his lips. In group shots, he was always close to the center, one or both of his arms wrapped around his friends. The photos taken during the next two weeks of his deployment showed some small changes. That was around when Eggerton had started to take pictures with the native population, and most of the pictures seemed to be with the same people, two women and three men. He still mugged for the camera with a smile, but now he was standing farther away from the center of the group shots.

During Eggerton's second month in Afghanistan, most of the pictures he was in were taken with some or all of those five Afghans. He seemed to be sitting or standing closer to one of the women, and smiling at her more than at the camera. The girl, for her part, seemed equally focused on Eggerton. In contrast, he was generally at the outer edge of any group shot, no longer embracing any of his fellow Marines. And in his solo pictures, his smile seemed increasingly forced, his eyes more serious. It was almost as though that Afghan family – if that's what they were – had supplanted his Marine unit in importance.

The photos taken immediately prior to Eggerton's disappearance showed yet another change, one that Reagan found very significant. Eggerton was hardly in any photos, and the girl he had been next to in so many of the earlier shots was nowhere to be seen. In fact, his only photo with the native population was with the two men Reagan assumed to be the woman's brothers, and Eggerton looked fairly downcast in that shot. He wasn't in any group shots with his fellow Marines, and the only other photograph Reagan could find showed Eggerton standing alone and slouched over, his hands in his pockets, his face angled towards the ground.

Collectively, the photos told a very simple boy-meets-girl story: Eggerton had met a local girl a few weeks into his deployment and grown close to her. But something had probably happened to the girl, and Eggerton didn't take it well. He seemed increasingly depressed and isolative, and then he deserted his unit. Finally, after several long days, Reagan felt like he was starting to understand the man better. He changed the view on his screen, displaying the geotagged location of the village and jotting down its coordinates. Next he wrote down the range of dates for the photographs in which Eggerton posed with the girl. He had quite the request in store for Special Agent Tommy Cho, and Reagan hoped the man was up to the task.

13

The only nice thing he could say about Kandahar Province so far was that the weather wasn't half bad for winter, Special Agent Tommy Cho thought. In fact, it wasn't far different from what he was used to in Italy, where he had been stationed at Capodichino in Naples. All things being equal, Cho would much have preferred to be back there than at the edge of the Registan Desert at FOB Jeremiah. The best thing he could say about this forward operating base was that it exceeded his expectations – Cho had grown up watching Vietnam War movies, and in his mind a FOB consisted of a couple of mud huts surrounded by sandbags and concertina wiring. FOB Jeremiah sprawled across several acres and had semi-permanent structures – and most of the amenities of home. It even had a small airstrip for supporting air operations, but no helicopters were parked there at the moment.

Cho had always been nervous about flying in those things; they seemed to fall out of the sky for no reason at all. He had all the more reason to be nervous due to the reason he had come to be sent to Jeremiah: to take over for Special Agent Matt Gunn, who had been one of three fatalities when his helicopter developed engine trouble and crashed. Although he had worked with Gunn in the distant past, he hadn't known him very well. His work seemed a little lackadaisical, and as Cho read the transcripts of Gunn's November interviews with the Marines serving with Eggerton, he was frustrated to see that Gunn hadn't pushed very hard for details. Cho was equally frustrated by the lack of direction from either Quantico or D.C.; Eggerton's unit had been restricted to base and all their electronic devices had been confiscated, so they knew something was up. And the more time that passed, the more time they had to rehearse their

120

answers. Cho resolved to call Director Smythe for guidance at the precise moment his phone rang.

"Tommy Cho," he said, recognizing the number on his display as coming from the Washington field office.

"Special Agent Cho, my name is Jack Reagan. I'm calling you from the Washington field office, where I've been going through the photos you sent. Doug Cannon gave me your number and..."

"I know who you are, Mr. Reagan. Doug filled me in," Cho interrupted. "He told me you're the one who came up with the bright idea for me to stay up all night uploading photos. Nice shooting, by the way. If we ever meet, I think I'd like to buy you a beer. What can I do for you?"

"Thanks," Reagan replied. He had gotten used to people stopping him in the hallways to shake his hand and offer to buy him a drink when this case was over. "I've got some follow-up questions for you, if you don't mind. First of all, did you just send over the physical media, or the cameras as well?"

"Cameras and smartphones. I didn't send the whole laptops though – I just popped out the hard drives. Why?"

Reagan explained the discrepancy in the timestamps. *Shit!* Cho thought, *I didn't think of that.* "Once you get the cameras, can you let me know what the difference is?" he asked.

"I can do you one better," Reagan replied. "I was thinking of having someone adjust the dates and times on the photos on the server."

"Perfect!" Cho laughed, grateful to have one less labor-intensive thing to do. "Find anything in the pictures?" He hadn't gotten around to reviewing them yet.

"Yes, as a matter of fact. You know the saying that a picture is worth a thousand words? Well, these pictures certainly seem to tell a story," Reagan said, explaining what he had found as Cho furiously scribbled down what he heard.

"That's quite some story, Mr. Reagan. I'll grant you that it makes a whole lot of sense, even though I haven't seen all the pictures yet, but it's a lot to conclude just from photos. Do you have anything else?"

"No. That's the reason I called you, though. I'm hoping you can fill in some of the details. The name's Jack, by the way."

"Ok, Jack. What do you have in mind?" Cho asked.

"Well for starters, Eggerton's fellow Marines probably know a lot more than what they said in their interviews," Reagan replied.

"You're probably right," Cho admitted. "Is this just a hunch, or do you have anything more solid to go on?" he asked hopefully.

"Nothing really solid," Reagan conceded. "A few instances of evasiveness here and there in the transcripts, but nothing more. Call it a strong hunch, maybe. I've deposed enough people to have a good sense when someone is holding something back or lying," he added. "Besides, now we have a better sense of what questions to ask."

"Fair enough," Cho replied. "Any other ideas? Just so you know, these guys have been sitting around for a few days. They probably know something's up and have had plenty of time to rehearse their stories."

"Do they have any idea Eggerton is connected to the shootings?" Reagan asked.

"I doubt it. Everyone has heard of the terrorist attack in the park, but Eggerton hasn't been linked to it. Besides, we took away their electronics."

"Good. Then you've got something to press them with – they aren't just covering for their friend anymore, they're co-conspirators in the murder of children if they don't spill what they know. They're aiding and abetting a terrorist," Reagan replied.

"Not bad, Jack. Not half bad," Cho said with a chuckle. "Can you e-mail me some of the photos – ones that show which Marines he seems closest to, and the ones you called the family photos?"

"Hold on, let me see if I can." Reagan double-clicked the Mail icon and was surprised to see that an e-mail account had been set up for his use. "Yeah, I'll do that straightaway," he promised. "One more thing – can you try to get IDs on the family, figure out who they were?"

"I can surely try," Cho replied. "I'm going to do some interviews first and see what pops, and then grab a translator and head out. Where am I going?"

Reagan read out the coordinates, which Cho repeated in verification.

"Where can I reach you with what I turn up?" Cho asked, then jotted down the cellphone number Reagan gave him. "Ok, Jack, I'll get right on this. Good talking to you, and good working with you, too," he added before hanging up. Both men had the exact same thought – *finally, some progress.*

Reagan spent a few minutes going through the photos, selecting the ones he thought would be most useful to Cho – about twenty in all – and dragged them into an e-mail. Then he spent another hour typing up his notes. When he finished, he re-organized them in another file and wrote a detailed summary. Satisfied with his work, he shut down his computer and went to find Watson. It had been a productive day, after all, and as tired as he was, Reagan was also elated by what he had found. More than that, he was confident that Cho would fill in the gaps to their knowledge, and a better picture would start to emerge as to what Eggerton was involved in.

The phone rang at the appropriate time and Reagan reached over to the bedside table, lifting the receiver slightly before dropping it back down. The Marriott, he knew, used a pre-recorded message for waking its guests, so there was no one to thank on the other end of the line. He got out of bed with less reluctance than usual, actually looking forward to getting a start on the day. He looked out the window as his coffee brewed, noting the snow that had fallen during the night. About an inch, he thought, with lots more on the way. Snow didn't bother him; Jack had a competent SUV and lots of experience behind the wheel, having driven through every weather condition and every possible terrain imaginable. As much as he loved to drive – for him it was a relaxing hobby – he remembered that Washington D.C. tended to shut down at the slightest dusting of snow. It wasn't the snow that was bad, Reagan thought as he climbed into the shower. It was the presence of unskilled drivers who had no business being on the roads.

"Good morning, Amanda," he said, opening the door on the second knock. "You look lovely this morning, as usual," he added with a smile, noting her wavy hair caressing her shoulders, free of the usual ponytail.

"Good morning to you too, Jack. You're in a good mood this morning," she remarked with a smile of her own. She hadn't slept well at all; she had nightmares of the Johnson children slaughtered in their apartment. But somehow Reagan's good mood was instantly contagious, and she drew positive energy from his enthusiasm.

"I guess I am," he replied. "I just have a strong feeling that we'll get some answers today."

"I hope so," Watson said. She hadn't quite made the same observations as Reagan about the photos, but then again she hadn't organized them as he had. "You're going to have to sit me down and show me what you found when we get in."

"With pleasure," Reagan responded, grabbing a bag and closing the door behind him. "A change of clothes, in case we get snowed in," he explained, seeing the quizzical expression on her face.

"Me too," she said with a laugh. "But the storm isn't supposed to hit until late tonight."

They listened to a news station on the radio as they drove in. The previous week's shooting was still receiving top billing, and an incensed caller was demanding that the government send in troops to deal with the terrorists on their home turf.

"What do you think about that, Jack?" Watson asked.

"It's a complicated issue," he allowed. "But it makes more sense to me to take an active role over there, rather than funnel weapons to unreliable assets who can just as easily use them against us." He could have said more than that, but this wasn't the time or the place. In his mind, Iraq had turned into a disaster because America didn't have the stomach to properly occupy the country, and Afghanistan was in very real danger of turning out the same way. People were too quick to forget the lessons of history. Germany and Japan had turned into stable and reliable partners because America had spent years in occupation after World War II, helping them rebuild their infrastructure, economy and civil society. That the Allies had not done the same with Germany after World War I had resulted in the rise to power of Adolf Hitler and the deaths of millions of people. America and England had understood that simple fact when Germany lay defeated in 1944, and had funneled manpower and money to help rebuild it, to everyone's benefit.

But not so today. Public opinion, fueled by liberal politicians and the media, had turned against the Iraq War very quickly, and the Bush Administration lacked the fortitude to make the hard choice to become an occupying power. Then came Obama, with easy promises of ending the war and bringing the troops home – great campaign slogans, but a poor strategy for bringing stability to the region. Even worse were the consequences of the so-called Arab Spring. Gaddafi and Mubarak had hardly been saints, but at least they were known entities whose interests in fighting Islamist terrorists were more closely aligned with America's than the regimes that replaced them. Much as Carter had done with Iran, so too Obama had chosen the wrong people to deal with – to America's detriment. As a result, the Middle East was more unstable and dangerous than it had ever been in Reagan's memory.

Watson could sense that Reagan had more to say – she was good at reading people, after all. "You know, you can talk politics with me any time you want to. I don't mind."

"It's been my experience that talking politics with people you like or respect can lead to disappointment, especially when they don't share your views," he replied with a chuckle. Reagan had never judged a person on the basis of race, gender or sexual orientation, but the older he got, the more he judged people on the basis of their politics. After all, life is too short to argue with people who see things in fundamentally different terms than you do.

"I know what you mean," Watson replied. She and her closest friends shared more or less the same views – morality, politics and even religion were all interconnected and, in her opinion, said much about a person's character. "But guess what? I'm willing to bet we see eye to eye on most things. Besides, you've heard what I listen to, and I know the campaign contributions you've made. Plus I think I know where you stand on gun rights. We're on the same page," she added with a conspiratorial wink. Amanda smiled as she pulled into the parking lot, focused on the first part of Reagan's last sentence. Jack smiled as well, having found one more thing to like about Watson.

Late in the morning, Special Agent Cannon called another status meeting to update everyone on the latest developments. Reagan took his place along the back wall in the large conference room, listening but not concentrating very well. Now that he felt he had a better handle on Lance Corporal Eggerton, he needed to figure out what Eggerton and his co-conspirators were planning – and it was proving devilishly tricky figuring how to go about doing that. *More data will help, Jack, so pay attention!*

Two things caught his attention during the briefing. The first was that using facial recognition software, they had a strong possible match – sixty percent – between one of the shooters

126

from the park and an Afghan man standing next to Eggerton in one of the pictures uploaded two days earlier. Reagan knew that photo well; it was one he had flagged and even e-mailed to Special Agent Cho the night before. This was the first concrete link, he heard Cannon say, connecting Eggerton to the terrorists.

The second thing that Reagan found important was that forensics had been able to access the SIM card found in Johnson's apartment, and that held all sorts of promising leads. They had been able to identify several calls exchanged with cellphones registered in Paterson, New Jersey, and were working to flesh out more details. *Paterson...I know that's important somehow, but how?* The answer hadn't quite come to him when he felt his phone vibrate, and he left the room discretely to answer it.

"Jack? Tommy Cho here," he heard on the other end of the line. "You know that beer I owe you? Well forget about it, pal – I'm going to buy you a whole fucking case. You were right, Jack!"

"About what?" Reagan asked, noting that Cho seemed outright elated.

"The story, the girl, everything. Even the approach. I interviewed a couple of Eggerton's buddies last night, and they folded the moment I told them they were being investigated as accomplices to the terrorist attack. Their first interview was complete bullshit – of course they knew more than they were saying." Cho wasn't just elated, he seemed positively giddy.

"So what did you find out?" Reagan asked.

"Got a pen, Jack?" Cho replied with a hearty laugh.

"Just a sec – I'm sitting down at my desk now. Ok, shoot!"

"The girl's name is Muska Abdali," Cho began, explaining in detail for close to twenty minutes. "That's some story, right? Anyway, I'm going to scan my notes and e-mail them to you. I'm going to start in on the other interviews now, and I don't know when I'll be able to type it up."

"Some story indeed," Reagan replied, setting down his pen and scanning several pages of notes. "Can you clarify something for me? Wait, it's easier if I send it to you again by e-mail," he said, selecting the photo that Cannon had showed in the conference room and sending it to Cho. "I just sent you a picture. When you get it, can you clarify which one is the girl's brother?"

"Sure, Jack. It just came through. Batoor is the one on the left, and the one on the right is the cousin whose name I don't have yet."

"On the left of the picture or on Eggerton's left?" Reagan asked.

"Sorry – I meant on Eggerton's left. Which means that he's the one on the right side of the picture," Cho clarified.

"Batoor is one of our shooters from the park," Reagan said quietly.

"Son of a fucking bitch!" Cho exclaimed. "How sure are you?"

"Sixty percent match. He was missing some of his face so that's the best they can do."

"That's your own fault, Jack," Cho laughed. "This is some pretty hot stuff!"

"It sure is," Reagan agreed. "Listen, I need you to do something else, soon as you can. If you can, that is."

"What's that, pal?"

"Go to the village and see what you can dig up. Verification, more details, more names, things like that. And DNA. *Especially* DNA," Reagan replied. "At this point, I think that's a little more important that the rest of the interviews."

"Jesus, you're not asking for much, are you?" Cho said in surprise. But the more he thought about it, the more sense it made. Besides, Cannon would probably ask him to do the exact same thing. "Yeah, I can do that, Jack. I can gather up some Marines and be there at first light. You're right, the other interviews can wait a little while longer. Do me a favor though – can you brief Cannon on this stuff?"

"I'll do that," Reagan promised. "Just as soon as I can organize this a little."

"Thanks, pal. My notes should be coming through in a few minutes. I'll call you as soon as I've got something," Cho said, ending the call.

Reagan went through his notes as he waited for Cho's e-mail, which he printed out and then read carefully. It helped that Cho had very neat handwriting. When he was finished, he started putting the details together into a cohesive story. Satisfied that he had reported every important detail, he picked up his phone and called Director Smythe's cellphone. "Director Smythe? This is Jack Reagan. I've got some things you need to know about," he began.

"Is it important, Jack?" Smythe's morning had not gone well. He had fought a turf battle with the Director of the FBI and Secretary of Homeland Security, both of whom wanted to take the lead in the investigation away from his people for lack of significant progress – despite the fact that both agencies were involved in the investigation and had so far come up with nothing. It didn't help that the FBI Director was a friend. Worse still, the Secretary of the Navy did not seem very enthusiastic in his support for NCIS. "Your people have taken a big hit, Francis," he had said. "Maybe it's better to let someone else take the lead."

"Very important, sir," Reagan replied.

"Ok then, go ahead." The Secretary of the Navy could wait a few minutes more.

"It's better if I tell you in person – it works better as a show and tell," Reagan said.

"I'm at Headquarters, Jack. It would take me an hour to get there and I've got a lot to deal with today." He paused, remonstrating himself for sounding so harsh. Cannon had kept him informed of what Reagan was doing, and both men were impressed with his work. Besides, Reagan didn't seem like the kind of guy who would jerk him around. "Is it really *that* important?" he asked.

"Yes sir, it really is. I could just brief Special Agent Cannon, but this is important enough for you to hear."

"Ok, Jack, see you in an hour." Smythe would just have to call SecNav from the car.

Reagan had one more call to make, and reached for the office phone to call Agent Watson. "Amanda? It's Jack. I need you to run a name for me, please."

"Sure, Jack. What's the name?" she asked, opening the appropriate program on her computer.

"Batoor Abdali," he replied, spelling it out.

"No hits," she said a few moments later.

"Can you try variations of the name," he asked.

"It's what I'm doing now, Jack. Still no hits. Who is this guy, anyway?"

"I'm pretty sure he's one of the shooters – the guy in the photo, I mean."

"How did you... Where did you come up with this?" Watson asked in surprise bordering on shock.

"I got it from Tommy Cho. I asked him to look into a few things last night and he came up with the name," Reagan explained. "I'll brief you fully when Director Smythe gets here in about an hour. Until then, can you cross-deck Abdali to other agencies? Maybe someone else has something."

"I'll do that," Watson promised, shaking her head in disbelief as she hung up the phone. She was starting to realize that Reagan would never stop surprising her.

14

The storm had come in earlier than expected, dumping enough snow to make driving a real challenge. As a result, it had taken Acting Director Smythe a little over two hours to reach the Washington office, his driver cursing most of the way. The phone call with the Secretary of the Navy – Smythe's titular boss – had gone pretty much as expected. The Secretary had legitimate concerns that this investigation was both too big and too close to home for NCIS, in light of the casualties they had suffered. Nevertheless, he had agreed to support Smythe in maintaining his agency's lead – provided that his agents could come up with a lead in the next 24 hours significant enough to justify their continued lead in the case. Such conditional support wasn't calculated to make Smythe happy, but Smythe didn't take it personally. Politics was politics, and all he could do was to encourage his agents to press forward as best they could. Besides, it sounded like Jack Reagan had come up with something, and the more he learned about Reagan, the more he liked.

Doug Cannon had kept him in the loop about Reagan's activities, and both men thought Reagan to be easily as bright as any of their young agents. Though he lacked the formal training in procedure and the familiarity with the resources that agents had available to them, Reagan knew his way around an investigation. His analysis was good, and he was always careful to distinguish what he could prove from what he merely thought. Most importantly, though, he knew how to ask the right questions, and had the capacity to seek answers to those questions in fairly creative ways. He was not bound by linear thought, and that was a good thing.

Smythe had asked Agent Johansen to continue doing background on Reagan, albeit discreetly, picking up where Agent

Watson had left off. There was never any question that Reagan was one of the good guys, but Smythe was always on the lookout for talent, so he took his time going over the dossier in the car, impressed with what he read. He looked over some of the briefs that Reagan had written, noting that he knew how to make a convincing case. He also noted that with one exception, Reagan had won every motion he had ever argued, and that was impressive in its own right. He was as well-traveled as he was well-educated; two decades worth of passport records showed that he had traveled extensively across six continents, though none of that was recent.

Equally interesting were Reagan's friends. He spoke with some frequency to a highly successful lawyer in Los Angeles and a well-known doctor in Chicago, both of whom had attended Columbia with Reagan. And then there were the friends from the wedding he had learned about indirectly from Watson – three highly decorated members of what until recently had been known as the Naval Special Warfare Development Group and an NSA section chief. These were the most interesting connections Reagan had, and curious as well. For Smythe, there were three types of friendships a person created: childhood (including college), situational, and occupational. What made these friendships so curious was that Smythe couldn't determine how they had been formed. He had checked all the service records and knew that none of the SEALs had gone to school with Reagan or lived in the same state at the same time as him. So how, then, had they met, let alone become such good friends? It was a mystery, but a mystery of the sort Smythe liked to solve. He could, of course, simply ask Reagan, but he rather suspected he would receive an evasive reply at best.

By the time Smythe walked into the conference room-turned-office accompanied by Agents Cannon, Pembridge, Hollerman and Watson, Reagan had reviewed his presentation and had had enough time to refine it further. He had also had the foresight to brew a fresh pot of coffee. Smythe poured himself a cup and sat down directly across from Reagan, with the other agents bringing in chairs around the table.

"Ok, Jack, what have you got for us that's so important?" Smythe asked.

"For starters, I've got an ID on one of the shooters," Reagan replied, turning his monitor to face his guests and pulling up the photo that Cannon had used earlier. "The man at the right hand side of the screen, standing to Eggerton's left, is named Batoor Abdali. He's the man who was identified as a sixty percent match with one of our shooters."

"Holy shit!" exclaimed Pembridge as Cannon asked Reagan how he came up with that name.

Smythe raised his hand, silencing his agents. "You've got our undivided attention, Jack. Go ahead."

"First of all, Amanda, were you able to find anything on Abdali?" Reagan asked.

"No sir – I mean no, Jack," Watson corrected herself, blushing in the process. "No other agency has anything on him that I've found yet."

"Thanks for checking. Let me take this chronologically," Reagan said, starting his briefing. "Lawrence Eggerton joined the Marine Corps shortly after his marriage failed. He told one of his friends in the unit that he did so because he had become bored with his life and wanted an adventure. His career in the Corps was fairly undistinguished, but he enjoyed it enough to re-enlist. At the time of his deployment to Afghanistan, he was considered a friend by most of the people in his unit, albeit not a particularly close friend. He enjoyed drinking, playing poker, and participating in other so-called 'normal' activities, like playing basketball, hunting and going to strip clubs. He wasn't known to have any girlfriends, and was considered fairly shy when it came to women.

"During the first two weeks of his deployment, he continued to be on good terms with the other Marines in his unit, and continued to play cards, play basketball, and engage in common recreation activities." Reagan paused, showing a number of pictures that reflected these activities. "Note the body language and facial expressions in these photos; he appears open and friendly, often near the center of action. In the third week of deployment, Eggerton's unit started patrolling the countryside around their forward operating base. One of the towns they passed through on every patrol – we don't have a name for this place yet, by the way – was located about five kilometers from the FOB, and its residents were particularly welcoming to the Marines. His unit spent upwards of an hour each day interacting with the people, cultivating relationships.

"According to his fellow Marines, one of the relationships Eggerton cultivated was with this family," Reagan continued, pausing to pull up a photo that showed Eggerton with his arm around a girl, surrounded by her family. "The girl's name is, or I should say was, Muska Abdali. That's her brother, Batoor," Reagan added, pointing. "This other young man next to him is her cousin, whose name we don't have yet, and the older man and woman are her parents. Eggerton began spending his time exclusively with Muska and her family, often causing the further movement of his unit to be delayed. According to his fellow Marines, Eggerton also snuck off base on at least two occasions, presumably to be with her. He said that he was in love with Muska, and indicated that he wanted to marry her and bring her and her family back to the States.

"During the second two weeks of his deployment, as he spent more and more time with Muska and her family, Eggerton became more distant from his friends. Note the body language and facial expressions during that period." Again Reagan paused, slowly scrolling through some more photos. "Compare that with his body language in these pictures taken by the other Marines that show Eggerton with Muska and her family. These other Marines, by the way, said that they didn't think Eggerton knew he was being photographed. In the fifth week of Eggerton's deployment, Muska and her cousin were visiting friends in another town at a time when another Marine unit was conducting operations in the area. Reportedly there was an exchange of fire between those Marines and unknown subjects, during which Muska was killed and her cousin injured.

"Eggerton took the news hard. He became depressed and started to have mood swings, lashing out at other Marines and assaulting one from the unit that had been involved in the firefight. This assault appears not to have been reported, in part because his friends hoped Eggerton would snap out of it, but also because they were afraid of what he might do. Note how isolated he is in the last of the pictures taken of him before he deserted." Reagan again paused, pulling up more photos. "He had become angry as well, with one Marine reporting that Eggerton said, and I quote, 'I'm going to make those assholes pay for this.' You'll find full attribution to sources in this report," Reagan concluded, passing around copies of the document he had worked on.

"Damn, Jack," said Hollerman as the agents flipped through their copies of the report.

"I see you've talked to Tommy Cho," said Smythe, as much a question as a statement.

"I called him last night and talked to him about what I observed in the photos, and we discussed how to follow that up," Reagan replied.

"So I see," Smythe stated. He was taking his time, reading the report in full. "This is quite something," he said, looking up when he finished.

"It's more than we had before, Director. It gives us a better understanding of Eggerton, and it does seem to confirm his involvement with the shooting in the park," Reagan responded.

"But?" Smythe asked.

"But it still doesn't tell us what his target is — what he's after," Reagan replied.

"So you still think there's something bigger going on? Why?" Smythe asked, thinking the same thing.

"I do. If the shooting in the park is all we had, I would just call it a strong hunch. But now we have three additional murders and two apartments that were thoroughly scrubbed – except for a SIM card that shows phone calls to New Jersey. That alone suggests that there's more going on here, but I just don't know what that is," Reagan admitted. *Yet*, he didn't add.

"Ok, so how are we going to find out? How are you going to follow up, Jack?" the Director wanted to know.

"For starters, when I spoke with Agent Cho this morning, I asked him to focus on that village. He's going to take some Marines at first light tomorrow – I guess tonight for us – and try to find out more about the Abdali family – firm up IDs and get some DNA if possible. Whatever he gets, I recommend cross-decking it to other agencies. Maybe the Abdali family is on someone's radar. I also think we should try to dig into the shooting that resulted in Muska's death. Were the Marines acting on any intel? If so, what was it? Who were the fighters they engaged, and how are they linked to the Abdalis? It might not be a coincidence that Muska and her cousin were there," Reagan pointed out.

"At the same time," Reagan continued, "I'm assuming we're digging deeper into that SIM card. I haven't seen any of that yet," he added.

"What do you think, Doug?" Smythe asked.

"I think this is a hell of a lot more to go on than we had before," he replied. "And I think Jack's approach is reasonable. Ryan, Joe, look into that firefight and try to figure out if we have any other players there. Amanda, go over the SIM data with Jack and help him with whatever Cho turns up. Anything else, Director?"

"Not that I can think of," Smythe said. "Jack, anything else?"

"Nothing I can think of right now, Director," Reagan replied.

"Ok guys, back to work, then," Smythe ordered. He watched his agents leave the room, noting that they seemed energized by the new information and new leads. He wasn't sure what, exactly, he had expected Reagan to come up with, but this had wildly exceeded his expectations. SecNav would certainly support his agency now. He stood to pour himself another cup of coffee and sat down again, this time next to Reagan. "Not bad, Jack. Not bad at all."

Reagan shrugged. "Nothing someone else wouldn't have come up with," he replied.

"Maybe, maybe not, but you did come up with this first, not to mention fast. You ask the right questions and sure as hell know where to look for answers. And you seem to look for answers directly, like you did calling Cho." Smythe observed.

"I did ask Agent Cannon's permission first," Reagan said, somewhat defensively.

"It's ok, Jack," Smythe said with a chuckle. "Don't misread what I said – I'm not mad. If anything, I like that you're taking a direct approach." He paused before continuing. "There's something I'm curious about. Why aren't you an agent? Or a cop, or in the service like your friends, for that matter? You certainly seem to have the aptitude for it."

"I may have the aptitude for it, and I did think about it at one time," Reagan admitted, "but that possibility was foreclosed to me a long time ago. When I was younger, in college and in grad school, I traveled quite a bit. I had the misfortune to fly with an ear infection, and as a result I lost most of the hearing in my left ear. Well, more precisely, I lost the ability to hear certain tones. That's something I wouldn't have been able to get a waiver for, at least not if I wasn't already an agent. Hence no career for me as a gun-toting special agent."

"How about taking the 'special' out of the equation – there are plenty of roles that don't require perfect hearing," Smythe said.

"That's true," Reagan replied. "But those roles don't really match my personality. First of all, unless you carry a gun you're pretty much considered a second-class citizen at most agencies. And second, and perhaps more importantly, it's not in my nature to *just* collect information. I want to be able to act on it as well. Being a lawyer allows me to do just that," he explained.

"Fair enough," Smythe responded, thinking that in the case of Reagan, an exemption surely should have been made. Certainly this man had no significant impairment, as his actions in the park had proven. "Anyway," he said as he rose, "I'm going to set a meeting for as soon as possible with the Director of the FBI and Secretary of Homeland Security. Maybe CIA too, in light of what you've come up with. I want you to run through your presentation again for them."

"Maybe it's better if someone else does that," Reagan suggested.

"Why's that, Jack? You don't strike me as the shy type," Smythe said with a laugh.

"I'm not. But I rather suspect you might get some pushback on having an outsider involved in this investigation."

"More than likely, but let me worry about that. Besides, you developed this information and you know it best," Smythe replied. "I'll go set it up, and let you know."

Reagan had just enough time to print some extra copies of his report, pack up his laptop, and most importantly, use the restroom before Smythe returned to collect him.

It was properly snowing now, Reagan observed on the drive to the Hoover Building, which houses the headquarters of the Federal Bureau of Investigation. The car's windshield wipers were barely making headway against the rapidly-falling wet snow. They drove in silence – or at least Smythe and Reagan did. Smythe's driver, on the other hand, was providing a running commentary on the other drivers on the road. After one particular criticism of blue-haired drivers with rear-wheel drive cars, Smythe turned to Reagan and rolled his eyes. Both men had to make an effort not to laugh, or at least not to laugh too loudly and so cause the driver to turn his wrath onto them. Eventually they arrived at their destination without mishap, and after a brief elevator ride were ushered into the FBI Director's spacious office.

"Good to see you, Francis. Retirement is treating you well," the Director said with a smile as he rose from his desk. "I keep meaning to set up a lunch so we can catch up – sorry I haven't done that yet."

"Don't worry about it, Dave. I've been pretty busy myself. How's Paula?" Smythe asked.

"She's good. You know, keeping busy. She's taken up baking, which hasn't been very good for my waistline, as you can see. Francis and I go way back," he explained, turning to Reagan. "Our wives were sorority sisters, would you believe? I'm David Goldberg," he said, shaking Reagan's hand.

"Jack Reagan. It's a pleasure to meet you, Director Goldberg."

"The pleasure is all mine – I've heard a lot of good things about you. And please call me Dave. Anyone who can shoot the way you do has certainly earned that right," he said with a wide grin. "Good job in the park, Jack. You know, I ran that little problem with my top HRT guy. He said you had a little bit of luck and a whole lot of skill – if he were in your shoes, he would have done pretty much the same thing, and that's high praise coming from him."

"I think he has it backwards, Dave. A whole lot of luck and a little bit of skill," Reagan replied, instantly taking a liking to the FBI Director. He and Smythe were two of a kind, honorable men who loved their jobs and who obviously valued achievement over politics.

"I can see why you like this guy so much, Francis. He's obviously good people," Goldberg said. "Anyway, Chip Gallagher is coming over from Langley. He's the Deputy Director, but don't hold that against him," he explained for Reagan's benefit. "I just spoke with him on the road; he says the snow is pretty bad. As for Secretary Jackson, he just left his office now. Since it looks like we have some time to kill and I can't find my deck of cards, why don't you give me a preview of your presentation?"

"Go ahead, Jack," Smythe said with a nod. Reagan set up his laptop on a conference table as Goldberg called another man into his office.

"Director Francis Smythe, Jack Reagan, this is Special Agent Paul Monaghan. He's running the investigation on our end," Goldberg explained as the men shook hands.

Reagan ran through his presentation as Goldberg and Monaghan crowded around his laptop, studying each picture carefully. "That's some story, Jack," Goldberg said when Reagan finished. "A lot more than I was expecting, to be honest. Fine investigative work, too. What do you think, Paul?"

"I think all the pieces fit. It feels real. But my first question is, to what end? What's the play here?" Monaghan replied.

"That's the same question Jack keeps raising, and that's what we have to figure out," Smythe said.

"What are you doing to follow up?" Monaghan asked.

"It's ok, Jack, you can tell them," Smythe said, and Reagan did so.

"It looks like you have this investigation firmly to hand," Goldberg observed. "Pretty smart play, bringing in a ringer," he added, tilting his head towards Reagan with a laugh. "What can we do to help?"

Reagan gave Smythe a look that asked permission and Smythe burst out laughing. "It's ok, Jack. Our rivalry with FBI ends well short of this door, and Dave is a friend. A real friend, I mean. You can speak freely with him – you don't need my permission. With Secretary Jackson, on the other hand, you're right to be guarded."

"He's short on experience and long on political bullshit," Goldberg added with a snort. Clearly he didn't think much of the Secretary of Homeland Security. "So how can we help?"

"Perhaps you can help us figure out how Eggerton and Abdali made it into the country," Reagan replied. "That bit of info would be fairly significant. As for the SIM card, I don't know if you have any resources we don't. I assume we all play off the same NSA playbook."

"Good assumption," Goldberg said with a nod. "But why us and not Customs and Border Protection? They might be in a better position to help, even if they do fall under DHS."

"With all due respect to Customs and Border Protection, they can't stop a guy dressed as Osama bin Laden from crossing the border illegally from Mexico. Not to mention everything else they fail to do. On the other hand, the FBI is the nation's preeminent law enforcement agency. How's that for a reason?" Reagan asked with a smile.

"Oh I really like this guy," Goldberg said to no one in particular when he finished laughing. "Yeah, Jack, we'd be happy to help run that down. Now Francis, let's you and I go catch up and leave our investigators to hash things out."

"Works for me, Dave," Smythe replied, as the two Directors went to sit by Goldberg's desk. Reagan and Monaghan remained at the conference table, reviewing the photos slowly. Reagan looked at his watch and frowned. As exciting as it was to be talking about the case in the office of the Director of the FBI, he would much rather have been back in his own office working the case instead.

15

Secretary of Homeland Security Moses Lincoln Jackson blew into the room like an angry Texas tornado prepared to leave a trail of devastation in his wake. He was not at all happy to be called out of his office on a snowy Monday – that much was evident the moment he spoke. "What the hell is so important that you dragged me out of my office in this weather?" he demanded, with a scowl on his face. He sat at the middle of the conference table without so much as a friendly greeting or perfunctory handshake. His entourage of four took seats on either sides of their boss, and a bodyguard remained standing by the wall next to a window.

Reagan took an instant dislike to Jackson, for his attitude as for the fact that he had felt the self-important need to bring a bodyguard into a meeting taking place in a highly secure government building full of armed sworn federal agents. Reagan remained standing as the other men sat around the table – Director Goldberg and Special Agent Monaghan representing the FBI, Director Smythe for NCIS, and Deputy Director Chip Gallagher for CIA. Gallagher had come alone and arrived a few minutes before; unlike Jackson, he seemed affable and likeable.

A projector had been brought in and connected to Reagan's laptop to make viewing his presentation easier. He passed around copies of his report and started his presentation for the third time that day, this time from memory. He saw Gallagher studying the pictures carefully as he spoke, taking careful notes in the margins of the report. Jackson, in contrast, seemed entirely disinterested, and his entourage merely looked confused and out of their depth.

It was Jackson who spoke first when Reagan finished his presentation. "I didn't find that very enlightening. The only thing you said, really, is that you think you know the name of one of the shooters, and that's only with sixty percent certainty at best. Do you have anything else?"

Reagan was about to say yes, having just realized the potential importance of the SIM card, but he thought the better of it and shook his head instead. "No, sir. Nothing at the moment."

"Very well. Please leave the room so we can discuss this further," Jackson said, waiting for Reagan to leave before continuing. "This was pretty much a waste of my time. All of this could simply have been done by phone. And I'm not at all happy that you allowed a civilian without security clearances to work on this, Smythe."

Smythe bristled at the remark, prepared to explain the significance of the information and defend his man, as he thought of Reagan, but Goldberg beat him to the punch. "Are you kidding, Moses? This is pretty hot stuff. It gives us a lot of new leads to track down. And Reagan is good people. Bob Angelo, my former S-A-C in Denver, speaks very highly of him, and besides, we've done a thorough check on the guy and Reagan is squeaky clean. More than that, he's known to us – we've talked to him in the past when renewing security clearances for people he knows."

"Ok, so the information *might* prove to be useful in the future," Jackson allowed, "but at this point in time you still have nothing solid. The President wants results and so far you haven't delivered any. So far all you've done is find more bodies. And 'good people' or not, I don't want Reagan working on this. God knows what he's going to tell the media. And besides, he has no experience – he's a nobody." Jackson waved his hand dismissively. "Am I right, or am I right?" he asked the men he brought into the meeting, all of whom nodded obsequiously.

"The information *is* significant, Mister Secretary. An investigation takes time to develop leads, and these are pretty promising leads," Gallagher chimed in. "And we don't have a problem with Reagan working on this. He seems to know what he's doing."

"Promising leads that haven't turned up anything yet. It's *possible* that they will some day, but they haven't yet and the President wants results," Jackson repeated. "Besides, it's not your call who works on an investigation," he continued, glaring down the table at Gallagher.

"You're right, Mister Secretary, it's not Chip's call. It's mine, and I say Reagan stays. He's sworn to secrecy and I trust him. Hell, if it'll make you feel better, I'll bring him on board as a consultant. But this meeting isn't about who developed this information," Smythe said, trying to get the meeting back on track. We're here to discuss how to proceed."

"You proceed by bringing me something important," Jackson replied arrogantly. "And a consultant isn't good enough. It won't fly and you know it. This meeting is about Reagan as much as anything. If you're letting outsiders run your investigation, I have to question your judgment, Smythe. You say it's your call, but I can make a call too," Jackson warned with all of the self-importance of a political hack.

"You're threatening me?" Smythe was outraged. "That won't fly either, Jackson. Consultant isn't good enough? Fine. I'll just appoint him my Acting Deputy Director of Operations," he said as he made the sign of the cross with his hand, finishing it off with a dismissive wave directed at the Secretary. "I've had a good career, and I have a good pension. I don't need this job. If you want to get me fired, go the fuck ahead," he continued, losing his temper. "Just think about how *that* will play in the media."

"Guys, this isn't a pissing contest," Goldberg interjected. "Now can we please talk about how we're going to proceed?"

"I already told you," Jackson said as he stood, his entourage following suit. "Bring me something concrete I can give to the President, and bring it to me fast. Don't waste my time with trivial nonsense." With that, the tornado blew out of the room.

"What an idiot," Gallagher said when the door was safely closed behind Jackson.

"Asshole, too," Goldberg replied, the other men nodding agreement.

"So what *are* we doing to follow up?" Gallagher asked.

"Bring Reagan back in and ask him," Smythe suggested, and Gallagher rose to get the door. "Did you catch any of that, Jack?" Smythe asked when Reagan entered.

"No – I suspect the door is sound-proofed. But I did catch a very dirty look when Secretary Jackson walked out. Productive meeting?"

"Hardly," Smythe replied. "I think I may have appointed you my Acting Deputy Director of Operations," he added with a hearty laugh. "Crazy meeting, actually. Ok Jack, tell us how we're following up," he ordered. Goldberg and Monaghan had heard it before, but Gallagher hadn't.

"Sounds good to me, guys," Gallagher offered when Reagan finished. "As far as I know, none of these people are on our radar, but I'll poke around and see what information we can turn up," he promised.

"Jack, you were about to say something before Jackson kicked you out but stopped yourself," Smythe remembered. "What was it?"

"It has to do with the SIM card found in Johnson's apartment. There were a number of calls made to cellphones in New Jersey. I just remembered that NSA picked up some chatter from northern New Jersey a few months ago, something to do with planes. I was wondering if perhaps there might be a connection," Reagan replied.

"What the hell? That's news to me," said Monaghan. "And potentially very worrying, if there's a connection."

"*If* is the operative word," Gallagher pointed out.

"Where'd you get this from, Jack?" Goldberg asked.

"A reliable source," Reagan responded, hesitating to say more.

"Your source won't get into any trouble, Jack. I promise," Goldberg said, to which Smythe added agreement. "Who's your source?"

"Brenda Angelo – well, Brenda Videtti now, I suppose. She's a section chief at NSA." Reagan figured he could trust these people, and besides, the source was important for them to properly assess this information.

"Bob's daughter?" Goldberg asked in surprise. "Pretty reliable source. How do you know her? Good call, by the way, in not bringing this up. Jackson would have flipped his lid even more."

"I've known her for a while," Reagan replied. "She just married one of my best friends on Saturday. Look, I know this chatter might be totally unrelated, but just to be on the safe side, I think it's worth looking into. Maybe at least try to track down the origins of the chatter and see if there's some kind of connection to this case," he suggested.

"Too bloody right we'll try," Goldberg spoke for everyone at the table. "Anyway, it looks like you're going to be with us for a while, whether Jackson likes it or not. What number can we reach you at, Jack?" he asked, taking out his cellphone and entering the number Reagan gave him. Monaghan and Gallagher did the same. "My cellphone number is on my card," Goldberg said, handing over his card when he finished programming his phone. "Call me any time you get something or need something." Monaghan and Gallagher followed the FBI Director's lead.

"You don't mind, do you?" Goldberg asked Smythe.

"Not at all, Dave," he replied. "This case is well beyond the reach of any agency rivalries. Call them with what you need, Jack. Cannon might take a little offense at this, but he'll understand."

The meeting ended, and Smythe and Reagan drove through the storm in silence, relieved that snowplows seemed to be making some kind of effort to clear the roads. Enough of an effort to allow people to get home, but not much beyond that. Six inches had already fallen, but the brunt of the storm was yet to come. The meeting had actually been successful inasmuch as it fostered inter-agency cooperation, but Smythe was still smarting from his encounter with Secretary Jackson. Loud, brash, obnoxious, incompetent and totally unsuited for his job, Smythe knew. He also knew he was taking a big chance with Reagan, but so far that had been paying off handsomely.

Neither Motrin nor Excedrin Migraine had helped ease the pounding in her head, and Special Agent Watson realized that her headache was probably due to the combination of stress and lack of sleep. Staring at a computer screen all day just made it worse. At least she had made good progress tracking down the phones connected with the SIM card they found in Ms. Johnson's sofa. Essentially, a SIM card contains network-specific data – such as an ISMI or international mobile subscriber identity – used to identify and authenticate a subscriber to that network. An ISMI is as unique as the actual phone number associated with it; once a cellular provider like AT&T or T-Mobile is provided with an ISMI, it can produce a detailed log of activity pertaining to the number.

The basic information in this log consists of the phone calls made and received, the time and date of those calls, and perhaps more importantly for this investigation, the identity of the cell towers that transmitted the calls. Each cell tower has a unique identifier that the cellular provider can use to provide a street address – or in remote locations, the GPS coordinates – corresponding with the tower. One final bit of useful data in the activity log, both for network engineers and for investigators, is the approximate strength of the signal of each call. From that, the distance between the cell phone and the cell tower can be inferred. If the make and model of the phone – and consequently the specifications of its antenna – are known, then the distance can be inferred with pretty good accuracy.

The activity log is not limited to this basic information; when a phone is turned on, it is constantly recording its location, and since modern phones are GPS-enabled, the location is fairly precise. The inverse of that is that when the phone is turned off, the cellular provider has no idea where it is, and if the battery is removed, it can't even be forcibly pinged by the provider to provide a location. In the case of the phones connected with SIM card from Ms. Johnson's apartment, it quickly became apparent that all eight of the phones had been kept powered off whenever they were not being used. This, of course, suggested coordination and planning, since how else would a person know to turn his phone on in order to receive a call.

All eight of the phones – actually nine, including the one missing a SIM card – had phone numbers associated with the area around Los Angeles, but none had ever been used there. In fact, none of the phone numbers had ever been used before January. The phone missing the SIM card, which Agent Watson had taken to calling Phone 1, had only been used in three locations: Eggerton's apartment complex, Rock Creek Park, and the general area to the northeast of the White House, of all places. The Rock Creek Park location was interesting, as it covered the area where the firefight had ensued. It had only been used there once, on the Thursday exactly one week before the shooting at approximately 2:30 p.m. From this Watson inferred that someone had scoped out the park. Whoever had done so had called the only other phone physically in the Washington D.C. area, and that phone – Phone 2 – had only ever been used in Eggerton's apartment complex. Additionally, Phone 2 had only been used to talk with Phone 1, and no one else.

Phones 3, 4 and 5 had only ever been used in New Jersey, predominantly in the Paterson area but also in Jersey City, Elizabeth and Atlantic Highlands. More than that, they travelled together and were used in sequence to place or receive calls to and from Phone 1 within the span of a few minutes every other day at roughly the same times. After talking for a couple of minutes with the owner of Phone 1, Phones 3, 4 and 5 would then immediately call Phone 9, which was always co-located with

148

Phone 1. Phone 9 and Phone 1, however, had never called one another.

Similarly, Phones 6, 7 and 8 had only been used in New Jersey, also in Paterson, Jersey City and Elizabeth, but not in Atlantic Highlands. They also seemed to travel together, and were used in sequence to communicate first with Phone 1 and then with Phone 9 every other day at roughly the same times. Phones 1 and 9 were the common link to all the other phones. It was a fairly straightforward task, albeit a tedious one, to organize these calls, but thankfully there were only nine phones involved.

The obvious conclusion suggested by the data was that there were two possible terrorist cells operating in New Jersey, in contact with one or two ringleaders in the Washington, D.C. area. As terrifying as this possibility was, Watson was elated by its discovery, finally feeling as though she had made a meaningful contribution to the case. Her first thought was to talk it over with Reagan, but he hadn't returned from the Hoover Building yet so she walked to Special Agent Cannon's desk to fill him in, only to learn that he and Pembridge had left to interview Eggerton's ex-wife and weren't planning on returning to the office until after the snow stopped falling.

Watson was about to head back to her desk when she caught sight of Reagan getting off the elevator. Her elation made her somewhat silly and impulsive, and she practically ran over to him, taking his hand and rushing him to his office. "I've got something pretty hot, Jack."

"You most certainly do," he replied with a grin, deciding instantly to tease her.

"Oh hush," she said with a wide smile. "Come on, let's get your coat off," she added, giggling as she helped Reagan shed his tan toggle coat and hanging it up for him. "Now sit," she commanded, pushing him firmly by his shoulders into his chair.

"You're certainly in a mood," Reagan remarked with a crooked smile.

"That's right, Jack. Because it's my turn to wow *you*," she replied. "And I want you nice and comfortable for this. So let's get you some coffee," she added, pouring him a fresh cup and presenting it with an exaggerated curtsy that caused them both to burst out laughing.

"I haven't seen this side of you before," he said. "I have to admit, I rather like it."

"I'm glad you like it, Jack," Watson replied with a wink. "Ok, now it's time for me to turn serious and impress you. I spent all afternoon obtaining records from the cellular service providers, following up on that SIM. When I got the records, I put them all together and organized them into this Excel file." She handed him a spreadsheet that ran to several pages and watched him flip quickly through it. "See anything interesting?" she asked.

"Two, maybe three terrorist cells reporting to one or two leaders?" Reagan asked in turn, looking up. He saw Watson's eyes go momentarily wide before she recovered, slapping her forehead with her right palm.

"Why, Jack, oh why do I keep letting you surprise me?" she asked with a chuckle. It had taken her about five minutes and three different colors of highlighter to come up with the same thing Reagan had seen in a matter of seconds. "That's it exactly. There seem to be two separate groups in New Jersey, and potentially another one in northern Virginia, all reporting to two cellphones here in the Metro area." Watson continued to explain, adding further details.

"You're right, this is definitely hot stuff," Reagan said when she finished. "More than you realize, actually. You remember Betsy, Nick's blushing bride? She told me that NSA had picked up some chatter a few months ago, something to do with planes. The chatter came from northern New Jersey." He went on to explain to Watson what had been discussed at the Hoover Building. "By the way, very nice work, Amanda," he added.

Watson smiled, and Reagan remarked that she was practically beaming. What he didn't realize was just how much his appreciation meant to her. "Thank you very much, Jack," she replied. "I have to admit, though, sifting through these numbers was fairly straightforward and simple. Other agents are working on the hard part. The SIM card we found was part of a batch of over twenty thousand prepaid cards that was sold to several distributors, who in turn sold lots to other businesses. Those other business re-sold either to consumers or other sellers, mostly online. Tracking down one particular SIM card is a lot like trying to find a needle in a haystack, and in other cases I've worked we haven't always gotten results. Anyway, as far as the chatter goes, it does all seem to be related, but we can't rule out the possibility that the chatter has nothing to do with this. So, what do we do now?"

"You're right, it can be just a coincidence. But the more we learn, the less likely it seems coincidental. To me, at least. And what we do now is brief the Director. He'll want to hear this," Reagan said, reaching for the phone and dialing the proper number. Watson, for her part, was more than a little nervous at the thought of briefing the Director. Nervous enough that her headache, which had disappeared with the excitement of discovery, had started to return. Approachable as Smythe was, he was still the Director, and that was enough to cause a junior agent such as herself to be apprehensive. Smythe routinely told agents to call his cellphone with anything, at any time, but no junior agent – and precious few senior ones – had ever taken him up on that. *Technically speaking, I'm not calling him. Reagan is.* That thought somehow made it better.

"Director Smythe? Jack Reagan. You're on speakerphone. I've got Special Agent Watson with me, and she's got something hot you need to hear." Reagan noted with some surprise that Watson seemed a little nervous as she went through her presentation.

"Hot is right," Smythe said when she finished. "Nice job, Agent Watson. Jack, did you tell her about the chatter?"

"Yeah, I did. The more information we develop, the less likely it seems to be a coincidence. At least that's how I see it. This makes getting details on the chatter all the more important," Reagan pointed out.

"Agreed," Smythe replied. "I made some calls but it will take a few days before we get it. Maybe not before the end of the week. Sorry, Jack – it is what it is. Agent Watson, what do you have in mind for follow-up?"

"Well, sir, since we know the exact dates and times these calls were made, plus a general sense of their location, I think we should see if we should canvas these locations. We might get lucky and turn up some surveillance video," she replied.

"Good idea, but we definitely don't have the manpower for that," Smythe observed.

"We may not have the manpower, but the Bureau does," Reagan pointed out.

Smythe thought about it for a moment before responding. "I'm ok with that, Jack. Go ahead and make the call. Anything else?

"Nope. Thanks for listening. Enjoy whatever it is that agency directors enjoy doing in a snowstorm," Reagan said, hearing Smythe laughing as he ended the call.

"So, Jack, what do we do now?" Watson asked, noting that not even Cannon spoke with the Director as Reagan just had.

"Now we pack up and head back to our hotel while the roads are still passable. I'm not looking forward to spending the night on the floor."

"It's barely past six though," Watson objected.

"Ok, so we'll grab some dinner and keep working at the hotel. How does that sound?" Reagan asked.

"That sounds like a plan," she replied, forming a smile. She realized there was little they could do at this point other than wait for something new to develop, and what better way to spend the time than getting to know Reagan better over dinner.

16

The drive to the Marriott took closer to an hour than the customary twenty or so minutes. The snow had stopped falling, but the plows had only done a superficial job of keeping the roads clear. Most of Washington had gone home early, and there was little point to cleaning roads that would soon be blanketed by even more snow. Watson and Reagan decided to eat in at the hotel, each of them secretly relieved that the other wasn't a foodie. It was simpler that way, not to mention more comfortable – this way they could talk without the worry of being overheard. Besides, the room service menu wasn't half bad.

Watson went up to her room to change. After hanging up the suit she had been wearing, she stood in front of the closet in her lingerie, suddenly realizing that she had no idea what to wear. She stomped her foot in irritation, thinking it would have been easier had they gone out to eat instead. That way she could have worn her little black dress, the better to accentuate her figure. She spent a few frustrating minutes going through her closet and two of her bags before settling on something at the other end of the spectrum from a dress: yoga pants, hot pink polo shirt, a loose-fitting gray hoodie with the logo of the U.S. Navy on the front, and sneakers whose colorful laces matched her shirt. This was the sort of thing she wore around the house and running errands, and she figured that Reagan would just have to get used to seeing her this way. *Besides, I look cute,* she thought as she took the time to brush her hair before putting it up in an elegant ponytail. Satisfied with her appearance, she grabbed her purse and the bag with work and headed upstairs to Reagan's room.

Reagan, she saw, had also changed into something more comfortable – khaki slacks and a navy blue polo shirt discretely emblazoned with Brooks Brothers' signature Golden Fleece. "You look amazing, as ever," he said, taking in how her pants accentuated her toned legs. "Thank you, Jack," she replied with a smile, dropping her bag and purse on the bed as she kicked off her shoes and sat on the bed, tucking her legs under her. "What's for dinner? I'm starving!" She had been so wrapped up in her work that she hadn't eaten anything all day.

As they waited for dinner to be brought up, Reagan asked Watson to explain the investigative process to him. He assumed there was a lot more going on behind the scenes, but was impressed at the sheer magnitude of very methodical work being done by a good number of agents he had never even met. Quite a few agents were tasked with tracking down copious amounts of data, which was then reviewed by yet more agents before the relevant information was passed along to agents like Cannon, Pembridge, Hollerman and Watson, who had the broadest view of the case. Reagan was surprised at how much of the work involved physical media; he had gotten used to television shows in which everything was magically pulled up on a computer screen. He knew from personal experience that this was merely a film fantasy, but somehow in his mind the fantasy had developed an aura of reality.

Dinner was brought up, and Reagan wheeled the room service table in front of Watson, pulling up a chair across from her. They lingered over dinner, talking about their childhood and life experiences, about politics and current affairs, about everything and nothing at all. They laughed a lot, and Amanda found herself opening up to Jack, more so than she had ever really done with anyone else. He was very easy to talk to, but more than that, they shared the same general world-view, morals and sensibilities. He spoke and acted with a confidence borne of competence and experience, and there was a certain intensity about him, an intensity that wasn't well hidden under the veneer of a laid back demeanor – at least not to anyone who knew what to look for. It was all in the eyes, and Watson couldn't help but smile every time she looked into them, finding herself increasingly drawn to this man.

With dinner over and the room service table pushed out into the hallway, Amanda knew it was time to turn to business, even though she would have preferred getting to know Jack even better. "So where do we start, Jack?" she asked, pulling out her notes and laptop. She was a very capable agent, but on cases of this magnitude she was used to looking to her seniors for direction and guidance.

"Well, how about as an appetizer you e-mail your spreadsheet to the FBI," he replied, realizing that he should have asked her to do it before dinner. He walked to the desk and retrieved Special Agent Monaghan's card, handing it to Watson.

"Ok, done," she said, having copied Cannon and Reagan on the e-mail.

"Thank you! Next, is there any way we can plot these locations on a map?" Reagan asked, pointing at the spreadsheet.

"There is," she replied, moving her laptop to the desk. "It's just going to take me a bit of time to type in all the coordinates." Reagan watched her as she worked. Competent, bright and morally centered, with a wit as sharp as her intellect, Amanda Watson was unlike most of the women Jack had known. Her smile was as captivating as were her eyes, and she carried herself with a graceful poise that accentuated her soft feminine features. As much as he avoided thinking about it, Jack felt very attracted to Amanda – more than that, he felt a connection that only deepened the more time they spent together. It helped that talking to her came very naturally, and Jack found himself letting his guard down and talking more about himself than he had with anyone save his closest friends.

Watson stood, taking off her sweater and tossing it on the bed. As she sat back down, her fingers poised above her keyboard, she tilted her head towards Reagan and flashed a mischievous smile. "I've barely known you four days and you've already got me in your bedroom taking my clothes off. Not bad, Jack!"

Reagan laughed heartily, about to reply when his phone rang. "Reagan," he said, still laughing.

"Jack? Paul Monaghan. Am I catching you at a bad time?"

"No," Reagan replied. "I was just watching a beautiful lady take off some clothes." He didn't see Watson grin into her computer at that remark. "What's up?"

"I won't keep you long, then," Monaghan said with a chuckle. "I got an e-mail from one of your people, Special Agent Watson, with a call log. I'm having my people check our database of cameras to see what's in the area, and I'm going to have some agents from our Newark office go and check these places out tomorrow. I spent some time in the Newark office not too long ago, and as far as I remember, we're most likely to get results from Elizabeth and Jersey City – those places have lots of security and traffic cameras. That part of Paterson is pretty much a no-go zone for us – few cameras and fewer people willing to talk. Atlantic Highlands doesn't seem to have much we can go on."

"Fair enough," Reagan replied. "Anything else?"

"Yeah, a heads up. We have some RICO cases building major steam in the city and northern New Jersey. We can spare some agents for a few days, but if nothing pops right away I won't have the manpower to keep at it. We can probably shuffle in some agents from elsewhere, but that's beyond my pay grade. Sorry, Jack."

"It is what it is," Reagan said. "Thanks for the info, and for the heads up."

"You bet, Jack. I'll keep you in the loop. Now go back to enjoying whatever it is you're doing," Monaghan said.

Reagan relayed the substance of the call to Watson. "That's how it goes," she said. "You and I are lucky – we can devote all our attention to this case. Even though this is a priority, everyone else has other things to work on as well," she pointed out.

Watson continued typing in coordinates as Reagan went over the spreadsheet carefully. They both finished at the same time. "This is pretty interesting," he observed.

"What do you see, Jack?"

"Elizabeth has two things, a port and Newark Airport. This location has warehouses and a clear line of sight to the airport," he replied, pointing at the screen. "I used to live in the area, remember. Jersey City has the Holland Tunnel. In other words, these calls were made from target-rich environments."

"How about Paterson and Atlantic Highlands?" Amanda asked.

"Atlantic Highlands has nothing I'm aware of. It's a nice area, with pretty views of the New York City skyline, but that's about it. Paterson is not such a nice area – the whole city is pretty much a giant inner-city neighborhood, if you know what I mean. I argued a motion in the courthouse there once. That's the only thing that comes close to resembling a target."

"So maybe they were scoping out targets?" Amanda offered.

"That's a reasonable assumption. They've got three juicy ones here. Or maybe not," Jack replied, zooming in on the map. "Look here," he pointed. "That's an IKEA, and not connected to the port. Unless they're targeting Swedish furniture, I'd say they were looking at the airport. And in Jersey City, these cell towers aren't exactly close to the tunnel, although I suppose they could have walked closer. Look at the timing of the calls, too. One group started and ended their day in Paterson, and the other did the same in Jersey City. It feels more like maybe that's where they're staying."

"Very interesting," Amanda replied, looking at the map more closely. "But what about Atlantic Highlands?"

"I don't know," Jack admitted. "That's the odd man out. Our guys – assuming they're from Afghanistan or the Middle East – can blend in nicely in Paterson or Jersey City, but not so much in Atlantic Highlands. I wonder..." He reached for his phone and called Agent Monaghan.

"Paul? Jack Reagan. You're on speakerphone. I'm here with Special Agent Watson. I wanted to run something by you," he said, explaining what he and Watson had just discussed.

"Already thought of that," Monaghan replied with a chuckle.

"I bet," Reagan said. "I've got a question for you, though. Is the Bureau tracking anything involving Stingers or large quantities of explosives?"

"Good question," Monaghan responded. "We've had attempted thefts of missile systems over the years, almost all on the West Coast, but nothing recent – and no one got away with anything. As for explosives, anyone with an internet connection can cook something up in their basement these days, but we aren't looking at anything specific at the moment. Well, a separatist group out West, but those kind of people generally target federal buildings, not transportation systems. I'll ask around some tomorrow," he promised. For Monaghan, the nice thing about working out of the Hoover Building was that he could keep relatively normal business hours. As a result, he was able to have dinner with his wife and son practically every night.

"What now, Jack?" Amanda asked when the call had ended.

"Now? How about we make another call," he said, searching through his phone for the right number.

"Hi, I'd like to order a pizza," Jack said when his call was connected, causing Lt. Cmdr. Sinclair to laugh on the other end.

"Thought you'd like that one," Sinclair said. "A throwback to the old days. Still in DC, Jack?"

"Still here, working the case. How about you?"

"Yeah, we're still here too. Jim and I met with our detailers today – our schedule got bumped around some due to the storm. It's amazing how much people panic at a little snow," his friend said with a snort. "What's up, Jack?"

"I wanted to run something by you," he replied, explaining what he had just talked over with Watson and Monaghan. "Any ideas?" he asked when he had finished.

"Target-rich environment is an understatement. Prescient question about the Stingers, though," Sinclair replied.

"What do you mean?" Reagan asked.

"Not over the phone, Jack," Sinclair cautioned. "Are you still staying at the Hay Adams?"

"No, I moved over to the Marriott near the Zoo."

"Works just as well. We're down the street at the Hilton. I'll walk on over so we can talk. You'll find this interesting," Sinclair promised. "See you outside in fifteen minutes," he added, ending the connection.

The snow had started up again and was falling at a steady clip, even as the temperature had dropped even further. Reagan stood in front of the hotel, under cover, watching the snow come down. As the wind picked up, the dim light of the street lamps seemed to bend around shadows, providing the illusion of ghosts dancing in streets devoid of cars or people. After a few minutes, a corporeal figure began to take shape, making its way towards him.

"Nice weather, guy," Peter Sinclair said from underneath a massive, hooded parka. "Almost reminds me of October back home." Sinclair had grown up in Alaska's Kenai Peninsula; for him, cold, snowy weather was at worst a trivial nuisance.

"I don't get what the big deal is with a little snow," Jack replied. Winter in the Adirondack Mountains wasn't all that much better than in Alaska, and he had gotten used to it. "We can go inside. I found a spot that isn't covered by cameras and is plenty loud."

They found some seats away from the watchful gaze of security cameras, near a group of middle-aged Germans loudly discussing an upcoming meeting. Sinclair casually but carefully studied the room before he spoke. "When you asked about Stingers, something clicked. It could be something, but it could just as easily be unrelated to your investigation. Either way, I think it's better that you know about it, in case you make some kind of connection we haven't. What do you know about Benghazi, Jack?"

"Only what I've read in the news," he replied, surprised by the question.

'Ok, but what do you *think*?" Sinclair pressed.

"Weapons transfer gone bad," Jack replied confidently.

"Give the man a cigar," Peter said with a chuckle. "Suffice it to say, our Ambassador wasn't there for a ribbon cutting ceremony at some mosque. Most of those weapons systems have gone missing. A number of them stayed in Libya, but we've tracked some down to Syria, Iraq, Yemen and Somalia. It sure seems like there's been a lively market for them."

"What kind of weapons are we talking about?"

"Not just weapons, Jack. Weapons *systems*. Including MANPADS." Sinclair was referring to man-portable air defense systems, surface-to-air missiles capable of being fired by an individual or a small team of people against an aircraft.

"Jesus Christ!" Jack's jaw dropped at the revelation. "What kind of MANPADS are we talking about?"

"Mostly Russian SAs, but also Stingers."

"I hope they were at least old stock!"

Sinclair shook his head in frustration. "No such luck. They were Block Is. But wait, it gets better. We got some intel last summer that someone was looking to smuggle some of the Stingers into the United States."

"Yeah, lots better. Who was trying to move them?" Jack asked.

"A Lebanese arms trafficker. He made sure we couldn't take him alive, but we bagged one of his associates. That guy sang plenty. He didn't know the identity of the people trying to move the weapons, but thought they were from the Caucasus."

"Who's working on this?"

161

"It's a pretty closely held special access program. About a dozen people from Langley plus a handful from NSA and DIA. We're doing the heavy lifting at JSOC, naturally," Peter replied with a chuckle.

"Is Chip Gallagher read into this?"

"The Deputy Director at CIA? Yeah, he is, as a matter of fact. You know him?"

"Just met him today, actually." Jack briefly summarized his meeting at the Hoover Building. "I don't know, Pete, I still feel like I'm not on the same page as these guys."

"Of course you're not, Jack," Sinclair laughed. "All the guys you've been working with are essentially cops, and they think like cops. You, on the other hand, are still thinking like a spook."

"Maybe that's it," Reagan said with a laugh of his own, cut short by a sudden realization. "That *is* it, actually. They're looking at what happened as a terrorist attack somehow involving a disgruntled Marine, but I'm seeing the hallmarks of a much more professional operation. The apartments were just too well scrubbed, and their phone discipline is just too good. Yes, I know, I know, the bad guys have learned a lot more about how we do things and they've gotten smarter in the process," he said, holding up his hands in submission. "But at the end of the day, that still suggests there is something more to come."

"For what it's worth, I agree with you. Your gut is telling you that whatever is coming is coming soon, isn't it?"

"It is, even though I have nothing pointing to an imminent attack."

"Trust your gut, Jack. We always did." Sinclair rose, putting on his parka to leave. "I meant what I said at the wedding. If you need anything, call me – on the books or off."

"Thanks, pal. I might take you up on that. By the way, I kinda expected Jim to come over, too. What's he up to?"

"Oh, he made it all the way to the elevator with me. And promptly picked up a girl in said elevator." Both men had a good

162

laugh at that. James Mason could pick up a nun on her way to mass. Probably had, for that matter.

Reagan returned to his room to find Watson laying comfortably on her stomach in his bed, watching the Fox News Channel. "You're missing the re-play of O'Reilly, Jack," she said with a grin.

"Anything good?

"The usual. I hate to say it, though, but he seems to be sounding more and more full of himself lately. What did Pete say?"

"He said he heard something last summer about someone from the Middle East wanting to smuggle some Stingers into the country," Jack said, carefully phrasing his reply.

"And?" she prompted.

"And this is code-word stuff, and I don't want to get him – or you – in trouble."

"Fair enough, I suppose. I trust your judgment." It didn't quite occur to her that a civilian attorney with no discernible security clearances had time and again secured more sensitive information than she had access to. "You know where my loyalties lie," she added, suddenly serious and trying to find the right words. "But I hope you know, Jack, that you can trust me. With anything."

"I do, Amanda," he replied with a reassuring smile.

"Good! Now what?"

"Now we wait. I have a feeling it won't be long before we hear from Tommy Cho."

"Ok then, O'Reilly it is," she said with a smile of her own, patting the bed beside her. This would be a new experience for her, watching her favorite news channel side by side with a unicorn that looked ever more pink.

17

Special Agent Tommy Cho was having the time of his life. Accompanied by two squads of Marines and wearing full tactical gear, he rode into the small unnamed village – nicknamed Friendlyville by the Marines – just before dawn. He watched with fascination as one of the squads secured the Abdali residence and the other squad deployed around the village. In many ways, he felt like one of the characters in the war movies he loved watching when he was growing up – and still watched in his free time.

The residence looked like it had been abandoned for quite some time; it had been thoroughly stripped of any personal items. Nevertheless, Cho had been able to pull some usable prints off a kettle as well as a washbasin. He even found some hair follicles near the washbasin – Cho hoped they belonged to the former occupants rather than the goats that had taken up residence in the deserted house. He treated the house as a crime scene, methodically examining every nook and cranny and taking plenty of pictures. Satisfied that he had found everything there was to find, he located his translator and went off to talk to the villagers that had gathered in the dusty street, woken from their sleep by the sudden burst of activity.

The Abdali family, he quickly discovered, had been a family in transit. They had arrived in the village the previous summer – no one seemed to know from where – and rented the house from one of the village elders, paying in silver. They had kept mostly to themselves, not allowing anyone into their house except for a Marine, whose name no one remembered. The Abdalis weren't well known or particularly well-liked by the other villagers. The most they had been seen outside their house was whenever the Marines had come through. Then, in early

December, they had simply vanished during the night, never to be seen or heard from again.

The village elder who owned the house at least remembered their names; Dawar and Balbala were the parents of Batoor and Muska Abdali. The cousin had arrived about a month after the Abdalis and had once introduced himself as Kerimsolta. At first, the villagers had thought he had come to marry Muska since the two had seemed very close, bordering on intimate. But then Muska had started to give her affection to a young Marine who had been seen sneaking into her house late at night on several occasions. That sort of behavior had not endeared the Abdalis to the villagers. Cho tried to get more information about Kerimsolta, but the few villagers he had spoken with – busybodies all – had been frustrated by their inability to learn more about him.

Perhaps most interesting was the statement from a young boy who swore on the lives of his parents that he had seen Muska hiding by a stream outside of town the day before her family vanished. Cho couldn't find anyone else who had seen her, but the boy's parents recounted that their son had told them what he had seen. They had been planning to confront Dawar about his promiscuous dead-but-not-dead daughter the next morning, but by then the family had disappeared. Satisfied that he had learned everything he could, Cho thanked the villagers, apologized for disturbing their sleep and signaled to his Marines, as he thought of them, that it was time to leave. He wasn't quite sure what to make of the information he had just uncovered, but was certain the agents back home would find it very interesting indeed.

"Jack? Tommy Cho here. Sorry to wake you, buddy!" Reagan heard on the other end of the phone. He had fallen asleep on his stomach watching some real estate show on the HGTV channel. His phone had been set on vibrate, but it had been close enough that he felt it ring.

165

"Never a problem, pal," Reagan replied. He felt Amanda stir at the sound of his voice – she had fallen asleep next to him, using his shoulder as a pillow – and gently nudged her awake. "I'm going to put you on speakerphone so I can take notes. What's going on?" he asked Cho.

"We went into town this morning. The Abdalis packed up and stole off into the night back in December. They didn't leave much of anything behind. I got some good prints but I wouldn't be too hopeful about DNA. I did find some hair, but even if it turns out to be human... well the place is being used as a barn now so you can imagine. All of that is on its way to D.C. as we speak. I've got some names for you," Cho said, reading off the names as Reagan and Watson wrote them down. Cho continued, reciting what he had learned in Friendlyville.

"So we've got a mysterious family that no one seems to know, an equally mysterious cousin – if that's what he is – and a live dead girl. Very interesting, Tommy," Reagan said when Cho finished his brief.

"Yeah, I thought you'd like that," Cho said with a chuckle.

"I imagine a lot of people have been displaced from their homes. Do you have any idea whether..."

"Pretty unusual, Jack." Cho cut Reagan off, having expected that question. "I had that thought as well and asked around some. People who are displaced from their villages tend to move around within their tribal areas, so to speak. If that isn't a possibility, then they find a relation somewhere else to take them in. The Abdalis and the cousin, if that's what he was, are unusual in that no one knew them at all."

"Have you learned anything about the firefight that resulted in the alleged death of Muska?" Reagan asked.

"Yeah, I read the reports and talked to some of the Marines. They were on a routine patrol when they took fire from four to six men who quickly disappeared on horseback. The Marines say they hit and probably killed at least one of the attackers, but his friends carried him off. This took place about five kilometers from the village, which was pretty unexpected. The Marines increased the frequency and number of patrols after the incident but they didn't find anything, and things have been quiet ever since."

"Unusual firefight, and an unusual family," Reagan remarked.

"That about sums it up, Jack. Any ideas for what's next?" Cho asked hopefully.

"Expand the search some, perhaps?"

Cho let out a long sigh. He had expected that, too; he had come up with the same idea. "A whole lot of ground to cover, pal. The Marines are already setting that up, though. Their CO is incensed by all of this, and he's offered all the help that I need. Still, I could use some help out here. I'm going to talk to Doug about that later."

"Maybe the Director, too," Reagan offered.

"Can't hurt. Maybe you can bring it up if you speak to him first. I imagine he listens to you," Cho replied.

"Will do, Tommy. And call me anytime, day or night."

"You sound like him too, Jack," Cho said with a chuckle, ending the call.

"Interesting stuff, Jack," Amanda said as she got out of bed with a yawn to run the names on her laptop.

"Very much so," he replied, heading for the bathroom to change out of his wrinkled trousers and into a pair of sweatpants he used as pajamas.

"Nothing on these guys," Amanda said when he returned. "I've already put in the request to other agencies. Watchlist, too. What now, Jack?" she asked with another yawn.

"Now we get some sleep. We can figure this out in the morning," he replied.

"Works for me," she said with a tired smile, shutting down her computer. She moved her bags off the bed and onto the floor, reaching for the phone to leave a wakeup call before climbing under the covers like it was the normal thing to do. Jack got in bed next to her and turned off the lights.

Amanda opened one eye and reached for the phone on its third ring, picking up the receiver and just as quickly replacing it. There was no point in talking to a computerized recording. She felt herself pressed up against Jack, whose left arm was wrapped around her waist. Her legs were twisted together with his and she had been using his right arm as a pillow, the fingers on her right hand intertwined with his. It was all very intimate, and Amanda realized with a start that she had never acted this way with anyone before. But it just came naturally, and felt comfortable and familiar. Exciting, too.

She felt Jack squeeze her right hand gently as he said good morning softly in her ear. He started to move his left arm away, but Amanda quickly took his hand and moved it back, holding it tightly. "Good morning, Jack," she said just as softly, turning her head slightly to him, resisting the very strong urge to kiss him. "I really don't want to get up," she added.

"Then don't," Jack replied. "It's still very early." Amanda shivered slightly, feeling his warm breath on the side of her neck. Neither of them wanted to move, fearing that doing so would somehow break the spell they were both under. "Ok," she replied with an unseen smile, pushing herself further into his warm embrace. They lay there together a good deal longer, drifting in and out of sleep, their hearts beating faster but together as one.

After a most enjoyable half hour, though, Jack had to reluctantly pull away to deal with the wakeup call he had set the previous evening. Amanda rolled over, looking past Jack and out the window. "It's still snowing!" she said in surprise. They both made their way to the window, quickly realizing that over a foot of snow had fallen during the night, on top of the six inches from the previous day. The snow had started to taper off, but the roads were covered in the stuff and there was no sign of life outside their window. They stood there watching for a few minutes,

Amanda leaning back against Jack, his left hand gently placed at her waist.

"I'm not driving in *that*," she said, just before her cellphone rang.

"Amanda? It's Doug," she heard Cannon say. "I made it to the office but don't bother coming in until the roads get cleaned. It's hell out there." It had taken him close to two hours to complete a drive that normally took him twenty minutes – in a 4x4 Chevy Silverado. "We'll do a status update by conference call around 9:30, so gather up Jack before then," he added, hanging up the phone before she had a chance to respond.

"I guess we're not going anywhere," she told Jack, relating the call. She reached for the room phone, ordering breakfast for both of them and then rushed to her room to shower and change before the food arrived. Jack headed for the bathroom as well, lingering in the hot shower. He had fallen asleep thinking of the information Cho had relayed, his mind mulling things over even as he slept. The shower helped him better formulate his thoughts, even if he didn't like what he was thinking.

Reagan turned off the water and, dripping wet, reached for his phone to call his friend.

"Good morning, buddy," he heard Peter Sinclair say. "Hey, can you believe that Jim *just* walked in, with a massive smile on his face, no less?"

"Boys will be boys," Jack replied with a chuckle before relaying the information Cho had provided.

"If I didn't know better, I'd say these people are players. And I don't really know better, do I?" Sinclair said when Jack had finished. "Odd sort of name, Kerimsolta. Sounds Turkish," he added.

"Not just odd, Pete. It's the wrong kind of name for the region," Jack pointed out.

"You're right about that," his friend interjected. He had spent enough time in Afghanistan to understand the significance of names.

"It could be Turkish, but it's also not uncommon for the Caucasus, and after our talk last night..."

"Yeah, these coincidences are really piling up, Jack. You have something in mind, don't you?"

"Yes, as a matter of fact. You know the phone calls? I keep coming back to Atlantic Highlands because it doesn't make any sense. Then I remembered that Sandy Hook is right there, and I've been to Sandy Hook enough times to know that under the right weather conditions, it's pretty much directly under the approach to Kennedy Airport."

"Jesus, Jack, that's nothing to wake up to!" Sinclair exclaimed. "It looks more and more like these guys are scoping out the airports."

"That's what it looks like to me," Reagan confirmed.

"You've got something in mind," Sinclair repeated.

"Yeah but it's a big ask, pal. The Bureau is going to be digging around for video, but no one expects them to find anything around Sandy Hook. So I was thinking that maybe you and Jim could head up there and take a look around. If you have time, that is."

"We can do that, Jack, definitely," Peter replied. "You think they're still scoping out the place?"

"I do. That's what their call pattern suggests, anyway."

"They stopped using those phones, though," Peter observed.

"Maybe they've gone radio-silent – that would make sense. Or maybe they've switched comms. Or maybe this is all a waste of time," Jack conceded.

"I don't think it is. It feels like you're on to something. Any suggestions for cover?"

"Fishermen, maybe? That seems to be a popular thing to do. Not many people around in winter that I recall," Jack said.

"Fish? In winter?" Sinclair had a good laugh at that one.

"Just an idea, pal," Reagan said defensively, thinking that most avid fisherman would find something to fish for no matter the season. Or reason.

"Not a bad one, necessarily," Sinclair admitted. "Any other ideas, Jack?"

"Yes, as a matter of fact. Think you can catch us a Stingray?" he asked, referring to the cellphone surveillance device.

"You don't ask for much, do you?" his friend said, laughing again. "Yeah, I might be able to cook one up. I'll fill Jim in on everything and we'll head up when the roads get cleared, most likely tomorrow."

Amanda returned to Jack's room just as the room service tray was being delivered. She looked fresh and relaxed, wearing pale denim jeans matched with a simple white blouse under a grey cardigan. She thanked Jack for his compliment as she sat on the edge of the bed and poured them both some coffee – she had ordered two pots, knowing how much of that stuff he drank. "I'm surprised you don't have an ulcer, Jack."

"I may be out of shape, but otherwise I'm perfectly healthy," he replied with a chuckle.

"Not so out of shape from where I'm sitting," she said with a smile. They talked over the case as they ate, trying to figure out how to summarize it cohesively during the conference call to follow. They both agreed that they had no new ideas about what to do next, other than wait for information to develop from the inquiries they had already made. They also agreed that they both hated waiting. Jack asked her what she would normally be doing while waiting; he was curious to learn more about how a typical investigation ran.

"Well for starters, I would be doing a lot less waiting," Amanda responded. "I mean, I'd be making calls and following up on our requests for information, pushing to get answers faster. That doesn't really apply here, though, because we are dealing with other agencies – agencies that well understand the magnitude of this case. Other than that, I'd be helping other agents track down things, or keep going through what we have and organize it better. And if there's still time left over, there are always reports to write, administrative stuff to go through, and of course preparing testimony for cases going to trial. Thursday was my first day back – well, Friday was, technically speaking – so I have a lot less on my plate than normal."

Jack found all of that very interesting, and they continued talking about policies and procedures. This, in turn, gave Amanda the chance to finally talk about her long assignment with DEA. She even vented some frustration at her own agency – something she knew she could never have done with anyone else. With Jack, it was just different. Time passed quickly, and the two of them were caught by surprise when both their cellphones rang precisely at 9:30 a.m.

The most significant developments in the case were the ones pulled together during the night and previous afternoon by Reagan and Watson. Watson ran through what they had discovered from the cellphone records, and related what they had learned from Cho. There was a general consensus that these were the best – and only – leads they had at the moment. Watson was surprised that Reagan didn't say anything, but surmised that there were too many people on the call and he was likely to talk things over later with just with the Director and Special Agent Cannon. She was proven right when Reagan's phone rang again seconds after the briefings concluded.

"Good morning Jack," Director Smythe said. "I've got Doug Cannon and Ryan Pembridge on the line. Feel free to bring in Agent Watson if you want."

"Good morning, gentlemen. You're already on speakerphone." Reagan replied.

"We wanted to hear your thoughts about these developments, but first, how are you at handling politicians?" Smythe asked. "Doug and Ryan went over to interview the

Congresswoman – Eggerton's ex wife – yesterday. That didn't work out very well. She had her chief of staff and a lawyer present, and pretty much didn't even want to admit having been married to the guy. On the one hand, she sees this as a political problem, and on the other hand, she's worried she might have been the target and is clamoring for special protection. She demanded a full briefing on the case, and I was thinking maybe you'd..."

"Pass," Reagan said, interrupting the Director. "I don't do well with those kinds of people. Besides, this is an opportunity for you to build some goodwill. Or something like that."

"Ok, Jack," Smythe said with a laugh. "It was worth the try."

"Is there any particular reason she thinks she might have been the target?" Reagan asked.

"None whatsoever," Cannon replied. "Basically she was the spoiled little cougar who married her bartender boytoy. Their marriage fell apart pretty soon after the honeymoon, and they haven't kept in touch. She's just being hysterical. I think it's safe to say that she probably wasn't the target." There was no doubt what he thought of the Congresswoman.

"So, Jack, any thoughts?" Smythe prompted.

"A few," he replied. "For starters, I think the cellphone calls are very important and we need to follow up on those locations."

"The FBI is handling that," Smythe reminded him. "It's a standard part of an investigation, and they will get to it in due course. Unfortunately, all we can do is wait for them to do it. You're still thinking this is part of something bigger?"

"The more we find, the more I think that, yes. When can we expect to hear something about that chatter about planes?" Reagan asked.

"I have a meeting at NSA on Friday morning," Smythe said. "Sorry, Jack, that's the earliest we can do it. They're notoriously tight-lipped when it comes to giving out information, especially when it comes to sources and methods."

"The other things have to do with Cho's report. He's going to expand his focus to other villages in the area, and he requested additional manpower," Reagan said.

"Yeah, he e-mailed the same request to me," Cannon observed. "We have a couple of agents in theater we can use."

"Ok, I'll have them report to Cho," Smythe replied. "What else?"

"The name Kerimsolta isn't a Pashto name. It sounds Turkish but it could also be from the Caucasus," Reagan said. "When you combine that with the manner in which the Abdali family mysteriously appeared and disappeared – and the issue of whether the girl is even dead – I wonder if that doesn't support the idea that there's something bigger going on here."

"That's an interesting thought," Smythe offered. "You're thinking what, that the Abdalis were there to try get intel from or to try to recruit an American, and they stumbled across Eggerton?"

"In part yes," Reagan replied. "I guess it feels to me like this has the hallmarks of some kind of operation, the objective of which is unknown. Maybe the CIA has some more information, or is in a better position to develop some."

"Look, Jack, I don't entirely disagree with what you're saying," Cannon said. "In fact, I think what you're saying is objectively reasonable. It makes sense. *But* you keep wanting to expand the scope of this investigation, and we simply don't have the resources to do that. We can assign every single agent at NCIS to track down the Abdalis and Kerimsolta and never accomplish that task. It's better to work with what we've got in front of us."

"I understand what you're saying," Reagan replied, standing firm. "But realistically, what we have in front of us is very little. Forensics have been a dead end so far. You've got quite a few agents tracking down the van, the cars, the ISP data, the trash even – things like that. I understand the importance of doing that. But at the same time, I don't think it's a good idea not to focus on Afghanistan as well. This started there, remember. Eggerton deserted for the love of a living dead girl whose brother was probably one of the shooters. We can't ignore that."

"We're not ignoring it, Jack, but we can only do so much. One more thought – in my experience, the more agencies that get involved in something, the more likely something is to slip through the cracks."

"The hell of it is you're both right," Smythe said. "Doug is right; we need to look at what's in front of us, and that includes focusing on the things that haven't resulted in leads *yet*. But Jack is right, too. All the leads we *do* have point elsewhere – New Jersey in the case of the cellphones, Afghanistan in the case of at least one of the shooters. Yes, involving other agencies does complicate things, but so far that hasn't been an issue. So, Doug, keep running the investigation the way you normally do. And Jack, run the Afghan stuff by Chip Gallagher and see what he says. You're been doing a good job not just turning up leads but also developing relationships with other agencies, and I think that will prove very useful as things unfold. David Goldberg really likes you, by the way. He couldn't stop singing your praises yesterday. So both of you, just keep doing what you've been doing. Good luck, everyone," he added, concluding the call.

Smythe was satisfied with his pronouncement; he thought he had split the baby rather nicely. He found the difference in approaches between Reagan and Cannon very interesting. Both men were very methodical in their work, but whereas Cannon was closely examining the details and seeing where they led, Reagan was in a sense working backwards, looking at the bigger picture and using every resource he could think of to fill in the details and see where things started. Cannon was acting like the cop he was, while Reagan was acting more like an intelligence officer. For this case, Smythe reasoned, both approaches were equally important.

18

Osman Mansuraev was not having a good day – the snow had come as an unpleasant surprise that could severely impact his plans. Shortly after he woke up, he received a call cancelling his meeting on Capitol Hill the following day. Naturally, he had rescheduled it for the following week so as not to arouse any suspicions, but he was disappointed at missing his final opportunity to reconnoiter the targets. Strictly speaking, that wasn't really necessary – he had already seen the locations of the doors used during an emergency evacuation, and had used his phone to obtain their precise GPS coordinates. Mansuraev had taken the three slightly different measurements of latitude and longitude, compared them with data from Google Earth, and calculated the midpoint of the four. That should be close enough.

The coordinates had already been programmed into a specially designed app for his men's jailbroken iPads – that wasn't the problem. The problem was that the launch coordinates had been programmed in as well and now, as a result of the snow, it was quite possible that these latter coordinates would need to be changed. His men knew how to do that, of course; they had practiced extensively in a remote region of northern Iraq and were quite capable of obtaining new coordinates, programming them in, and launching – all under fire. Mansuraev still worried, though, so instead of his meeting on the Hill, he would spend Wednesday afternoon walking around the National Mall and the Capitol Building to check whether the locations he had selected would still be accessible. That was an unwelcome risk, though. There were far too many surveillance cameras in that area, and that really made Mansuraev unhappy.

Still, he was very pleased with the operational concept, and more so with the thought that the Americans would finally learn what it was like to have their own technology used against them, to devastating effect. *Praise Allah*, he thought sarcastically, for delivering Adil to him. The young man was every bit as wise and insightful as his name suggested. A sheer genius with computers, it had taken Adil barely a week to create the app, and another couple of days to simplify it to the point that even a monkey could use it. Not that Mansuraev's men were monkeys – they were all bright and highly experienced combat veterans of multiple campaigns across the Middle East. It had taken Mansuraev years to groom them, win their loyalty, train them further and then get them into place.

As confident as he was in his men and in his plan, Mansuraev still worried. It was in his nature to do so, and being slightly paranoid had helped him survive more than a few close calls with death over the years. *The snow, the damned snow!* Mansuraev grew impatient, realizing that there was little he could do at the moment. He would have to wait until the next day to walk around and see whether the mission was still capable of being pulled off. Cancelling or postponing it was as simple as editing the listing for his auction on eBay – that wasn't the problem. The problem was that getting to this point had required years of patience on his part, and now, as the time for action approached, Mansuraev's patience was wearing thin. He decided to take a long shower and head to the building's gym, hoping that a good exercise would relax him. After all, he had nothing else to do on a snow day.

A mere twenty minute walk away, Jack Reagan and Amanda Watson had nothing to do at the moment, either. Snow plows were just starting their rounds and it would be hours before they could head in to the office. And even then, they had nothing to do, really, but wait for information being developed by others. Waiting was not something that came easily for either one of them, but today was different. Today they had time to sit and talk – to get to know one another even better – and that was something they had both been looking forward to. Both of them were fairly reserved, rarely discussing themselves, let alone their thoughts, opinions or feelings. But together, they had a special chemistry that kept the conversation flowing. More than that, each found the other very interesting, and they both realized that they would never run out of things to talk about.

Peter Sinclair and James Mason were as annoyed by the snow as everyone else. They had things to do, but were prevented from doing them by the weather. Both men thought their friend was on to something, and his idea to scout out Sandy Hook was not a bad one. They had come to trust Reagan's judgment and even his instincts, and both men thought that Reagan hadn't missed a beat, despite not having worked with them for over a decade. Sinclair spent the better part of an hour running Reagan's idea up the chain of command, using the encrypted satellite phone he always carried. His bosses agreed that it was something worth pursuing, even if they weren't quite willing to commit more people to it than Sinclair and Mason. *Yet*, they had emphasized. It took less than two hours for them to secure permission to proceed – they would have done so anyway, but this way Reagan's off-the-books request had taken on a patina of black, approved in some special operations log that no one outside the special operations community would ever see.

A Stingray device was on its way to Andrews from MacDill; it had helped that Reagan was still somewhat of a known entity, and well-regarded by people who had come up through the ranks and were now in positions of some authority. Their mission approved and a plan formed in their heads, by noon Sinclair and Mason had nothing to do but wait – and waiting was easy. Mason closed the curtains and both men got in bed to sleep. They had learned from doctrine and long experience that rest was a weapon.

For Doug Cannon, the quiet solitude of a mostly empty office was just what he needed. He sat at his desk, hand writing letters of condolence to the families of the four agents – *his* agents – who had fallen in the line of duty. He struggled for words that would somehow make sense of the tragedy and bring a measure of comfort to the families; the words did not come easily, but the pain flowed freely. After many false starts, Cannon gave up trying to make sense of the evil that had taken place and instead decided to focus on the goodness of his agents. He remembered very personal anecdotes about each and related them instead – it was better for their families to remember the amazing people they had been rather than the manner in which they had died.

By early afternoon, as agents started trickling in to work with the reopening of the roads, Cannon was satisfied with the letters and set them aside. Later that evening, he would drive to Andrews Air Force Base to hand the letters to agents who would be escorting the bodies of Annie Jenkins and Fabian Barr to their families in Oklahoma and California. The other two letters he would himself hand to the parents of Jay Tompkins and Thomas Nicholson – both were former Marines who would be interred at Arlington National Cemetery on Friday afternoon.

Hard as it was to do so, Cannon switched focus back to the Eggerton investigation. He was frustrated that no new information had developed yet, but he could hardly fault his people. They knew their jobs and were doing everything they could. Their main focus at the moment was on Eggerton and the apartment he had used. Cannon was not at all happy that he had to rely on the FBI to follow up the leads in New Jersey or, for that matter, that he had to rely on Customs and Border Protection to try to identify the shooters. He had a nagging doubt that CBP was incompetent – in four days, its agents had been unable to match photos of the shooters with people entering the country. Not even Batoor Abdali, who had clearly been in Afghanistan just a few months earlier, appeared in any immigration records. *How the hell did he get here?* Clearly he – and Eggerton – had somehow entered the country. If not by plane, then most likely by boat, and Cannon had agents checking freighters but so far to no avail.

Cannon thought back to a question Reagan had posed at one of their meetings. If they came in by boat, what else did they bring with them? It had been merely an interesting question at the time, but with the paucity of information the investigation had developed – and with the apparent sophistication of Eggerton and his cohorts – the question seemed increasingly prescient. A few days earlier, Cannon had thought it only possible that the attack in Rock Creek Park was part of something bigger. Now he thought it increasingly likely, and wondered what had made Smythe and Reagan so certain from the very beginning.

Far from the nuisance Cannon had expected him to be, Reagan had turned out to be unusually helpful. He asked the right questions but more importantly, he knew how to connect the dots and find answers. The Director was very impressed by him – which was a remarkable thing by itself since very few people impressed him at all – and was relying on Reagan almost as much as on Cannon. More than that, the other agents liked him and readily accepted him as one of their own. Cannon liked him too, but was still somewhat bothered by the fact that Reagan didn't seem to follow any procedure. He was an information whore, pulling in intelligence from any source he could – even farming out work to other agencies so he could benefit from what they turned up. At first that had offended Cannon, but he quickly realized that part of what made Reagan so effective was that he was unburdened by procedure and chain of command. Still, he wondered why Smythe was putting so much faith in him, allowing him to talk freely to a very senior agent at the FBI and the Deputy Director of the CIA...

Son of a bitch! That's it, isn't it! Cannon sat ramrod straight at his desk, as though jolted by electricity when the realization hit him. Days earlier, the Secretary of Homeland Security had sought to put together a task force, but that idea hadn't gone anywhere. Except that it had, Cannon realized. Reagan was coordinating with the FBI and CIA – in fact if not in name, he was setting up that very task force, and even running it, reporting his findings to NCIS. The only reason it worked for Reagan and not for Secretary Jackson was that there was no ego involved; Reagan was a complete outsider, with no agency to please and no career ambitions to further. Cannon chuckled at his realization. He had allowed himself to forget just how clever his Director really was. That even explained why Smythe had loudly declared he might appoint Reagan to his old job – it gave Reagan the aura of authority he needed with other agencies.

Watson and Reagan had been reluctant to leave Jack's hotel room – they figured that their day would be full of waiting, and it was far more comfortable to wait on a soft bed than sitting behind a desk. But they couldn't do *that*, not when so many other people were braving the weather to head to the office. So by mid-afternoon, they pulled into a freshly-cleared parking space; it was the right decision, even if not the most logical one. It didn't take long for them to be summoned by Cannon to the large conference room. Cannon was there, along with Pembridge, Hollerman, and one other agent neither Reagan nor Watson had seen before. She looked rather nervous, Reagan thought as he walked in.

"We have an interesting development from Eggerton's apartment building. Special Agent Katia Ross here is going to fill us in," Cannon said, convening the meeting.

Katia Ross was every bit as nervous as Reagan thought her to be. She was brand new to NCIS, having just completed training two weeks prior, and presenting before Cannon was nerve-racking – he was one of the best, most experienced and storied agents, a man who could very easily have been in a much higher position but for his preference to remain an investigator. He was also a stubborn perfectionist who demanded the best from anyone he worked with. Pembridge's career was almost as impressive as Cannon's, and despite his jovial manner, was known as a harsh critic of inferior work product. Then there was Reagan, whom she had initially thought was an outsider until she had heard another agent refer to him as senior staff; this made sense to her, since he dealt almost exclusively with the Director and Cannon. All of this made Ross extremely nervous, even though she was only reporting on the work of others.

"I called Detective Baker of the Manassas Police Department to follow up as to whether any additional residents at the Manassas Arms have been interviewed," she said. "Detective Baker reported that he had spoken with a Jeremiah Black, the man who lived under Eggerton's apartment, on the ground floor. Mr. Black had been visiting his ex-wife and children in Georgia and only returned yesterday morning, before the storm. Mr. Black stated that he didn't know Eggerton personally but had approached him on several occasions to introduce himself. He did so thinking that Eggerton was a Muslim, like himself. He believed this because he witnessed a man visit Eggerton on several occasions, said man being dressed in what Mr. Black believed to be typical attire for an imam or other important religious teacher. Mr. Black did not talk to this alleged imam, and did not observe what vehicle he was driving. Mr. Black also stated that he did not see Eggerton receive any other guests or talk to any residents." When she was finished, Ross looked up, hoping there would be no questions. She was wrong.

"What was Black's basis for believing the visitor to be an imam?" Cannon asked.

"According to Detective Baker, Mr. Black stated that the man dressed in a long white robe and skullcap almost identical to what his own imam wears," she replied. "Detective Baker obtained the name of Mr. Black's imam and the address of his mosque, and he is going to go there today or tomorrow, depending on weather, to interview the imam in the hopes that he has some knowledge of Eggerton."

"How about a prayer rug – did Black see either men with a prayer rug?" Cannon asked.

"Yes! Sorry, sir, I forgot to mention that. According to the witness, the visitor always carried what he believed to be a prayer rug, but he never saw Eggerton with one," Ross replied. She seemed a bit pale at her mistake.

"How about anything that either man carried to or from Eggerton's apartment?" Pembridge asked.

"No sir, the witness didn't see anything being carried other than a prayer rug."

"You said that Black didn't see Eggerton receive any other guests or talk to any residents," Reagan said. "Did Detective Baker ask who else might have seen?"

Ross looked through her notes, hoping to find an answer but knowing there was none. "Detective Baker didn't say, and I didn't think to ask him that, sir."

"You'd be surprised how little that sort of question gets asked, Jack," Cannon said.

"Really?" Reagan said in surprise, swiveling his chair towards Cannon. "Pretty much any time a witness tells me they don't know something, my next question is well, who would know? Miss Ross, do you have Detective Baker's phone number?" Reagan pulled the speakerphone closer to him, making it clear that he intended to call Baker right then and there. Ross read the number as Reagan dialed. Cannon, for his part, leaned back with a wry smile. He had done the same thing as Reagan was now doing many times in his life.

"Detective Baker? This is Jack Reagan over at NCIS. You're on speakerphone with Special Agent Cannon and several other agents. We were just going over your interview with Mr. Black. Did you happen to ask Mr. Black who else might have seen who was visiting Eggerton – or Ms. Johnson, for that matter. Also, who might know more about him?"

"Sorry, Reagan, I didn't think to ask that. You know what, I just pulled out of the parking lot. Give me a couple of minutes and I'll find out for you. Can I call you back on the number on my caller ID?" he asked.

Reagan looked up at Cannon and saw him nod. "Yes, this number is fine."

"Any other questions you want me to ask?" Baker asked.

Reagan looked around the table and saw everyone shake their heads. "No, that's all for now. Thank you very much."

"This is an interesting and rather unexpected development," Cannon remarked to no one in particular. Reagan didn't entirely agree but kept his counsel; to him, it was entirely expected that Eggerton had converted to Islam. The next ten minutes passed mostly in silence as everyone in the room seemed to stare at the phone on the table. Finally, the phone rang.

"Reagan? Baker. Grab a pen," everyone heard when Reagan answered the call.

"Ok, shoot," Reagan said.

"Three things," Baker said. "First, the nuns at St. Margaret's Sisters of Charity here in town used to stop by a couple of times a week with meals for the older residents. Our officers haven't seen them around, though. Second is Marco's Pizza, the only place around here that delivers. But we already interviewed their driver and he doesn't remember anything. And third, Mr. Black says that up until two weeks ago when he left town, some hookers were working the area. My guys haven't seen them around the last few nights – our presence probably dampened their enthusiasm for this corner. Want us to follow up with any of this?" he asked helpfully.

"I'd appreciate it if you can get us some more information on the hookers," Reagan replied. "If your vice people don't have anything, maybe you can use a more discreet vehicle the next few nights in the hope of luring them back. We'll follow up with the nuns and pizza place, but thanks for offering."

"The pizza place is a dead end – we spoke with the driver," Baker reminded him.

"Driver, singular," Reagan replied. "Are there any other drivers? Were there any other drivers working during the relevant time period who are no longer employed there?"

"Good point, Reagan. Glad to help, and good luck." Baker said, a little embarrassed not to have seen that sandbag descending towards his head.

Cannon couldn't resist a soft chuckle. "That, Miss Ross, is how you follow up," he said when Reagan ended the call. "Ryan, you and Joe go talk to the nuns and the pizza delivery drivers. I'm going to hold off updating the Director until you do that," he said, drawing the meeting to a close.

19

The nuns had been most gracious hosts, fussing over Special Agents Pembridge and Hollerman with tea and cookies. They had also been rather helpful; Sister Mary Catherine had distinctly remembered the Imam, as they had taken to calling him. She, too, had thought him to be a man of God, based primarily on his manner of dress. Better still – and despite her advancing years – Mary Catherine had perfect recall when it came to faces. She provided a highly accurate description of the man she had seen less than half a dozen times in passing. Her memory for faces came from nearly three decades teaching math at a Catholic School in Richmond. She *had* to remember her students, she had said as she retrieved her coat and put it on. Pembridge had offered to bring a sketch artist to her, but she had flatly refused, insisting she accompany them to their office. "CSI is my favorite show," she had explained.

Before paying a visit to the nuns, Pembridge and Hollerman had stopped at the pizza place. "Looks like Jack was right," Pembridge had said upon learning from the store's owner that he employed a total of six drivers, two of whom were in the store at that moment. The first driver – a young woman so large that Hollerman wondered how she fit behind the wheel of a car – had been entirely unhelpful. The second driver, on the other hand, vaguely recalled the "neatly dressed guy with the weird thing on his head." The pimple-faced teenager had remarked that the Imam parked on the street rather than in the parking lot of the Manassas Arms. Even better, the kid was fanatical about cars and described his vehicle as a 2008-2010 BMW 325i, silver with four doors and 19" chrome rims. Best of all, the car had Virginia plates and a long, deep gash that ran halfway across the rear bumper.

Hollerman had already called in a B.O.L.O. on the car even before they stopped at the convent. Now he sat in the back seat with a wide smile on his face at the significant progress they had made in just a few hours. He didn't even mind sitting in back; he had gladly given up his seat to Sister Mary Catherine, who was grinning broadly as Pembridge sped through traffic that parted at the sound of his siren and sight of his flashing lights. Mary Catherine had asked and Pembridge had obliged; in part he did so to thank the nun for her help, but more than that, after twelve years of Catholic schools, Pembridge was simply used to doing what nuns asked of him.

The man Sister Mary Catherine described in great detail bore little resemblance to any of their shooters, but Special Agent Cannon had showed her their photos just to be sure. The nun had even started to pray for the terrorists after seeing a picture of one missing half his face, but she stopped herself quickly. These men were pure evil, she reminded herself. They had killed children and were consequently burning in the pyres of Hell. Her prayers were best saved for the innocents. Cannon had showed her pictures of the villagers in Afghanistan as well, hoping that perhaps she might recognize someone from those pictures. The nun studied each of them very closely – she seemed to be dragging things out so as not to leave – but she didn't recognize any of them. Cannon, for his part, thanked the nun by finding an agent to give her a tour of the building.

It turned out that there were a whole hell of a lot of silver BMWs registered in Virginia. The agents would start with the sixteen that had been reported stolen just in the previous six months, expanding their search backwards while also prioritizing owners whose names appeared to be foreign. It would be a very long night – probably a very long couple of days – but Cannon was optimistic that they would come up with something. Special Agent Watson was assigned some records to examine, and she offered to call a taxi for Reagan so he could go back to the hotel and rest. He had politely declined and sat next to Watson, seeing

187

what she was doing and listening to her as she explained her work. After a while, he thought he had it figured out and went to Cannon, asking for some records to review on his own.

"I don't have a problem with that," Cannon said after thinking it over briefly. "I assume Amanda showed you what to do?" he asked, seeing Reagan nod. "Any particular place you want to start, Jack?"

"Yeah, the oldest people you can find, please" Reagan replied at once.

Cannon raised an eyebrow, printing out a list of a little more than seventy vehicle registrations and handing it to Reagan without a word. He was a little surprised at the request, but had given up trying to figure out how Reagan's mind worked.

It took Reagan just over three hours to find what he was looking for – naturally it had to be the second to last name on his list. He started each search by comparing the name of the car's owner to the Social Security Administration's Death Index. The seventy-first name he pulled up was Robert Keller. Keller had passed away on June 14, 2014, but his vehicle registration had been renewed – in person – on October 1. Reagan excitedly called Cannon to his office to show him what he found. Cannon agreed that it was something worth pursuing immediately, and sent Pembridge and Hollerman to interview Keller's widow, despite the fact that it would be close to 11 p.m. by the time they arrived in Fredericksburg. On further thought, he asked Reagan and Watson to go as well, in case either of them came up with any outside-the-box questions.

"Mrs. Keller, my name is Ryan Pembridge. We're federal agents with the Naval Criminal Investigative Service. Sorry to disturb you at this late hour, but we have some questions we need to ask you." The three agents had walked around the house before ringing the doorbell, making sure that nothing appeared out of the ordinary.

"The Navy? My Robert was in the Army, not the Navy," Mrs. Keller said, a little confused as to why four Navy people would be on her porch at this late hour.

"We're federal agents, ma'am," Pembridge repeated. "We'd like to ask you about your late husband's car."

"Robert's car? I sold that thing last summer, after he passed. What do you want with his car?"

"Who did you sell it to, ma'am?" Pembridge asked.

"Oh I don't remember his name. A nice young man, though. Did I do something wrong?" she asked, suddenly worried.

"No, ma'am," said Hollerman. "You've done nothing wrong. We're just interested in the man who bought the BMW. What do you remember about him?"

"Not much, I'm afraid. He was a nice young man. A Latino, I think, but he spoke very good English," Mrs. Keller replied. She was only able to give a vague description of a thin man, probably in his 40s and anywhere from 5'4" to 5'10" tall, with indeterminate facial features. She had kept no paperwork from the sale, and hadn't written down his name anywhere.

"Do you recognize any of these men?" Pembridge asked, showing her photos of Eggerton, the shooters, and the men from the village in Afghanistan.

"No, none of them look familiar." Mrs. Keller was tired and more than a little confused as to why these strange men and woman were showing her pictures of even stranger-looking men.

"How did he pay for the car, Mrs. Keller?" Reagan asked.

"In cash. I don't remember how much," she responded, somewhat guardedly.

"Ma'am, we're not with the IRS," Reagan said, correctly guessing what was on this widow's mind. "We think the man who bought your husband's car may be involved with some very bad people – very dangerous people – and we're trying to find him. That's all," he said, seeing Mrs. Keller nod her head. "Now, how much did he pay, and do you still have any of the cash?"

"He paid $5,500. I spent most of it, but I think I still have a few hundred tucked away," she replied.

"Can we see those bills, please?" Pembridge asked. "We'd like to take them with us and have a closer look at them – check them for fingerprints, that sort of thing."

"Oh no, I couldn't do that," Mrs. Keller replied, shaking her head. "It's my money and I need it."

"I promise we'll have it back to you in a couple of days," Pembridge said.

"No, I can't do that," Mrs. Keller said, growing somewhat alarmed. "I'm a widow, you see, and money is very tight."

Reagan decided to try a different tack. "How about I exchange the bills this man gave you with money from my wallet," he suggested, taking out his wallet in the process.

Mrs. Keller thought it over for more than a few seconds. "Well, I suppose that's ok. You all wait right here while I go find the envelope." She closed the door, leaving her visitors outside. The agents and Reagan traded amused looks as they heard the latch lock into place and the scrape of a chain being secured. It took close to ten minutes for her to return with a white envelope in her hand.

"There's five hundred dollars here," she said, looking through the envelope as Reagan opened his wallet and handed her five one hundred dollar bills. He started reaching for the envelope but stopped mid-reach.

"Is this your envelope or did the buyer give it to you?" he asked.

"He gave it to me," she replied.

Reagan backed away, letting Pembridge take the envelope with a gloved hand and place it in an evidence bag.

"Thank you very much for your help, ma'am," Pembridge said as the group turned to leave.

Something caught Reagan's eye from the neighboring house – some kind of very small and dim red light behind a window that came on for a second and then disappeared. He instantly thought the light to have come from the laser focus of a digital camera. "Mrs. Keller, one more thing," he said, turning back to face the widow. "What can you tell us about your neighbor?"

"Doris? She's the busiest busybody in the world!" Mrs. Keller replied with a chuckle.

"Do you know her last name?" Reagan asked.

"Yeah, Rose. Doris Rose. She's as prickly as her name suggests," Mrs. Keller said, letting everyone know what she thought of her neighbor.

Reagan thanked her and led the agents across the snow-covered lawn to the Rose house and up the front steps.

"What's going on, Jack?" Hollerman asked.

"Humor me for a second, guys," he replied, knocking loudly on the door after failing to locate any doorbell. "Mrs. Rose, we're federal agents. We'd like to ask you some questions about your neighbor, Mrs. Keller."

The door opened rapidly, revealing a short and significantly overweight pensioner with wild eyes and wilder hair. "What's she done?" she asked a little too eagerly, sizing up the credentials held up by Pembridge.

"We have reason to believe her late husband's car may have been used in connection with violent crime," Reagan said. "We're trying to track down the person who bought it."

"Some Hispanic man, last summer," she said at once. "Way too many of them around these parts lately. I only hire white people to mow my lawn." Mrs. Rose had no qualms expressing her feelings.

"Can we please see the pictures you took of him?" Reagan asked. "It would be very helpful in our investigation."

"I don't have them with me. I forgot my camera at my boyfriend's beach house at Myrtle Beach last October," she explained. "I've only got this cheap piece of shit now," she added, holding up a small Cannon digital camera. "Hey, how did you know I have pictures?" she wanted to know.

191

"Are you sure you have photos of the man who bought the car?" Reagan asked, ignoring her question.

"Yeah, I'm positive. They're on a 32 gigabyte memory card that's still in the camera, and the camera is probably in a dresser drawer along with my collection of bikinis," Mrs. Rose explained.

Reagan cocked his head at Pembridge, who obtained the boyfriend's name, addresses and contact information. Reagan didn't know what he found more disturbing, that this woman had a boyfriend, or that she had a collection of bikinis.

"Fuckin' A, Jack," Pembridge exclaimed on the way to the car. "Very nicely done. But how'd you know?"

"Saw the red laser thing from her camera. No big deal," Reagan replied, shrugging his shoulders.

"No big deal my ass, pal," Pembridge said with a laugh. "Ok, what now?" he asked, trying to resist the temptation to turn the car south for the six hour drive to Myrtle Beach. He was very excited at the prospect of seeing the photos and finally having something concrete to work with.

"How about we ask the local cops to sit on the place until we figure out who goes down to get the photos?" Reagan suggested.

"Good idea," Hollerman replied, taking out his phone to do just that.

Pembridge called Cannon to relay the information, speaking as he drove. Cannon was as eager to get his hands on the pictures as they were, and he decided to send two agents down by car just as soon as he could secure a warrant. It would take at least twelve hours for them to return with the photos, but it was well worth the wait.

Thanks to the snow event, Tuesday had turned into a very long day for all the essential personnel who had no choice but to brave the weather and go to work. Special Agent Paul Monaghan was no exception. He looked at his watch and quickly realized that this was by far the latest he had ever stayed at work in the two months he had been assigned to the Hoover Building. He also realized that this fortuitous assignment would not last indefinitely. The administrative position he now held – coordinating investigations between offices and with other agencies – was a reward of sorts for the very successful completion of an operation against organized crime during which he had spent close to a year undercover with an up-and-coming mob family in Philadelphia. His marriage had suffered terribly as a result of his prolonged absence, and Monaghan was grateful that his more reasonable hours seemed to be restoring a sense of balance in his family. He only had one more call he needed to make before he could head home and enjoy a very late dinner with his wife, who most surprisingly was waiting up for him.

"Jack? Paul Monaghan. Hope I didn't wake you!"

"Wake me? Hell, Special Agent Monaghan, it's barely midnight. Plenty of hours left in the work day," he heard Reagan say. This was followed by a hearty laugh. It was hard not to like the man; Monaghan knew that his Director thought very highly of Reagan, and had been overheard musing that they should steal him away from NCIS. Monaghan thought Reagan knew his way around an investigation fairly well, even if he didn't follow any procedure Monaghan was aware of. *That's not entirely true*, he corrected himself, realizing that Reagan reminded him a lot of the people he has worked with earlier in his career – in the Counterintelligence Division. *Yeah, he'd fit in there very nicely.*

Monaghan couldn't resist a laugh of his own. "I've got some information for you. I'm afraid it's a case of good news-bad news, though." At first, he had been wary of sharing sources and methods with Reagan, but his Director had overruled Monaghan, pointing out that the NCIS Director had essentially legitimized him as senior staff of that agency.

"Thanks Paul," Reagan said. "How about bad news first?"

"The bad news is that we only found usable cameras in Elizabeth and Jersey City. The Elizabeth ones are at the IKEA, by the way, and they're pretty poor quality. There's only one vehicle that shows up at the relevant times. It's a white panel van with no apparent markings. The really bad news is that we can't read plate numbers, and we can't get a good look at the driver or the front seat passenger. We're going to try to clear up the image a bit but our tech guys aren't optimistic. Best guess is they're both males, ages unknown. They never step out of the van, by the way."

"Ok, that's not *that* bad," Reagan replied. "What's the good news?"

"The good news is that the area in Jersey City around the Holland Tunnel has nothing but cameras, and many of them are very good quality. The problem, of course, is that all of the phone calls from Jersey City were made at peak rush hour times. Even if we limit ourselves to white panel vans – which is what we've done for now – that still leaves well over a dozen of them that appear during the relevant times. We're going to track down as many as we can, but because of the way vehicles are packed in there at rush hour, we haven't been able to get plate numbers on some of the vans. Worse than that, most of these vans are probably regulars – they commute at the same time each day. So being able to track the van we are interested in is going to be very tricky and labor intensive."

"Do you have enough people to do that?"

"We do," Monaghan said. "That's part of the good news. We've got analysts to do that kind of thing, and that frees up our agents to go back to what they were working on," he explained.

"Any idea how long that might take?" Reagan asked next.

"I wouldn't expect anything before the end of the week, Jack. I'll call you as soon as I have something, one way or the other. Anything new on your end?"

Reagan relayed the information they had developed in Fredericksburg and Manassas, naturally downplaying his role.

"So what do you make of all this?" Monaghan asked when Reagan had finished.

"At the very least, the involvement of more people suggests that there's more going on here – probably part of something bigger."

"Fair enough, Jack, but keep something in mind – the number of cellphones we've got matches exactly the number of shooters in the park, plus whoever it is that set off the explosives and got away. It could just be that these guys from New Jersey ditched their cellphones and headed to Rock Creek Park," Monaghan pointed out.

"That's a distinct possibility," Reagan admitted. "Quite a few people in this office have that idea as well. It doesn't sit well with me, though, and I think it's very important to track that van you mentioned and figure out if it shows up more recently. Especially if it shows up *after* last Thursday's attack."

"Why doesn't it sit well with you?" Monaghan pressed.

"Well for starters, it doesn't make sense for the people in New Jersey to develop a pattern of calls and travel around some very significant potential targets, only to drop everything and head to Washington. I mean, why would they do that?" Reagan asked, then suggesting answers to his own question. "One possibility is that the calls in New Jersey were meant as a misdirect, suggesting an attack in a place other than where the true target was. The problem I have with that, though, is that it presupposes that the people who made those calls thought they were being surveilled. And if they were being surveilled, it would stand to reason they would also be followed to wherever their true target was. In other words, the very premise of a misdirect is faulty."

"Makes sense," Monaghan conceded. "What else?"

"Another possibility is that the original targets were mean to be in New Jersey, but the bad guys got orders changing the target to Rock Creek Park. That really doesn't sit well with me, though, because a major transportation route, airport or port are all much juicier targets than NCIS agents and some children. If you're a terrorist, what's a juicier target – armed federal agents or a passenger plane?"

"Fair point," Monaghan admitted. "But that kinda presupposes these terrorists think the same way you or I do," he pointed out.

"That's true enough," Reagan replied. "But if the targets were the NCIS agents, to what end? That doesn't seem like a valid end, but more like a means to an end – and *that* suggests something more is coming."

"You raise some valid points," Monaghan agreed.

"One more thing," Reagan added. "We now have two more individuals connected to Eggerton who were not among the shooters in the park. One of them, the Imam, seems to be a point of contact to Eggerton. The other one – the one who bought the Imam's car – sounds a bit like a fixer, doesn't he? And *that* suggests a network larger than the nine men in the park."

"I hadn't thought about it like that," Monaghan admitted. "Interesting point. I'll give it some more thought. Anyway, I'm off to a late dinner with the wife. Catch you later, Jack." Monaghan grabbed his parka and headed for the door, thinking that Reagan would fit in very well indeed with the counterintelligence people.

20

Lieutenant Commander Peter Sinclair crossed the Anacostia River using the Frederick Douglass Memorial Bridge and instantly regretted it. The approach to Suitland Parkway was thoroughly backed up, and Sinclair couldn't tell whether there had been an accident or whether there was merely a high volume of cars that morning. He looked over at his partner and saw that Lieutenant James Mason had given up trying to figure out the traffic feature on the car's satellite navigation unit, instead using the map app on his phone to figure out the cause of the delay.

"Accident blocking all lanes about a quarter mile ahead," Mason said. "No way around it."

Sinclair gripped the steering wheel tighter in mild frustration, but he had come to expect Washington traffic to be bad. Yet one more reason to avoid this place, he thought. "Should have left earlier," he grumbled.

"Aye aye, sir," Mason replied. "Sorry about that!"

"No you're not!" Sinclair said with a laugh. Mason had gone downstairs for dinner the night before and returned slightly before 5 a.m. with two different shades of lipstick on his collar.

"You're right, I'm not," Mason replied with a chuckle of his own, thinking back to the very prim and proper lobbyists he had convinced to loosen up after they invited him back to their room. It turned out that they were neither prim nor proper, and Mason didn't mind trading sleep for this particular diversion. "Mind if I take a nap?" he asked, leaning his seat back and closing his eyes. The drive to Andrews would take well more than the usual half hour.

The car, at least, was luxurious, supple and extraordinarily comfortable. Sinclair and Mason had talked Bob Angelo into giving them the keys to his daughter's car. Bob had laughed approvingly at their idea, agreeing that a black Porsche Cayenne S would make for great reverse stealth in northern New Jersey. Sinclair really looked forward to opening the car up on the road; he was not at all worried about police because the Stingray device they were heading to pick up came with credentials identifying them as Deputy U.S. Marshals. This accommodation had been devised by the Attorney General under the previous Administration, as much to provide cover to JSOC personnel on those rare occasions when they worked domestically as to avoid falling afoul of the Posse Comitatus Act. That the current Administration had allowed this accommodation to continue was nothing less than a miracle, and spoke volumes about the underlying concern for the President's safety – most domestic deployments had been to augment his security.

Sinclair reached for the car's owner manual as Mason closed his eyes, thinking that he might as well take the opportunity to read up on all the buttons and switches that stretched from the center armrest to the top of the center console. The car cabin looked and felt more like the cockpit of a fighter jet, and that excited him. Sinclair, like so many of his colleagues, was somewhere along the path towards obtaining a civilian pilot's license. His entire unit, in fact, collected skill sets with much the same eagerness as a young child collects baseball cards. That had made them all fierce and awesome warriors long before the public ever heard of their operation to kill Osama bin Laden.

Jack Reagan woke to the sound of the phone ringing and reached for the room phone, thinking it to be his wakeup call. He was well and truly tired, and it took him several seconds to realize that the ringing noise in fact came from his cellphone. He felt Amanda stir next to him; she was still spooned up against him, and Jack realized than neither one of them had moved an inch all night. He smiled when he felt her hand squeeze his as he fumbled to find his cellphone. He couldn't help but smile waking up next to this amazing, brilliant and beautiful woman.

Amanda smiled as well. She felt warm and safe wrapped up in Jack's arms – and excited as well. More than that, it felt right and natural, even though this sort of thing was completely out of character for her. Jack, she realized, made her feel comfortable and at ease with herself in a way no one else had before. He also made her feel like the person she had always wanted to be – a better version of herself – and that was decidedly special. It had taken her the duration of the drive back to their hotel at 2 a.m. to come up with a very simple excuse to go to his room; she asked him to order room service for the both of them as she left the elevator on her floor, and hurriedly showered and changed into comfortable clothes before heading up. Nothing was awkward when they were together – the awkward part was finding a reason to be together in the first place.

"Jack Reagan," he spoke into his phone, his voice betraying his exhaustion.

"Hey Jack, it's Tommy Cho. Wake up, buddy, you're wasting daylight," he heard on the other end of the phone.

"Hey Tommy, how are you? What's up?" Reagan replied.

"I'm great, thanks!" Cho replied. He was thoroughly enjoying his current assignment, and delighted in helping the Marines plan their maneuvers through the villages in the area in search of the mysterious Abdali family. He had even taken to chomping on an unlit cigar around base, much to the amusement of the Marines and the two agents who had been sent to help him. "Just wanted to give you a little update. Earlier today we went into a village around 35 klicks from here – I'll send you the coordinates by e-mail; you sound too tired to write them down properly," he said with a laugh. "Anyway, this next part is really going to wake you up, Jack," he said, drawing up the suspense.

"What's that, Tommy?" Reagan asked, as expected.

"It's really interesting. In fact, I'm sure you're going to find it extremely interesting," Cho replied, drawing Reagan in further.

"Ok, Tommy, I'm awake and listening."

"Are you sure, Jack? This is pretty big!" Cho was playing up the suspense as much as possible.

"Yes, Tommy, I'm sure," Reagan said with a laugh. The suspense was great at waking him up.

"Ok, Jack, but you're not going to believe it. I'm not sure I believe it myself. I showed around the usual pictures of the Abdali family and our shooters. One of the people who lives in this village used to be an Economics professor in Kabul back in the '90s. He swore on the Holy Qur'an that he recognized Dawar Abdali. Are you ready for this, Jack? He says Dawar was some kind of an official in the Taliban regime – the one before 9/11, I mean. He thinks he was an intelligence officer."

Reagan sat bolt upright in bed with a look on his face that almost made Watson reach for her pistol; Reagan's face, which seemed to hold a perennial and good-looking tan, had turned completely pale. "How sure are you about this, I mean how sure is this guy?" he asked.

"He's as sure about this as he is that the sun rises in the East and sets in the West, Jack."

"Ok, tell me exactly what he said, and assess his credibility," Reagan ordered.

"He seems credible as hell. His name is Tabaan Durrani. He opened up a box he keeps hidden in a hole under his garden and showed me some things from his past – his diploma and pictures of him in a classroom with students at Kabul University. Obviously a diploma can be faked and I have nothing to compare the photos to, but it feels very real. His tone and body language were right, too. Anyway, Tabaan said that after the Taliban came to power, he was called to deliver several lectures on the mechanisms of international finance to Qari Ahmadullah, who was the Minister of Security up until the time we killed his ass in December 2001. There were three other people present for these lectures, and Tabaan distinctly remembers that Dawar Abdali was one of them. Jack, this is pretty big. What do I do now?"

"Did you copy any of the things he showed you?"

"In a manner of speaking. I took pictures of them. I guess you want me to send them to you?" Cho asked.

"Fast as you can, Tommy. Have you told anyone else yet?" Reagan asked.

"You'll have them in a few minutes," Cho promised. "And no, not yet. Director Smythe told me to reach out to you first whenever I get something. How do I even follow up on this stuff?"

"I'll call the Director right now and fill him in. As for follow up," Reagan paused, his mind going into overdrive. "I don't know that you can, to be honest. I think all you can do is keep asking the questions you've been asking. I'll give it some more thought and let you know if I have any ideas."

"Thanks, Jack. Told you it was interesting!" Cho said with a chuckle, ending the call.

Reagan scrolled through his contact list to find the right number as Watson looked on, noting that his face was regaining its color.

"Director Smythe? Jack Reagan here."

"Good morning, Jack!" Smythe seemed to be in a good mood. "Really nice work last night. I talked to Doug and he said..."

"I've got something important, sir," Reagan said, interrupting the Director. "I just spoke with Tommy Cho. He interviewed someone who identified Dawar Abdali as an official in the old Taliban regime, possibly an intelligence officer."

"Jesus Christ!" Smythe remarked, as stunned as Reagan had been a minute earlier. Watson was equally stunned as she heard Reagan relate what Cho had told him.

"This is big, Jack, very big," Smythe said when Reagan had finished. "Where do we go with this from here?"

"Do we have any sort of database of Taliban officials?" Reagan asked.

"We do. It mostly comes from CIA."

"In that case, I'd like to take this to Chip Gallagher at Langley. They probably have the best information – and they can assess the photos Tommy took and see if Tabaan's story holds up," Reagan suggested.

"Approved," Smythe said at once. "Work fast, Jack. The more I hear, the more inclined I am to think something bigger is going on here. Any other thoughts?"

"Just one. We need to start looking where we haven't been looking," Reagan replied, his words not quite keeping up with the speed at which his mind was processing his thoughts.

"You've lost me, Jack."

"Ok, let's assume that this information is accurate and Dawar Abdali was an intelligence officer," Reagan thought out loud. "A former Taliban intelligence officer and his family mysteriously appear in a village within walking distance of a Marine base. The daughter captures the attention of a Marine, who falls in love with her. The daughter dies, allegedly at the hands of other Marines and Eggerton deserts as a result. Only the daughter isn't really dead, and the family mysteriously vanishes. This sounds an awful lot like some overly complicated honey trap."

"That's exactly what it sounds like, Jack. Go on." *Why the hell didn't I see that sooner*, Smythe asked himself.

"Ok, next, we have Eggerton pop up in Washington, calling his Congresswoman ex-wife to arrange a meeting. Only he never shows up at that meeting – at least not so far as we know. Instead, the undead girlfriend's brother shows up with seven of his Kalashnikov-wielding friends to take on NCIS. It seems to me that Eggerton was used to set us up. Set up NCIS, I mean."

"Yeah but to what end?" Smythe asked.

"As a diversion from something yet to play out," Reagan explained. "We're funneling all of our resources into finding Eggerton, and what do we turn up? Pretty much nothing. An apartment – no, excuse me, *two* apartments – that were pretty thoroughly sanitized, even though we did get lucky with the SIM

202

card. Whoever set this up *knew* we would be looking for Eggerton. They're making it more difficult, and as a result we're expending more effort to find him. Not just us, but the FBI too. We're looking left, when we should be looking right."

"I'll admit, Jack, what you're saying makes a lot of sense," Smythe replied. "If whoever is behind this is anticipating our response, wouldn't they also know we've increased the threat alert level?"

"They probably would. But what if that's part of it?" Reagan said, remembering something Nick Videtti had initially suggested. "What if, for example, our heightened security posture actually helps facilitate whatever they have planned?"

"That's a scary thought," Smythe admitted. "Any ideas what that might be?"

"Sorry, no." Reagan replied. "But I think we need to focus more on New Jersey – that's the best lead we have."

"That seems like the reasonable place to look," Smythe said. "After you talk this over with Gallagher, give some thought about how to proceed with respect to New Jersey. Meanwhile I'll call David Goldberg and bring him up to speed. Thanks, Jack – call me if you need me."

"Will do, Director." Reagan set his phone down and decided that before he did anything else, he really needed some coffee. He started in the direction of the coffeemaker, but Watson beat him to it. She started pouring water into the machine, her brain trying to catch up with what she had just overheard. She had never worked on anything even approaching the magnitude of this case, and part of her thought it sounded like something out of a bad movie. But everything Reagan had said made perfect sense, and more than that, her Director seemed to agree. Both were among the smartest people Watson knew, and the possible implications of their collective judgment were almost too terrifying to contemplate.

Jenny Draper was just too new and inexperienced to fully realize that while curiosity is a very good attribute for an employee of the Central Intelligence Agency, it isn't always something to be acted upon. Her boss had left work the previous week when his wife went into labor, but the baby had come a bit too early and the delivery was not without complications. He had spent the past five days at the hospital by her side, and would be with her still as she was released later that day. Baby Jonah would be staying in the neonatal intensive care unit a while longer - and his parents were having a hard time coping. Draper had sent some colorful flowers to the hospital in a heartfelt but ultimately unsuccessful attempt at helping the new parents feel better.

Draper looked through the alerts on her boss's computer, relieved to see that there was nothing new. Monday had seen two searches related to Agency personnel, but since both had originated with local police agencies checking license plate information, Draper was fairly certain those had been routine traffic stops. On the other hand, the single inquiry into Jack Reagan by NCIS the previous Thursday had been followed by multiple inquiries from that same agency as well as the FBI. More than that, there were requests from Homeland Security, the Metropolitan Police Department – and even one from inside CIA. All of this made Draper very curious.

She sat at her boss's desk and tried to decipher the acronyms appended to Reagan's name. Eddie Lancaster was a very good person to work with – he took the time to explain things simply and clearly – and Draper remembered enough to understand that Reagan had been an outside contractor and then an Agency employee. She knew the procedure Lancaster followed in cases like this: first, he checked Agency records to determine who the person was, and then he called the most senior person at the agency that made the request to try to figure out why it had been made. After that, he notified the DDCI, who took it from there. Draper didn't have a high enough clearance to access personnel records, but she figured she could still help. Lancaster had enough to worry about with his family, so what could it hurt to at least figure out for him why other agencies were interested in this Reagan person. This way her boss would have one less thing to do when he stopped by the office later that day, and he could go home sooner and be with his wife.

But first Draper needed to figure out whom to call. She was reluctant to call either the FBI or DHS – both of these were institutional rivals of the CIA. She knew little about NCIS, but a quick search revealed that its Director had once worked in this very building, in the Directorate of Intelligence. That would make him an ally, probably, and Draper reached for her boss's encrypted phone after she found the right number, not realizing that she had no authority to make such a call.

"Director Smythe? My name is Jenny Draper. I work with Eddie Lancaster at CIA. I have a question for you regarding Jack Reagan."

"Is there a problem?" she heard a tired-sounding voice say on the phone. "I asked him to reach out to Deputy Director Gallagher on an urgent matter."

"I don't know anything about that, sir. I'm calling because your agency has made several inquiries about Mr. Reagan and I'm trying to determine what that's about," Draper said.

Smythe had been caught off guard and was now a little confused. "Wait, who did you say you were again?"

"My name is Jenny Draper and I work for Eddie Lancaster."

Smythe vaguely remembered talking to Lancaster once or twice. He was the person at CIA who was responsible for...*Son of a bitch, Jack!* Smythe finally made the connection, and sat in stunned silence.

"What can you tell me about Mr. Reagan," Draper prompted, hearing nothing but silence.

"He's helping us with a very important investigation," Smythe finally replied. "What can *you* tell me about him?"

"I'm sorry, sir, I'm really not at liberty to say anything," Draper responded – at least she got that much right.

"I see. Thank you for your call," Smythe said, setting down the receiver. It all made perfect sense now. Reagan was acting like an intelligence officer because that's exactly what he had been. Probably.

Smythe reached into his desk and pulled out Reagan's file. Now that he knew what he was looking for, it didn't take long for him to connect the dots. It had to have been before his law career – the law firm Reagan had worked for was not one to tolerate moonlighting, and it was clear that whatever else he had been, Reagan had also been a very successful litigator. Smythe looked at the dates in Reagan's bio, comparing them to his passport file. His foreign travel had really picked up in his last years of college and lasted until law school. He had even lived in London, which made his side trips short and easy. *You could have told me, damn it!* But Smythe was too professional to be cross at Reagan – obviously the young man took security and classification very seriously and *couldn't* have told him.

All this time, Smythe had thought Reagan to be a very gifted amateur, but he was clearly more than that. Well, *probably* more than that. He needed more information, and thought about how to obtain it. He could simply ask Reagan, but doubted he would get a straight answer one way or another. He could also call the DDCI, but that might just confuse things and the investigation was much too important to risk that. Smythe looked at the dates, searching his memory, trying to remember who the Deputy Director, Intelligence and Deputy Director, Operations had been during the relevant time period. The former, he remembered, had passed away shortly after he left CIA. But the latter was living out his retirement somewhere in Virginia horse country – Smythe exchanged Christmas cards with the man. Reagan's talents seemed to reach across both Directorates, so Smythe thought it likely that John Quincy, the former DDO, would at least have heard of him. He reached for his phone and called Quincy, arranging a meeting on Friday morning in Rock Creek Park. This was not the sort of thing to talk about over the phone.

Smythe put Reagan's file back in his desk and briefly considered calling Doug Cannon to talk this over with him. *Probably better not to,* he decided; he didn't want Cannon's institutional prejudices getting in the way of his working relationship with Reagan, and Smythe needed both men to carry on the investigation. He allowed himself a smile, realizing that with Cannon and Reagan, he had a pair of pocket aces – if anyone could figure out what Eggerton and the terrorists were planning, they would.

21

Amanda Watson pulled into a parking spot in the visitors' lot at the Central Intelligence Agency and accompanied Reagan through two separate security screenings before the pair were escorted into the anteroom of Deputy Director Chip Gallagher's office. They didn't have long to wait before the officious-sounding secretary announced them and led them into Gallagher's office. Watson was rather in awe of her surroundings; she had always been fascinated by the secretive and mysterious workings of the CIA. Reagan, on the other hand, seemed unaffected by his surroundings.

"Good morning, Jack," Gallagher said with a friendly smile and a wave. "Sorry to drag you all the way out here, but I much prefer discussing things in person."

"Not a problem, Deputy Director Gallagher," Reagan replied, shaking the man's hand. "This is Special Agent Amanda Watson. I'm working with her at NCIS."

"Miss Watson," Gallagher acknowledged, shaking her hand as well. "Have a seat, Jack – and call me Chip. I'm not much for formality," he explained. "What's this information you've tumbled across?"

Reagan recounted the information developed by Tommy Cho, adding his own analysis as well. He spoke slowly, noting that Gallagher took copious notes.

"Very interesting stuff, Jack," Gallagher said when Reagan finished. "This is news to us, by the way. We've already checked on the Abdali family and turned up nothing. Of course, those might just be the names they're using now – not the ones they were using back in '01."

"Now that we have a better idea of what we're looking for, can you cross-reference the Abdalis – at least the photo of Dawar

– with whatever information you have on the Taliban intelligence services?" Reagan asked.

"We can do that – it shouldn't be too hard," Gallagher hoped. "If there were only a handful of people at those economics meetings, Dawar was probably some mid-level or senior official, and we have some workups on those types, even if we don't have names or pictures. You know what the problem is? We bagged the top guys very quickly – just as soon as hunting season opened, actually. Most of the senior guys scattered after that, trying to blend in with the populace of their native tribal areas. That didn't work out too well for them, and we bagged most of them too. The really smart ones – not that many of them, luckily – scattered to the winds. We hear things about a few of them now and then, but still haven't developed enough information to find them, let alone figure out who they are."

"Do you have any assets in-country you can turn loose on this?" Reagan asked. "It's pretty important," he added.

"More than pretty important, Jack," Gallagher said with a chuckle. Despite the fact that he was a presidential appointee, Gallagher was an experienced intelligence analyst who had come up through the ranks at CIA. "I'll talk to my people just as soon as we're done here, and have the Station Chief turn his people loose. Carefully, of course. As important as this is, we have some other things going on that I don't want to risk."

"Fair enough – just so long as you keep NCIS in the loop on anything relevant," Reagan replied.

"I'll do that," Gallagher promised. "Anything else?"

"Yes, actually," Reagan said, handing over a small USB drive. "These are the photos Special Agent Cho took of Tabaan's diploma and pictures. Can you have your imagery analysis people run through them – just to be sure we aren't barking up the wrong tree?"

"Not a bad idea," Gallagher admitted, taking the drive. "We almost definitely have photos from inside Kabul University. The diploma is probably a dead end though; records from that place are prone to catching fire. If we had the original we could try to analyze it, but that wouldn't be conclusive. Any other ideas?"

"Unfortunately, no. You?"

"Me either," Gallagher said, shaking his head. "Anyway, I'll let you know if we find something." He rose and extended his hand, signaling the end of the meeting.

"Thanks," Jack said, shaking his hand. "And Chip, please let me know if you *don't* find something, too."

Gallagher had himself a good chuckle at that one. "Will do," he said. "Miss Watson, nice to put a face to the name. Oh and Jack, in case no one has told you, you're doing a damn good job."

"I'm just the messenger," Reagan shrugged with a smile, then turned to follow Watson out the door.

"Bullshit, Jack... Bullshit," Gallagher told the receding figure with another good chuckle.

"So what did you think?" Reagan asked Watson when they were back in her car.

"What did I think..." she repeated. What she had thought, watching in silence as Reagan spoke with Gallagher, was that she had never met anyone like Reagan before. He never stopped impressing her. As self-confident and self-assured as she was – *had* to be, as a federal agent – Reagan was in a whole different league. She had just seen him walk into CIA and secure the cooperation of its Deputy Director – "call me Chip," he had said – quietly and entirely without histrionics, something that not even Doug Cannon could pull off. People listened to Cannon because they *had* to; his authority came from his long experience, rank and badge. But people listened to Reagan because they *wanted* to. He held authority simply by virtue of being smart, confident – and seemingly always at least one step ahead of everyone else. More than that, he saw things and made connections that others didn't.

"I think I feel a little like Alice in Wonderland," Watson replied with a grin. "That place is just different, you know. It has a certain mystique that gets to me. It didn't seem to faze you any, though."

"Maybe I just have a good poker face," Reagan offered with a smile.

"Maybe," she replied, turning to study his face. "But you know what, one of these days I'll have you all figured out and then we can really play. Poker too, if you want," she added with a playful wink, putting the car in gear. She had never acted like this with anyone before, but she had stopped worrying about it days earlier. She was a different person around Jack – a better version of herself, she thought. She felt a connection with him unlike any she had felt before, even in her most intimate relationships. All the while working the single most important case in her career. *How about that*, she thought as she turned south on the George Washington Memorial Parkway.

Reagan sat in his office looking through still images from the video sent over by the FBI. It must be maddening work, he thought, looking through thousands upon thousands of frames of videos showing thousands of vehicles, trying to narrow down which car their suspects drove. He wondered how long the average analyst lasted on the job before being escorted to a padded room for a long rest. Whatever the level of their sanity was, those agents certainly did good work – they had narrowed things down to the same nine vans and two sedans that passed through the same set of traffic lights at the same time each day. Most of them were probably ordinary commuters maintaining their monotonously normal schedule. But lurking among the innocent drivers were some potentially very bad actors.

Not for the first time, Reagan wished the bad guys had horns and a tail, the easier to be recognized for what they were. Looking at the pictures, he simply couldn't tell who the bad actors were. The pictures themselves were very high quality, but the angle of the sun in every photo meant that the drivers were sitting in shadow, and in the case of the vans, high enough that only the lower portions of their faces were partially visible. Worse still, they thought they had license plates on only six of the vans and the two sedans. You couldn't tell from these pictures, though, because the vehicles were packed in, bumper to bumper. Had they been driving towards the toll booths, the FBI analysts could have simply advanced the video and matched license plates as they rolled through the EZ-Pass lanes or stopped to pay the toll. Unfortunately, the vehicles were all going the wrong way at the wrong time of day, and that made everyone's job harder.

Reagan wondered whether that, too, had been planned by the terrorists, or whether it was merely a happy coincidence for them. Probably the former, he thought, setting the photos aside and switching to the workup on the vehicles for which license plates had been visible. The vans were registered to a catering company, three general contractors, an electrician and a plumber. One of the cars was registered to a nurse and the other to an eleventh grade English teacher. Nothing Reagan read struck him as particularly suspicious, let alone noteworthy.

The Bureau, at least, was taking the developments in Afghanistan very seriously – a number of agents had been assigned to check out the vehicles and their drivers in preparation for interviewing all of them. Reagan read the information compiled by the Bureau very carefully, and then re-read it, noting that the catering company had been created only a few months earlier, while the other companies had been in existence for years. By itself, that didn't mean anything, though. Terrorists could plan things remarkably far in advance. Reagan looked up and smacked his forehead in frustration, only to see Doug Cannon standing in his doorway, with Pembridge, Hollerman and Watson nearby.

"You look cute when you focus, Jack," Cannon said, finding humor in the moment.

"Meh," Reagan replied as he broke into a grin.

"Doh!" Pembridge chimed in with a grin of his own.

"Ok boys, settle down. This isn't the Simpsons," Cannon said, levity in his voice. "Joe's got something for us, but first, Jack, would you mind calling the Director? He should hear this too."

"We've found the silver BMW," Hollerman said when the Director was on the line and everyone seated. "It was torched and then partially submerged in a pond in the Shenandoah Valley. Hikers found it this morning. We've got forensics people on their way now to take a look. They say that the fire works in our favor, but the water doesn't."

"Either way, it's going to be a while before we get anything. If we get anything," Cannon corrected himself.

"Does the location tell us anything?" Reagan asked.

"It suggests that the person who dumped the car knows the area. This pond is accessible only by a dirt road off a rural county road. No cameras around, obviously. The State Police is coordinating a grid search with the local constabulary and will be interviewing the people that live around there. Not many of those around, though." Hollerman replied.

"Was the dirt road plowed or snowed in?" asked Smythe.

"Snowed in - we're waiting for a plow so we can get the car towed out. That tells us it was dumped before this week," Hollerman reported.

"So we have another potential lead, but one that doesn't tell us very much," Smythe said, his frustration showing.

"At least we know not to keep looking for the car," Pembridge said lightly.

"So what do we look for instead?" Smythe asked testily. It was a very good question, everyone thought, but no one knew how to reply.

"Jack, any thoughts?" Smythe asked when no one spoke.

"Maybe," Jack replied. "Joe, tell me more about the area – you said not many people live around there."

"That's right. Only a handful of people live there year-round. A lot of summer residences and cabins for seasonal use.

Probably a lot like where you live, actually. No real attractions, at least nothing that's on the map."

"Where I live, people tend to notice outsiders driving around," Reagan said. "Whoever dumped the car probably scouted the location some time in advance – as early as last summer when it was acquired. So maybe we can track down the owners of those seasonal residences and ask them if they remember seeing anything."

"Can't hurt to do that," Cannon agreed.

"Anything else, Jack? What are you working on at the moment?" Smythe wanted to know.

"I've been going through the information the Bureau sent over from New Jersey. Nothing jumps out at me. As you know, I spoke with Chip Gallagher this morning but he hasn't gotten back to me yet. I'm planning on calling him now. The only other thing... well, I was thinking of taking a drive up to New Jersey tomorrow and taking a look for myself."

"Think the Bureau missed something?" Cannon asked in surprise.

"No, not at all. I just want to see things for myself though. Maybe it will help me get a better feel for things," Reagan explained.

"I don't have a problem with that," Smythe said. "We can spare you for the day, Jack. Do keep your cellphone on, though. And take Agent Watson with you."

"Works for me," Reagan replied. "I'll call Gallagher and then head out to get some rest. We'll drive up in the morning."

"Do you want me to send someone else up with Reagan and Watson?" Cannon asked his Director over the phone when he returned to his desk.

"Expect there to be any trouble?" Smythe asked in return.

"No, not at all," Cannon replied. "It's just that sending one agent alone isn't exactly..."

Smythe interrupted him with a laugh. "Since when have we strictly followed procedures and protocols when it comes to Reagan? Why start now? Besides, there are plenty of other things for our agents to work on."

"Fair point," Cannon conceded. "But there's always a risk," he pointed out.

"Just so that you and I both feel a little better, make sure Watson brings along a backup weapon. Preferably an M1911 if you can dig one up, but a P226 will do in a pinch. So have you warmed to Reagan any?" Smythe asked.

"I like him just fine," Cannon said, somewhat defensively. "He's doing good work and has been pretty damn helpful. And he does think like a cop once in a while. I guess my only problem with him is that sometimes he seems to think a little too much like a spook, but I'm trying to overcome my prejudices."

"It's always good to overcome one's prejudices," Smythe replied with an unseen smile. "Besides, I'm thinking that maybe we can find a way to keep him around when this case gets resolved. What do you think about that?"

"We could do worse," Cannon admitted. From him, that was high praise indeed.

Osman Mansuraev started his afternoon with a taxi ride to a seafood restaurant on Water Street SW, where he found the Maryland crab cakes particularly fresh despite the fact that they were months out of season. He lingered over a pleasant bottle of Chardonnay until he was as sure as he could be that none of the vehicles in the parking lot or on the street contained counterintelligence agents. After settling his bill in cash, he walked down to 1st Street SW. Certain that he wasn't being followed, he turned down some side streets and made his way to the Randall Recreation Center, where he was pleased to find that the parking area right next to the baseball diamond had been thoroughly cleared of snow. Even more promising was the absence of cars; his men would have an easy time finding their pre-selected spot on Friday.

Mansuraev maneuvered along the edge of the tennis courts, turning left on S Capitol Street SE and walking until he reached the Spirit of Justice Park. He adjusted the hood on his parka to better hide his face from the multitude of cameras in the area. Thankfully it was cold enough to justify the heavy coat, and Mansuraev saw many people dressed even more warmly than him. He lingered in the park, studying first the Rayburn House Office Building and then the Longworth House Office Building. Seeing nothing that would cause him to alter his plan, he continued onwards to the Capitol Building, crossing over to Constitution Avenue NE and turning right.

This took him right past the three Senate Office Buildings; first came Russell, then Dirksen, and finally Hart. He turned left on 2nd Street NE and left again on C Street NE, walking fully around the three buildings before heading into Union Station Plaza. Again he was relieved to see that nothing had changed that would cause him to alter his plan. More than that, the snow had been thoroughly cleared in the vicinity of Union Station, including on H Street NE directly behind it. Mansuraev caught a taxi at Union Station and headed down to the Jefferson Memorial, which was just in the process of being cleared of snow. His driver waited with the meter running while Mansuraev played tourist, snapping a few shots of the monument before getting back in the cab and asking to be driven past the East Potomac Golf Course and around Hains Point before heading back to Union Station.

Mansuraev was excited to see that most of the parking spots at Hains Point had been cleared pretty thoroughly. In fact, the snow worked even better for his purposes, since it would make it more difficult for responding forces to approach his men on foot. Their approach would be limited to just the east or west side of Ohio Drive, which would make it easier for his men to hold them off. His men were highly skilled and knew their tasks – they would inflict the brunt of their damage long before authorities were alerted to their presence. Mansuraev was especially pleased to have found Hains Point on one of his many scouting trips. Even the White House was within range.

It took Armando Diaz less than five minutes to install the secure phone that Reagan had requested for his office. Reagan watched as he did so, slightly puzzled by the large screen and multiple buttons. "Where do you stick the key in?" he asked Diaz when he had finished.

"No key needed for this one, sir. It's fairly new – the Sectera vIPer. Same principle as the STU-III you're thinking about but it works slightly differently," Diaz said, showing Reagan how to work the phone. "It's a good piece of equipment, but the screen does tend to get a little finicky."

After Diaz left, Reagan called Chip Gallagher, watching the screen to confirm that a secure connection had been established. "Chip? Jack Reagan. Anything turn up on your end?"

"Hey Jack, I see you found yourself a secure phone. That'll come in handy. Just a few small things to report so far. Our people took a look at the photos of Tabaan Durrani and his students and they check out. Better still, we did find a photo of Tabaan from the late 90s in our records and he seems to check out. As far as Dawar Abdali goes, he might – I emphasize might – be a match with a description we have of a senior Taliban intelligence officer from around 2001. The problem, of course, is that it's hard to match a photo with a mere description of someone from fourteen years ago. He wasn't on our radar back then."

"Anything you can do to try to develop more information?" Reagan asked.

"Truthfully, not much. Our people have instructions to beat the bushes carefully, but there aren't that many bushes left in that place. The only good news, if you can call it that, is that we know pretty much everyone who had been directly involved in plots against us from that time period, and this guy doesn't seem to be one of them."

"If you ask me, it sounds more like bad news, since he definitely seems to be part of a plot against us now," Reagan said.

"Well yeah, there's that," Gallagher said with a chuckle. "Do you mind if I ask you something, Jack?"

"Sure, go ahead."

"Does your current Director know you used to work for us?" Gallagher asked with an unseen grin.

"Hmm?" Reagan replied noncommittally, surprised by this unexpected development.

"I just got done reviewing your file, Jack," Gallagher said. "I was an analyst at the Latin America desk when you were out running around for John Quincy. Wish we'd met back then, if your file is anything to go on."

Eddie Lancaster had stopped by Gallagher's office earlier to inform him of outside interest in several Agency employees and one former employee. Gallagher had been stunned to learn that Reagan had worked both in the DI and DO, and had immediately requested his file from Archives. After ordering a driver to take the exhausted Lancaster home to his wife, Gallagher had spent the better part of half an hour reading up on Jack Reagan, impressed with what he saw. Reagan had been a very capable analyst – and more. He would have had a promising career had he not resigned from the Agency so abruptly. There was nothing in the file to suggest why Reagan had left, and as curious as Gallagher was, he refrained from asking.

"That was a long time ago, Chip," Reagan said cautiously.

"Not so long ago, really, and besides, you've obviously still got the chops. You should tell Smythe – he used to work for us too, in case you didn't know – but before your time. He'll like you better for it, if that's even possible."

"We'll cross that bridge *if* we get to it," Reagan replied.

"Do what you think is best, Jack. In the meantime I talked it over with the Director and he said that even though your clearances have lapsed, we can read you in to whatever we get on this little affair."

"In that case, I've got a question for you," Reagan said. "What do you know about connections between Afghanistan and the Caucasus – have there been any ties between the Taliban or other groups and entities in Russia's southern states?"

"More than a few, actually. Back in the 90s, quite a few Taliban cut their teeth fighting in the Caucasus – Chechnya, Dagestan, the usual places. And quite a few Islamists from the Caucasus paid for the privilege of training in Afghanistan. Since 2001 that hasn't really been the case, although lately there seems to be an uptick in that kind of activity. Why do you ask?"

"How about arms shipments?" Reagan pressed.

"Only small-arms stuff, and that's infrequent. Most of the heavy stuff comes through either Pakistan or the former Soviet – stans. What are you thinking, Jack?"

"This might be totally unrelated but it's been keeping me up at night," Reagan replied. "Kerimsolta sounds an awful lot like a name found in the Caucasus."

"We think so, too," Gallagher interrupted. "Sorry, go on."

"I heard that there may be a connection between the Caucasus and the Lebanese arms dealer who was trying to smuggle Stingers into the States. On top of that we have the NSA pick up chatter about potential terrorist activity, and next thing we know, Kerimsolta's cousin is shooting up a park in Washington DC – and he's linked to a cellphone that exchanged calls with two groups in northern New Jersey who seem to be casing Newark Airport – maybe JFK, too. I just can't help thinking it's all connected," Reagan replied, relieved to finally be able to tell someone what had been on his mind.

"Or it could just be a coincidence," Reagan added, noting that Gallagher wasn't saying anything.

"Neither one of us is trained to believe in coincidences, Jack," Gallagher finally responded. "What you're saying fits, but it's very disconcerting."

"I've always had the sense that this is all part of something bigger, and everything I've seen – from the actions of the shooters to the cleanup in Lance Corporal Eggerton's apartment – it all fits better with a clever intelligence op than it does with a single and isolated terrorist attack."

"We see it the same way here," Gallagher said. "We haven't really connected all the dots like you just did. I'll run it by my people and see what they think. I need to sit down with our Caucasus experts – I'm pretty weak in that area," he admitted. "Anyway, I'll see what we can develop – and we'll keep in touch. You've given us a lot to think about, Jack." Gallagher had taken Reagan seriously from the very beginning, despite Secretary Jackson's histrionics, but knowing the man's history made what he had just said all the more disconcerting. Gallagher reached for his office phone and called the head of the South Caucasus Desk up to his office. They had a lot to discuss.

22

Their drive to New Jersey had been plagued by traffic accidents and delays, and had taken much longer than either Peter Sinclair or James Mason expected. They arrived shortly after dark and drove around for a while to orient themselves. Much to their surprise, the Sandy Hook National Recreation Area was still open after dark, but they decided they wouldn't be able to see much and went off in search of a McDonald's instead. They ate inside out of respect for Brenda Videtti's Porsche and then went to find a hotel, checking into a La Quinta Inn a number of miles to the south of Sandy Hook. The hotel was clean and comfortable, but Mason found it too quiet – meaning that he hadn't spotted any single women yet.

"Jim, do you ever *not* think about women?" Sinclair asked his friend as the two unloaded their bags from the car.

"I generally don't think about them when we're working – and before you say it, we're not on the clock until morning," Mason pointed out. "Speaking of which, we need a name for this little op. Which do you like better, Hard Freeze or Frozen Tide? We're at the beach, after all."

"You're not feeling cold, are you?" Sinclair asked the Florida native.

"I'm from Miami – anything below 70 and the little old ladies bring out their fur coats. Of course I'm cold, you Eskimo!" Mason laughed.

Sinclair, for his part, would never admit that he felt cold, too. As well he should, since the temperature was hovering in the single digits. "I can definitely see you in a mink coat," he said with a grin.

"If you're offering to buy, I'd rather have a sable one," Mason replied. "So what's it going to be – Frozen Tide or Hard Freeze?"

"I'm leaning towards Frozen Tide," Sinclair admitted as he locked up the car parked in view of their room's window. He didn't figure there was much crime in the area – there was a Porsche dealer practically across the road – but it was always a good idea to keep an eye on their ride. Any wannabe car thief would be in for a very nasty surprise.

"Frozen Tide it is, then," Mason declared. "Too bad Nick isn't here – he's great at coming up with names."

"That's for sure," Sinclair agreed. "Much better than the computer generated ones, anyway."

"Mind if I hit the gym first, Pete?" Mason was feeling stiff from sitting down for so long. Even a Porsche has its limits.

"Ok, go ahead. I'll watch some TV." It would have made more sense for both men to use the gym at the same time, but they couldn't very well leave their equipment and tactical gear unattended, even in an empty hotel. Mason headed off as Sinclair sat on his bed and flipped through the channels, wondering what the next day would have in store for them.

Reagan and Watson were almost out the door when Joe Hollerman came running up to let them know the photos taken by Mrs. Rose had just arrived. They would soon see the mysterious purchaser of the silver BMW that was still stuck in a pond in the Shenandoah Valley. The trio joined Ryan Pembridge by Cannon's desk, watching as Cannon slipped the memory card into his computer. The memory card defaulted to a slideshow view, and the very first image came up on the screen.

"What the *hell* is *that*?" Cannon demanded, surprised and very revolted by what he saw.

"*That* is Miss Doris Rose," Pembridge said, unable to suppress a laugh. "Quite the hottie, isn't she!"

"She's single if you're interested, boss," Hollerman chimed in.

"You know guys," Cannon said, crossing his arms as he leaned back in his chair, "I have seen some of the worst crime scenes imaginable, and have had the displeasure of seeing the most disturbing things done to the human body. But nothing in my long career has prepared me for *that*." He shook his head as he pointed at the picture of Doris Rose posing in front of a mirror in a bikini top and nothing else.

"If you like that one, you should know she has a whole collection of bikinis," Pembridge said as everyone laughed.

"I just hope I don't have to sit here all night and see that thing on my screen," Cannon replied.

It took just five minutes to find all 137 photos Doris Rose took of the man who bought Robert Keller's BMW. The group crowded around Cannon's monitor and studied the photos, looking carefully at the man's features. He looked to be in his early 40s, with short black hair that was neatly parted on the right side. Full black eyebrows made for a marked contrast with his bright blue eyes set above high cheeks. Except for a small scar next to his cleft chin, the rest of the man's features were unremarkable. He was thin but came across as somewhat athletic, and he had excellent posture. His height couldn't be determined with precision without a more thorough analysis, but he looked to be short – between 5'6" and 5'9".

"I've never seen blue eyes before that were so lifeless," Pembridge said.

"Neither have I," Hollerman replied, commenting as well on the falsity of the man's smile.

"At least the pictures are pretty good," Cannon offered. "Doris seems to have captured every possible angle on this guy. Ryan, get the better pictures set up for facial recognition and also send them out to other agencies."

"Overseas too?" Pembridge wanted to know. "You know, it's funny – Mrs. Rose said he was Hispanic but he doesn't look particularly Hispanic to me," he added.

"Yeah, overseas too. And I agree, this guy doesn't look particularly Hispanic to me, either," Cannon replied. "Whatever he is, let's track him down, people."

Special Agent Watson was very excited, but tried her best to hide it. As much as she loved her job, some aspects of it appealed to her more than others – and nothing appealed to her more than being out in the field. More than that, she was going out into the field with Jack, and that made it doubly special. He was every bit as good a mentor as Doug Cannon and if nothing else, working with Jack was making her a better agent. But there *was* something else, of course – the easy chemistry between them that made it feel so normal for her to start and end the day wrapped up in Jack's arms. Amanda had started to yearn for his touch even as she couldn't help but smile at the sound of his voice.

Work came first, however, and Watson remembered that she didn't really know what they would be doing in New Jersey the following day. By now, Cannon would probably have briefed her, or at least given her instructions. "What, exactly, are we doing tomorrow?" she asked as they walked towards the hotel elevators.

"We're going to start with the IKEA around Newark Airport and have a look around, and then head over to Sandy Hook and meet up with Pete and Jim," Jack replied.

"Your friends are there?" Amanda asked in surprise.

"Yeah, they drove up today. They're going to keep an eye on Sandy Hook for us and see if anyone interesting visits the place."

"Oh," she replied. A lot of questions suddenly flooded her mind, but now wasn't the time for them. Clearly Jack had something in mind, but whatever it was, he was holding his cards close to his vest. As much as she hated it, she was used to

224

working with less than full disclosure, but she was certain he would tell her what she needed to know when the time was right – if she needed to know, that is. Her Director trusted Reagan, as did she. For now, that was enough. "How long are we staying?" she asked instead.

"We'll probably come back Friday evening, if that's ok with you."

"I go where you go," she said with a smile. "Now come help me pack," she added, playfully pushing Jack out of the elevator when they reached her floor.

Jack sat on the edge of Amanda's bed and watched as she went through her closet and luggage, pulling together an assortment of clothes. "You know, I think I might need a drink for this," he said, taking off his coat.

Amanda looked at Jack, a sheepish grin on her face. "Yes, Jack, when it comes to clothes, I'm like every other girl you know."

"Amanda, you are hardly like any other girl I've ever known," he replied with a grin of his own.

"Ok, how about this?" she asked, holding up a dark gray pantsuit as she studiously ignored the compliment.

"That'll work, but bring along a couple of sweaters. Different colors, if you can, so you can change your appearance on the fly."

"Oh, ok," she replied. She had never done that before. Whatever Jack had in mind for New Jersey, it would be a new experience for her. Suddenly she worried that she didn't have the right clothes for this; her favorite colors for clothes were limited to white, gray, navy and black. The most colorful things she owned were a couple of polo shirts. Well, not *just* polo shirts, but she could hardly wear *those* out in the field. She did, however, pack them in her suitcase when Jack wasn't looking – just in case.

"All done!" Amanda proclaimed a mere fifteen minutes later. She had packed two bags, a small one for the car so she could change her appearance quickly, and a larger one that would go in the trunk. Jack saw that she also had a backpack she had taken from the office and asked her about it.

"Laptop, camera, binoculars, gloves, evidence bags and this," she said, retrieving a Sig Sauer P226 along with some extra magazines. "Doug said Director Smythe wanted to be sure you know where it is, just in case."

"Not a bad idea," Jack admitted. "Now how about some dinner? We could head out and try..."

"Room service is much more convenient, Jack," she interrupted with an impish grin. "Go order us up something while I have a shower."

Reagan headed up to his room and ordered a couple of steaks and soft drinks. He looked over the wine list but didn't see anything he remotely recognized, so he settled on a bottle of Moet instead. Ordinarily Reagan wasn't much of a drinker – he presumed that Watson wasn't, either – but his mind had been working overtime at night during the previous week, and the only way he could really push things out of his mind at night was with a little alcohol. He was fairly limited in what he liked, with a preference for champagne. Somehow, those delicious bubbles didn't affect him the way they did other people; he could easily consume more than a bottle without being the worse for wear for it.

He lingered in the shower, letting the warm water soothe his skin and massage away the aches that came from all the sitting he had been doing lately. Reagan didn't know what to expect from his trip to New Jersey and was already thinking about next steps. He kept coming back to the link between Dawar Abdali and Kerimsolta – a probable Taliban intelligence officer and a terrorist who more likely than not came from the Caucasus. In a way, that relationship was not unlike the one between the Taliban and al-Qaida in the run-up to September 11, 2001, with the Taliban providing outside actors with assistance in planning an attack against America. Factor in the attempted smuggling of Stinger missiles into the United States and you had the makings of another major terrorist attack in the New York City metropolitan area.

The next step after his field trip, Reagan decided, was to talk to Chip Gallagher and ask to be brought onboard in some limited capacity to work on the Caucasus connection. This was the Agency's bailiwick, after all, and except for whatever additional information Tommy Cho developed, it was unlikely that NCIS would be the source of any new significant leads. Now that Gallagher knew his background, he just might be able to persuade him.

Just as Reagan was toweling off, his phone rang – appropriately enough it was Gallagher. "Jack? I just tried your office but they told me you already left."

"Hi Chip – I was just thinking about you, actually. I left a little early so I can head up to Jersey tomorrow and take a look around."

"Well good luck with that," Gallagher said. "I'm not going to go into details over an unsecure line but I wanted to let you know that I ran that thing you said in our meeting by my people, and we all agree that it's got merit. So we're going to start digging into it."

"Great!" Reagan replied. "Actually, that's why I was thinking about you. I was thinking that maybe you can use an extra set of eyes on this."

"I figured you'd ask," Gallagher said with a laugh. "I'm inclined to say yes, but I still need to find the right way to bring it up with the Director. You seem to be on Secretary Jackson's shit list, and it's going to have to be the Director's call whether we want to risk his wrath. As a practical matter, we can expedite clearances. You've been thoroughly checked out since last Thursday. Why don't you give me a call when you get back from New Jersey and we can talk about it some more."

Amanda knocked on his door just as he ended the call with Gallagher, and Jack rushed to put on a shirt and sweatpants before opening the door. He remarked that the green of Amanda's polo shirt brought out the richness of her eye color, even as her gray yoga pants emphasized her toned legs – impossibly long despite the flats she was wearing on her feet.

"You needn't have bothered getting dressed on my account, Jack," she said with a wink, tussling his still-wet hair before heading for the television remote on the bed.

"Yeah, but what would people think?" Jack asked with a chuckle as he headed back for the bathroom to dry his hair.

"Who cares!" declared Amanda loud enough for Jack to hear. In point of fact, she did – she had always guided her behavior with at least some consideration given to what other people might think of her. Yet one more thing about her remarkable relationship with Jack, she realized, was that she didn't really care what other people might think. This relationship was uncharted territory for her, but she hardly felt out of her depth. Everything was just so natural between the two of them.

"What's for dinner?" she asked moments before room service knocked on their door.

"Steak and champagne, if you want some," Jack replied.

"But of course! It's my favorite," she laughed as the hotel employee excused himself, a knowing smile on his face.

"I just need to make one quick call before I can eat, but feel free to start without me."

"I don't mind waiting for you," Amanda replied, smiling at the double entendre. "I will, however, open up the champagne. Hey, I don't suppose you know how to open it with a sword, do you?"

"But of course," Jack said with a laugh as he scrolled through his contact list for Tommy Cho's number. "I'll show you some time," he promised as the call connected.

"Tommy? Jack Reagan. Hope I'm not calling you too early."

"If I were back in Naples this would be way too early, but over here these Jarheads seem to like waking up at 0500. I'm used to it by now. What's up, Jack?" Cho hated waking up early almost as much as Reagan did, but he found his current assignment exciting enough that the early hour didn't bother him so much. He loved riding around with the Marines, who seemed exceedingly eager to please, and he enjoyed helping them plan their "missions" to track the Abdali family. In many ways, Cho felt like he was living out his childhood fantasies, influenced as they were by his favorite war movies.

"Did you get the photos Doug Cannon sent you?" Reagan asked.

"Yeah, along with a short explanation. I assume you want me to show this photo around, too?" Cho said.

"You assume correctly," Reagan replied. "One more thing, though. When you're talking to people, don't just ask about the subjects we're interested in. Try to get a sense of who has been passing through the area, as far back as they can remember. And if the villagers you talk to can remember any languages that were spoken, that would be helpful as well."

"I've been doing some of that already, but not consistently," Cho admitted. "Word of warning, though – some of these villagers barely know their own language. I don't know how helpful they'll be remembering other languages."

"Good point, Tommy, but at least they might remember *if* another language was spoken. And hell, you were able to dig up a university economics professor living in the middle of nowhere. Who knows what else you'll find."

"The Ark of the Covenant, perhaps," Cho said with a laugh. He liked Indiana Jones movies, too. "Anything particular you're looking for, Jack – language-wise, I mean?"

"The languages of the Caucasus, but I'll take what I can get. I'm basically looking for any foreigners, whatever languages they speak," Reagan replied.

"Jack, what the hell *are* the languages of the Caucasus? I know next to nothing about that area of the world. I'll try, of course, but I can't guarantee I'll come up with anything," Cho warned.

"All I'm asking is that you try, pal," Reagan said. "When you're digging around out there, just keep in mind that I'm looking at possible connections between Kerimsolta and the Abdalis on the one hand and foreign actors – probably from the Caucasus – on the other."

"Ok, Jack, I'll keep that in mind. Call you if I get something," Cho promised, ending the call and heading out to a waiting Humvee, signaling his waiting Marines that it was time to get going. God, how he loved this job.

"You've got some catching up to do, mister," Amanda said as she handed Jack a flute of champagne, her cheeks made radiant by the drink. Her eyes sparkled hypnotically, the dancing bubbles reflected in her eyes as she lifted her flute to her lips and paused, forming a smile at once shy and enchanting. Jack smiled in return, at once mesmerized by this beautiful and amazing woman who was truly unlike any he had ever known. His heart always seemed to beat just a little faster around Amanda, and he wondered how much longer he could keep trying to ignore what he felt for her.

23

The sun was merely a hint on the horizon when Osman Mansuraev opened his eyes, long before his alarm clock was set to go off. Sleep had come hard lately without drink, but the same magical elixir that helped put him to sleep also caused him to rise early, more often than not feeling poorly rested. That had never been a problem for his father, Mansuraev remembered – the Colonel could drink an entire bottle of vodka and then wake up late the next day feeling refreshed. The Colonel had needed to drink himself to sleep every bit as much as his son, though; it was late at night that their demons came, and alcohol was the only thing that seemed to keep them at bay.

It was too early to get up for a day that would be long with flights, first to Miami and then onwards to Rio de Janeiro, but Mansuraev found it difficult to fall back asleep. He was simply too excited. In less than 36 hours, the plan that he alone had perfected would be set in motion, and America would never be the same. Its people would finally realize how illusory their safety and security were when its own weapons were used against them. As a practical matter, the government would be crippled and the economy would suffer significantly in the immediate aftermath.

More than that, though, what leadership was left would overreact; based on incomplete information it would submit to the clamoring of the masses who were already out for the blood of Muslim nations in response to the minimal attack in Rock Creek Park. America would be finally and fully at war with Islam and, like the Soviets in Afghanistan, it was a war that would damage its morale, prestige and economy. America would fall, and Mansuraev's country would rise in its place. That thought was pleasing enough to allow him to fall back asleep.

The anticipation of the day that lay ahead had kept Amanda Watson from getting uninterrupted sleep – she kept waking up to check the time. There were only two other occasions in her life when she had been unable to sleep due to excitement: when her parents had taken her to Disneyland at age 8, and the night before Josh Harmon had taken her to the senior prom. She had continued to date Josh through college before the two went their separate ways, agreeing that their relationship wasn't going anywhere. Josh was a good man, who went on to become a very successful real estate developer preoccupied with revitalizing Wayne County. But he couldn't hold a candle to the man that lay sleeping in front of her. No man could, Amanda had concluded.

She lay on her side facing Jack, resting her head on his arm inches from his face, her feet kept warm between his, her right hand gently pressed against his chest, feeling his heart beating. She studied his face, taking in features she found very handsome. She was drawn to his green eyes – eyes that were always full of expression and communicated volumes, even when they were closed in sleep. She could tell from the way his brow was scrunched and his closed eyes narrowed that he was processing some thought as he slept, and Amanda filed that away as yet one more remarkable thing about the man she was falling for.

The ringing cellphone caused Jack's eyes to open suddenly and then narrow as they adjusted to the dim light. He could see Amanda facing him, awake and looking into his eyes, and he smiled as he always did when he saw her. He reached for his phone, feeling her hand pressing gently on his chest as he answered.

"Sorry to wake you so early," Joe Hollerman said. "I'm downstairs in the lobby. Director Smythe wanted me to rush something over to you before you left and we weren't sure when you were heading out."

"Ok, come on up, Joe," Reagan replied, giving him the room number. Amanda took her cue from that, groaning as she

232

got out of bed and went into the bathroom, closing the door behind her. Jack was almost awake by the time Hollerman knocked on the door, handing over an unsealed manila envelope. As Reagan pulled out the contents, Hollerman peered over Jack's shoulder. A trained investigator, he could read the signs very clearly – the single large indentation in the middle of the bed suggested that Jack hadn't been alone, and Amanda's purse and backpack were right there on the floor next to the bed. *Good for them*, he thought, trying hard not to smile.

"Safe trip today, Jack. And if you need anything, call us, *boss*," Hollerman emphasized before heading back down the corridor.

"What was that about?" Amanda asked, coming out of the bathroom when Jack knocked on the door.

"Here, have a look," he replied, handing over the envelope. She looked inside and pulled out a set of credentials identifying Jack as the Deputy Director of Operations at NCIS, along with a handwritten note from Director Smythe. *Jack, I thought this might come in handy. I trust you'll know when to use it, and when not to. Best of luck, Francis.*

"Wow, Jack," was all Amanda could say.

"Wow indeed. Now come back to bed – it's too early," he replied, getting back in bed.

"Whatever you say, boss," she replied with an engaging smile. She was glad to climb back into bed and curl up next to him, feeling his arms wrap around her as they spooned. Amanda closed her eyes and fell back asleep with a smile on her face.

"Kick it loose, Lieutenant," Peter Sinclair told his friend as he gently shook him awake. "The park is open and it's light enough outside to get oriented. Let's go scout things out and find a place to observe people coming in," he said as Jim Mason got out of bed.

"Aye aye, sir," Mason replied. "Looks like Frozen Tide is a go."

It took a couple of minutes for the men to dress in casual attire before taking their bags to the Porsche and heading out, first stopping at McDonald's to pick up some breakfast. A few minutes more along roads entirely devoid of traffic and they arrived at Sandy Hook.

"The entrance is a good choke-point," Mason pointed out as they passed unmanned toll booths.

"We can come back and park in one of these lots. One way in, one way out, and great visibility," Sinclair agreed, heading down what was so far the only road in the park. It turned out that the park was quite a bit larger than either man expected despite the fact that they had thoroughly studied the map the night before. The park opened up considerably; there were many parking lots, old military fortifications, and even a decommissioned Nike facility – not to mention the old barracks and some kind of Coast Guard station at the far end. There was even some kind of school in the park, they realized.

"This is our best bet," Sinclair said as he pulled into one of the parking lots closest to the entrance after driving a complete circuit of the park.

"Seems that way," Mason agreed. "A lot of ground to cover for just the two of us, though. Especially if it gets busy."

"Yeah, I'll call it in and see if we can get some support," Sinclair said. "Why don't you see if there's any car rental place in the area – it would help if we could at least use a second car to get you mobile. That way one of us can stay here and the other can go take a closer look at anyone who looks interesting."

"Nearest Hertz is about an hour away, nothing closer. But Jack's on his way with his girlfriend, so they can go get us a rental," Mason replied after checking his iPhone. "How do you want to play it?"

"For now let's just sit in the car and enjoy a very slow breakfast. We passed some kind of concession building that has good sightlines from the second floor, so maybe a little later we'll reposition there."

"Works for me," Mason said. "I suppose I'm taking the first shift?"

Sinclair responded by grunting, lowering the back of his seat as he closed his eyes.

Watson had expected that Reagan would want to use his car. He knew where he wanted to go and it was, after all, his op. She also wasn't surprised when, after loading their bags in the back, he held the door for her. It was clearly in his character to do so, just as it was in his nature to maintain a fastidiously clean car. The only thing that surprised her was that Jack took off his duffel coat and got behind the wheel in a short-sleeved shirt despite outdoor temperatures in the single digits that weren't expected to climb out of the teens.

"Aren't you cold, Jack?"

"Not really," he replied. "I'm furry and besides, we've got heated seats," he pointed out, showing her how to work the controls. Against her better judgment, Amanda took off her coat as well, and a minute later was glad to have done so – the car seat kept her warmer than her jacket ever could.

"Nice feature," she said, lamenting that she didn't have heated seats in her car as Jack turned onto Connecticut Avenue. She studied the way he drove and, finding him to be a relaxed and competent driver, she began to relax as well. By the time they turned east on the Beltway, she had even kicked off her shoes and tucked in her legs under her, at ease with Jack's driving as with everything else about him. They made good time up until Baltimore, where the heavy volume of rush hour traffic slowed them nearly to a standstill.

"I notice you tend to drive with just one hand," she pointed out. "Any particular reason?" she asked, her curiosity getting the better of her.

"I learned to drive on a manual," Jack laughed. "I guess even after all these years, I'm still used to keeping my right hand free to shift gears. How about some music?" he asked, finding a gap in free-flowing traffic and slipping smoothly into it.

"Sure! But I don't have much of anything on my phone. What do you have on yours?"

"Help yourself," Jack said, unlocking his phone with his thumb and passing it over. "Just avoid the DropBox app, please – I've got legal stuff on that."

Amanda scrolled through his music folders and playlists. "Wow, Jack, quite the variety." Somehow she had expected to find only classical music, but there was a little bit of everything on his phone. She found a playlist heavy with dance music that she liked and selected that. "Can I take a look at your pictures, too?" she asked.

"Go ahead," he nodded. "Not much to see, though."

Amanda scrolled through the photos, admiring some lovely nature shots before finding the few pictures that had Jack in them. Almost all of those were with his mother, his arm wrapped around her and a big smile on his face. The progression was remarkable, and Amanda could see Jack's mother become smaller and frailer, appearing weaker as the photos progressed. *He must have gone through sheer hell*, she thought, the pain clearly visible in Jack's eyes making her heart churn. She wished she had known him then, to be there for him and comfort him. She clutched the phone to her chest and turned her face to look out the side window so he wouldn't see the tears streaming down her cheeks. Eventually, though, she discreetly wiped away the tears and turned back. There was nothing she could do about the past, but she would make sure Jack never had to go through anything like that ever again – not alone.

Mansuraev arrived at Reagan National earlier than he would have preferred, concerned that he might be bumped from his flight. He had seen on the local news that there were still a lot of cancellations and delays stemming from the airport's closure due to Tuesday's storm, and some passengers on flights that had not been affected were being bumped to make room for those that had. As it turned out, Mansuraev needn't have worried – a full-fare First Class passenger is rarely, if ever, bumped. He made his way to the lounge and found the bar, ordering a gin and tonic to kill the time.

His men would be starting their last reconnoiters right around now, Mansuraev realized. During the past month, they had been going to their pre-assigned locations daily at around the same time, the better to blend in as a regular and expected part of the landscape. He had checked in with them every few days during the first two weeks, but after he was satisfied that they had aroused no suspicions, he had discarded his phone and instructed them to do the same. The Americans were just too good at intercepting communications – he had always known that, of course, but Edward Snowden's revelations made it all the clearer just how clever and dangerous the Americans really were. The only way he had to communicate with his men right now was through innocuous-seeming auction listings on eBay, each signifying a predetermined message. Mansuraev took his phone out and checked his eBay app, but found nothing amiss.

The hardest part of the mission ahead lay in the hands of the Imam, as Mansuraev had come to think of the most religiously zealous of his men. At present, the Imam was babysitting that fool Eggerton, who had turned out to be a little crazier than Mansuraev expected. At first, the Imam had visited Eggerton every couple of days, spending hours inculcating the values of Islam and the praiseworthy goals of jihad. Eggerton was an eager student and had become a devout Muslim, greatly impressing his teacher. But then he had just snapped, torturing his female neighbor and her young sons for no apparent reason before butchering them in an attack so full of hatred that even the Imam – no stranger to butchery – was taken aback.

As a result, they had moved Eggerton to an isolated farmhouse in rural Virginia that Mansuraev had purchased years ago as a safehouse. The Imam sat with him day and night now, keeping Eggerton under control. In just over 24 hours from now, the Imam would dress Eggerton in a bomb-laden vest and deliver him to the Capitol Building, where he could take revenge on the government that had killed his beloved Muska. Mansuraev couldn't care less what happened to Eggerton after that – he figured he would probably be shot by snipers well before he even reached a door to the building. That didn't matter, though. Eggerton was merely a creative diversion.

"You can hardly feel the speed," Amanda remarked, seeing that the speedometer hovered above 85 on the fairly empty stretch of road. Their car rode exceptionally smoothly for the behemoth SUV it was – but then again, it *was* a Range Rover.

"Want me to slow down?" Jack offered.

"Only if you want to. I tend to drive a little fast myself," she admitted. Luckily, Amanda had managed to bat her eyes out of a fair number of tickets.

Jack suddenly slowed the car, dropping speed quickly but smoothly, and Amanda was about to tell him that she really didn't mind the speed when the radar detector went off. She looked around but failed to see any police cars, instead seeing Jack point at an overpass coming up in front of them. She turned her head as they passed, finally seeing the State Police cruiser.

"Ok, Jack, how the hell did you know he was there?" Amanda demanded. "You don't have x-ray vision, do you, Superman?" she added with a grin.

"Hardly," he replied with a laugh. "Just deductive reasoning. What little snow there is up here looked to have been a little disturbed in that area, and the area just felt right."

"Felt right?" she asked.

"Driving at speed is a cross between tank warfare and aerial combat maneuvers," Jack explained with a laugh. "You study the terrain and try to figure out where the cops are hiding, which usually turns out to be the same sort of a place you'd hide a tank – a reverse slope, or a ditch, or a cutaway in the trees, for instance. Places where you can't see them until it's too late. You also study the terrain for evidence that the ground has been cleared away or disturbed – tire treads in the grass, snow cleared away, that sort of thing."

"And aerial combat maneuvers?" Amanda asked, laughing heartily.

"You don't want them to get a lock on you so you hit the brakes and take evasive maneuvers. You know, slip behind another vehicle for cover and let the guy behind you take the ticket."

"Jesus, Jack, you really don't think like anyone else I know, do you!" Amanda declared, unable to stop laughing. She saw him smile sheepishly in reply and reached over to squeeze his hand, pulling it to her lap. "That's a good thing, by the way. A very good thing."

"Heads up," Sinclair said, nodding in the direction of a tan Ford Explorer that had just entered the park and was making its way slowly up the road. They had decided that it was just easier to stay in the car in the parking lot closest to the entrance. Several cars had pulled in after the sun came up – most of these carried bikes to ride or dogs to walk. None was the least bit suspicious, and they served to provide adequate cover.

"No phones," Mason said, looking up from his laptop on the back seat as the Explorer drove past them. "Three people, all men. They could be Latinos or Middle Easterners. It's about the right time of day, too," he added, jotting down the license plate number.

"Let's see where they go," Sinclair replied, pulling out when the Explorer was far enough away. It turned out that they didn't have far to drive; the Explorer turned right onto a small road that dead-ended at a beach used by fisherman a short distance off. "Shit! We can't follow them in there without being made."

"Go park and work our way in on foot, maybe?" Mason suggested. They had seen a trail running through that area, and they could always just walk up the beach.

"Maybe," Sinclair allowed. There was barely an inch of snow, not enough to be a bother but just enough to be a potential problem. "I don't much like the idea of leaving tracks behind." He pulled over to the side of the road, far enough past the side road that he wouldn't immediately be seen but close enough so that he could see movement in his rearview mirror. "Let's call Jack."

24

Reagan was making good time on the Garden State Parkway, listening to Watson singing along to one of her favorite songs. Her hair may have been up in a neat ponytail, but it was otherwise fully down now, and Jack was captivated by her beautiful voice – a voice that somehow seemed to make his heart skip a beat whenever he heard it. He reluctantly turned the radio off when his phone rang.

"Jack? How far out are you?" he heard Sinclair ask.

"About 30 minutes. What's going on?"

"We got possible targets here. Three men, right age and ethnicity, in a tan Ford Explorer. No phones, and the time of the day is just about right," Sinclair replied.

"Did you get the plates?" Reagan asked. Watson cued in on his question and reached for a pen, writing down the license plate number that Reagan conveyed.

"They've gone down a dead-end road and we can't figure a good way of taking a closer look at them without being made," Sinclair added. "I'm thinking you and Amanda might fit in better – you know, take a romantic stroll down the beach or something, so hurry it up."

"Will do, pal," Reagan replied. "Call me if they move."

"Want us to follow them if they leave before you get here?"

"Yeah, absolutely. We'll set something up on the fly," Reagan said, ending the call and relaying the information to Watson, who in turn called Ryan Pembridge and asked him to run the plates.

"The car is registered to Rosita Velazquez of Paterson, New Jersey," she said a few minutes later. "Fifty four years old, no wants or warrants. Ryan wants to know if you want him to look up more info on Velazquez."

"Couldn't hurt," Jack replied. "Ask him if there are any new developments, while you're at it." Both he and Amanda had forgotten to check any sooner, and Reagan quietly remonstrated himself for that.

"Nothing new," she said, which was pretty much what they were both expecting.

They covered the remaining distance fairly quickly, yet still found it agonizingly slow. Almost exactly half an hour after Reagan had ended the call with Sinclair, he pulled into a parking lot at Sandy Hook just to the left of Brenda Videtti's Porsche.

"Hey Jack, Amanda," Sinclair called out through Watson's open window. "Glad you two made it. Our suspects are still tucked away on that side road. It's about two miles down this road, second right after the Ranger's station. There's a sign that reads 'Fishing Beach.' We drove by a couple of times but there's nothing on the Stingray. Kinda odd that three people in this part of the world drive around without cellphones. Anyway, how do you want to play it?"

"Tell me about the Park Rangers," Jack said.

"They patrol around every two or three hours. More like a lackadaisical drive than a proper patrol – every time we see them they seem completely uninterested in anything. Usually it's a man and a woman, but sometimes its two men. They last came by around two hours ago." Sinclair replied.

"Ok, Amanda and I will figure it out. You two hang here for a bit. If they come out before we do, follow them."

"Works for me," Sinclair said. "Oh, before you drive off, Jim has something for you. Back seat, buddy," he added.

Reagan reached for his coat, putting it on as he stepped out into the blustery cold. "Hey Jim," he said, opening the rear door of the Porsche.

"Got something for you, Jack," he replied quietly, handing over a holstered M1911A1 not unlike Jack's own. "Seven in the mag and one in the chamber, safety is on," Mason said, handing the weapon over surreptitiously along with four extra clips.

Reagan slipped the holster under his jacket, clipping it to his belt at the small of his back. He put two of the magazines in his front left pant pockets, and the other two in his left jacket pocket. "One more thing," Mason added, handing Jack credentials that identified him as a Deputy United States Marshal. "This thing is ok for show and general use but it won't survive serious scrutiny," he said, watching Jack put it in his right jacket pocket.

"Thanks, pal,' Reagan said, walking back to his car. "Hey, what are we calling this thing?" he asked through Amanda's window before pulling out.

"Frozen Tide," Sinclair replied with a chuckle.

"It's definitely cold enough," Reagan laughed, closing his window and driving off. He found the side road Sinclair had identified, driving past it before circling back to the Ranger station. Although there was a large parking lot by the station, empty except for a Park Service pickup truck, Reagan continued looking until he found a small area off the road, sheltered from view by some bushes. There he parked and shut off the engine, walking over to Amanda's door and holding it open for her.

"What are we doing, Jack?"

"For starters, we're going inside to talk to the Park Rangers," he replied, and the two crossed the road and walked into the building. Once inside, a man stood up from a desk behind a counter. He was about Jack's height but heavier, sporting the makings of a goatee. There was a woman inside as well, sitting on a slightly tattered armchair. She was too engrossed by her phone to even look up.

"Can we help you?" the man asked, surprised not to see a car in the parking lot outside.

"I think you can," Reagan replied cheerily, holding out the credentials Agent Hollerman had delivered that morning. "My name is Jack Reagan, Naval Criminal Investigative Service. This is Special Agent Watson." He nodded his head towards Amanda, who held up her credentials as well.

"Is there a problem?" the Ranger asked, still more surprised than alarmed.

"No. Well, probably not," Reagan said. "We're tracking down a deserter, and we received some information that his car was spotted in one of the parking lots here. The tip is probably bad, but we came over to check it out anyway, and we'd like to use your pickup truck to drive around a little. Just in case it *is* his car – and it probably isn't – we figure he won't get too spooked that way."

"Glad to help," the Ranger replied, readily handing over his keys. There had been something in his training sessions many years in the past about working with federal agencies, but he had forgotten all about that. He was happy to have a story to tell his friends after work – his participation in things naturally embellished.

"Thank you very much," Reagan said with a smile. "While we're at it, can we borrow your jackets and hats as well?"

"Not a problem. Want us to come along with you?"

"Thanks for the offer, but that won't be necessary, not right now, anyway," Reagan replied. The jacket he tried on was a little too big and the jacket Amanda put on was a little too small, but altogether it was just right for cover in a pinch.

"Should I bring my camera?" Amanda asked as she got in the passenger seat.

Jack shook his head. "Too obvious. Maybe your cellphone if you can do it discreetly." He pulled out of the parking lot and turned down the side road, driving slowly. They could see the Ford Explorer ahead, parked off to the side of the road in a little bit of snow, but its occupants were nowhere to be seen.

"Maybe out on the beach?" Reagan suggested.

"No, up on the right on top of that bunker," Watson said, having spotted them first.

"Put those on," Reagan said, pointing at some sunglasses on the dashboard. Amanda did as told, understanding the purpose of concealment. Or at least she thought she did. With Jack, the surprises never stopped.

"Two men, in their twenties, standing on the bunker with binoculars. They seem to be looking out towards the ocean," Amanda reported as they drove past slowly. "Third guy is sitting on the edge of the bunker. Also mid-twenties, no binoculars. They're all clean shaven and look... well they look like they could be from the Middle East." She risked turning her head to look directly at them just as they drove in front of them, and saw that the sitting man looked at her and waved. She smiled and waved back.

Jack reached the end of the road and stopped where the sand began. His head moved as though he were scanning the beach, but he kept his eyes on the rearview mirror, studying the men. He counted out thirty seconds and then turned the truck around, slowly driving back the way they had come. He took out his phone and opened the camera app, holding the phone up to his left ear and pretending to talk as he drove past the bunker, which was now on his left side. His thumb pressed on one of the volume buttons to snap pictures. The men seemed fairly ordinary to Reagan – but they reminded him a good deal of the men he had dismissed as soccer players the previous week in the park. When he reached the main road, he stowed his phone and drove around for a few more minutes so as not to arouse anyone's suspicions.

They returned the truck, jackets and hats to the Ranger Station, thanking the man for his help and letting him know that the car was not the one they were looking for. Thankfully, neither of the Park Rangers had been the least bit curious; the young woman had never even looked up from her phone. Reagan and Watson returned to their Range Rover and drove back to where Sinclair and Mason were still parked.

"Well?" Sinclair asked.

"We borrowed the Ranger's truck and did a drive-by," Reagan said, relating what they had seen.

"This feels real," Sinclair said, to everyone's agreement. "What do we do now?"

"Now we follow them and see where they take us," Jack replied. "If they're our guys, they're probably going to turn west on Route 36, cross the bridge, and follow that to the Garden State. Why don't you two head over now and stop just past the bridge. We'll signal you when they leave the park – you can follow them from in front and we'll take them from behind."

"Sounds like a plan," Sinclair said, with Mason nodding agreement. "What if they don't head over the bridge, though?"

"Only other way they can go is south along the coast for a bit. You can do a u-turn pretty easy if they go south. If I recall correctly the road opens up to two lanes a few miles down, and we can maneuver some then."

"Yeah, I know where that is," Peter replied. "Our hotel is down around there. What about comms? We've got some spares in the back."

"Let's just use cellphones for the moment. Now off you go," Jack said.

"Aye aye, sir," Sinclair said with a chuckle, heading out of the park as planned.

Watson was fairly excited; everything she was doing was new to her, though she would never admit it. She had done surveillance work before, but that had been of fixed locations, never of a moving car. She had trained in techniques for trailing vehicles, of course, but she had never actually done it other than for practice. She turned to her partner and saw how relaxed he looked, as if this was the most normal thing in the world. She was about to ask him where he'd learned about tailing cars when she caught sight of the Ford Explorer driving towards the park exit.

Jack saw it too, dialing Peter's phone. "Heads up, on the move. All three targets inside. Keep the line open," he said. A minute later, it was clear that the Explorer was indeed heading west on Route 36, and Jack told Peter to start off ahead of their target. The hard part, they soon found out, was timing the traffic lights. On occasion Reagan would get stuck a little behind and then he would have to race to catch up. Similarly, Sinclair would pass through more lights, forcing him to slow down significantly and wait for the other vehicles to start to catch up. It was a lot like a very complicated dance routine, made even harder by the light volume of traffic. More cars would have allowed them to work closer in, but this way the Porsche and Range Rover were just too easy spot.

Eventually they reached the Garden State Parkway, and as expected, the Explorer turned north in the express lanes. Traffic volume was still unexpectedly light, but at least the target was going a steady 65 mph. "Trade off soon, Jack?" Sinclair asked.

"In a few minutes. I want him to forget me a little first," Reagan replied, easing off on the throttle and allowing himself to fall further behind. About a quarter mile behind the Explorer, they lost sight of it at times as it went into turns.

"Aren't we a bit too far behind, Jack?" Amanda worried.

"Distance depends on circumstances," he replied. "In this case, there aren't any exits or turnoffs – not for a few miles, anyway. These guys can't go anywhere without us seeing them. I'm not particularly worried about them dropping something from their car or doing a stop-and-dash, so I don't think we need to be any closer – for now," Reagan explained.

A few minutes later, satisfied that the occupants of the Explorer had probably forgotten about them, Reagan decided it was time to swap positions. "Ok, Pete, time to slow down and let him pass," he said, accelerating past the speed limit to catch up.

Sinclair did just that, gradually slowing to a respectable 60 mph, letting the Explorer pass. None of its occupants looked his way, a fact he quickly relayed to Reagan. A few seconds later, Reagan passed him, too, and then passed the Explorer as well, slowing down to match its speed about two hundred yards ahead of it. The terrorists, if that's what they were, didn't pay any attention to him, either.

"Where do you think they're going, Jack — Paterson?" Sinclair asked.

"That's my guess. I don't know this area as well as I should, but I figure they'll keep using the Garden State and then turn west on I-80." He noticed that the volume of cars was increasing. That made sense — it was past 3:30 p.m. and schools would be letting out. People would be leaving work soon, too.

Sinclair saw that traffic was starting to slow down a little and had the same thought. "What do you say we tighten this up a bit, Jack?"

"Good idea," he replied. A few minutes later, Reagan and Sinclair had maneuvered to within a few car lengths of the Explorer, keeping a few random cars between them and their target.

"We don't have enough cars to do this properly," Sinclair remarked, seeing a significant number of additional vehicles on the road as they approached a massive bridge that spanned at least ten lanes in each direction.

"You're right. Let me see if I can get us some help. I'll hang up for a little but call me back if he twitches." Reagan found himself regretting that he didn't take Sinclair up on his offer of comms. He scrolled through his contacts and dialed Special Agent Monaghan's number.

"Hi Jack," he heard on the other end. "I was going to call you," Monaghan said apologetically. "We've ruled out most of the vans but still don't have a plate on one of them."

"Thanks but that's not why I'm calling, Paul. I'm in New Jersey, tailing a car we found a little suspicious over at Sandy Hook. We're northbound on the Garden State, probably heading towards Paterson, but traffic is picking up and we don't have enough cars for a proper tail. Do you have anyone in the area who can help us out?"

"I'll find out and call you back as soon as I can," Monaghan promised.

As they waited on Monaghan, Reagan gave his phone to Watson and had her call Sinclair from her phone so they could maintain an uninterrupted connection. They didn't have long to wait.

"Jack, I've got Special Agent Anita Edwards on the line. She and her partner were on their way to Newark from Atlantic City, so they're somewhere behind you on the Garden State," Monaghan said.

"Where are you now, Special Agent Reagan," Edwards asked.

Jack looked at his GPS and gave his approximate location, speed and direction of travel. "Call me Jack, it's easier that way," he added.

"Ok Jack, I'm Anita. We're only about twenty miles behind you. We'll catch up as quick as we can," she said, turning on her lights and siren as she kicked down the accelerator on her powerful vehicle. "What's everyone driving," she asked, and Reagan gave her the details on all three cars.

"Jack, before I step off the line, is there anything else we can do?" Monaghan asked. "Do you need us to run down the plates and send some people over?"

"No, not yet. I mean, we've run the plates and are checking up on the owner – Rosita Velazquez of Paterson. I'd rather you give this some thought and set up a surveillance package on her. We don't want to spook anyone just yet," Reagan replied.

"Makes sense. We'll figure it out," Monaghan said.

It took Edwards just about fifteen minutes to catch up, turning off her lights and siren and slowing down as she approached. "Jack, the Porsche is a few cars in front of me. I can see the Explorer further ahead and you out beyond that. What now?"

"Now I'm going to trade places with the Porsche and in a few more minutes you'll swap positions with me," Reagan replied. "What are you driving?"

"Black Charger," she replied, reading off her plates. They continued driving north for another forty minutes, the traffic getting incrementally worse. Sinclair was having a hard time keeping in front of the Explorer, who often switched lanes without signaling.

"Think we've been made?" Sinclair asked through Watson's phone. "He's driving more erratically now."

"I don't think we've been made. Maybe this is standard counter-detection for him," Reagan suggested.

"I've been meaning to ask, who are these guys? What can you tell me about them?" Edwards finally asked.

"We think they might be connected to the terrorist attack in Rock Creek Park," Reagan replied.

"Oh," Edwards said, trading a look with her partner. She knew the shooters in the park had used Kalashnikovs, and that worried her. She had a two-year-old at home and another one on its way in seven months. "Jack, we're not equipped to handle something like that."

"Try not to worry about it, Anita. We haven't seen any weapons on these guys, and we can handle anything that comes up," he replied confidently.

Traffic had come almost to a complete stop just past the junction with Route 46. All four cars were in the center lane, with Sinclair still in front. Five cars behind him came the Explorer, with the Bureau Charger just two cars behind that. Another two cars separated the Charger from Reagan's Range Rover. They were all crawling forward slowly, but the Explorer had started to leave a large gap in front of it, and more cars jumped in, further separating the Porsche from the group. Just past the left-hand exit for Route 19, the Explorer found a small gap in front of a truck illegally travelling in the left lane and suddenly cut across it, almost diagonally and then slightly into oncoming traffic, veering quickly onto the ramp for the exit they had just passed.

"Fuck! He just went out on Route 19," Edwards called out. She tried following the Explorer but was blocked off by the truck.

Reagan, meanwhile, was blocked in by the traffic behind the truck. Despite leaning on the horn and flashing his lights, it took him well over a minute to maneuver out the exit, followed closely by Edwards. Sinclair eventually made it to the left-hand shoulder and backed up before darting up the exit ramp to join the chase. Reagan and Edwards weaved through traffic as quickly and safely as they could, but no longer had eyes on the Explorer.

"I messed up, Jack. I'm sorry. What do we do now?" Edwards asked.

"You didn't mess up. Traffic is what it is. Turn on your lights and sirens and head on up the road. If you see our subjects, though, leave them alone. Pass them and keep on going, but call in their location to us."

"I can do that," Edwards promised, riding between the left lane and the shoulder. Traffic slowed down even more to make room for her to pass – exactly as Reagan had expected – but a few minutes later Edwards came back on the line sounding grim. "I'm on Ward Street in Paterson. We didn't see them, Jack. They're gone."

Reagan barely managed to hold in the expletives that came to mind, but apparently Sinclair was vocalizing them quite nicely. He couldn't quite hear what he was telling Watson, but she was trying to calm him down. Unsuccessfully.

"What do we do now, Jack?" Edwards asked. The disappointment in her voice was obvious.

"Wait for us there and we'll figure it out," he replied, ending the call. Reagan pulled up behind her a few minutes later, followed by Sinclair a few minutes after that. Reagan waved his friend over, and together they walked up to Edwards' open window.

"Jack Reagan," he said, shaking her hand. "This is my friend, Pete Sinclair." Edwards started to apologize for losing the Explorer but Reagan cut her off with a smile. "No need to apologize, Anita. These things are unpredictable and it's really my fault. I should have planned this better. Do you have some time to help us out now?"

"I'm here for as long as you need me," she replied.

"Good. In that case, I'd like you to escort Pete to a police station so he can secure his car, and after that Pete and his partner are going to ride with you on a tour of the neighborhood in which the car is registered. The Porsche would stand out too much," Reagan explained. "If you find the car, let me know and see if you can sit on it discreetly until we can get a surveillance package set up."

"And if they make us?" Sinclair asked.

"Use your best judgment," Reagan replied. "A living bad guy can provide more usable intelligence than a dead one, but don't take any unnecessary chances." He saw Sinclair and Edwards nod in agreement. "If you don't find them – and to be honest, I don't think you will – pick up the Porsche, head over to Newark Airport, and get Jim into a rental car."

Reagan and Sinclair returned to their cars, and Sinclair followed Edwards to a police station, which turned out to be fairly close by. Edwards' partner went inside to explain their request to the local constabulary while Mason and Sinclair offloaded some equipment into the Charger. Edwards watched them place a laptop bag and larger duffel in her trunk before getting into her back seat with large cases obviously meant for automatic weapons. She felt much safer with these gentlemen in the car, observing that they carried themselves a lot like her husband, who had served three tours in Afghanistan as an Army Ranger. They were probably good shooters, too. NCIS obviously had a few of those – there wasn't an agent in the Bureau who hadn't heard about the NCIS agent who shot four terrorists in the head with a pistol at extreme range. Her partner returned to the car, and Edwards set off to find the elusive Ford Explorer.

25

Reagan and Watson sat in the parking lot of a well-lit gas station, waiting for Sinclair to check in with them. They both felt somewhat safer in the bright light – neither one thought much of their surroundings, and Jack observed that Amanda kept her purse open in her lap, her weapon within easy reach. He also noted that she was still riding an adrenaline high, and he knew from experience how exhausting it felt coming off of those. Luckily they didn't have long to wait; within forty-five minutes, Sinclair called to tell them that after a thorough search of the Velazquez neighborhood, the Ford Explorer was nowhere to be seen. Sinclair and Mason were off to retrieve their car and head over to the Hertz counter at Newark Airport before heading back to their hotel, where they would all meet up later for a confab.

"Let's go have a chat with Mrs. Velazquez," Jack said, putting her address into his GPS. It turned out they were only a few minutes away. Mrs. Velazquez lived on the ground floor of a row house in what passed for the nice part of town. They could tell that her television was on, and saw through her curtains that she had set up dinner for herself on a small table in front of the TV. She opened the door quickly when they knocked, but her eyes were guarded and full of suspicion.

"Mrs. Velazquez? I'm Special Agent Amanda Watson, Naval Criminal Investigative Service. We'd like to ask you a few questions about..."

"I no criminal," Velazquez responded in anger. "No hablo ingles," she said, starting to shut the door.

Reagan quickly stuck his foot in the door and held up the badge Mason had given him earlier. "Deputy U.S. Marshals, ma'am. We really need your help," he said. That immediately got a better reaction from Velazquez. She had never heard of NCIS but she was very familiar with the Marshals Service. Every once in a while, they would apprehend one fugitive or another in the area, and her neighborhood was much improved as a result. "Do you own a Ford Explorer, ma'am?" Reagan asked.

"Si, yes, the car of mi hijo. My son," she said, in broken English.

"What's your son's name, ma'am?" Reagan asked, smiling politely.

"Raul. Raul Ernesto Velazquez," she replied. "He is good boy, very good boy."

"Yes, ma'am, I'm sure he is. Is he here now?"

"No, he is in El Paso. He good boy," she repeated.

"When is the last time you saw him or spoke to him?" Watson asked.

"He call me few weeks ago and send money. He found job in El Paso," Velazquez said. "You are la migra, no?" she asked, growing skeptical.

"No ma'am. We are not immigration. We don't care about papers," Reagan said, trying to think of a way to get the woman to open up. He looked past her and saw a large number of icons and crosses nailed to the wall, along with several religious figurines lined up neatly next to her television. "We really need your son's help. A few weeks ago, a pregnant woman was attacked by two men when she was coming out of church after evening mass. Your son helped her – he came to her rescue. He saved the woman and her unborn child, Mrs. Velazquez. We really need your son's help to identify those men and arrest them before they hurt anyone else. Do you understand what I just said?"

She clearly understood, and that lie did the trick. Mrs. Velazquez was so proud of what her son did that she opened up the door and invited Reagan and Watson inside. Jack sat to talk with the woman while Amanda wandered around the room, discretely taking a picture of the son's photo with her cellphone. Meanwhile, Reagan learned that Raul had left home back in

October and had called her to say he found work in El Paso – but didn't say what that work was. It turned out that Raul wasn't up for any trophies as a son; his mother had no idea where he was staying and didn't even know his phone number. His last call to her had been Christmas Day. But at least she was happy he was such a good boy, helping a pregnant woman. Reagan thanked her for her help and headed outside with Watson. Both were relieved that their car was still there and in one piece.

"Nicely done, Jack," Amanda said, showing him the picture she had taken. "He doesn't look like any of the people in the car."

"Yeah, he's not one of them. Interesting that they're driving his car. Did you get the sense that Mrs. Velazquez was holding anything back?"

"Not at all. She seemed a bit sad at how little contact she has with her son," Amanda replied. "What's next?"

"Next you send that picture to Doug Cannon to add to our collection. Send it to Paul Monaghan at the Bureau, too. We're going to need to talk to both of those gentlemen soon, but first let's get back to civilization," Jack said, heading off in search of the Interstate. They had no sooner found I-80 than Reagan's phone rang.

"Hey Jack, it's Paul. Your agent just sent me a photo. Is that one of the people you were following? Sorry they got away, by the way."

"It happens," Reagan conceded. "No, that's the son of the car's owner," he said, explaining what they had found.

"Interesting stuff," Monaghan said. "You know, it could just be that Raul is still up in New Jersey, lying to his mother. Maybe he lent his car to some friends who went down the shore for the day. I'll grant you, they do sound a little suspicious, but still, there could be a simple explanation."

"How about the lack of cellphones?" Reagan asked.

"Hey, I know most people are always playing with their phones, but just because you didn't see them in use, it doesn't mean they didn't have them," Monaghan said with a chuckle.

"If they had them anywhere in that car, they were turned off. We would have known otherwise, if you catch my meaning. And three phones turned off is suspicious enough," Reagan said.

"Yeah, I'll admit, that does make things more suspicious." Monaghan understood full well what Reagan had just said. He was surprised that NCIS had a Stingray; he hadn't known about that. "What do you propose we do with this information?"

"Can you follow up for us? Maybe you can track down Raul from his call to his mom on Christmas, and then build from there," Reagan suggested.

"You mean a phone tree? Why not just interview him, if we find him?"

"A phone tree would be helpful. That's how we stumbled on these guys to begin with, from a SIM card. And if Raul does turn out to be a player, we want to know who else is involved without spooking anyone. Maybe follow him around some, see what turns up," Reagan replied.

"A phone tree we can definitely do," Monaghan promised, "but I need to kick the rest upstairs. I suppose you're going to stick around New Jersey for a while?"

"That's the plan. I'm betting we see these guys again really soon, and next time we'll be ready for them."

"Ok, Jack. Let me know how it goes."

Reagan had barely finished his call with Monaghan when Doug Cannon called Watson. She filled him in on the day's events, but left out the involvement of Sinclair and Mason. She had heard Jack's report to Monaghan and sought to match it in detail – no more, and no less. After all, that's what partners do. Cannon, to his credit, didn't think it a stretch of the imagination to suppose the men they had followed were probably bad actors. In part he was learning to trust Reagan's judgment, but also, it was just too much to write off as coincidence. Unfortunately, he explained, there wasn't a whole hell of a lot he could do to help.

The drive back to Sandy Hook took considerably less time than their drive from it, and by 9 p.m., Reagan and Watson pulled into the La Quinta a few miles south, securing a room across the hall from Sinclair and Mason. They dispensed with the pretense of separate rooms, and didn't even bother requesting a room with two beds. Watson's adrenaline had worn off, and she was every bit as exhausted as Reagan had thought she would become; all Amanda wanted to do was to curl up in bed with Jack.

Just as soon as she lay down on the bed, she realized that their day probably wasn't over yet – Jack would want to talk things over with his friends. More than that, her stomach had started to remind her that neither she nor Jack had eaten anything all day. Amanda was about to suggest that they order something to eat when there was a knock on the door and, as if by magic, a pizza arrived. "I thought you might be a little hungry – hope you like it," Jack said, setting it on the desk, along with the bottle of Diet Coke that had been delivered as well.

"Thank you, thank you, thank you!" Amanda said, quickly getting off the bed and giving Jack a very tight hug before turning her attention to dinner. "Looks delicious – and hey, I didn't even hear you order!"

"There's an app for that," Jack said with a chuckle.

"I suppose you want to talk to Pete and Jim. Why don't we just take the pizza over to their room and save some time?" she suggested. "Besides, this thing is too big for just the two of us."

"Works for me," Jack replied, grabbing the bottle as Amanda carried the pizza. They walked across the hall and knocked on Sinclair's door.

"Pizza's here!" Amanda announced with a smile, walking into the room. She took two steps inside and stopped dead in her tracks, her mouth ajar at the sight in front of her. Jim Mason was sitting on his bed, halfway through field-stripping some variant of an M-4 assault rifle. Another M-4 was propped up next to his bed, and Watson could see two more weapons – H&K MP7s with suppressors, she thought – on Mason's bed, along with a suppressed MP5. On Sinclair's bed she saw three sets of night vision goggles and communications gear, both of which were unlike any she had seen before. Even the desk was filled with equipment. Watson quickly tried to regain her composure, closing her mouth before asking, "Where do you guys want it?"

"How about over here on my bed," Sinclair said, packing away the gear that was on it. "I guess you must be feeling a little apprehensive right about now," he said with a smile.

"I'd be feeling a lot apprehensive if you weren't Jack's friends and I didn't know what you guys are," she replied truthfully.

"What, exactly, do you know about what we are?" Sinclair asked.

"I know you're Navy SEALs, right?"

"More than that," Mason said with a chuckle. "We're what used to be called DEVGRU – Naval Special Warfare Development Group. We're called something else now, obviously, after all the press we got after bin Laden."

"You're part of Seal Team 6?" Amanda asked, stunned at the revelation.

"Guilty as charged, ma'am," Sinclair replied. "Naturally, that information doesn't leave this room – in fact, you can't discuss anything you see or hear here with anyone other than Jack. Do you understand?"

"I do," Amanda replied, still somewhat in shock. "I always just assumed that you were here helping Jack out as friends."

"Oh we are," Peter replied. "But we're here with the blessing of JSOC as well. Some of the things that Jack has turned up, like a possible connection to some Stingers we've been looking for, are of great interest to us, and our bosses have enough faith in Jack's judgment that we're kinda-sorta attached to him for this little op."

"Frozen Tide, in case you forgot," Jim chimed in, proud of the name he had selected.

"What's the connection to Stingers?" Amanda wanted to know.

"Sorry, ma'am," Peter replied. "Not even your Director is read in on that one. Technically speaking, Jack isn't either, but he's just too damn good at making connections and figuring stuff out. Can you live with not knowing more, at least for now?"

"I guess I can – I have to, don't I?" she said, starting to smile. Clearly these very experienced warriors, and their bosses, trusted Jack's judgment every bit as much as she did. That made things ok. "So, what's on the agenda for tomorrow," she asked, noting that everyone turned to Jack for the answer.

Reagan reached for a slice of pizza, thinking before he spoke. "We all agree the guys in the Explorer are probably players, right?" he asked. Everyone nodded agreement. "Right. Is that red Mustang outside your rental?" he asked Mason.

"Yup," he replied. "I had a hard time choosing between that and a minivan, but I figured a single guy wouldn't be as creepy driving a Mustang," he added, causing everyone to laugh.

"Ok then. How about we stage a little accident?" Jack asked. "If you can rear-end our target, maybe you can plant a tracker when you get out to check the damage. I haven't been able to come up with any other way to do it – they seem to hang out too close to their car to do it otherwise."

"I can't think of anything better," Peter admitted. "Hope you bought insurance, pal," he said to Jim, who merely nodded his head as he winced.

"The only other thing I could think of would involve a helicopter. I don't suppose you can get us one of those?" Jack asked Peter.

"As a matter of fact, Jack, I already thought of that," he replied with a smile. "We'll have a Black Hawk standing by at

259

McGuire-Dix-Lakehurst starting at 0700 tomorrow. I know, I know, it's not the best platform for tracking a car in suburbia, but it's all we could get. Besides, it's good to have handy in case we need it."

"Good thinking," Jack said. "As far as tomorrow goes, why don't you two head over in the morning and take up positions in the same lot as today. Get some good pictures when the targets come in – if they come in tomorrow, that is. Amanda and I will make our way in a little later, like today. Maybe take a walk in their AO and get a closer look. Should be easier for us to come up with a cover than for you two."

"What's an AO?" Amanda wanted to know.

"Area of Operations," Jim replied. "And I'm betting they'll be back tomorrow. We won't be able to get great pictures of all three when they're in the car, though."

"Any chance you can work your way in on foot, or maybe set up before they arrive?" Jack asked.

"We can, but there's just enough snow that they might spot our trail, if they're looking," Peter answered.

"Better to do it from the car, then," Jack said. "Also, let's use your comms tomorrow. They would have come in handy today. More than that, I really don't know. I'm kinda making this up as I go along," he admitted.

"So are we, Jack," Peter laughed. "And for what it's worth, we don't have any other ideas, either. What do we do if they make us?"

"Then we stop them and have us a nice chat," Jack replied.

"And if they come out shooting?" Jim asked.

"We won't be taking any unnecessary chances. Not after Rock Creek Park," Jack said, seeing everyone nod in agreement.

"By the way, I brought along an MP5 if you want it," Jim said.

"We'll see tomorrow," Jack replied.

"Your funeral, pal," Peter chimed in. "I meant to bring along a baton for you, but I forgot," he said with a wink.

"Hey, I was young and foolish," Jack said with a laugh.

"You may not be that young anymore, but you're still foolish. A 9mm up against Kalashnikovs, Jack? You know better," Peter said with mock gravity.

"Yeah, I suppose I do," Jack replied. "Now eat up. I don't know about you guys, but I'm exhausted."

Amanda sat on the only chair in the room, finishing her second slice. She hadn't said much in the meeting, realizing that she was well and truly out of her depth. Causing an accident to plant a tracking device was not part of her training, though she suspected Doug Cannon would readily approve of the idea. Even the trailing they had done that afternoon was far more advanced than anything she had ever practiced. Everything these men did and talked about doing was at a much higher level of sophistication than anything she could have imagined doing herself. Normally this would have caused her to be at least a little anxious, if not worried. But all she felt now was excitement.

"I'm going to go shower and get ready for bed," she told Jack. "Don't stay up too late playing with your friends," she said, pointing at the weapons with a smile on her face.

"Yes, dear," he replied with a sheepish grin.

Jack spent only a few more minutes with his friends before he excused himself. It had been a long day, after all, and he was tired. But more than that, he was really looking forward to curling up in bed with Amanda. He returned to the room just as she was getting out of the bathroom, wearing a deep red silk robe that he hadn't seen her pack. He was a little surprised when she walked over and hugged him, but the surprise quickly faded as he wrapped his arms around her and held her tight, her warm breath on his neck sending shivers of pleasure through his body. She moved her hands up against his chest and rested her forehead against his as his hands moved down to her waist.

"You smell amazing," Jack said with a smile.

"Only for you," she replied, with a smile of her own. "Now go shower – I'll wait," she said, pushing him away gently.

Jack took his pajamas and dopp kit from his bag and headed to the bathroom. He showered quickly before brushing his teeth; he avoided looking at himself in the mirror, wondering how much longer he could maintain his self-control. That thought left his mind just as soon as he turned the light off and went into the bedroom. The room was illuminated only by the soft glow of the lights from the parking lot, and he saw Amanda leaning against the desk, her robe slightly open, revealing a hint of pink and black lingerie underneath.

"Come here, Jack," she said softly, the trace of a smile on her lips.

Jack walked to her, standing in front of her, holding her waist as her arms moved up around his neck.

"You don't realize what you do to me, do you?" she asked, slowly pulling his head down to her. She tilted her head slightly as their lips connected in a soft kiss that lingered. Another kiss followed, and another. He gently parted her lips with his, feeling the tip of her tongue gently caress his upper lip, then the lower. He responded in kind and their shared passion grew in intensity along with their kisses. She held onto him tighter as he moved his arms under her robe, holding her firmly, feeling her soft skin against his hands. He kissed her neck as her robe slid off, feeling her respond with a shiver, and then a soft moan. Her right leg wrapped around his left as she leaned back more, his kisses moving slowly down her neck, down her chest.

He felt her breathing faster as she pushed him back and stood, her arms on his waist, kissing passionately as his shirt came off. He felt her shiver and press against him as his hands traced slowly down her back, then up again. Her left hand came up to his cheek as the kisses became longer and harder, his hands reaching behind her to squeeze her rear. She brought her hand slowly down from his cheek, pressing against his chest with her fingertips, slowly going lower, feeling his excitement grow, hard and ready. She smiled, as did he, and together they took the two steps into bed.

26

Osman Mansuraev had not slept well on the overnight flight out of Miami, despite the comfortable bed and free-flowing vodka in First Class. At first he thought it was just nerves, that he was anxious about how well his plan would unfold later that day. But it wasn't that at all, he realized somewhere over the Caribbean Sea. It was the ghost of his father that kept him awake. The Colonel had been a demanding man who required perfection, attention to detail and above all, unconditional obedience. He was a man who had never uttered the words 'please' or 'thank you' in his entire life, except perhaps in the presence of the Chairman and the General Secretary. Those men, and many others, tolerated the Colonel's abusive and vicious behavior without comment. He was, after all, the best man they had planning offensive operations against their many enemies.

No one had said a word when the Colonel shot a young captain in his office, simply for failing to fully understand some of the nuances of the Colonel's order. The blood-stained carpet had been replaced by the next morning without comment, and the young captain's body had disappeared quickly – probably disposed of in the building's furnace. The Colonel's abusiveness carried over to his personal life as well. Mansuraev had been subjected to innumerable beatings over things as trivial as saying 'kindly pass the salt' in English, instead of the more widely-used 'please pass the salt.'

His mother, however, had taken the worst of the beatings; oftentimes Mansuraev and his younger sister had hurriedly helped around the house because their mother had been beaten too badly to move from bed. Remarkably, she stayed with the Colonel despite the beatings and abuse – she had loved him fiercely. Not that she had any choice but to stay; she would probably have disappeared into a furnace had she tried to leave. Besides, there was a lot of prestige to be had as the wife of a senior Colonel in the KGB, not to mention access to closed shops full of Western goods.

Mansuraev needed his mission to fully succeed – not just for his country and for the sake of his own immense ego, but also to please his long-dead father. His country, of course, was Russia. Osman Mansuraev had been a clever identity crafted for Anatoly Lavrov when he was a 22 year-old lieutenant following in his father's footsteps at the KGB. In fact, the operational concept had been laid out in general terms by the Colonel himself shortly before his death. The cause of death had been listed as liver failure, but Anatoly knew the real cause to be a heart broken by the disintegration of his beloved Rodina at the hands of the Americans under Ronald Reagan and George H.W. Bush. His hatred for America had subsequently grown by leaps and bounds, and Anatoly wanted nothing more than to avenge his father – and his country – and push America into the abyss.

The sun had risen just above the treetops when Director Smythe's driver pulled into a parking space near the entrance to the very park where his agents had been massacred the previous week. The tranquil white field of snow masked the tragedy that had occurred, but as the icy wind whipped up loose flakes of snow, Smythe couldn't help but feel that the ghosts of his men were still there, fighting for their lives. Maybe they could finally find some peace when their bodies were put to rest later that afternoon, following a somber memorial service planned at the Washington field office.

Smythe wrapped his scarf tighter around his neck as he approached the solitary figure standing a few feet into the park, whose long black coat and cane provided the only contrast between the white of the snow and the white of his hair. Former Deputy Director (Operations) John Quincy looked considerably older and frailer than Smythe remembered from when he last saw him at CIA close to two decades earlier, but he carried himself well nevertheless, his back ramrod straight from many years of service in the Navy earlier in his life.

"This is where it happened, isn't it?" Quincy asked as Smythe approached.

"It is," Smythe replied. "It all started with Lance Corporal Lawrence Eggerton," he said, starting an explanation that included a very detailed account of the battle that had taken place.

"I'm sorry for your loss, Francis," Quincy said, shaking the man's hand after Smythe concluded his story. "Glad it wasn't worse."

"Thanks, John – and so am I," Smythe replied. "Jack Reagan worked for the CIA, didn't he?"

Quincy had not known the reason for their meeting before, but after hearing the story, that question was the very one he expected. The location of their meeting was a nice touch, too, if a little theatrical. "He did," Quincy said, forming a little smile. "I'm glad for his sake that he graduated to guns. The last time he went up against terrorists with Kalashnikovs, all he had was a tactical baton."

Smythe's eyes went wide in surprise; there were many things he had expected to hear, but that was not one of them. "What can you tell me about Jack? He's been helping us with the investigation, by the way."

"And he's turned out quite a few gems, has he?" Quincy asked with a knowing nod. "Do you remember Max Peterson?"

"Sure – he was a legend!" Smythe replied. "He was in the original OSS, first in the Middle East and then in France, as I recall. He was one of the first officers to join the CIA when it was formed and had a storied career up until he retired in the 70s, I think."

"He retired in the 70s, but he stayed active. He was a Special Assistant to the DDI right up to the time he died in the late 90s," Quincy explained. "When he wasn't consulting for us, he was teaching – at Columbia, among other places. He's the one who discovered Jack Reagan and brought him to us. Reagan was one of his best students at the time, and he had a very keen mind. He knew how to ask the right questions and was able to figure out where to look for answers all on his own. More than that, he knew when to read between the lines as well as when not to. Max got him cleared and started using him as an assistant on the things he was working on. Reagan impressed the people on the seventh floor enough that when Max passed away, they brought Reagan in to continue his work."

"So Jack was an analyst, then," Smythe said. Obviously still a very good one, he thought, having been trained by the very best in the business.

"Not hardly," Quincy replied with a chuckle. "The problem with Reagan is that we didn't really know what to do with him. Do you remember the attack in Paris on the Israeli peace delegation?"

"That was back in the 90s, too, wasn't it?" Smythe asked. "Our ambassador was having a late dinner with the chief Israeli delegate at his private residence when some Hamas terrorists crashed the party. They were apprehended by security before they could do any damage, I think. I had left the Agency by then so I'm relying on my memory of news accounts," he admitted.

"Pretty close, but it wasn't the ambassador. It was the Secretary of State. She decided to have a secret and private dinner meeting, so she only took along a couple of her protective officers instead of her full detail – there were some Tier 1 assets on her, but I don't remember the details myself. There were four terrorists. They had somehow found out the location and drove up late in the evening. The ones we took alive later said they had no idea SecState was there – their target was the Israeli delegation. Anyway, they drove right up to the front of a house near central Paris and came out shooting. They killed both outside security personnel the French had assigned, as well as one of the two Israelis on perimeter. Two of them made it all the way to the front door and were about to kick it in when they realized they were all alone."

"Jack's doing?" Smythe asked, his eyebrows raised.

"Jack's doing," Quincy confirmed with a nod. "Just like in this park here, he was in the wrong place at the wrong time. He was simply on vacation, visiting a great-aunt in Paris. He was walking back to his hotel and just happened to be right in front of the Israeli delegation when the terrorists showed up. He got down between some cars when the shooting started, and quickly pieced together what was happening. Thankfully he was carrying a tactical baton – an ASP – for personal protection, and he made good use of it. One of the terrorists came up next to him and Jack gave him a good whack in the head and disarmed him, then he moved around the car behind one of the other terrorists and took him out too. The first one he killed, by the way, but we never told him that."

"And the other two?" Smythe asked, fully engrossed in the story.

"They tried to get away but a couple of local cops heard the shooting and responded very quickly. They exchanged fire with the terrorists and eventually apprehended them. As for Reagan, this is where the story gets interesting. He had the presence of mind to hide the baton and his ID in the tailpipe of one of the parked cars, and he just sat quiet and listened. His French is very good so he figured out what was going on and decided that it was better for there *not* to be any CIA involvement. So he played the part of a drunk German tourist – his German is fluent, by the way – and he talked his way pretty quickly out of trouble. By the time the police arrived en masse, he was already at our embassy, explaining what he had done."

"Quite some story," Smythe remarked. "The baton and ID?"

"One of our people retrieved them some time the next day," Quincy shrugged. "What's also interesting is the friends he made at the embassy. The people who were tasked to protect

SecState but had been left behind – SEALs, I think – took him out for drinks to thank him for doing their job and they really hit it off. They positively loved the guy and even wanted to drag him kicking and screaming through OCS and then train him to work with them. They made inquiries, and word of *that* got back to Max. Max, in turn, had an idea of his own for Reagan's future." Quincy paused, lighting a small cigar.

"Anyway, as you may know, every once in a while over the years, we kept toying with the idea of integrating the DO and DI better – this was before the post-9/11 reorganization, mind you. The idea was always the same – provide intelligence support to our operations people in the field, and have faster, on-scene analysis and follow-up suggestions for our intelligence officers. Max floated the idea to have Reagan do that. He was coming along nicely as an analyst, but more than that, he was pretty swift on his feet. The DCI really liked the idea, but I have to admit I was more than a little reluctant to go along. I would much rather have had Reagan go through the Farm and join my team directly. Reagan was pretty adamant about not doing that, though. Given the choice between Intelligence and Operations, he made it very clear that he would prefer the DI. Max finally convinced him to accept a cross-over role, so we put him through some training."

"The Farm?" Smythe asked.

"In part, yes. For general tradecraft. We were more keen on him learning how things are done rather than having him do them himself, mind you. For other things, his SEAL friends devised a training program for him, mostly at Coronado and Bragg. That was part of the problem, actually – we really didn't know what to do with Reagan. He had one foot in the DI, one foot in the DO, and had his fingers in the paramilitary side of things as well. Everyone wanted him exclusively, and we couldn't figure out how to share him. Eventually the DCI stepped in and decided to send him off on discrete assignments, supporting various things we had going on in the Middle East, Europe and North Africa. Mostly, though, he was assigned as a liaison of sorts with the special operations community. Those people absolutely loved him."

"Sounds complicated," Smythe remarked.

"What made it complicated was that a lot of my people were reluctant to deal with him. How can I put this delicately... the officers whose main goal was doing their job loved him and were glad to have his help, but the ones whose main goal was to further their own career resented him. More than one Station Chief tried to cut him out of the loop completely, and I ended up making Reagan one my Special Assistants just to cut through the some of the resistance from my own people. After a rough start, it started working pretty well. Reagan was good at plucking a diamond from a coal mine, so to speak. He was also good at developing sources and information all on his own. That caused some friction with my people, too."

"Under a cover?' Smythe asked.

"Once or twice, but generally no. He was a legitimate grad student, and then had a legitimate post-graduate fellowship. That was pretty much all the cover he needed. He didn't actually recruit or run agents, mind you, but he easily could have. He recommended some of his sources to our field officers, and some of them *were* subsequently run as agents."

"It sounds like things were going well indeed. So why did Jack leave?"

"The system wasn't ready for him then, and it probably still isn't ready for someone like him today," Quincy said, shaking his head before laughing. "Crazy, isn't it? The bureaucracy can be stifling, and I'm as much to blame for having been part of that. Reagan reported to too many people – he served too many masters, often with conflicting directions and orders. When he worked with smart people who let him do things his way, everything turned up roses. With the military especially. But Reagan chafed at having to report to people who couldn't get their heads out of their asses, to use his words. I'm partly to blame for that, too. After Max died, I didn't support him as strongly as I should have, and I still regret that.

"As for why he left, the short version is that he had become increasingly frustrated with the bureaucracy and quit. That's the official version, too. Unofficially, though, it was because of an assignment in Istanbul. We sent him there to assess the reliability of an agent the Station Chief himself had recently recruited. Reagan concluded that the information was probably good, but that the agent was probably some kind of a plant. The Station Chief didn't buy it, and set up a meeting between one of his officers and the agent. Reagan, all on his own initiative, went out and scouted the location. He came back and told the Station Chief his concerns about the location. He wanted to tell the officer as well but the Station Chief didn't allow him to. In fact, he even had Reagan detained by the Embassy Marines until after the meeting.

"It turned out that Reagan was right; the agent had been a plant, and the meeting itself was an ambush. Our officer escaped by the skin of his teeth, but a family of American tourists was gunned down during the course of the ambush. As soon as Reagan found out, he decked the Station Chief and resigned the next day. We canned the Station Chief a week later and asked Reagan to come back, but he refused. He decided to go to law school instead."

"That's quite some story, John," Smythe said. He was very much impressed by what he had just heard, but at the same time not at all surprised. He had read Reagan correctly from the very beginning. "I liked him pretty much as soon as I met him without really stopping to figure out why, but now that I know his story, I think I like him even more."

"I take it from your interest that you've got something more in mind for Reagan after this Eggerton matter is resolved," Quincy stated.

"I've given it some thought," Smythe replied. "I've got lots of great cops, former military, and even some intelligence types. I don't have anyone like Jack Reagan, though. Any words of advice?"

"Francis, I've known you for a fairly long time, and I've known Reagan too. You two are a good fit. Especially if you give him enough autonomy to do things his way and you don't burden him with bureaucracy. But if you ever have him work under someone less capable or smart than you are – or Reagan is, to be more precise – you'll have fireworks. One other thing. If you bring him in now, you might just be creating a mess for the next Director. Unless, of course, you're planning on staying."

"I've been thinking about that, too," Smythe admitted. Rebuilding morale after the massacre in the park was proving to be tougher than he had imagined, not just in the Washington field office but across the agency. Ironically, perhaps, the agents handling it best were the ones actively involved in the investigation – especially the ones working with Reagan.

"If you want my advice about *that*, take the job if it's offered," Quincy said. "Retirement is no fun, let me tell you. There's only so much bingo and canasta you can play. Then again, you're young enough to still have some fun."

"I've taken up sailing," Smythe said with a laugh.

"That's not a bad hobby," Quincy replied, laughing as well. He had been an avid sailor. "But you know what's better than a hobby? Work. For people like you and I, the lack of intellectual stimulation is a real killer."

"I'll keep that in mind," Smythe chuckled. "Thanks for meeting me, John – and glad to see you looking so well. I've got a full day today. I have to head over to NSA and convince them to read me in to some intercepts about a possible attack. It's supposed to be easier than this," he lamented, shaking his head.

"I've heard that for over fifty years," Quincy replied. "Every time someone has a bright idea to reform a bureaucracy, all they end up doing is creating a whole new layer of bureaucracy on top of what already exists. Everyone eventually gets captured by the system. Well, maybe not you and Reagan."

Smythe headed back to his car, thinking of all the work he needed to catch up on. Today would be a relatively unproductive day, with what he anticipated would be a drawn-out meeting at NSA followed by the memorial service and funerals for his agents. The weekend would be long, too – he would be flying out to pay his respects to the families of the fallen agents. Yet despite all the things he had to do, Smythe felt as though a weight had been lifted off his shoulders. His meeting with Quincy had wholly erased any lingering doubts he may have had about Reagan's role in the investigation and, not for the first time, he thanked Providence for guiding his snap decision to allow him to participate that first, fateful night.

27

Amanda Watson opened her eyes slowly, hoping that last night hadn't just been an amazing dream. No, it had been very real, she realized, seeing Jack's ruggedly handsome face inches away from hers. He was sleeping on his back and she was draped over him, using his right shoulder as a pillow as she pressed against him, her right arm on his chest and her legs wrapped around his. Unlike the previous mornings, she could feel his warm skin pressed against hers – they had fallen asleep without dressing after they had consummated their passions. She liked it better this way, and couldn't help but smile as she saw Jack stir and start to open his eyes. She had never done anything like this before – it took her weeks of knowing someone before she felt comfortable enough to be intimate with them, and many potential suitors had quickly given up on her. But with Jack everything was different, and everything was just *right*. She had barely known him for a week, but felt like she had known him her entire life.

"Good morning, beautiful," she heard him say and felt her heart melt.

"Good morning, handsome," she said, leaning in to kiss him softly. His lips felt very good against hers.

"I rather like waking up like this," he said, smiling with his eyes as much as with his lips.

"Me too, Jack. Me too." She leaned in for another kiss, longer and more passionate this time, as her right hand caressed his chest and moved slowly lower... "You're up early today," she said with a playful grin.

"What can I say, you always get a rise out of me," he replied sheepishly.

"Always, eh? That sounds very promising." She touched him playfully as she gazed into his eyes. "Well you can't very well walk around like that all day... Whatever am I going to do with you?"

"I'm sure we can think of something," he replied, kissing her again as he slowly ran his fingertips up her arm and down her chest, feeling her shiver as he reached lower.

"I'm sure we can," she repeated softly as Jack rolled her onto her back and kissed her neck. She closed her eyes, feeling her heart flutter. It was late, but work could wait.

Sinclair and Mason had arrived at Sandy Hook just as the sun started to peek above the horizon. They wanted to get a better look at the area the potential terrorists seemed interested in, and it was better to do that as early as possible, when no one else was around. They walked down the side road slowly, studying the terrain carefully in case they needed to approach surreptitiously on foot. The foliage was pretty thick, even for winter, and would afford them excellent cover. The major problem was the snow – with overnight temperatures again in the single digits, the snow had frozen and now crunched when stepped on. They could approach without being seen, but not without being heard.

The two men climbed to the top of the bunker, careful to step only where their footprints would blend in with those of the men who had been there last. Sinclair took out his phone and looked at the photos Reagan had taken the previous day, seeing where the potential terrorists had stood and looking out in the same direction they had. What he saw immediately alarmed him – a KLM 747 was descending on approach to Kennedy Airport.

"How far away would you say that plane is?" Sinclair asked Mason.

"I'd guess about 3 miles, maybe less. Hold on, let me check." Mason removed a sophisticated laser rangefinder from his rucksack and aimed it, locking on to the plane. "I have it as 11,088 feet. That's a little over two miles, straight line."

Sinclair felt a chill; he knew that distance was well within range for a Stinger missile. "Unless these guys happen to be really weird plane buffs, I think we may have found who has our missing Stingers."

"I hope you're wrong, Pete," Mason said, knowing that he wasn't. Both men took out pads and sketched the terrain approaching the bunker.

"I can't see any good approach that's silent," Sinclair said.

"Me either. Let's go check out the beach — it's closer than the main road."

"It is, but it's also directly in their line of sight," Sinclair pointed out. "Let's check out the bunker first."

Mason quickly picked the cheap lock securing the bunker and took out his flashlight, illuminating the graffiti on the windowless room, damp from water that had seeped through a roof vent. Except for some empty beer bottles, probably dropped in from the vent, the 15x15 foot room was empty. Mason closed the door and replaced the lock in the exact position he had found it before the men continued their walk down to their beach.

"Frozen Tide indeed," Mason laughed, pointing at sheets of ice that were starting to form over the ocean, seeming to freeze some of the waves in place.

"We sure picked the right name for this one," Sinclair chuckled. "At least the beach here is wide enough and flat enough to land that Black Hawk."

"What did the driver say?" Mason asked. He had been in the bathroom when Sinclair had called the base.

"He said he's on standby and can be here in just over fifteen minutes. He seemed competent enough."

"Not for the first time, I wish we had more people for this," Mason thought as the pair walked back along the road towards their cars.

"Me too. Depending on what we see today, I'm probably going to call in tonight and make the case for getting more people up here. I'm also going to ask for some wireless cameras to set up. We're sitting blind here – if the bad guys suddenly decide to lob some missiles, we won't have any warning."

"Good point," Mason agreed. "What do we do about the IKEA site, though?"

"Yeah, we really do need more people for this," Sinclair admitted with a frown. "Maybe Jack and Amanda can stake out that place on Monday while we stay here – assuming we don't get more people to help."

"Monday, hell, what's wrong with tomorrow? The bad guys made calls on weekends, too," Mason pointed out.

"Ok then, *tomorrow* we'll ask Jack and Amanda to head over."

"What do you think about Amanda, by the way?" Mason wanted to know.

"She seems very bright but also very green," Sinclair said at once. "She's got good potential, though. Jack sees it too, obviously, or he wouldn't have brought her along."

"I think he sees more than just potential, Pete," Mason laughed.

"You picked up on that, did you?"

"Kinda hard not to." Both men laughed at that. They got back in their cars and drove to the same parking lot they had used the previous day, parking in a different area. Mason joined Sinclair in the Porsche as the wait began.

Anatoly Lavrov had decided against continuing on to Argentina right away. He hadn't gotten much sleep lately and he couldn't afford to make any mistakes in Buenos Aires. Besides, Rio held a certain attraction, he thought, looking at the women walking down the beach in bikinis that were barely there. He had checked into the Caesar Park Ipanema, taking a suite on a high floor overlooking the ocean. He sat at the marble dining room table and took in the view, contemplating what to order for a late lunch. All the televisions in his suite were tuned to CNN, the better to see the effects of his operation. He would eat, watch his success, and then go out to celebrate with any one of the lithe creatures that blossomed in this part of the world. As tired as he was, he was also very excited. He decided that a filet mignon with some Dom Perignon would be most appropriate.

"Jack? We think we may have something on Raul Ernesto Velazquez," Reagan heard Special Agent Monaghan say as he answered the phone, turning off the shower in the process.

"Fast work. What do you have?"

"We think we may have Raul himself – in the El Paso morgue listed just under the name Raul Ernesto. He was brought in Monday last, found in a dumpster behind some bodega. Does that suggest anything to you?" Monaghan asked.

"That's around the same time Latasha Johnson and her sons were killed," Reagan remembered.

"That's right. We don't think it's mere coincidence, either, since the SIM card in Johnson's apartment led you to the guys driving Raul's car."

"Raul wasn't involved with coyotes by any chance, was he?" Reagan asked.

"How'd you know?" Monaghan asked, the surprise clear in his voice. "Yeah, local police have a small file on the guy. They think he was involved with a people smuggling ring. Once over the border, Raul would help them get north. We've got agents heading over to see the files and get the coroner's report."

"I don't like what I'm hearing," Reagan said, squinting his eyes as he spoke. "We've been wondering how our shooters got into the country – well, Batoor Abdali, anyway. We were thinking freighters but now it sounds like maybe they crossed over from Mexico."

"That's a scary thought, Jack. I'll grant you, it's definitely possible."

"Any idea how far along the local police investigation is?" Reagan asked.

"Not really, but it sounds like the locals have had their hands full with the massive waves of illegals coming over the border. I mean, from what I understand, this investigation isn't a top priority. They're stretched pretty thin."

"You know, everywhere I turn I keep hearing that line. It's getting old, pal." Reagan's frustration was showing.

"I hear you, Jack. I'm frustrated too. Sometimes it feels like we're fighting a herd of bulls with just one quadriplegic matador dressed in red. You know how it is – well actually, I guess you don't, not really. You don't know the bullshit we go through, fighting for money and resources and then being told by political hacks which laws to enforce and which to ignore. It never used to be this bad before, either." Monaghan was even more frustrated with the bureaucracy than Reagan; he had to deal with it on a daily basis.

"Sorry, Paul. I didn't mean to touch on a nerve."

"A raw one at that," Monaghan laughed. "But it's ok. It's not your fault. It's the system."

"What can we do to get more information on that human smuggling ring, maybe figure out who they smuggled?"

"Not much, unfortunately," Monaghan shook his head at his speakerphone. "The one down there is being handled by a task force between the Border Patrol people and local cops. Homeland is running it. They're not going to give us shit unless we sit around for days justifying what we want, and then they're going to demand to run this investigation, too."

"Ok then, how about we go around them? Deal with the locals directly," Reagan suggested.

"That would be nice if it were possible," Monaghan said with a laugh. "Even though it's human trafficking, I'm not sure we have a jurisdictional basis, not when Homeland is already running a task force."

"Terrorism still falls within the Bureau's purview, doesn't it?"

"Well yeah, but..."

"And here we have a potential terrorist crossing state lines, don't we?" Reagan pressed.

"I suppose that's something we can build on," Monaghan admitted. "What are you suggesting we do?"

"See if you can develop information about what people this ring was bringing in. If they're just Latinos, then leave that to Homeland. But if it turns out the people might be from the Middle East, we need to know, and we need to pursue that."

"I'll run it by my Director and we can give that a try. Can't hurt anything to try," Monaghan thought.

"When you talk to your Director, can you also put in a request for some people in New Jersey, too?" Reagan asked. "We've got Sandy Hook covered for now, but I don't really like that we're ignoring that IKEA area."

"I think he'll go for that now, Jack. Probably the soonest we can set something up is tomorrow."

"That should be ok. I've got nothing to suggest anything is going to go down today," Reagan said.

"Yeah, we've got nothing, either," Monaghan agreed. Neither man had any idea how wrong they were.

Special Agent Doug Cannon arrived at work unusually late. Annie Jenkins' mother had called him the previous evening to thank him for the kind note he had written. She had wanted to know more about the work her daughter had done with her other family, as Annie had thought of NCIS. The conversation had been surprisingly painful for Cannon, and he had needed a few stiff drinks to fall asleep. Unfortunately, he had forgotten to set his alarm clock and only woke when the sun started to light up his bedroom. His foul mood at waking so late was only worsened when his car wouldn't start, and it took him far too long to find a spare battery to jump-start it. But today was not a day for foul moods, not with a memorial service and two funerals.

Cannon sat at his desk, going over Watson's report from the previous evening. Raul Ernesto Velazquez certainly seemed like a lead worth pursuing, but Cannon lacked the resources to do so himself. He picked up his phone to call Special Agent Monaghan, only to discover that Monaghan had just spoken with Reagan and received his marching orders. That news was enough for Cannon's bad mood to resurface just as his Director stopped by.

"I just called Paul Monaghan at FBI to follow up on something and he told me that he already spoke to Reagan and was working on it. Nice to be kept in the loop," he said sarcastically. Just then Cannon's phone rang, his display showing Reagan's number. "Speak of the devil," Cannon said.

"Be nice," Director Smythe warned with a chuckle. "I'll wait."

Cannon forced himself to be polite as he listened to Reagan's report of his conversation with Monaghan. After hanging up the phone he turned to Smythe and shrugged.

"Feeling better now, Doug?" Smythe said with a hearty laugh.

"Yeah, yeah, yeah," Cannon replied, raising his hands in mock surrender. "You want to hear the developments?"

"Actually, no," Smythe replied. "Keep me in the loop as needed, but I trust you and Reagan to run this. Both of you," he added.

"Just once, Francis, it would be nice if people remembered who Reagan works for – which technically is no one."

"Not these days, anyway," Smythe said, a sly smile forming on his face.

"These days?" Cannon asked, his eyes narrowing.

"There are some things about Jack Reagan you should know," Smythe said, relating the conversation he had a few hours earlier with John Quincy. He noted the surprise in Cannon's eyes, even if his jaw hadn't quite dropped to the floor.

"That's some history, Francis," Cannon said, leaning back in his chair. "No wonder you like him so much."

"You should get used to liking him too, Doug."

Cannon took the hint for what it was. "Planning on adopting him, are you?" he asked with raised eyebrow.

"Something like that. He seems to fit in around here but more than that, he's our kind of people."

"I guess he is," Cannon replied, allowing himself a smile.

Reagan and Watson arrived at the beach just before 10 a.m. and spent a couple of hours driving around, occasionally getting out to walk a little. They used as cover the very real couple they were, walking hand in hand. To even a professional observer, they seemed like a couple playing hooky on a blisteringly cold Friday, laughing and carrying on inbetween very intimate displays of affection. Yet as much as they genuinely enjoyed one another's company, they were also studying the park very carefully.

"It looks like they chose the best position in the park," Amanda said as they finished their circuit and drove towards the parking lot where Sinclair and Mason were positioned.

"Easy car access, a convenient choke point and clear line of sight over the water? Yeah, looks ideal for their purposes," Jack agreed. Both of them had noted how close the planes seemed as they approached Kennedy Airport.

"So what did you see?" Sinclair asked. All four were casually standing behind the Porsche – four friends enjoying a cold Friday at the beach.

"It's a really nice park, especially when it's empty," Reagan replied. "Other than that, our guys seem to have picked the best spot available. Looks hard to get in there on foot undetected."

"Pretty much impossible," Sinclair agreed with a nod of his head. "We were thinking maybe set up a camera somewhere.

We're too far out to get in there quickly if they decide to do something bad, and the road is an effective choke point.

"Not a bad idea," Reagan agreed. "Air support?"

"Pilot seems competent," Sinclair shrugged. "He can be here fifteen minutes after we call. His crew chief has some kind of new laser toy he wants to use to try to track the car. We also requested some additional support on the ground. Jack, something else. We're a little uncomfortable at leaving the IKEA uncovered. Maybe you and Amanda can head up there tomorrow?"

"Already thought of that. I asked the Bureau to do it, but if they don't, we will," he promised. "Anything else?"

"Nope," Sinclair replied. "Now we sit and wait."

"And we just love waiting," Mason chimed in.

Watson smiled. Normally she hated waiting, too. But today, sitting with Jack, it wouldn't be so bad.

"Actually, I just remembered something," Reagan said. "Let me call Director Smythe – he had a meeting at the NSA this morning." Reagan looked through his contact list, finding the right number.

"Director Smythe? Jack Reagan."

"Hello Jack! I was just talking about you, actually."

"Nothing bad, I trust," Reagan said with a chuckle.

"No, not at all. But we should sit and talk about your future when you get back. Still heading back this afternoon?"

"No, I think we'll stay here a few more days, at least until we can get things properly set up," Reagan replied.

"Fine by me, Jack. I trust your judgment. Nice tail, by the way," he chuckled. "Dave Goldberg filled me in last night."

"Not a very successful one," Reagan admitted. "I was wondering if you pried anything out of NSA."

"A little, actually. The short and the long of it is that they picked up on a phone call between a Lebanese arms dealer and a burner cell in northern New Jersey. The subject, in code, was monitoring airplanes. That's all. The burner cell isn't one we're on to, by the way. Does this mean anything to you?"

"Actually it means a great deal, sir. It's something we need to talk about in person, though."

"I told you, Jack, it's Francis. And as I just said a moment ago, I trust your judgment. I imagine you have some sources you can't clue me in to, but I'll look forward to what you have to tell me. Good luck out there, and nice work."

"What's wrong, Jack?" Amanda asked as he slipped his phone back into his shirt pocket. He had turned a little pale, and that worried her.

"The NSA chatter? Phone call between a Lebanese arms dealer and a burner in New Jersey."

"Jesus, Jack," Sinclair said, going a little pale himself. "I'm going to call the office right now. This is probably enough to get the whole fucking team mobilized."

Watson wasn't sure what they were talking about, but kept her counsel, reminding herself that next to these men, she was a rank amateur. Mason opened the trunk of the Porsche and removed a gun bag, placing it on the back seat of the Range Rover. "Loaded and good to go," he said. "Six extra mags, too." Reagan nodded, conceding the logic of it.

"What now, Jack?" Sinclair asked, checking his watch.

"Now you make your call. Amanda and I are going to go get everyone some coffee, and then set up one parking lot over in Area C. Meanwhile let's all give some thought to whether we really need to wait for these guys to do something or whether we want to take them down now. While we're here, let's set up the comms and test them."

"Works for me," Sinclair said, reaching into another bag in the trunk. "A lot's changed since you last used one of these, so pay attention."

28

The last of the coffee had long been finished, and Reagan and Watson passed the time talking. As much as they talked, they never ran out of things to say – something they both agreed was a very good thing. As the clock ticked slowly past 1 p.m., they talked about favorite vacation destinations; they both loved the beach, the fewer people and more isolated the better. They laughed about how badly they needed to get away to a nice, quiet beach when all of this was over. What they left unsaid, but both understood, was that they needed to get away together.

"Heads up, here they come," Sinclair said.

"Got 'em," Mason replied from his Mustang a few yards over. "Something's different – can't tell what, though."

"I don't know, it looks... rear axle. The car's riding lower," Sinclair realized.

"I see it too," Mason said a second later. "There's a brown Ford Taurus right behind them. Might be with them."

"Coming your way right around now, Jack," Sinclair estimated.

"Got 'em here," Reagan replied. "Explorer has 3 people, Taurus has only one I can see."

"Three and one," Watson confirmed.

"How do you want to play it, Jack?" Sinclair asked.

"We'll give it fifteen minutes and then Amanda and I are going to take a stroll down there."

"Copy that. Watch your back, Jack," Sinclair said.

Reagan got out of the car and took his jacket off, thinking it a little too constricting to drive in or, if necessary, shoot with. He put on a heavy wool sweater and started taking his spare magazines out of the coat. "Check your weapon," he told Amanda. He had already done so when she went into the McDonald's to

285

get the coffee earlier. Next, he dumped out the contents of his messenger bag, putting his extra pistol magazines in the outer pocket. Then he unzipped the gun case and transferred all the spare magazines for the MP5 into the center pocket of his bag. Finally he checked the weapon, making sure it was within easy reach on the back seat, before placing his messenger bag next to it. He still had two magazines for his pistol in his left front pocket, and felt the .45 dig into his back when he climbed back behind the wheel.

Watson checked her weapon and replaced it in her purse, which she left open and slung across her shoulder and onto her lap. She had moved her backup weapon to the car door, also within easy reach. Her heart was beginning to race, and she looked over to Jack, wondering how he managed to stay so calm and collected. "Jack..." she started to say, but she stopped herself. She felt excited and worried at the same time, and didn't really know how to say that, let alone whether to admit it.

"It's ok," he said with his usual warm smile, reaching over to squeeze her hand. "We're just going to take a little drive to the end of that road and look out on the beach. Maybe we'll get out to stretch our legs, but probably we won't. Just a quiet Friday afternoon at the beach, I promise. Now, let's figure out where we want to go when we finally bag these guys. How about Miami Beach?"

"Way too many people," she replied with a smile of her own, instantly at ease. "I've always avoided going for just that reason. Besides, I don't speak Spanish. How about Hawaii? It's a long flight but hopefully that discourages mass tourism."

"True, and it's always beautiful in Hawaii. Not Oahu, though. It's too touristy and neither one of us speaks Japanese."

"There's always the big island – definitely fewer people," Amanda said with a laugh.

"Maui is a good compromise," Jack suggested.

"How about the Caribbean? Much closer but probably a lot of tourists."

"Not necessarily. Actually, my favorite place is in Jamaica. Same place I recommended to Nick and Brenda for their honeymoon, actually," Jack said.

"Ok then, that's settled. We're going to Jamaica," Amanda declared with a smile warm enough to melt the snow.

"Jamaica it is!" Jack agreed, giving her hand another squeeze. "Now let's go see what our friends are up to," he said, putting the car in gear. "Seatbelt off, please," he added, watching as Amanda unbuckled. He drove slowly, turning right onto the dead-end road.

"We're heading in," he spoke into his mic. "The Taurus is parked about a hundred and fifty feet up the road – probably with our targets. Confirm."

"Roger Jack, Taurus is one-fifty feet up, probably with targets," Reagan heard in his earpiece.

"Going off comms," he said, tucking his earpiece into his sweater as Watson did the same. He drove slowly, as if taking in the sights. The driver of the Taurus was still sitting behind the wheel, but about 250 feet further up the road, the trunk of the Explorer was open and all three men were standing by it.

"Shit," he said softly. Watson saw the open trunk as well and wondered what they were doing. Reagan looked into the rearview mirror as he slowly drove up the road. He saw the driver of the Taurus open his door and quickly walk to the middle of the road when they were about fifty feet away. He was fumbling with something, lifting it...

"Gun!" Reagan shouted, slamming on the brakes. "Get down," he ordered just as the driver of the Taurus fired, the burst shattering the rear window of their Range Rover. Reagan quickly glanced up; the three men by the Explorer had been alerted by the gunfire but hadn't started to move yet. He only had seconds in which to act, Reagan realized. He quickly put the car in park and opened his door, stepping out, drawing his weapon and taking the safety off in one swift, well-practiced move. He moved quickly towards the back of the Range Rover, pistol up and pointing in his direction of travel.

Reagan crouched by the rear tire as more rounds hit the Range Rover. He thought he heard Watson call his name but he couldn't focus on that right now. A second later, the fire seemed to shift a little towards the right side of his car, so Reagan took two steps forward, aiming for the man standing in the middle of the street about sixty feet away. He fired two rounds at the man's head and saw him fall straight down, his weapon clattering to the ground a few feet away from his body. For good measure, Reagan fired two more rounds aimed at the center mass of the body lying in the street before turning his attention to the front of the car.

Watson, he saw, had crawled across the center console and over the driver's seat, dropping to the ground and sheltering behind the front left wheel. "Jesus, Jack," she yelled as a fresh burst of fire hit the front of the car from the direction of the Explorer up the road. "Stay down," he yelled back, pulling his earwig out of his sweater and replacing it in his ear. "Taking fire," he said loudly. "One tango down at the Taurus, three active shooters with Kalashnikovs. Get your asses up here and call in that air support."

"On our way, sit tight," Sinclair said as Mason ran to the Porsche, getting in the back seat. Sinclair sped off as Mason placed one of the MP7s on the front seat before opening his window and readying his own MP7, braced between the seats.

Reagan maneuvered behind the Range Rover, careful to keep his head down. He peeked around the side quickly and saw that one of the shooters had climbed to the top of the bunker. Another one was making his way up as well, while the third lay prone in the street. He fired off his remaining shots towards the shooter in the street, but the distance was too great. He quickly ejected his empty clip and reloaded, replacing his pistol in his holster as he moved back to the left side of the car. "Cover fire," he told Amanda, reaching into the back seat to sling his messenger bag across his shoulders before retrieving the MP5, all as Watson stood quickly and fired a dozen rounds in the direction of the shooters. "Switch positions," he commanded, moving forward as Watson moved to the rear of the car.

"Two shooters on top of the bunker, one in the street," Reagan spoke into his mic as Sinclair and Mason arrived, shielding the Porsche behind Reagan's car.

"Roger that," Sinclair said. "On the count of three, give us suppressive fire on the guy in the street. We'll work our way up on the right side. When I call hold, switch fire to the bunker and we'll take the guy in the street."

"Copy. On your three count," Reagan replied, flipping the safety off on his weapon and calculating the approximate position of his target.

Sinclair and Mason maneuvered behind the Range Rover, weapons up and ready to move. "One...two...three!"

Reagan stood and fired in short bursts as Sinclair and Mason crossed to the edge of the road, sheltered from view of the bunker, and started forward.

"Bunker shooters repositioning," Reagan called out when he saw them start to come back down off the bunker. "Prone shooter moving towards bunker," he called out a second later.

Sinclair and Mason dropped to the ground for cover as Reagan took careful aim at the formerly prone shooter, who had just fired his weapon at the lock on the bunker door. His shot just missed, but the shooter's didn't, and he yanked the door open and flung himself into the bunker. "One went in the bunker," Reagan called out in surprise. It seemed the absolutely worst tactical move to make. A few seconds later, the other two shooters ran into the bunker as well. "All three shooters inside the bunker." Reagan reported as he ejected his empty clip and reloaded.

"What the hell!" Sinclair and Mason said as one. They, too, thought the terrorists had maneuvered idiotically. "Jack, switch off with us. Head up the right side of the road – we'll take the left."

Reagan did as told, moving to the right, his weapon continuously aimed at the bunker door as he walked slowly towards it. Watson, he saw, was following about thirty feet behind him, her pistol aimed down at the ground. Sinclair and Mason were equally spread out, their weapons never leaving their target.

"Door closing," Mason reported. "What the hell are they up to?"

"I don't know, but let's move in now," Sinclair said, racing up the road. He and Mason positioned themselves to the left of the door, leaving Reagan to cover behind the Explorer, almost directly in front of the door. He took a quick look in the back. "We just found some of your Stingers," he reported. "Got any flash-bangs?"

"Yeah," Sinclair replied, edging his way to the door and pulling it gently with his left hand from the cover of the thick concrete walls. He shook his head and made his way back a few feet. "Door's barricaded somehow. We don't have charges, and if I try to force it open, I'm dead."

"Roof vent?" Reagan asked, seeing the shape on the roof. Sinclair looked at Mason, and both of them nodded in unison.

"Amanda, come to us, please," Sinclair said, explaining to her what to do with the flash-bangs. She made her way carefully behind the bunker and managed to reach the top without slipping on the ice. "In position," she reported.

"Ok, on three, drop them both in like I told you, and we're going to breach. Jack, hold your position."

"Roger that," Reagan confirmed, followed immediately by Watson.

"Here goes nothing," Sinclair said, making the sign of the cross as he and Mason edged closer to the door. "One...two..." He repositioned quickly directly in front of the door. "Three!" Watson pulled the pins and dropped the flash-bangs through the vent. A second later they detonated as Sinclair yanked open the door, allowing Mason to rush in first. He followed quickly, weapon up and ready to fire. Reagan came in shortly after Sinclair, reaching in his bag and retrieving a flashlight.

All three terrorists were on the ground, writhing in pain. None of them had held on to their weapons. "Jack, secure their weapons," Mason said. Reagan collected three Kalashnikovs and one pistol, taking them quickly outside and placing them in the back of the Explorer while Sinclair and Mason kept their weapons trained on the men. When he returned, Mason handed his MP7 off to Reagan and drew his sidearm, expertly searching each terrorist and securing his wrists with zip ties as Reagan and Sinclair covered. "All clear," he announced a minute later. Neither Sinclair nor Reagan relaxed their aim any, though their fingers moved to the trigger guards.

"What now, Jack?" Sinclair asked.

"How far out is that helo?" Reagan asked. He watched Sinclair switch to his command radio and ask.

"Five minutes or so," Sinclair reported. "What are you thinking?"

"Have him land on the beach. Jim, see if you can find the keys to that Explorer and drive it down to the beach. When the chopper lands, have the crew chief help you get those missiles onboard. Anything else you find that's of use. Amanda, go up the road and secure whatever weapons that shooter had. Search his car and grab any papers and electronics devices. Bring everything back here. Pete and I will stay here and cover these fuckers."

"Works for me," Sinclair said, nodding his assent. "Get to it."

Mason found the keys in the ignition and chuckled as he drove onto the beach. He reached into a pouch on his tactical jacket and took out some flares, marking a landing zone for the Black Hawk. He searched the car, finding only an EZ-Pass, which he pulled off the window and pocketed. Next he checked the trunk, surprised to find not just two launchers and eight missiles, but an RPG as well. The helicopter flared and landed just as he finished his search of the vehicle, and Mason jogged on over to tell the crew chief what needed to be done before heading back to the bunker.

Watson approached the body laying in the street carefully, her weapon drawn and aimed. She needn't have bothered, she realized as she got closer. She could see the entrance holes from two rounds, neatly drilled just above the right eye, separated by less than an inch. Two more rounds, also separated by around an inch, perforated the lung on the left side of the body. She searched his pockets, finding a wallet and cellphone. Then she switched her attention to the Taurus, where she found a bag full of extra magazines for the Kalashnikov. She put the wallet and phone in the bag and collected the bag and assault rifle before heading back to the bunker, arriving at the same time as Mason.

"Wallet, phone and a lot of rounds for his rifle," Watson reported as she walked into the bunker, holding up the bag.

"Thanks," Reagan replied. "Now collect these things and put them in the bag, too," he said, pointing at the assorted wallets and phones on the ground. "Jim, get the crew chief to help you get that body on the chopper too, then get all your gear onboard as well."

"It's a crime scene, Jack," Watson immediately objected. She noticed that Mason shrugged off her statement and headed back towards the chopper. "The missiles and weapons I understand, but we can't just move the body."

"We have bigger problems here, Amanda. Please trust me."

"You know I do, Jack. I'm sorry," she replied, reproaching herself.

"Nothing to be sorry for," Reagan said, smiling at her. "Whenever you have a thought or an idea, just tell me. He turned his attention to the terrorists, studying their faces in the glow of his flashlight. A minute later, Mason returned, reporting that the crew chief was taking care of the body and their gear. He hadn't offered to help, expecting that Reagan had something else in mind.

"Ok guys," Reagan said, handing Mason's weapon back to him. "Let's get these jokers outside, lined up against the wall, please. Reagan and Watson went out first, covering as Sinclair and Mason brought out their prisoners, backing them up against the bunker wall. None of the terrorists spoke, but all three were trading glances.

"Jack, maybe we should get hoods on them," Sinclair suggested.

"Not yet," Reagan replied, walking up to his friend and whispering in his ear. "I want to find one to talk to. Keep your eyes open for the weak link and back my play." He handed off his MP5 when he saw Sinclair nod, and proceeded to walk closer to the terrorists. He stopped suddenly and turned to Watson. "Amanda, maybe you should head over to the helicopter. I don't know that you should see this."

"I trust you, Jack, but you have to trust me too. No matter what happens," she said.

Reagan nodded and turned back to the terrorists. "Which one of you little shits wants to talk to me?" he asked.

"Fuck you," the one on the left said. "Allahu Akbar!" All three of them started chanting "Allahu Akbar" right up to the moment Reagan walked up to the one on the left and hit him hard in the throat with the butt of his pistol. As the man started to drop to his knees in pain, Reagan brought up his right knee, striking him hard in the face, knocking him unconscious. Reagan knelt down by the unconscious man and looked up at his two comrades, now stunned into silence.

"Would you like to see what I do to terrorists?" he asked, taking hold of the unconscious man's legs and dragging him around thirty feet down the road towards the beach, moving his body to the snow on the side, hoping this was far enough away. "This is what I do to terrorists," he yelled, kneeling down above the body and placing his pistol next to the man's head before pulling the trigger. Reagan walked back to the bunker slowly, his eyes never fully leaving the remaining terrorists' faces. He did, however, glance quickly at Watson, seeing her turn paler than the whitest snow, her mouth open in shock. He couldn't worry about that now, but deeply regretted that she had to see that.

As he got closer, he became more certain that he found someone to talk to. While the terrorist now on the left had regained his composure and glared at Reagan, the one on the right seemed to be in shock. His eyes were wide with fear and he trembled a little. "Right?" he asked Sinclair as he passed him.

"Right," Sinclair confirmed.

"Right," Reagan repeated as he approached the two remaining terrorists. "Which one of you do I talk to and which one do I kill?" he asked, alternating his aim between the two. "Hmm... I think I'll talk to... you," he said, aiming at the one on the left. "Jim, bag this one and get him on the chopper. Then deal with the body over there." He backed off and waited for Mason to head off with his prisoner before approaching the remaining terrorist.

"Now what to do with you?" he asked, resting his chin theatrically on his left fist as he waved his pistol around for effect. "What to do, what to do... Oh, I know!" Reagan holstered his pistol and reached into his bag, pulling out his folding combat knife. He flipped the knife open right under the terrified eyes of his prisoner, resting the tip of the blade against his neck.

"Where do I start?" he asked, slowly moving the knife down to the man's belt, slipping it behind and then slicing through the belt. He then moved the knife to the single button on the jeans, slicing it off as well. "I assume you must be pretty dirty down there," Reagan said with a vicious smile, reaching into his bag with his left hand and pulling out a latex glove. This he put on his left hand as dramatically as he could, all the while smiling at his prisoner.

"There, that's better," Reagan said, reaching into the man's pants with his gloved hand and taking a firm grip of his genitals. Next he lowered his knife into the pants as well, resting the blade on the terrorist's genitals as he pulled with his left hand. The man's eyes went wide with terror and he started to cry.

"No, please no," the man said, gasping for air between tears.

"If you want me to stop, all you have to do is talk to me," Reagan said, his voice even and reasonable. "Or else I could just cut a little." He emphasized his point by pressing the blade more firmly against the genitals.

"No, I'll talk! I'll talk!" the man cried.

"Ok then," Reagan said, releasing his grip on the genitals and removing his hands from the man's pants. "Let's talk. My name is Jack. What's yours?"

"Adil," the man replied, obviously relieved to be out of immediate peril and trying to regain his composure.

"Ok, Adil," Reagan said with a smile. "Tell me about your plan – and your targets."

"Planes," Adil said at once. "As many as we could shoot down. Maybe eight."

"When?" Reagan asked, observing that Adil spoke excellent English.

"Two thirty. Then we fight off police," he replied. "I was not supposed to be here," he added defensively.

"There's more," Reagan said, gesturing with his knife as a reminder to Adil.

"Newark. IKEA parking lot. Same time. Missiles."

"How many men?" Reagan asked.

"Three, maybe four," Adil replied, still unable to breathe properly.

"What else?" Reagan demanded, his peripheral vision noting that Mason had rejoined them.

"Washington, D.C."

"Airport?"

"No. Congress, buildings around Congress, offices."

"Congressional office buildings?" Reagan asked, and then saw Adil nod. Adil was a broken man, perfectly willing to cooperate now. He was so scared, however, that he could barely speak.

"How? When?" Reagan demanded.

"I don't know! At three, I think. Mortars. Many mortars, from park, and behind train station, and a peninsula with golf course."

"How many men?"

"I don't know."

"How many men, damn it!" Reagan pressed.

"Twenty. Maybe thirty, spotters nearby," Adil whimpered.

"Spotters where?"

"I don't know," Adil said as he started to cry again.

"Thank you, Adil. If you continue to cooperate, I will continue to let you live." Reagan turned to Mason. "Get him on the chopper right the fuck now and tell the pilot to get ready to take off."

"Jack, did I just hear what I think I heard?" Sinclair asked incredulously.

"Kinda shocks the conscience, doesn't it," Reagan said grimly. "Call your people. I'll get the word out, too." He walked over towards Amanda, who was herself starting to regain her composure, relieved that Jack hadn't killed anyone else. "Let's go, Amanda – on the chopper. This isn't over yet."

"What do you mean?" she asked, stopping in her tracks. She hadn't been close enough to hear what Adil had said.

"Come with me and listen in on my call," Jack said gently, taking her by the hand as he scrolled through his phone for the right number.

29

"Hi Jack," Reagan heard Director Goldberg say on the other end of the phone. "I've got my senior staff here for a meeting. Can I call you back a little..."

"Shut up and listen," Reagan interrupted. "This is urgent – CRITIC stuff. Put me on speakerphone."

"Ok, Jack, we're listening."

"I'm at Sandy Hook in New Jersey," Reagan explained, speaking rapidly. "We just had a firefight with four hostiles. One tango down, three in custody, zero friendly casualties. They had eight Stinger missiles and two launchers, armed with Kalashnikovs and an RPG. Their targets were flights into Kennedy Airport, with the attack to commence at 1430 hours."

"Holy shit! Is this for real?" someone said before being quickly silenced.

"I interrogated one of the terrorists. We have two more attacks imminent, at 1430 hours and 1500 hours. First target are flights at Newark Airport using Stingers from the IKEA parking lot at 1430 hours. Three, possibly four hostiles. Second target is Capitol Hill, most likely the congressional offices, using mortars at 1500 hours. Twenty, possibly thirty hostiles, firing from behind Union Station, from an unknown park, and from a peninsula with a golf course that I believe to be that land next to the Jefferson Memorial. They're using spotters, locations unknown. That's all I have for now."

"Jesus Christ, Jack, it's 1410 right now!" Director Goldberg exclaimed.

"Yes, sir. I advise you shut down air traffic at Newark immediately and suspend all flight operations. I also recommend that you mobilize in Washington. It's probably safer to get Congress and staff into the tunnels instead of evacuating by street. Maybe shut down the cell towers, too – our guys had cellphones but no radios"

"We'll get right on it," Goldberg promised. "Anything else? Do you need any help, Jack?"

"No, sir. We've secured the weapons and terrorists and are about to head to the IKEA site by Black Hawk to see what we can do. Please advise Director Smythe of the situation at your earliest convenience. I'll call you back with any developments," Reagan said, ending the call as they reached the helicopter. The rotor started to turn as they climbed aboard, and Reagan helped Watson buckle up before strapping in himself. She looked particularly pale, obviously still trying to process what she had just seen and heard.

More than anything, Amanda was stunned that Jack had shot – no, executed – an unarmed prisoner in restraints. She knew him well, and intimately, and would never have thought him capable of anything like that. It bothered her to the point that she couldn't get it out of her mind. The way in which Jack had interrogated the last terrorist didn't bother her at all. He had merely suggested torture, not actually carried it out. But if he was capable of cold-blooded murder, she wondered what else he might capable of.

She tried to shake that thought, looking up finally to see the inside of the helicopter. She had never been in one before. She was strapped in next to Jack on jump seats behind the pilot, with Sinclair and Mason strapped in across from them, behind the co-pilot. Or was it the other way around, she wondered, realizing that she couldn't tell which one was the pilot. Amanda looked to the rear of the cabin and saw the crew chief watching over the three prisoners as he repositioned several bags containing ropes. *Three* prisoners, she realized, her jaw dropping in shock as she saw that the terrorist Jack shot wasn't shot at all. He merely looked uncomfortable, secured to the seat with a gag in his mouth and hood over his head.

Amanda squeezed Jack's hand and leaned closer to be heard over the sound of the engines. "He's alive!" she exclaimed.

"Of course he's alive, Amanda. I'm not a psychopath, you know!" he replied with a chuckle. He felt her squeeze his arm tighter as she rested her head on his shoulder.

"I'm sorry, Jack," she said, taking a deep breath. "I know it's no excuse, but I've never been in a situation like this before and I overreacted."

"You have nothing to apologize for," he replied as the Black Hawk lifted off, turning his head to kiss her cheek. He caught sight of Sinclair waving to him, gesturing for him to put his headphones on.

"Gentlemen, my name is Major Cahill. I'll be your pilot this afternoon. Where exactly are we going, and what's the plan?"

"Major, I'm Peter Sinclair. We spoke earlier. Across from me is Jack Reagan. This is his op, so it's his plan." Sinclair grinned, knowing full well what his friend was going to say next.

"Major, we have an imminent terrorist attack against aviation at Newark Airport, most likely using Stingers. We expect three, possibly four hostiles, probably armed with Kalashnikovs and RPGs as well. You're going to fly us over to the IKEA that's to east of the airport, just next to the New Jersey Turnpike, and then we're going to figure out how you can insert us so my friends and I can go have a chat with the terrorists. Fast as you can, please."

"Just a chat, huh?" Cahill chuckled, trading a glance with his copilot. They had driven around enough spec-ops guys over the years to know exactly what they meant by 'chat.' The thought of Stingers, on the other hand, was nothing to laugh about. They could just as easily be used against his Black Hawk as a commercial jet. The only good news was that his Sikorsky was designed with a HIRSS – a hover IR suppression system that cooled engine exhaust gasses when hovering and in forward flight. That would make it harder, but not impossible, for a missile to get a lock. "I've flown over the area some. Unless the parking lot is empty, there's no good place to set down close. We do, however, have lines for your rappelling pleasure."

Reagan felt the helicopter pick up speed rapidly, its nose edging down slightly in a race against time. He watched as Sinclair and Mason checked their weapons and gear, redistributing their loads. The crew chief had finished setting up the lines and was preparing the harnesses, which he passed out to the three men. Reagan slipped out of his belt and managed to remember how the harness went on just as the pilot called "five minutes."

"Major, can you take us in from east-southeast, low over the warehouses?" Reagan asked, remembering the layout of the IKEA with respect to the airport and other buildings. He knew that store well, having shopped there on many occasions. It was a local institution – the flat-packed and small-scale furniture was the right size for getting through the narrow stairs and hallways of New York City apartments. Reagan had bought his favorite leather chair from that very store over two decades earlier, back when IKEA still had some higher-quality pieces. The store's parking lot, he knew, bordered the New Jersey Turnpike, to the west of which was Newark Airport. Coming in from the east-southeast would provide a modicum of cover, since the bad guys were probably going to be looking in the wrong direction to see their approach.

"Will do," Major Cahill replied, altering his course a little. He glanced back and saw the three men getting into their harnesses and readying their gear. He had never worked with these particular soldiers – sailors, he corrected himself – before, but they had the same cool and collected demeanor as the Delta soldiers he had ferried around Iraq years earlier. They clearly knew their job, and trusted Cahill to do his. He would do his best not to let them down; the imminent threat to civilian life posed by the terrorists had a palpably greater urgency than any of the other missions Cahill had flown. "Airport's in sight now," he said, watching an Airbus with Air France markings lumbering down on final approach.

Sinclair and Reagan looked forward and saw the Air France touch down and perform its roll-out. "Damn it, they haven't suspended flight ops yet," Sinclair said over his headset.

"Major, how about after you drop us off you go hover over that runway?" Reagan suggested.

"Sorry, sir, I can't do that," Cahill said at once. "That's too dangerous. It will cause..."

"It will cause planes to divert," Reagan interrupted. "It will shut down the airspace and save lives."

"What the hell, I can try," Cahill shrugged. It was no less crazy than inserting a special forces platform in a store parking lot in suburbia.

Sinclair and Reagan continued looking at the airport, watching a Boeing 777 with United markings speed down the runway and lift off. Both men would later swear that seconds later, they saw an object streak across the sky towards the plane, exploding just behind the port engine. Their co-pilot saw it too, calling out "Holy shit!" in his headset.

Takeoff had been perfectly routine for Captain Joseph Belmont, in command of United flight 318 from Newark to San Francisco. His co-pilot had called V1, followed shortly thereafter by Vr and V2, at which point Belmont had pulled back on his control stick, lifting the Boeing 777 off the ground at precisely the right angle for his climb-out. The controls were responding normally, and Belmont double-checked the flap settings as the plane rose into the sky. Seconds later, however, the plane shuddered violently and alarms started to blare, indicating they had lost all power in the port engine. Belmont immediately started to level the plane and adjust power to the starboard engine while his co-pilot verified that the automatic extinguishers had functioned properly and suppressed any fire.

"Port engine is out, fire is out," the co-pilot informed Belmont before getting on the radio to inform the tower of their situation.

"Check," Belmont replied. "Tell the tower we'll go around and land." In those few seconds the plane had seemed to be responding properly, albeit very sluggishly. The starboard engine had more than enough power to get them back down safely, and Belmont wasn't particularly alarmed. He had practiced this situation many times on the simulator. But two seconds later, he felt another, much more powerful vibration and loud noise as the port wing sheared off by the engine. The plane was no longer responding to his commands, and Belmont barely had time to utter "Oh my God" before the plane started to tip over towards starboard before falling to the ground. The 187 passengers and 8 crew never really stood a chance.

Everyone on the Black Hawk had their eyes on the United 777. After the explosion the plane had started to level out, but it also slowed down and, for a moment, it appeared to be suspended motionless in mid-air. A second later, they watched in horror as the port wing seemed to just tear off the plane. The plane then tilted slowly to starboard, and an instant after that plummeted rapidly towards the ground. The fireball on impact was massive, easily seen from miles away. No one on the helicopter spoke; the emotions they felt were simply not capable of being reduced to words. The men turned their attention to the ground, searching for targets – the IKEA was in sight now. "Southwest corner of the parking lot," Sinclair said, having spotted the terrorists first.

The parking lot was fairly large, easily capable of holding several hundred cars but at the moment containing merely a hundred or so, all parked close to the building. At the far end of the lot, near a tall chain-link fence separating it from the highway, a white cargo van was parked at a right angle to a burgundy minivan, effectively screening two men from the rest of the lot and from the street approaching the entrance to the south of the IKEA some three hundred feet away. The two men behind the vehicles, it was instantly clear, had fired the missile and were readying another one.

About three-quarters of the way between the vehicles and the entrance, two more men were approaching two State Police cruisers that had blocked the entrance. From the helicopter, it was readily apparent that the trooper from the lead car and the two troopers from the second car hadn't had time to fully assess the situation before getting out of their cars; all three bodies were visible on the ground, feet away from their open doors. In the distance, they could see the lights of other police vehicles approaching from both directions on the Turnpike, but it would be minutes before they arrived.

"Taking fire," Major Cahill reported calmly, having seen muzzle flashes oriented in his direction. "Where do you want to insert?" he asked. The parking lot *was* large enough, but the only spot to set down was between the terrorists' vehicles and the store exit to the north, and there was only one solitary car parked in that area – not enough for cover.

"North side of the building," Sinclair said at once, feeling the helicopter sideslip into position and lower to rooftop level before hovering. "Call us in to the locals," he added. "Let them know we're here."

"Will do," the co-pilot replied, searching for the right frequency on his radio as the crew chief kicked the rope bags out the doors, two on the starboard side and one to port.

"Hook up," Sinclair ordered, pointing Jack to the port line. The crew chief handed Reagan a helmet and verified that that the rope was properly threaded through his descender, checking its link to the carabiner as well before giving him the thumbs up. All three men checked the safety on their weapons and stood in potion.

Only then did Watson realize that Jack was no longer sitting next to her. She had been totally transfixed by the fireball still rising into the sky, unable to look at anything else. When she finally overcame her shock and turned around, she saw Jack move to the door, hooked into the rope. She was surprised; for some reason, it hadn't occurred to her that he would be rappelling down with Sinclair and Mason. She wanted to tell him not to go – she desperately wanted him to stay with her in the relative safety of the helicopter. More than anything, she didn't want to lose him. But she knew he had to go, so she smiled bravely at him and mouthed "good luck."

Jack turned to Amanda and saw her smiling at him, wondering how she was so calm and collected when he was so anxious and even a little afraid. He smiled bravely at her and mouthed "see you soon," just as Sinclair ordered them to stand to over their comms. Reagan started to lean backwards out the door, kicking off when Sinclair yelled "Tally-ho!"

Reagan reached the ground quickly but softly, rapidly unhooking his descender and moving off towards the wall of the warehouse, raising his weapon and taking off the safety. When he reached the wall, he crouched down, verifying that his fire selector switch was set to the 3-round burst mode. He was immediately joined by Sinclair and Mason, who lined up in front of him and started off around the building, their weapons raised and ready to fire.

As they rounded the building into the far end of the parking lot, Reagan caught sight of their ride move over to the airport, hovering low over the runway. They jogged along the wall of the building in a crouch, sheltered from view by the cars parked alongside. Around three hundred feet from the terrorists, they stopped; the cars thinned out farther down and their risk of being spotted would be much greater. The terrorists standing near the police cars had seen and shot at the Black Hawk, but didn't seem to realize that they were no longer alone in the parking lot; the building had effectively shielded their insertion from view.

Sinclair pointed to a handful of cars parked roughly halfway between them and the terrorists, the last cars that could serve as cover before open ground. "Let's work our way there," he said. "Jim and I will leapfrog over, and Jack, you follow. Jim, get to the front of the Mercedes at the far end parked diagonally and I'll join you at the rear. You take whichever target is on the left and I'll get the one on the right. Jack, set up behind that Saab," he said, pointing. "Cover the bad guys behind the minivan."

"How do we deal with the two behind the minivan?" Reagan asked, looking in that direction. There was no good way to approach them from cover, and they had a clear field of fire over the entire parking lot.

"I'm open to suggestions," Sinclair admitted.

"Use the chopper?" Mason suggested.

"I'm not too fond of that idea," Reagan said at once. He understood exactly what his friend meant – and worried about Amanda. "Why not just wait for the cavalry? There's nothing for them to fire at," he said, pointing to the sky miraculously devoid of planes. "If they try to run, they'll just be easier targets and we can take them then. I mean, why rush things?"

"Fair point, Jack. We'll try it your way," Sinclair said. "But...I'm going to have our pilot position to the south, at least to keep the bad guys looking that way. If I feel like they're getting squirrely for any reason, I'll have the pilot line up a touch-and-go as a distraction and we'll rush their position. Agreed?"

"Makes sense," Reagan said as Mason nodded agreement. Sinclair called Cahill over the command net and told him the plan.

"Good to go," Sinclair reported. "Jim, lead us off. Nice and careful."

It took the three a few minutes to cover the distance; the terrorists by the police cars were scanning their surroundings continually. Reagan wondered what had happened to the police cars he had seen – none had yet arrived. Sinclair and Mason reached the Mercedes and lay prone on the ground at either end, sheltered by the tires as they took careful aim at their targets. Reagan knelt by the rear of the Saab, bracing slightly against the rear quarterpanel as he covered the van and minivan.

"Got him, Jim?" Sinclair asked.

"On target," Mason replied, his aim never leaving his target's head.

"Ok then, on the count of one we'll take them. Three...two...one." Both men fired simultaneously in burst mode, and the two terrorists fell to the ground, each with three perfectly aimed rounds in their foreheads. The minimal noise from their suppressed weapons didn't carry far enough to be heard.

"Two tangos down," Sinclair reported over their comms as well as over the command net. "Have the cops start in," he told Major Cahill.

Less than a minute later, Reagan saw one of the remaining terrorists peek out from behind the minivan and duck down quickly, probably having seen that his compatriots were no longer among the living. A few seconds later he peeked out again before dropping back down. "Heads up, guys," Reagan said. "One of them just peeked out from behind the right side of the minivan. They know they're alone now."

"Bad angle for us, Jack," Sinclair replied. "Can you get a shot?"

"Yeah," Reagan replied, aiming where he had last seen the head slightly less than two hundred feet away.

" Ok. If he sticks his head up again, take him."

"Roger that," Reagan said, steadying his aim and controlling his breathing. Not a moment later, the head popped up again and Reagan gently squeezed the trigger. He had forgotten just how quiet the integrated suppressor made his weapon; as he watched the body fall to the ground, he could just about swear he heard a thud. "Tango down, one shooter left."

"Nice shooting, Jack!" Sinclair exclaimed. "Now how about we...the fuck?" He saw he side door of the minivan slide open – the last terrorist was crouched inside with... "RPG!"

Sinclair screamed, throwing himself to the ground and covering his head as the car ten feet away from him exploded.

Reagan had seen the door open and the terrorist fire; he had been too slow to get down and the blast wave from the explosion knocked him on his ass away from the shelter of the car he had been crouched behind. He quickly scrambled back to cover and called out to Sinclair and Mason over the radio. He tried again but got no response. Reagan made his way towards the front of the Saab to get a better look, but couldn't see anything through the thick black smoke of the burning wreckage. "Pete, Jim, you guys ok?" he called out loudly.

"No, Jack," Sinclair yelled back. "Hold position, cover the cars and if that fucker shows his head, blow it off."

Reagan wondered what was wrong, but now was not the time to ask. He moved back to the rear of the Saab and lay prone on the ground, taking aim at the still-open door of the minivan. "Come on, asshole," he said softly. "Stick out your head."

Sinclair's radio had somehow been damaged in the blast, though the command radio still seemed to work. Aside from a cut on the back of his left hand, he was unhurt. But Mason was unconscious. He had been crouching next to the Mercedes when the blast propelled him backwards. It looked like he had hit the back of his head against the car's side mirror hard enough to dislodge the mirror. Sinclair quickly looked him over and found no penetrating injuries. His breathing, pulse and heart rate seemed to be fairly normal, all things considered. Sinclair made sure his friend was safely behind cover before heading off to find a better vantage point.

All of a sudden, the white cargo van came to life, lurching forward an instant later with a screech of its tires. The last remaining terrorist had decided to make a run for it – that or use his van as a weapon. Reagan immediately fired multiple bursts into the engine compartment, not sure where, exactly, the engine block was located. He saw the van sputter and slow, its engine no longer working properly, and quickly reached into his bag for a fresh magazine. Sinclair, having seen Jack shoot into the engine, focused instead on the driver's seat, riddling it with bullets as the van crawled to a sputtering stop, smoke billowing from the hood.

"Where's Jim?" Reagan called out.

"By the cars, unconscious but ok," Sinclair yelled back. "See any movement?"

"No. You?"

"Me either. Cover me from there, I'm going in for a closer look." It was somewhat of a gamble, but Sinclair decided to take the chance, walking forward slowly with his weapon raised. As he got closer, he could see blood stains on the driver's seat. He cautiously approached the window and looked in, seeing a bloody body crumpled in the front passenger footwell. Sinclair couldn't tell for certain whether he was dead, so he fired a burst into his the man's head, resolving any doubt.

"Jack, come and cover me from here," Sinclair said, pointing at where he wanted his friend. "I'm going to check the back." He waited as Reagan moved up carefully, and then headed around to the back of the van. The door was open and there was no one inside. "We're clear. Four tangos down," he said, finally lowering his weapon.

"Where's Jim?" Reagan asked again.

"Over there," Sinclair pointed, and both men saw their friend start to stand, rubbing the back of his head. "All clear," he shouted, to which Mason replied with a wave.

"Where are the cops?" Reagan wanted to know, thinking they should have certainly arrived by now.

"Cahill called them off when he saw the explosion," Sinclair said. "I've still got comms to him but my team radio stopped working. What's next?" he asked his friend.

"Tell Cahill to keep the cops back a little while longer and ask him if he can land right here. I think we should get the missiles out of here."

"He says he can do it," Sinclair said, watching the Black Hawk already start in their direction. "Why don't you go check those bodies out there and I'll look over things here."

Reagan nodded and went off towards the shot-up police cars. He secured the two Kalashnikovs and bags of extra magazines, taking the men's wallets and phones as well. He was about to head back towards their ride as it prepared to land when he stopped in his tracks, realizing that they probably wouldn't have room onboard for the bodies. He took out his cellphone and took several pictures of each man before returning to join Sinclair. Mason had made his way to the helicopter, still rubbing his head, and the crew chief helped him climb aboard before trotting over to Sinclair to help load the seven Stingers, two launchers, RPGs and assorted other weapons.

"Phones and wallets?" Reagan asked Sinclair, who held them up in reply.

"Why don't you go have a seat and figure out what to do next, Jack, while we get this stuff loaded," Sinclair suggested.

30

Reagan stood in the parking lot of the IKEA, far enough from their helicopter that he could be heard, and placed his call. His call was answered on the first ring. "Jack? We have reports of a plane down at Newark Airport. What's going on? Are you ok?" the FBI Director asked, concern in his voice.

"We got here too late. We saw the plane go down. We engaged four hostiles armed with AKs. Four tangos down, one minor friendly injury from an RPG but he's ok," Reagan reported. His voice sounded mechanical and hollow, he realized, and he barely had the energy to speak at all. "We're clear here – just securing the Stingers now. Do you have people who can secure the scene here, and at Sandy Hook as well?"

"We can do that," Director Goldberg promised. "Are you ok, Jack? You sound a little shaky."

"It's been a rough afternoon," Reagan admitted. "What's going on in Washington?"

"We've got two terrorists dead and one in custody behind Union Station. They had some kind of mortar tube in the back of a pickup truck. They shot it out with some of my agents but my people are ok. That's all I know for certain right now. We also got a call from two of our agents who reported coming under fire at Hains Point, but we lost the connection and haven't been able to raise them," Goldberg said, sounding worried. "SWAT – ours and Metro's – should be on scene any moment now and we'll know more. We also have reports of a suicide bomber walking into the Capitol Building, but we don't have more details on that, either. As far as parks go, we've got every law enforcement officer we could reach searching parks, but no word on that, either."

"What can we do to help?"

"You've done enough, Jack. More than enough, actually. You go and take care of yourself. We're going to need you to help piece this all together when it's over, so go get some rest. I'll keep you in the loop."

Reagan replaced his phone in his pocket and slowly walked to the helicopter.

"What's next, Jack? What's happening in Washington?" Sinclair asked, correctly guessing who his friend had just called.

"Not enough information," Reagan shrugged. "I'm open to ideas. Maybe we can head..." his voice trailed off as he looked back at the bodies of the dead terrorists.

"To base and refuel?" Sinclair suggested.

"Not yet." Looking at the bodies had given him an idea. "Bring the talker out here," Reagan commanded. Sinclair gave his friend an odd look but climbed into the helicopter, returning a minute later with the still-hooded Adil. "Let's go for a walk," Reagan said, heading over to the bodies. When they were right on top of the bodies by the police cars, Reagan turned and removed Adil's hood and gag.

"You might recognize your friends here," he said, kicking Adil behind his left knee, causing him to fall on top of one of the bodies. Reagan reached down and grabbed the hair on the back of the man's head. "This is what happens to people who fuck with me, understand?"

Adil's eyes went wide with fear, staring at the face of a dead man he had never met before. He nodded slowly.

"Tell me more about the attack in Washington," Reagan commanded.

"I said everything I know," Adil protested.

"You mentioned a park. Where is the park?"

"I don't know!"

"Trust me when I tell you that you do *not* want me to ask again," Reagan said, slipping his pistol out of its holster.

"Park is next to a highway. There's a sports stadium close," Adil said, starting to shake in fear.

311

"See? That wasn't very hard to remember," Reagan said with a smile. "Now how about the spotters? Where are they located? What do they look like?"

"I don't know. It's the truth. I helped program the coordinates but I don't know any of the people, I swear. Only the people I was staying with, only them."

"What did you use to program the coordinates?"

"My laptop computer. It's at the house," Adil volunteered, unable to look away from the body in front of his face.

Reagan and Sinclair traded a look. "Just two more questions for now, Adil," Reagan said. "Answer them truthfully and you can live. Where is the house?" He flipped the safety off his pistol for effect. Adil very rapidly gave him the exact street address, adding that it was a detached house on a quiet street.

"Last question. When we go to the house, how many people are we going to find there?"

"No one," Adil said in surprise. "It was just the four of us there!"

"Ok, Adil," Reagan said, helping the man to his feet. "Good job, thank you!" He patted the man on the shoulder, causing Sinclair to roll his eyes and snort. "Take our friend back to the helicopter, please."

Reagan reached for his phone and called Director Goldberg again, watching Sinclair escort their new friend back to the Black Hawk. As before, his call was answered on the first ring. "What's going on, Jack?" Goldberg asked.

"Some new information. The park is next to a highway, with a sports stadium close by."

"That'll help," Goldberg exclaimed. "Just got word from SWAT – they're exchanging fire with an unknown number of subjects at Hains Point. Call me if you get anything more."

"Will do," Reagan said, jogging back to the helicopter and climbing aboard. As he sat down next to Amanda, she reached over and gave him a tight hug. He could see she had been crying. "Are you ok?"

"Lots better now," she replied with a smile.

"Where to, gentlemen?" Major Cahill asked once Reagan put his headset on.

"Back to base, please," Reagan replied. "Pete, as soon as we get back, see if you can't get some more people up here. I want to hit the house tonight, and I'm not sure we can trust our new friend here that it's empty."

"I can make the call now, Jack," Sinclair said, his face breaking into a grin. Clearly his friend hadn't told the FBI everything.

"Why wait?" asked Mason, holding up his rifle with a grin of his own.

"Tempting, but I don't want to go in blind," Reagan replied, leaning back in his uncomfortable seat and closing his eyes. He felt Amanda take his hand and squeeze it before she rested her head on his shoulder.

Despite the horrors of the burning wreckage of the United flight half a mile away, Major Cahill couldn't help but smile as he overheard the conversation. He looked over at his copilot, who had a smile of his own. Both men were thinking the same thing; the men in the back of their aircraft were some very serious players. They had just bagged eight heavily-armed terrorists in two separate locations and were already planning to go out again. Just as exciting as the operations tempo in the Sandbox, even if it was way too close to home.

"You are a very brave Muslim, Mohammed – a true warrior for Islam," the Imam had said to Lawrence Eggerton a mere hour earlier, using the new name Eggerton himself had selected when he had converted to Islam in Muska's house, her parents and brother looking on with pride. The Imam had come under cover of darkness, escorted by Kerimsolta, who had stood watch outside. "Today you will make the infidel demons pay for their crimes against our faith, and for their murder of your beautiful Muska." The Imam had then checked the explosives-

313

laden vest worn by Eggerton under his parka and hugged him – carefully, of course – before Eggerton got out of the car in front of the Capitol Building.

"Salam alaykum," Eggerton had said with a smile, saying goodbye to the man who had spent so many hours teaching him about his new faith.

"Wa-alaykum salam," the Imam replied with a smile of his own, certain that the idiot now leaving his car would die a glorious death. Even a fool has his uses, the Imam thought.

Eggerton had walked up a long series of stairs to a visitor's entrance, waiting patiently in line to pass through the metal detector. He walked through, smiling as the alarm pinged, disregarding the police officers when they ordered him to stop. He walked into the middle of the large lobby and unzipped his parka, revealing his explosives to the many people going about their business, many of whom stopped dead in their tracks and gasped. Eggerton took the bomb's trigger in his hand and turned slowly towards the police officers, lifting his arms in prayer as people in the lobby started to scream and run. When he finished praying, he flashed an eerie smile and yelled "Allahu Akbar!" as his thumb moved to press the button on his trigger, and...

...a very pissed off Sergeant Bob Collins of the Capitol Hill Police Department knocked Eggerton unconscious with a perfectly timed blow to the back of the head with the butt of his shotgun. "Get the bomb squad over here right now," Collins ordered, turning the man carefully onto his back after cuffing him so he could get a better look at the device. He knew a few things about explosive devices, having trained as an Explosive Ordinance Disposal Specialist before a bad infection scarred his lungs, resulting in discharge from the Army.

The device in front of him looked exceedingly simple, even rudimentary, except for a cellphone connected to a circuit of some kind that he couldn't see. He didn't like that one bit, since it meant that someone else could set off the device. Collins had already ordered the lobby to be cleared and sent out his officers

314

as well, having decided to disconnect the cellphone. From what little he saw of the circuitry, he figured that the bomb and phone probably needed a call to come in before the circuit was completed. It was very risky to pull out the phone, but in his mind it was even riskier to leave it in place.

Phone in hand and with a sigh of relief, Collins stood slowly and looked at the man in front of him, for the first time noticing that he looked like an average white guy from middle America. "You piece of shit," he said, even angrier than he had been two minutes earlier. His brother had been killed by an IED in Iraq, and this piece of human garbage in front of him offended his memory. "Cocksucker," he said, giving the already-unconscious man a good, swift kick to the head before spitting in his face.

The Imam waited in his car for a few minutes, waiting to see the explosion that would serve as the opening act of the main attack. But no explosion took place, and after a few more minutes, the Imam reached for his phone and called the number attached to the bomb. Nothing happened. Confused, he called the number a second time, and still nothing happened. He was positive that the explosion would have been easily large enough to be seen and heard outside the building, so something must have gone wrong. He cursed silently and drove away quickly; this had not been expected. Then again, it didn't really matter, either; the mortar barrage would still take place at 3 p.m.

The location "behind Union Station" turned out to be a parking lot bordering H Street NE, accessible from 2nd Street NE, just blocks away from the Washington Field Office of the FBI. Within minutes of getting the call, four teams of agents were heading to Union Station, and it didn't take long to spot the pickup truck parked with the motor running and three men sitting in the cab. Their behavior gave them away – they couldn't stop fidgeting in their seats when two agents drove slowly through the parking lot, and they were very quick to avoid any eye contact. As soon as the agents stopped their car and started to get out a safe distance away, the driver of the pickup truck put it in gear and careened towards the exit, running directly into an SUV containing more agents.

The front seat passenger in the pickup truck was dazed by the impact of his head against the dashboard when the driver slammed on the brakes. The driver and rear seat passenger quickly got out and brought their Kalashnikovs to bear on the FBI SUV, completely disregarding the two agents thirty feet behind them in the parking lot. It wasn't strictly speaking fair shooting those mutts in the back, Special Agent Pierce thought, holstering his sidearm to cuff the survivor – but you couldn't expect fair if you tried to shoot FBI agents with a machine gun.

Pierce's partner pulled back the tarp covering the back of the pickup and called Pierce over, pointing to the strange tube bolted to the bed. "Is that what I think it is?" he asked.

"If you think that's a mortar, it's exactly what you think it is," Pierce replied. The information conveyed by the Director had been right in every detail. His next thought was to call EOD; if the rest of the information was anywhere near as accurate, there would be a waiting list for ordinance disposal by the end of the day.

The Bureau's luck ran out at Hains Point. The first agents to arrive had just left Reagan National Airport when the call came in over the radio, and it was a very short drive over the Rochambeau Memorial Bridge. They drove slowly and turned into the parking lot after passing the golf course, noting the presence of several pickup trucks parked near the middle of the lot, each with cargo concealed by tarps. That was as suspicious as the half dozen or so men milling by the trucks, seemingly not bothered by the frigid afternoon temperatures. The two agents were carefully studying the men and trucks, but they ignored the three men sitting in a white Mazda in the very first parking spot in the lot.

Just as soon as the FBI sedan passed by, the Mazda's front-seat passenger quickly got out of the car, braced his Kalashnikov against the roof of the car, and splayed the FBI sedan with bullets. The agent driving pushed down on the accelerator, driving quickly past the pickup trucks as his partner worked the radio to call for backup. The driver noticed that as they were approaching the parking lot exit, a man got out of a gray minivan parked at the far end, carrying some kind of tube that he started to raise to his shoulder. Both agents realized what it was at exactly the same time, cringing as they saw a flash of light before the RPG hit their sedan, killing them instantly.

The leader of this group of terrorists cringed just as badly, at once angry that his man had used a rocket-propelled grenade where bullets would have done just as good a job. The report of a Kalashnikov would carry, but nor as far as an explosion. He looked at his watch and saw that they still had close to fifteen minutes to go before they could fire. This was an unwanted complication, but one they had trained for. The leader cursed as he heard sirens – obviously those police officers had gotten the word out. He ordered his men to set up the launch tubes and switch to the secondary target, which they did quickly and easily, calculating the direction and elevation using a very clever app on their iPads.

The Mazda and minivan pulled out of the parking lot in both directions, driving about a hundred feet north before blocking the roads with their cars, effectively cutting off the only road approaches to the pickup trucks. The large amount of snow would force the police to keep to the roads, they figured, and it would take time to organize boats or helicopters to try approaching from another direction. Three men got out of each of the two vehicles and stood behind them holding their rifles, listening to the approaching sirens. A couple of them smoked to quiet their nerves as they waited for the police to arrive.

They didn't have long to wait; FBI SWAT was on scene less than five minutes later. The terrorists weren't overly concerned – they had expected to be eventually found out, and to a man they expected to die like good soldiers of Allah. They expected a set-piece battle, with the FBI moving slowly and cautiously down the roads, setting up positions and then eventually exchanging fire with the blocking force. The men responsible for the mortars would have enough time to launch all their shells before grabbing their weapons to engage the federal agents once they made it through the blocking force. By then, they expected, many of the officers would already be dead.

The FBI, however, was not about to accede to the expectations of terrorists. The approaching vehicles separated into two veritable convoys as they drove down both branches of Ohio Drive SW, each led by a heavily armored Mine Resistant Ambush Protected (MRAP) vehicle. Instead of slowing down as they approached the blocking vehicles, the MRAPs picked up speed, pulling ahead slightly from the vehicles behind them and running straight into the Mazda and minivan. Once through the blockade, the MRAPs, still trailed by several SUVs, continued into the parking lot, smashing into two of the pickup trucks before finally coming to a rest. The terrorists in the parking lot had not been expecting this. By the time they had recovered enough from shock to grab their weapons, the FBI agents were already out of their vehicles, their weapons up and ready for action.

The terrorists fought back – or tried to. Only two of them even got shots off, and none of those came remotely close to hitting anyone. In less than ten seconds, the battle was over and all six terrorists in the parking lot lay dead. The terrorists by the Mazda had jumped out of the way of the MRAP, dropping their weapons as they did so. They quickly scrambled back to their weapons, but by then several vehicles had stopped and unloaded agents. Unarmed and surrounded, the three men raised their hands in surrender. The terrorists that had been standing behind the minivan, on the other hand, never got the chance to surrender. The MRAP flipped the minivan over on top of them, and long trails of blood smeared the pavement where they had been dragged for over thirty feet before being pushed out of the way, in pieces.

The three men sitting in the Chevy Tahoe in the parking lot of the Randall Recreation Center were having a lively argument about premiership football – this time over a taped match they had just seen of a game in which Arsenal narrowly beat out Newcastle, scoring a supremely lucky goal in the last seconds of regulation play. At least two of them thought it was lucky; their friend thought it was all skill. These men had become good friends during the past few months, finding that they had more in common than just their willingness to kill in the name of Allah. All of similar age and upbringing, they had practically the same tastes in movies, music, and even women. They had become lifelong friends, and despite knowing that their lives would end that very day, they looked forward to Paradise together.

The men wrapped up their conversation and exchanged handshakes and hugs before exiting the car – not without some sadness – to set up the launch tube, using a special tool to bolt it into the ground before retrieving their iPad to properly orient it in direction and elevation. Task completed and mortar ready to fire, the men sat in the open trunk of the Tahoe and smoked cigarettes as they looked around. It was just a few minutes to 3 p.m., and they wanted to be precise. They watched in amazement as an old man walked a small dog right past them, not paying any attention to what they were doing. When he was well past, they traded amused looks and even a chuckle – but then they heard the sirens.

After a few seconds, the men realized that they were getting closer – from every direction. It sounded like every single police car in Washington, D.C. was heading their way. Two police cruisers stopped short in front of the park on South Capitol Street, and officers emerged with weapons drawn. Of the three terrorists, two were meant to work the mortar while the third held off the police for as long as possible. The latter of the three reached for his Kalashnikov and took off across the field to engage police, leaving the other two to their work. But the men had become good friends, and they couldn't just let their friend face the police alone; the two grabbed their rifles and chased after him, ignoring the mortar altogether. In the end, two police officers lost their lives and several more were wounded in the exchange of fire that lasted several minutes. The terrorists were dead as well, and along with them, Osman Mansuraev's plan.

31

The Black Hawk flared as Major Cahill pitched the nose up with the aft cyclic and reduced collective. As the helicopter decelerated rapidly, Cahill raised the collective, adding power to maintain altitude and rotor thrust. Just before losing effective translational lift, he pitched the nose down using forward cyclic and flew a normal approach to the landing spot that had been marked out for him. The sudden movement of the helicopter before landing caused Jack Reagan to jolt fully to consciousness.

"Welcome back, Jack," Sinclair said with a grin, seeing his friend wake so suddenly. "We're landing at McGuire-Dix. Our people called ahead, and it looks like they're setting us up in our own hangar where we won't be disturbed."

"Or where no one will be disturbed by their screams," Mason joked, tilting his head aft toward their prisoners.

"We've got a couple of more people on the way up but they probably won't get here till late tonight at the earliest," Sinclair continued, shaking his head at Mason. "If you still want to hit the house tonight, it might have to be just us."

"Let's think about it after we have a more thorough chat with our new friend Adil," Reagan replied. "At the very least I want eyes on that place in case someone goes in to clean it."

Sinclair nodded agreement. "I'll have a chat with the base commander and see if we can't find some transportation." No one spoke again until after the engine had powered down and the rotors stopped spinning – everyone was thoroughly exhausted.

The silence and the inactivity were not good for Reagan. His mind started to wander, thinking back to the United 777 he had watched fall out of the sky, and all the lives lost with it. It was all his fault, Reagan knew. If only he had been faster getting Adil to talk, or driven down that side street only a few minutes earlier...or, for that matter, gone to Sandy Hook much sooner. All the dots had been there for anyone to see, but he had failed to connect them. If only he had, and acted sooner, none of this would have happened. *You fucked up, Jack, and people are dead as a result.*

Watson could tell that Reagan had something on his mind, but wondered if she would ever know Jack well enough to know how his mind worked. It was well worth the effort, she thought, squeezing Jack's hand. He squeezed back and turned to smile at her, but she sensed something was wrong. "What's wrong, Jack?"

"I'm just a little tired, I guess," he replied with a shrug as they entered the hangar. "Long day and all. How are *you* doing?"

"I'm ok. Tired too – first time on a helicopter and I slept through half of it!" she laughed. "Still trying to process everything. There's a lot to take in," she pointed out.

"Very true," he replied, wondering what Amanda must be thinking about him after his very massive failure. Hard as it was to do, he had to set aside that thought for now and focus. He needed to talk to Adil again, but in a more structured setting. "Pete, Jim, I want to talk to Adil again, sooner rather than later. I'm going to find a quiet place to sit and think up an approach and some questions. Can you find a suitable room and set up a camera?"

"Can do," Sinclair said as Mason nodded. "We've got cameras in our gear."

"Super. Back in a few minutes," Reagan said, walking towards an office he saw along the wall of the hangar.

As soon as Reagan was out of earshot, Watson turned to Sinclair. "Something's up with Jack."

"Probably just tired," Sinclair said. "It's been one hell of a day."

"No. When he's tired he's punchy and a little feisty, even. This isn't tired." Of that Amanda was sure.

"What do *you* think it is?" Peter asked.

"I think I fucked up," Amanda said at once. "Back at the beach, when I though he shot the guy we had in custody, I kinda freaked out a little."

"Not that we noticed," Peter observed.

"When we got on the helicopter and I realized Jack hadn't really shot him, I was a little too relieved, if you know what I mean."

"I know exactly what you mean, actually," Peter replied with a chuckle. "Do you know why so many of us are still single? It's hard to find a girl who gets that sometimes good people have to do bad things. That's a minimum threshold for a relationship, by the way."

"What do you mean?" Amanda asked, confused.

"I mean, to even have a relationship with someone like Jack, Nick, me or even Jim, you need to first accept that sometimes good people have to do bad things. Not just for this job, but even as a lawyer. I mean think about it, if he's defending a doctor against a malpractice claim, he's fighting to prevent an injured person from getting money. Or a criminal defense lawyer representing a murderer or a rapist – thank God Jack doesn't do any of that, by the way."

"Ok, that's first," Amanda replied, starting to understand. She hadn't quite thought of it that way. "What's next?"

"I'll tell you what, Miss Watson, why don't you run me through your thoughts on Jack's actions, and then I'll tell you your future."

She hesitated for a moment before responding. "At first, I was shocked when I thought he executed that guy. I know Jack's killed people, obviously, but this looked like murder – shooting an unarmed prisoner wearing restraints. And it bothered me like crazy to think he's capable of murder, especially since we..." she blushed, but Sinclair waved his hand dismissively, waiting for her to continue. "Then, on the helicopter, I was relieved to see that Jack wasn't a murderer, but in the back of my mind I kept wondering what he's capable of if he can come up with an idea like that." She paused, taking a deep breath.

"Then I saw that plane go down. As horrible as that was, it made me suddenly realize that I was looking at things the wrong way. The only reason Jack pretended to shoot that guy was to prevent something like that from happening – to prevent innocent people from being killed, Jack pretended to kill a terrorist who had shot at us. I realized something else, too, after I saw the plane. Even if Jack had shot him for real, I wouldn't be the least bit bothered by it. There's a lot more at stake – a much bigger picture, and I guess I didn't really appreciate that until then."

"So sometimes good people have to do bad things?" Peter asked.

"Actually, no, not exactly. Sometimes good people have to make very difficult decisions and do things others may perceive as bad, even though in the grand scheme of things, they're really not that bad."

"Not bad," Sinclair nodded approvingly.

"Jack can never be a murderer," she added. "He's a killer, yes, but that's entirely different. I know that might sound a little odd, but..."

"Not at all," Peter interrupted with a chuckle. "Everyone I work with is a trained killer, but none of them – none of us – is a murderer. And it's more than mere semantics. Ok, so what's the conclusion you've reached from all this?"

Amanda thought for a moment before replying, "Sometimes you have to do the thing that's right, even if it doesn't seem like the right thing to do."

"Nicely said," Peter grinned. "And Jack?"

"Jack is the best man I know. After everything we've been through together, I trust him to know what the right thing to do is, and to do the thing that's right. That's it – it really is that simple isn't it?"

"It really is," Peter replied. "The people I work with – Jack, too – we all live in a world that has a little white, a little black, and a whole lot of shades of gray. Colors shift all the time, except for one thing – the only thing, really, that always stays white. It's the trust we place in one another to, as you say, do the thing that's right, even if it doesn't seem like the right thing to do."

"And my future?"

"I now pronounce you man and wife," Sinclair said, laughing as he made the sign of the cross. "Jack's a lucky guy; you get it. Only other woman I've known who gets it is Brenda, and look how that turned out. You two will become fast friends, and I can see her as one of your bridesmaids. Start planning your wedding, kid!"

"So you don't think Jack is upset with me? You think we're ok?" she asked. She had to be sure.

"He may not show it like other guys do, but he's crazy about you," Peter laughed. "Besides, he doesn't really get upset with other people. He only gets upset with...oh shit! Amanda, you go in there and talk to him, right the hell now."

"About what? I don't understand what..."

"Jack only ever gets upset with himself," Peter interrupted. "You say something's up with Jack? He's probably sitting there blaming himself for all the people who died on that plane."

"That's not his fault! If it weren't for Jack – for all of you – a lot more people would have lost their lives today," she objected.

"I know that, and you know that, but he doesn't. I've seen this before," Peter said, shaking his head. "He takes failure very personally, especially when there's loss of life. Go talk to him, Amanda. Right now he really needs you."

"Thanks for listening, Pete. Just so you know, I'll always be there for him," she promised, turning to walk to the office she had seen Jack enter.

"She's a pretty remarkable girl," Mason said, having heard most of the conversation as he was unpacking video equipment. "Smart, too. She gets it."

"That she does," Sinclair nodded agreement. "It's not hard to figure out what Jack sees in her."

Reagan had scribbled some notes on a pad he found in the unlocked desk, and was now looking out the window, lost in thought. He didn't notice Watson come into the room until she sat on the edge of the desk right in front of him, a bright smile on her face. As lousy as he was feeling, he smiled, too. With her, it came naturally.

"Penny for your thoughts, Jack."

"I'm afraid they're not worth that much," he replied with a shrug.

Amanda leaned in slowly and kissed him softly, first on his cheek and then on his lips. "Tell me anyway."

Jack took a deep breath, trying to find the courage to admit his failure. He lowered his head as he spoke – he just couldn't look her in the eyes right now. "I screwed up, and people died as a result."

"Jack, look at me," she said softly, placing her palms on his cheeks and tilting his face to her. When he opened his eyes, she could see tears welling up. "You didn't screw up. You didn't screw up at all. You *saved* lives. If it weren't for you, a lot more people would be dead today."

"But I didn't..." he started to say. Amanda stopped him by putting her finger on his lips, pressing her forehead against his.

"You did everything you could, Jack. A lot more than anyone else did – a lot more than anyone else would even *think* to do. You stopped this from being much, much worse. *You* did that – you were the one on the ground risking your life. Don't ever do that to me again, by the way," she said, placing her hand over his heart. "I really don't want to lose you." She paused, seeing her words start to sink in. "You know I'm right – you know that a lot more people would have died today if it weren't for you. Just think about it."

Jack nodded slowly, and the smile he formed was more heartfelt.

"You're carrying the weight of the world on your shoulders," Amanda said. "Granted, they're big, strong shoulders," she added, smiling as she squeezed his shoulders. "But just remember, you're not alone. Not in this, and not in anything else. You've got some pretty amazing friends backing you up, and you have me, too."

"I do, do I?" he asked, raising an eyebrow.

"Yes, you definitely do," she said, leaning in to kiss him again. "In case you haven't figured it out, Jack, I'm falling in love with you. And nothing is going to change that – nothing you do, nothing that happens, *nothing* is going to change that. I promise."

Jack looked into her eyes, thinking about what she had said. "How did I get so lucky to find someone so amazing as you?" he asked, leaning forward to kiss her.

"We both got lucky," she replied, with a smile that melted Jack's heart. "Ok. Now that that's settled, let's figure out what to do next."

"I suppose we should call Washington and find out what happened," he said.

"You mean you haven't found out yet?" she asked in surprise, reaching into his shirt pocket and pulling out his phone. "You've got a couple of missed calls here from the FBI Director and Director Smythe. Where do you want to start?"

"FBI," he said, taking the phone and calling the number before putting it on speakerphone.

"Jack? I've been trying to get in touch with you. Is everything ok?" Director Goldberg asked.

"Yes. Sorry, sir, we were in the air. We're at Joint Base McGuire-Dix-Lakehurst right now. What's going on in Washington?" Reagan asked, concern in his voice.

"I keep telling you, call me David." *If anyone had ever earned the right to call me by my given name, it's that guy,* the

327

Director thought. "We've got 14 terrorists dead and 4 in custody. Lawrence Eggerton, too – he showed up at the Capitol with an explosive vest but had his ass handed to him by a pissed off cop. A couple of police officers were killed or wounded in the shootouts, but no civilian casualties. We got to them in time – not a single mortar was launched. Not a single civilian casualty," he repeated. There was already a celebratory attitude around the FBI Headquarters and Washington Field Office.

"Thank God," Reagan said, breathing an audible sigh of relief.

"From your lips to His ears, Jack," the Director said with a laugh. "We couldn't have done it without you. We owe you a massive debt of thanks, pal."

"I wish I could have done more," Reagan admitted.

"You did a lot more than anyone has a right to ask. Do you have some time right now? I'd like to discuss next steps with you."

"I'm listening, Director – David."

"No, Jack. We're the ones listening," Goldberg replied. "Just so you know, I just spoke with Director Smythe on a secure line. He filled me in on some of your...past activities. I gather you haven't always had the support you needed in the past, but you've got our full support now. You've acquitted yourself very nicely, so call your play and we'll back it."

"Do you have IDs on the shooters?"

"No, not yet. They all had fake papers. No hits on fingerprints or DNA, and it'll be a while before we get through facial recognition. Did your guys have ID on them?"

"They did, but I haven't gotten to it yet," Reagan admitted. "Cellphones, too."

"Our guys had cellphones as well. We're putting together call logs right now."

"Can you please e-mail copies to Special Agent Watson? I'd like her to go over them as well. She's the one who found the connection with New Jersey."

"We'll do that. Want us to run your IDs too?"

"Yeah, that makes sense. I don't know about logistics, though. My car got pretty shot up," Reagan said, wincing at the thought of his poor car, and then at the thought that his insurance company would probably cite a terrorist attack exclusion to deny coverage.

"So I heard," Goldberg said. "I've got agents there now – they count several shell casings and a large pool of blood. Where'd you stash the body? And do you want us to get the cars to you?"

"We were in a hurry so we took the body with us." Reagan thought for a moment before continuing. "Do you think you can find a couple of flatbeds and bring the cars to us? The Porsche, I mean, and a red Mustang in the second lot from the entrance, a rental from Hertz."

"We can do that this evening. What about your car?"

"Fuck if I know," Reagan said. He really loved that car. "Maybe you can box up the contents and send them over with the cars."

"That works. And we'll figure out what to do about your car," Goldberg said, laughing as an idea popped into his head. If the Bureau didn't end up buying this guy a new car, for damn sure every agent would happily contribute some money to the cause.

"One more thing – since your agents are already in the area, can they check us out of our hotel and bring our things down as well?" Reagan asked, providing their room numbers at the La Quinta.

"Not a problem, pal," Goldberg promised.

"Any way to narrow down where the IDs may have come from?"

"We're looking at that too, but we're not very optimistic. Too many cheap printers on the market are good enough to do that sort of thing these days."

"El Paso," Reagan said at once. "It would explain how these guys got into the country, too."

"That's our thinking as well. I've kicked loose our El Paso Field Office and everyone there is working on this as a priority."

"I think that's where we need to focus our attention," Reagan emphasized.

"Duly noted. Jack, do you think this was it, or is something else in the works?"

Reagan let out a long sigh. "Right now I've got nothing to go on except my gut, and my gut tells me this was it. But there's someone I want to talk to about that."

"The, umm, other gentlemen you picked up?" Goldberg carefully avoided calling them prisoners.

"Yeah," Reagan said with an unseen nod. "We already have an address to look into."

"Do you want to set something up with my agents? This is all priority now."

"I'd prefer to use my people for now," Reagan demurred. "I don't know how fast we can get that going – probably early tomorrow – but I'm planning on setting up an overwatch tonight."

"I don't have a problem with that," Goldberg replied. He along with half the world had watched the news channels replaying a shaky video of three men rappelling into the IKEA parking lot from a Black Hawk that lacked any markings. It didn't take much of a stretch of the imagination to figure out who Reagan's people were.

"As soon as we finish having a look around, I'll call you so your people can process the scene," Reagan promised. "That brings us to the six hundred pound gorilla in the room. I'm privy to something that neither one of us is read into, but in light of today's events, I think you and Director Smythe should demand access. If you'll allow me to mix metaphors, that cat is well out of the bag by now, and it's loudly meowing for food."

"I'll talk to Francis and we'll make the call together," Goldberg replied, laughing heartily. "Speaking of clearances, we're working to expedite yours. It'll be about a week or so. If I were a betting man – and I am – I'd wager Francis already has a position in mind for you. And if he doesn't, I'd be happy to snap you up."

"We'll cross that bridge when we get to it," Reagan said. "I'm willing to follow this investigation as far as it goes, but I don't know that I'm the right fit for government work."

"You are most definitely *not* the right fit for government work," Goldberg said, laughing again. "That's one of the reasons Francis and I like you so much. And it's probably one of the reasons why you've been so damned effective. When you come in to debrief, let's the three of us put our heads together and try to find a place for you. Your country needs you, Jack."

"We'll see," Reagan replied. "I'll go have a chat with my new friend, go check out the house, and then head back to D.C."

"Sounds like a plan. Call me if you need anything – and damn good work, Jack."

Amanda leaned in and kissed Jack softly after he ended his call. "That's just a reminder that I need you too," she said softly. "Your 'past activities' sound interesting, by the way," she added with a sly smile. "I have to admit that I've been imagining all sorts of things the last two days, but I'm betting the truth is far more interesting."

"Why didn't you ask?" Jack said in surprise.

"I figured you'd tell me some day," she replied. "You know, some night when neither of us can sleep because our babies are keeping us up," she added playfully.

"How about after we get back to Washington, the two of us sit down and talk about it. And figure out just how many babies you want," he said with a chuckle.

"I've got a better idea, Jack. How about after you get debriefed, we find a nice, quiet beach somewhere, curl up on the sand, and talk about it then? And practice this whole baby-making thing too, while we're at it?"

"I like your idea more," he admitted, realizing just how fortunate he was to have met this amazing woman.

32

Anatoly Lavrov gripped the champagne flute so tightly in his hand that it shattered when CNN played the amateur footage of soldiers descending from a helicopter in the IKEA parking lot. Something had gone wrong. Lavrov leaned in towards the television as the short segment of tape was replayed, noting that the time-stamp on the video read 2:28 p.m., two minutes *before* his attack was to commence. That meant that the Americans had known – must have known – in order to have a special operations team at that location at precisely the right time. Suddenly Lavrov was gripped with fear, unlike any he had ever known before, when CNN switched to live footage from Washington, D.C.

The live feed, from atop some building whose name he didn't catch, showed a sea of flashing lights from police vehicles. The news anchor was reporting multiple shootouts with police and federal agents, the extent of casualties unknown. As he spoke, the words "Terrorist Attack Thwarted" scrolled across the screen; Lavrov realized that not only had something gone wrong, but something had gone terribly, horribly, terrifyingly wrong. The Americans had known his plan, despite the rigorous operational security he had employed. And so he was gripped with fear, still clutching the broken champagne glass in his hand as he looked towards the door to his suite, expecting Brazilian police to burst through any moment with guns drawn.

Minutes passed before Lavrov started to relax a little. The most the Americans would have were a name and maybe a description, but Osman Mansuraev was neither the name on his passport nor a name he would ever use again. As for his description, he had already started to subtly alter his appearance, and he would continue to do so when he made it to Buenos Aires in a few days. For now, he was safe. He stood and stretched before heading to the bathroom to clean the blood off his hands.

A few minutes later, after having taken a shower as well, he returned to the sofa in a fluffy robe to watch continuing coverage of his failed plan. He was still very much disappointed that the plan he had spent years carefully putting together had somehow come undone at the last minute, and he just couldn't figure out how. Something had clearly gone wrong, but *what*? Still, one plane had been shot down, and the media had already reported that a missile had been used. Combined with the panic ensuing in the nation's capital, Lavrov realized that he had succeeded in terrifying the American people, and that was, after all, what the purpose of his plot had been. As disappointed as he was that the full magnitude of his scheme had not been realized, his mission had not actually failed. It had succeeded. He switched his television to Sky News and smiled when he saw the caption on the screen: "Muslim terrorists attack America." His mission had definitely succeeded.

Lavrov stood slowly and walked over to pour himself some more champagne, disappointed that it had already gone a little flat. He called room service to order another bottle and retrieved his laptop, powering it up on the marble dining table overlooking the ocean. He barely had time to open the anonymizing software that masked his IP address when the doorbell rang. Lavrov tipped well enough to merit prompt and attentive service, but not well enough that he would stand out too much or be remembered for too long. He opened the new bottle and poured himself a drink, calling up the White House schedule of events in his browser as he waited for his drink to settle.

The President, he saw, was scheduled to depart for his holiday in Hawaii early Thursday afternoon, leaving the White House aboard Marine One. Although terrorist attacks had just taken place, Lavrov thought it safe to assume that the President would not alter his schedule – this one loved his holidays and his golf a little too much to allow such minor nuisances to interfere with his plans. He logged on to his eBay account and started listing an ancient blue Chevy Nova for sale, with the auction end date and time coinciding with the President's scheduled departure. He also listed a "Buy it now" price of $5,001 dollars, a simple message that instructed his men to track the President's schedule themselves and alter their attack to coincide with his actual departure, if it should be altered.

Lavrov had always known that this attack was highly unlikely to even come close to succeeding, and he was sure that it was bound to be stopped by increased security in the wake of today's events. But, he thought, this third attack, coming so closely on the heels of Rock Creek Park, Sandy Hook, Newark Airport and Capitol Hill, would succeed in pushing America over the edge. Its people would feel a fear unlike any they had known in this lifetime, and in response would demand a global war against Islamic terrorists. This attack, Lavrov was sure, would push America into the abyss.

The two men sat in a darkened room illuminated only by the soft glow of a solitary incandescent bulb from a small, industrial desk lamp. An iPhone on the desk streamed the live broadcast from Classic FM in London, currently playing Beethoven's Piano Sonata No. 14 in C Sharp Minor. The pianist was Daniel Barenboim, and both men found him a very skilled player. Coffee in fine white china sat mostly untouched near the phone, along with an ashtray half filled with the remnants of the pack of Dunhill that now sat in the trash bin. Both men smiled as they listened to the music, sharing their preferences for piano and the violin, respectively. It had already slipped from their minds that they weren't amicably chatting in a flat in London, but rather in a disused office on a military base in New Jersey. The only things seemingly out of place were the video recorder mounted to a tripod and the small recording device sitting discreetly to the side of the desk.

Adil had felt a wide range of emotion as he was led to the office, only to find his restraints removed and be offered coffee and a cigarette by the man who had very nearly emasculated him on the beach. Jack was all smiles, shaking Adil's hand and thanking him for helping prevent the deaths of innocent women and children – even quoting a passage from the Holy Qur'an. Whatever fear and anxiety he was feeling had quickly evaporated, and Adil opened up to the man sitting across from him; soon they were talking very much as friends.

It hadn't taken much prompting for Adil to relate his life story. He was a Palestinian born in Iraq, where his family had fled to after the Israeli invasion of his homeland in 1947. He had grown up in a middle-class family in a suburb of Baghdad and had excelled in his studies before the Americans invaded his adoptive country, driving his family from their home much as the Israelis had done before them. They had survived as virtual refugees along the border with Jordan until a distant relative in Lebanon had arranged their transit to that country. At first, they had looked forward to resettling on the outskirts of Beirut, hoping to find a return to some kind of normalcy.

But the squalid conditions of the solitary room with makeshift kitchen and bathroom facilities, coupled by their inability to find work, had destroyed the spirits of Adil's family even more than when they fled Baghdad. Still, his parents had managed to scrape together enough money to pay for Adil to sit his entrance exams to the American University of Beirut, often by foregoing such luxuries as a decent meal. They sacrificed still more to pay his tuition, and Adil had always felt the debt weigh heavily on his shoulders.

At University, he was instantly fascinated by computers and realized he had a natural facility for understanding how they worked. He had studied computer science for a few years, attaining very decent grades. Increasingly, however, he found himself distracted from his studies by the virulent anti-American and anti-Israeli sentiments expressed by his family and friends.

Such hatred was inculcated in the young across the Middle East, but nowhere more so than among people who felt very personal suffering at the hands of these colonialist oppressors. Every discussion, even on topics like the weather, eventually switched focus to the Great Satan and Little Satan.

Adil increasingly felt obligated to do something to fight the Americans, as many of his cousins had done. By his third year at University, he had lost interest in his studies and had started to spend all his time searching for ways he could join the Holy Jihad. Eventually, he came across a web site that seemed to be recruiting, and he had entered into a lively exchange with a man who called himself Mahmud. After a few weeks of dialogue, Mahmud had offered to meet Adil, and they got together for some coffee at a little shop in Beirut. That first meeting led to many others, and Adil quickly realized that Mahmud was sounding him out and evaluating him. He knew all the right things to say, of course; though Adil wasn't particularly religious, he had heard many people quoting from the Holy Qur'an when cursing the Americans. All he had to do was repeat what he had heard, and apparently that was enough to convince Mahmud of his sincerity. Mahmud had promised that he would find a special use for Adil, and they parted ways.

Several months had passed without word, leading Adil to conclude that perhaps he hadn't passed Mahmud's tests after all. But then, out of the blue, he received a text message arranging another meeting. Adil was instructed to pack a change of clothes and tell his family he was going on a trip for school, and he met Mahmud in Beirut. After a few days of travel, Adil realized that they were somewhere in northern Iraq, but he had been so thoroughly disoriented by their modes of travel – and the fact that they only travelled at night – that he had no idea where, precisely he was.

In Iraq, he was introduced to a man who had called himself Osman. He met with Osman several times, sharing some particularly bitter coffee as he impressed his host with his

337

knowledge of computers. Eventually, Osman took him to a small barn and showed him a mortar tube. Would it be possible, Osman asked, to come up with a simple program that anyone could use to calculate the precise angle at which the mortar needed to be set up to hit exact coordinates? Adil was very excited to see such a sophisticated weapon in the hands of his compatriots, and after a brief demonstration of how the thing worked, he returned to Beirut with Mahmud to research what he would need to do.

It only took him a few weeks to come up with a computer program, and a few more weeks for Mahmud to arrange their trip back to Iraq – to a different village, this time. Osman had been very pleased with the proof of concept Adil created, but wondered if it would be possible to make it even simpler – perhaps even program it into an iPad. Adil was very eager to try, and spent another week learning how to program for the iPad and refining his program. He then watched Osman and several other men use the program to great effect. Everyone was very pleased at the results, and Adil was very proud to have found a way to contribute to the jihad.

He spent several weeks back home, keeping his activities hidden from his family, until Mahmud asked Adil whether he would be willing to travel to America to help in the attacks. Osman had personally requested him, and Adil considered it a great honor. Together with Mahmud, Adil flew to Tunis and then headed across North Africa in a series of cars and busses, eventually arriving at a small port. There they boarded a freighter and a few weeks later disembarked in a strange land full of tropical plants where the people spoke Spanish. Adil had been purposely kept disoriented, and was not aware of their port of departure, point of arrival, or even the name of the ship he had been on.

Once off the freighter, he had accompanied Mahmud to what he understood to be a safehouse. There he briefly met four other men; two of them, he thought, were Iraqis, and the other two seemed to be Libyans. By the time he woke up the next morning, the men were gone, and he was left all alone with Mahmud. A few days passed, during which Adil never left the house, before Mahmud introduced him to two scrawny Hispanic men. These men, he explained, would get him the rest of the way to America, and he was to do whatever they said, so long as he didn't discuss anything he had done with Osman.

Adil travelled with the Hispanic men for five nights and four days until they crossed a river he understood to be the Rio Grande. "Welcome to America," one of the men had said, slapping him across the back. They took him to another safehouse, this one in a suburb of a large American city, where Adil remained for nearly a week before another Hispanic man came to get him. He introduced himself as Raul and told him he would take him to Osman. They spent a few days driving north in a pickup truck before they reached a very isolated farmhouse in what he thought was Virginia. Osman was waiting for him, and had prepared a sumptuous meal in his honor.

The very next day, Osman had given him a nice new suit that fit very comfortably. They then drove together into the very heart of the Great Satan, Washington, D.C. Osman drove him to a couple of locations, telling him that these would be the places from which the mortars would be launched. After they returned to the farmhouse, Osman gave Adil a large number of iPads onto which to recreate his program and prepare the coordinates. And then Osman left with the iPads, leaving Adil alone in the farmhouse for close to two weeks. Luckily, there were enough provisions to make his stay very comfortable, and he passed his time watching satellite TV, wishing that at least he had been left with a computer to play with.

Just as he was growing anxious about the lack of contact, he saw a silver BMW pull up to the door of the farmhouse. Osman got out, all smiles, and asked Adil if he felt like taking another trip. Adil readily agreed, and they drove to a house in New Jersey, after sleeping a few hours in the car at a truck stop somewhere along the way. Once at their destination, Osman introduced him to three men – all Lebanese – before taking Adil into a bedroom and showing him a shoulder-fired antiaircraft missile system. The Stinger, Osman showed him, was reporting some kind of error code and he was worried it wouldn't work. Amazed to see such a ferocious weapon in front of him, Adil set to work. It only took a few hours for him to reset the thing, and Osman rewarded him with such high praise as he had never heard before.

After a celebratory dinner, Osman had left Adil at the house, telling him that someone would be in touch to arrange for his travel back to Mexico and onwards home. He was a very valuable commodity, Osman explained, and much was expected of him in the struggle against America. Adil stayed at the house for over a month without ever being contacted. During that time, he became close friends with the three men whose house he shared. They were all of similar age and background, and shared many of the same interests and hobbies. Almost every day, the men would leave in the morning and return in the evening, explaining that they were going to the beach. Eventually they took Adil with them, and when they weren't sitting at home playing on the X-box or watching pornographic movies, they went to Sandy Hook to watch and photograph birds and other wildlife.

Another man was supposed to have come up from Mexico to help them in their mission, but he never arrived. So as the day of their mission drew closer and no one had contacted Adil about his return home, Adil decided that he would help his new friends succeed in their mission. At first the three friends had rejected his offers, but that morning, he gave them no choice but to take him along. He had gone into the SUV and refused to leave. It turned out that the men hadn't even tried to coax him from the car; they were happy to see he was willing to die with them and join them all in Paradise.

Adil eventually admitted that he had been more than a little uncomfortable with the thought of shooting down civilian airplanes, even though he understood why it was necessary to do so. He had no qualms about bombing American politicians in their houses of parliament, and nor would he object to using missiles to shoot down warplanes over his adoptive country. But killing innocent people going about their business didn't sit well with him, and he was even a little relieved that Reagan and his commandos had prevented them from doing just that.

In many ways, Adil felt just as relieved to be finally able to tell someone what he had been doing, and he found the man sitting across from him a very receptive and sympathetic listener – or so he thought. In the end, he ended up telling Reagan pretty much everything he knew, and Reagan had asked a few follow-up questions that had helped him remember even more. At first, Adil had been terrified by Reagan and loathed him and everything he stood for. But as they talked, Adil got the sense that the only thing Reagan really cared about was preventing civilian loss of life. He spoke very respectfully about Islam and even seemed to empathize with his plight and desire for revenge. Adil hadn't expected that, and quickly realized that the man sitting across from him, while not exactly a friend, was also not quite an enemy. Reagan was just too easy to talk to, and the coffee and cigarettes helped, too.

"What happens to me now?" Adil asked as the conversation started to draw to a close.

"I imagine that some more people will want to talk to you over the coming days and weeks," Reagan replied. "Just continue being honest and truthful, and you'll be ok. Nothing bad will happen to you. After all, you're a hero – you might not think so right now, but you saved the lives of a lot of innocent people today. That's something to be proud of – something the Holy Qur'an deems very noble."

Adil nodded, very much wanting to trust and believe his new friend. He wondered how it was possible for a man to act so ruthlessly one minute, yet show so much compassion the next. There was so much about America he didn't understand, but he was quickly learning. As much as he still hated this country, Adil was starting to realize that if the man sitting across from him was typical of its soldiers, his jihad would only ever end in failure.

Just as soon as Adil was on his way back to the brig under the watchful eyes of Mason and a handful of MPs, Reagan reached for his phone to call Directors Goldberg and Smythe. He filled them in on the highlights of the interview, emphasizing the manner in which Adil had gained entry to the United States. Raul Ernesto Velazquez and the connection to El Paso, they all agreed, was of paramount importance and would become a major focus of the investigation. They also decided that instead of handing over the evidence collected at Sandy Hook and IKEA to agents from the Bureau's Newark Field Office, it made more sense to fly everything – including the prisoners – down to Quantico in the morning. The Bureau's Laboratory Services were located there, and that was the best place for a thorough forensic examination of the evidence.

33

By the time the conference call had ended, Brenda Videtti's Porsche and Jim Mason's rental Mustang had been hauled over to the base from Sandy Hook. Mason and Sinclair had the foresight to offload all their gear into the Black Hawk on the beach, but Watson had left behind her bag in the Range Rover. She quickly found it in one of the boxes the FBI had used to pack the contents of the shot-up car and retrieved her laptop, thankful that it still worked. Despite the day's excitement, Watson felt like she hadn't contributed nearly enough. She thought she had acquitted herself well enough in the action at Sandy Hook – that, at least, she had been somewhat trained for. But everything from the field interrogation to the takedown at the IKEA had been handled by Jack and his friends. All she had done was sit and watch, unable to help with something that she knew was well and truly beyond her expertise.

At least with her laptop, she could finally do something. She checked her e-mail and saw that the FBI had sent her the raw data from the terrorists' call histories; this, at least, was something she could work on. Watson started reviewing the files, taking careful notes, when she heard a helicopter flare outside in preparation for landing. She watched as two men in civilian attire got out and walked towards the hangar as some ground personnel ran to offload gear. When the men reached the hangar, Sinclair trotted over to get Reagan, who was just wrapping up a phone call, and waved for Watson to join them.

"Jack Reagan, NCIS Special Agent Amanda Watson, these are Master Chiefs Bernard Cohen and Dennis Tang," he said, introducing the new arrivals.

"Bernie," said the taller of the two, shaking their hands. "I've heard a lot about you, Mr. Reagan. It's a pleasure to be working with you."

"The pleasure is all mine, Bernie – and it's Jack."

"Commanders Videtti and Sinclair have told us more than a few stories, Jack," the shorter Tang said. "It's an honor to meet you."

"Welcome to Frozen Tide, gentlemen" Sinclair told the newcomers.

"Nice name – who picked it, Mason?" Cohen asked.

"Someone talking about me?" asked Mason, entering the hangar with Major Cahill, who promptly introduced himself to the new arrivals.

"Ok, now that we're all here, I think we have enough people to take down the house," Sinclair said. "Let's all pull up some chairs and discuss plans."

"I'm just going to go back to the phone logs," Amanda told Jack, feeling slightly out of place.

"Nope. You're part of this team, and you're going to sit through the briefing," he replied. "First you watch and learn, then you do," he added with a wink, seeing the skepticism on her face. He pulled up a chair for her and sat down next to her.

The group studied satellite photos of the house and the neighborhood, and decided on an operational concept that was simple and straightforward. The four SEALs would drive there in the Porsche, dropping off Cohen and Tang on the street behind the house. As they would make their way to the back door and prepare to breach, Sinclair and Mason would drive around the block to the front of the house. Once Cohen and Tang signaled that they were in place, Sinclair and Mason would breach from the front at the same time Cohen and Tang entered through the rear.

Once inside, all four men would sweep the first floor. After that, Sinclair and Mason would clear the upstairs before returning to the ground floor to provide cover for Cohen and

Tang, who would then check the basement. Reagan and Watson would provide overwatch and serve as the backup team out front in the Mustang while Cahill, having overseen the installation of fuel pods on his Black Hawk, would provide coverage from the air. He had also identified a field about 400 yards to the north that was on a list of fields used by Medivac choppers. He figured that in an emergency, he could set down there. After the house was secure, Reagan and Watson would go in as well to help search the place, while Cohen and Tang would take up positions outside.

"Shouldn't we let local police know we're there?" Watson asked.

"We generally don't like to announce our presence," Sinclair replied. "Done right, no one will even know we're there, and we should be in and out fairly quickly. The FBI will do a full sweep tomorrow, too."

"The only problem I can see is that it's a good 90 minutes by car in each direction," Mason pointed out.

"You're right – I don't know what's worse, driving for 90 minutes in New Jersey or flying over Indian country for that long," Cohen laughed. Like Reagan, he was a native New Yorker who held New Jersey in some disdain.

"Settle down, people," Sinclair said with a laugh of his own. "Let's leave here a little after midnight. That'll give us a couple of good hours of sleep." Everyone thought that was a particularly good idea. Someone, they saw, had had the foresight to bring in a half dozen cots, complete with bedding. "Let's check weapons and catch forty winks," Sinclair commanded.

That proved quickest for Watson, who only had two Sig Sauer pistols to clean and load. When she finished, she went over to the cots and carried a pair of mattresses, some pillows and sheets to the office Reagan had been using. She figured the floor was comfortable enough for her purposes. When she saw Jack finish, she waved him over, smiling as he approached. The phone logs could wait; right now, she really needed to feel his arms around her.

"I'm up," Jack told the door, looking at his watch. Someone had scratched at the door – the Ottoman Empire's equivalent of a knock. He wasn't feeling particularly refreshed or awake, but at least he hadn't had any nightmares. The nightmares might actually never come, he realized, softly kissing the neck of the dream curled up against him.

Amanda moaned softly in response. "What time is it?" she asked, followed by a yawn that Jack found incredibly cute.

"Zero dark hundred," he replied softly. "Time to wake up and get to work."

A short sigh was followed by another moan. "I'm up, I'm up," she said, squeezing Jack's hand and turning to kiss him softly on the lips. "Good morning, handsome."

"Good morning, beautiful," he replied, smiling.

She responded with a smile of her own, realizing that the way things were going, this was likely to be their wake-up routine for years to come. She had been in a number of relationships over the years, but her feelings had never been as intense as with Jack. In every other relationship, she had been able to envision living her life with her partner. With Jack, it was subtly but significantly different – she couldn't envision living her life without him.

The drive up to Paterson – technically Fair Lawn – took less than the 90 minutes they had expected, and by 2 a.m., everyone was in position on the quiet street. Master Chief Cohen tagged the house with a laser designator; the Black Hawk circling quietly overhead was equipped with a device that read heat signatures and Major Cahill reported moments later that the house was probably empty. Not that the SEALs relaxed any – they breached silently and carefully, calling out a few minutes later that the house was empty and secure. Reagan and Watson went inside as Cohen and Tang took up positions outside. No lights had come on even in the houses feet away from their target; their entry had gone unnoticed by people well into their sleep.

346

"Ok, Amanda, this is your show now," Reagan said. "Treat it like you would any other crime scene, but leave prints and DNA to the FBI. Focus on computers and other items."

"Sure thing," she replied, happy to finally be in her element. "Let's all be careful what we touch so we don't..." Her voice trailed off as she realized that everyone else was already wearing gloves. Watson took out her camera and photographed each room before searching it carefully. The only thing of interest on the ground floor – other than a game console that Mason quickly packed away along with every media he could find – was a Rand McNally road atlas of the United States with Sandy Hook circled in red on a tabbed page. After the sofa was searched, Reagan sat down to look through the atlas, wondering what else it might reveal. Watson went upstairs with Mason to continue the search.

"Heads up, car turning onto the street," they heard Major Cahill report.

"He's pulled up to the house," Tang reported a moment later. "Two door coupe, single male occupant. He's getting out now, seems to be looking up and down the street." By this point, every man had flipped off the safety selectors on their weapons.

"He's walking slowly towards the house," Cohen whispered. "Doesn't feel like a cop," he added.

"Jim, Amanda, stay put upstairs," Sinclair commanded over the radio. "Jack, into the kitchen. If he comes in, draw him there and I'll take him down," he said, moving into the shadows behind a large armoire. "Bernie and Dennis, eyes up for any other threats."

A moment later, Sinclair and Reagan heard a key scratching at the lock before turning the latch. The door opened slowly. "Adil?" they heard the voice say before adding something in Arabic. Reagan turned on the tap in the kitchen sink. "Adil?" the voice asked again, still by the door. As Reagan started whistling Anchors Away, the man started to walk tentatively towards the kitchen. "Adil?" he asked yet again, walking into the

347

kitchen. The moment he saw Reagan, standing there smiling at him, the man reached under his jacket as though to bring out a gun, only to feel Sinclair's powerful left arm around his neck, squeezing his circulation as Sinclair brought up his right hand to the man's head. The man started to go limp as he lost consciousness, and Sinclair carefully brought him to the ground before turning him over and binding his wrists, securing his pistol in the process.

"All clear – subject in custody," Sinclair said a moment later.

"All clear outside, no one else coming," Tang reported, a fact confirmed immediately by Cahill circling overhead.

"I wonder who this fucker is," Sinclair said as he turned the man over to look at his face. "Not Osman, that's for sure."

"Even money it's the Imam," Reagan suggested.

"Whoever he is, what do we do with him – take him with us?" Sinclair asked. "We're already full up in the Porsche." They had planned to use the Mustang to carry whatever they recovered from the scene.

"Yeah, put him in the Porsche," Reagan replied. "Jim will ride with us – we have a little detour to make, anyway."

"How're we doing with the upstairs?" Sinclair asked over the radio.

"Less than five minutes, boss," Mason responded.

"I'm going to go bring the car around. You ok covering him, Jack?" Sinclair watched his friend nod before heading out.

It took a little more than five minutes to bring down the two laptops and iPad they found upstairs, along with a number of books and magazines, and then load them into the Mustang. Sinclair and Mason then carried the gagged and hooded unconscious man and strapped him into the Porsche, with Tang getting in beside him. "Back to base?" Sinclair asked Reagan.

"Yeah, you guys head on ahead. I've got a stop to make first, but we won't be far behind you."

"Fair enough," he told his friend. "Ok, Major, we're splitting off. We are RTB in the Porsche. Pace us back, please," he spoke into his radio.

Less than half an hour later, after calling the FBI and asking them to secure the residence they had just searched, Reagan pulled up to a storage facility and typed his access code into the keypad by the gate, waiting for the gate to open fully before driving around back to his unit.

"What's here, Jack, your weapons stash?" Mason joked.

"Not quite," Reagan laughed, dialing in his combination before lifting up the garage door and flipping on the lights.

"This is just like that last Bond movie, Skyfall," Watson said with a grin as Reagan removed the tarp and fitted cover that had been keeping his car safe. "Surely you don't expect me to ride in *that*," she said with a laugh.

"Well, we could always walk," Reagan replied with a chuckle as he retrieved his keys from their hiding spot and unlocked the door, disconnecting the battery charger in the process. He was relieved that the engine growled to life without hesitation, and after allowing the car to warm up a little, carefully backed it out of its spot, letting it idle while he secured his lock-up.

"I do love your taste in cars," Watson said approvingly, admiring the silver Porsche Carrera Turbo S as Reagan walked around to hold the door open for her.

"Just so long as this one doesn't get shot up, too," he replied, a touch of sadness in his voice.

As the sun started to rise above the horizon, Master Chiefs Tang and Cohen supervised the loading of the Stingers onto the chopper that had brought them to New Jersey. They would accompany the missiles to Andrews AFB, and then onwards to wherever their bosses wanted them delivered. Meanwhile, Major Cahill's copilot and crew chief loaded the evidence boxes and terrorists' weapons onto their Black Hawk for the flight down to

Quantico. The terrorists would be loaded last, brought up from the brig where they had been secured. They would be blindfolded and gagged, with noise-cancelling headphones on their ears for good measure, and watched over for the duration of the flight by Pete Sinclair and Jim Mason.

The sound of the first helicopter taking off finally roused Cahill, Sinclair and Mason, all of whom were just tired enough to sleep through the burst of early morning activity occurring in the hangar around them. They stumbled out of their cots in various states of undress and headed straight for the coffeepot, where they were joined by Cahill's copilot. "Nice flying yesterday, guys," Sinclair said through a yawn.

"A smooth ride is a nice ride," Mason agreed as he worked the coffee machine. "So what do you say, Pete, can we keep them?"

"I've got no objection. Let's ask Jack what he has in mind first, though. What's your current detail, Major?"

"That's kinda up in the air right now, so to speak, but I can make myself available," Cahill grinned. He did have orders to report as a flight instructor, and as cushy and appealing a job as that would ordinarily be, he would much rather fly these guys around for a while longer. Three operations in twelve hours, with terrorists captured or killed in three different locations – these guys sure as hell knew their jobs, and for Cahill, nothing beat driving professionals. "What team are you guys with, anyway?" he asked. Both he and his co-pilot had them pegged as based in Little Creek, but they disagreed as to whether they were most likely Team 2 or 10. A fresh twenty dollar bill was riding on the response.

"DEVGRU," Mason replied, winking as he handed Cahill his coffee. In retrospect, the answer didn't really surprise Cahill – these guys had way too much pull to be anything else. "Morning, Jack...Amanda," Mason called out, seeing the couple stumble into the hanger. They looked as tired as everyone else, but they both seemed to have a bit of a spring to their step.

"Hey guys," Reagan called back. "Anything to eat out here?"

"I was just about to ask the same thing," Sinclair chuckled. "I suppose there's a mess hall somewhere, right?" he asked, turning to a young lieutenant who was hovering by the door, instructed by the base commander to give these men whatever they needed. "If not, we could always spit roast one of the terrorists. Who knows, it might get the others to open up and talk."

"I'll have some breakfast brought right over," the lieutenant promised, walking to a phone. He hadn't been told who, exactly, these people were, but it hadn't been all that hard to figure out. His first hint had been the collection of cars parked outside the hangar – two Porsches and a Mustang. Pretty much every naval aviator he had ever met drove a sports car, but then so did a good majority of special forces officers. The second hint had been their civilian attire, and the third and clearest hint was the collection of tactical gear scattered around the hanger – many of a type that the lieutenant had never seen before.

"So, Jack, what's next?" Sinclair asked as he handed his old and new friends mugs of coffee. "Our bosses are exceedingly happy at the way yesterday turned out, casualties notwithstanding. They're thinking of making Frozen Tide an ongoing thing, and we're yours until we hear otherwise. Oh, Jim found himself a new puppy – he wants to adopt the Major here," he laughed.

Reagan sat down with his coffee to pull together his thoughts, even though it was pretty clear to him what needed to be done next. "Any experience south of the border, Major?" he asked.

"Some, but none recent," Cahill replied. "Colombia and Peru, with one rather harrowing trip into Nicaragua as well."

"How about farther north, like Mexico?"

"No, nothing like that," he said, his eyebrow raised. He had once talked to a bird colonel who had delivered some Deltas

351

to Mexico, but he never did get the full story. Whatever had happened was blacker than black.

"El Paso, Jack?" Mason asked.

"That's where we start," Reagan nodded. "Inevitably it will lead us further south, though. How's your Spanish?"

"Muy bien, jefe," Sinclair chuckled. It turned out that of the six of them, only Cahill and Reagan had ever been to Mexico – Cahill to Acapulco and Reagan to Puerto Vallarta. None of them had ever desired to vacation there much.

"I know it's way too early to know how things are going to play out, but what's your best guess?" Mason asked Reagan. One of the many things these operators liked about Reagan was that, much like a chess master, he always seemed able to see several steps ahead.

"We're going to track the movements of Raul Velazquez back as far as we can," Reagan replied. "Even money says that his friends in El Paso are going to lead us to some kind of boss – maybe cartel – down Mexico way. There we'll probably need to apply some pressure to get more information on whatever pipeline they were using. I doubt any of the players will know names, at least not the names we really want to know more about. But they'll eventually get us to whatever freighters were used, and then we'll have another place to look, probably in North Africa."

"So off to El Paso we go," Sinclair said.

"Yeah, but before you do, try to see if you can't get anyone else in on this. As good as you two gentlemen are, I don't much fancy just the three of us taking on the cartels."

"We can absolutely do that," Sinclair replied. "Nick will be back from his honeymoon next week, and he'll definitely want in on this. He'll get a kick out of us putting the band back together again."

"How about us?" Cahill asked. He damn sure wanted in on this, whatever *this* turned out to be.

"First, figure out where you can park that thing in the El Paso area," Reagan said, pointing through the closed door in the direction of the Black Hawk. "After that, start going over maps of Juarez and get yourself oriented. It'll probably take us a week or so to figure out which area, exactly, we'll be operating in, but once we know, we'll probably want to move fast. You know the drill, Major – flight times, fuel loads, extraction points, that sort of thing."

"Figure on six or eight men in your ride, plus gear," Sinclair added. "I'll have orders cut for you by the time we get to Quantico, and I'll probably see about getting us at least one other bird.

"Fine by me," Cahill grinned. Three successful operations in less than a day and now these men were essentially planning to take on terrorists *and* the cartels, and all before breakfast. He'd worked with top operators before, but never quite like this. All of this, of course, made him very excited.

Watson, for her part, wasn't sure what exactly she was feeling. She had worked with Doug Cannon long enough to have watched him plan operations, too – most notably against a minor drug kingpin who had been trying to recruit sailors to deal for him. But however complicated, dangerous and even thrilling that had seemed at the time, it paled in comparison to what these men were discussing. Jack had pulled back the curtain and revealed a world she had always known existed, yet never would have otherwise seen. Right now he was essentially putting together – on the fly – the outline of a sophisticated covert operation into a foreign country.

Professionally, she was loving every minute of this – it was the experience of a lifetime. But personally, she worried about Jack. The way everyone was speaking made it clear that his participation was expected, so she couldn't really ask him not to go. Not for something this important to national security. She would just have to figure out a way to go with him, she decided. She had no illusions about her role in things; all of these men operated on a whole different level, not just from her but from everyone she worked with. But, she figured, she was the only one

353

with actual training as an investigator, so she could contribute *something*. And more than that, maybe she would be able to persuade Jack to step back from the more dangerous parts of the mission – for both their sakes.

34

The drive back to Washington turned out to be mercifully quick, aided in large part by a Maryland State Police trooper in an unmarked car Reagan unwittingly passed going twenty miles over the speed limit. As excited as the trooper was to ticket a speeding Porsche, he was even more excited to see a pair of NCIS credentials held up as he approached the car. That agency had been all over the news, responsible for preventing a major attack and killing the terrorists who had shot down the United 777. The ticket book was quickly put away, replaced by a cellphone and a request for a group selfie. After Reagan and Watson obliged in good humor, the trooper insisted on escorting them to the state line and took off at speeds bordering the obscene. The trooper was a Nascar fan and happy for the opportunity to open up his souped-up cruiser, but was a little disappointed that he couldn't pull away from the Porsche, hard as he tried.

Even for a bitterly cold Saturday afternoon, traffic was exceedingly light as they turned off the Beltway and drove south through Chevy Chase and into the District. All the parking lots they passed were largely deserted; suburbia, it seemed, had decided to stay home today. If the intent of terrorism is to terrorize, then surely the attacks that had failed a mere twenty four hours earlier had achieved a chilling success. The vast majority of cars they saw on the road were police cruisers, sent out en masse to reassure the people that they were safe. Instead, their presence had the opposite effect, with people thinking that surely some new attack must be coming, otherwise the police wouldn't be out in force. Osman Mansuraev may not have gotten the results he wanted, but he nevertheless achieved his goal.

Reagan pulled into the parking lot of the Marriott, and both he and Watson sighed simultaneously, turning to face one another to laugh at their shared reaction. "Home sweet home," Amanda said. "I suppose it's early enough that we should probably head to the office after we shower. And burn our clothes."

"I guess we probably need to be debriefed." Jack took out his phone to call Director Smythe and figure out what would be in store for them. "We're going to have a meeting at the Hoover Building at eight," he said when he ended the call. "Sounds like a group debrief," he shrugged, already guessing who would be in attendance and not looking forward to it one bit.

"That gives us plenty of time to relax," Amanda replied with an impish smile.

"That it does," he replied, leaning in to kiss her. Thirty six hours with little time to do more than splash water on their faces, her lips never tasted better. They dispensed with even the pretext of ordering room service, heading directly to Jack's room.

"Come here, Jack," she called from the bathroom after turning on the shower. "Let's get these off you," she said, lifting off his sweater and unbuttoning his shirt. She had never been this forward with anyone before, but she had stopped caring about such things with Jack days earlier. "I never noticed that," she remarked, caressing a small scar well hidden by the hair on his forearm.

"Old wound, old story," he replied, suddenly a little self-conscious.

"Which you'll tell me soon enough on our beach holiday." She smiled, bringing his arm up slowly to kiss the scar. "You have to promise me one thing," she said, suddenly serious. "I realize you know what you're doing, but please, Jack, for me – no more running off into battle like you did yesterday. I was worried sick, and I really don't want to lose you."

"You won't," he promised, wrapping his arms around her and holding her tight.

"Good," she whispered in his ear, squeezing back as tightly as she could.

They took a taxi to the Hoover Building, where they were surprised when the uniformed officer at the security desk asked to shake their hands, and even more surprised when a round of applause broke out as they were escorted to the elevator. Both of them were embarrassed by the attention and glad when the elevator doors closed. Their relief, however, was short lived – once they reached their floor, the corridor was lined with more people wanting to shake their hands. The mood in the Director's office was no less congratulatory, with handshakes and even hugs exchanged along with words of high praise that made Reagan and Watson more than a little uncomfortable.

"Great work, Jack. You saved a lot of lives – both of you did." Director Goldberg was all smiles. Special Agent Monaghan sat next to him, while Director Smythe and Special Agent Cannon were there for NCIS. Deputy Director Gallagher and one other person were there for the CIA, and a stenographer and videographer rounded out the group.

"Thank you, Director, but I just wish we had gotten to Newark Airport sooner." Reagan still blamed himself for the United flight that was shot down, and it was not something he could easily let go of. "How many casualties?" he asked.

"One ninety or so," Goldberg replied. "You can't blame yourself for that, though – not at all. As best we can figure, the terrorists in the IKEA parking lot fired early. The State Police response was too uncoordinated, and we think the arrival of the first officers on scene forced their hand," he said, referring to the terrorists. The Director and the heads of SWAT and the Hostage Rescue Team had already reviewed the amateur videos being shown nonstop on the news, and they felt that had Reagan and his people arrived first, they would probably have prevented the launch. It was just bad luck that the police had gotten there first. "What was your plan, come in low behind them and combat-rappel right on top of them?"

"That or land right on top of them," Reagan nodded. "We didn't have the right gear aboard to fast-rope, which is just as well because that terrifies me."

"You went in with the SEALs?" Monaghan asked in surprise. Smythe and Cannon had already been briefed to some extent by Watson, but none of the others had heard all the details yet. Neither Goldberg nor Gallagher were particularly surprised, though.

"Yeah, I figured three shooters was better than two," Reagan replied simply, followed by a shrug.

"Let's do this a little more formally, for the record," Goldberg said, taking control of the meeting. "I'm going to say this again in a moment, but you have nothing to be worried about – nothing at all. As far as the Bureau is concerned, every single thing you did was necessary, proper and in the interests of national security. As far as anyone else is concerned, you were acting under the color of authority provided by both NCIS and the FBI. Do you understand?"

Reagan nodded. What that meant was that he would not face criminal prosecutions for his actions. Probably. It did not, however, preclude the Congressional investigation he was sure would someday follow.

"Ok, then, let's begin." Goldberg nodded to the videographer and stenographer. "Tell us about your activities the last two days," he commanded.

"We called the operation Frozen Tide," Reagan said, starting his debrief. He provided a fairly thorough account of his actions, except that he declined to name Sinclair and Mason as the SEALs involved, referring to them simply as Shooter 1 and Shooter 2 instead. He spoke for close to forty-five minutes, with only a few interruptions for clarification or follow-up questions. The men listened attentively and, for the most part, impassively – neither Goldberg nor Monaghan did a very good job, however, at concealing their surprise at the scope of the operation Reagan had put together using outside resources.

Director Smythe was surprised as well, albeit for an entirely different reason. He had already heard all of these details from Watson, and was surprised at the extent to which Reagan played down his role, both at Sandy Hook and in the IKEA parking lot. To hear him tell it, it was almost as though he had never left the car or the helicopter. While it was, unfortunately, not unusual for someone to embellish details a little so as to play up his role in an action, Reagan was doing exactly the opposite. He had no qualms acting decisively when necessary or taking responsibility for his actions and shortcomings, but he also had no interest in praise or accolades. He did what he did because it was the right thing to do, not because it would look good for his career.

Reagan didn't even have a career in government – he was under no obligation to do anything at all, and could just have gone home at any time. The fact that he didn't spoke to his character and a sense of duty and honor that few people possessed. Smythe could count on his fingers the number of people he had met in his entire life who were like Reagan or, for that matter, Cannon or Goldberg. That realization made his decision easier, and he finally made up his mind. He would stay on as Director, provided that Reagan stayed too.

"How did you get this Adil to talk," Monaghan was asking.

"I asked questions, and he answered them," Reagan replied with a shrug.

"Thank you Jack, I think we have everything we need. We're done with the debrief," Goldberg said, nodding at the videographer and stenographer. He waited for them to leave and for the door to close behind them before continuing. "Now, off the record, Jack, how *did* you get him to talk?"

Watson watched the men's faces as Reagan explained, wondering if their reactions would be at all similar to what hers had been. The FBI Director and CIA Deputy Director had their lips turned up in partial smiles, while Cannon was trying hard to suppress a chuckle. Director Smythe sat fairly impassively, leaving only Monaghan with his mouth wide open.

"I would have shot him out of hand," Goldberg was the first to say.

"Me too," Cannon added. "I don't think I could have shown your level of restraint."

"Pretty risky play, Jack," Smythe offered, beating Gallagher to saying almost the exact same thing.

"Not too risky, actually," Reagan replied. "That's part of the reason I dragged him so far. I mean, aside from his comrades not being able to get a good look at what I was doing, it gave me a good deal of time to assess how unconscious he was. He was well and truly out, so I didn't think it much of a risk at the time."

"And if he had shown signs of moving while you were dragging him?" Goldberg asked.

"Then I wouldn't have aimed *behind* his head," Reagan answered without hesitation, seeing most of the men around the table nod in agreement.

"That would have been cold-blooded murder," Monaghan objected. "Of an unconscious, unarmed prisoner in restraints, no less. Even terrorists have rights." He was shocked, if not quite outraged, by what Reagan did, not to mention by what the other men – including his *Director* – were saying.

"Save your outrage for someone who gives a shit," Goldberg suggested. "That *terrorist* was preparing to use missiles in an attack against civil aviation – to kill people. Surely you don't mean to suggest that mutt had more rights than the people he was trying to kill."

"But he *hadn't* fired any missiles – they prevented him from doing so, and he was in custody," Monaghan replied.

"That's true, but at the same time, Jack had a very good reason to believe that at least one other attack was imminent," Smythe pointed out. "He exercised sound judgment trying to prevent those attacks. Besides, he didn't actually shoot the guy. He just wounded his pride a little."

"And if he *had* shot him?" Monaghan wanted to know.

"Then he would still have our unconditional support, in light of the totality of the circumstances," Goldberg declared.

"But that's not what the rules say," Monaghan continued to object. "I mean, what..."

"There's a quote I'm particularly fond of," Gallagher interrupted. "The relevant part of which states that rules are meant for the guidance of the wise. They're not always absolute. Sometimes we have to trust our man in the field to make the right call, even if we don't necessarily like it or even agree with it. And it should be clear to you by now that we all trust Jack."

Rules had always been sacrosanct to Monaghan, so he had trouble accepting that the top leaders of three different agencies were all suggesting that sometimes the rules didn't apply. Still, he realized that this was not an argument he was going to win. Something Gallagher said did get through, however, and Monaghan was starting to understand that these men knew a lot more about Reagan than he did. They had to, to place their trust in him like that.

"Sometimes we have to trust people like Jack to do the thing that's right, even if it doesn't seem to us like the right thing to do." Watson had been unable to stop from coming to her partner's defense, even though it was entirely unnecessary. Though facing Monaghan, she caught Smythe suddenly smile after she spoke.

"I see," Monaghan conceded, although he still didn't necessarily agree.

Smythe saw something as well. It struck him that Watson had covered for Reagan – she had left out his field interrogation of Adil from her description of events. That in itself didn't surprise him too much and only vaguely troubled him. Clearly after working side by side with the man for a week, Watson saw Jack as her partner, and partners did tend to cover for one another. What *did* surprise Smythe was the fact that Reagan had covered for Watson as well. He had just said that she had not been in a position to observe his interrogation, but Smythe didn't believe that for an instant. Reagan needn't have said that – clearly his actions were approved of by the men around the table – but his instinct had still been to protect Watson. And *that* meant... *Well, good for them,* Smythe thought, leaning back in his chair.

Amanda Watson was a promising young agent, even if still a little green. Smythe had reviewed her file before sending her off with Reagan, and liked what he saw. She was naturally talented as an investigator, and had been brought along nicely by Doug Cannon until the DEA borrowed her. Her bright future had been delayed a little by that useless little assignment, but Smythe was very impressed by what he had just heard her say. That sort of observation usually came from many more years of experience, and not all agents reached the point in their careers where they could analyze things in such terms. That thought made him smile.

More than that, from what he had seen of her in the last week, Smythe could tell that she was starting to come out of her shell gradually. Her reviews indicated that she was fairly conservative and reserved, but she didn't seem the least bit fazed by her presence in this high level meeting. Reagan's influence was obvious, and he clearly was every bit as good a mentor as Cannon. Her partnership with Reagan – which clearly extended outside of work – would be very good for both of them. Besides, they were very good people who had been through a lot in their lives. They deserved whatever happiness they could find together.

"So, what now, Jack?" Goldberg asked. They still had a few minutes to conduct some business before Secretary Jackson arrived, more than likely with his usual hysterics.

"Right around now, a nice rest sounds like a good idea. Maybe even a drink first," Reagan smiled.

"You definitely deserve both," Goldberg chuckled. "But after that, how do you want to proceed with the investigation?"

"Well I'm not exactly an investigator..."

"You're also not exactly *not* an investigator," Goldberg interrupted him. "We've heard about some of your, um, history," he pointed out.

Reagan's eyes darted over to Gallagher who merely chuckled. "I didn't tell them jack shit, pal. I could guess who did, though."

Reagan took a deep breath and leaned back in his chair before replying. "If yesterday's batch of terrorists are anything like the ones from last week, you're probably not going to get much in terms of usable forensics. Their phones are probably going to be the most interesting thing to look at. It's worth trying to get the Imam to talk – I tried a little this morning but he wasn't the least bit cooperative. Adil, on the other hand, is very helpful, but I don't know how much more he knows."

"Probably not very much," Cannon interrupted. "I went through the video of your interrogation this afternoon and I think you've pretty much tapped that well. Very good approach, by the way." Cannon was not one to be satisfied with an interrogation unless he was conducting it himself, but in this case, Reagan's approach had been very thorough. Watching the video, Cannon had started to mouth follow-up questions to what Adil was saying, only to find Reagan ask pretty much the same thing a second later. "As for the Imam and the others, I doubt we'll get anything at all from them. You were in a better position to do so before they were officially in our custody, and I don't think we'll get any farther," he admitted.

"Right now, I would say that the best bet is to pursue Raul Ernesto Velazquez and the El Paso connection. That seems to be how these guys got across the border, and maybe we can track them back all the way to their countries of origin. The more we find, the closer we'll get to Osman, and he seems to be the ringleader of this whole mess," Reagan offered.

"We think so, too," Goldberg said. "We've got a field office down there, in case you didn't know, and I've turned my people loose to track down Raul's associates. Special Agents Monaghan and Cannon will be flying down later this week to interview them."

"Can I make a suggestion?" Reagan asked. "Don't interview them. Set up discreet surveillance and figure out where they go, who they meet, who all the players are. Run this more like an intelligence op than a police investigation."

"You don't ask for much, do you," Goldberg chuckled. "We've thought about that, Jack, but as many resources as we can bring to bear, it's not going to be enough. Human traffickers run with the cartels, and it's for damn certain that the cartels know exactly who our people are. They would see us coming a mile away, and then Raul's associates would disappear and we'd be left with nothing."

"How about using someone else's people, then?" Reagan pressed.

"We do have some Spanish-speaking agents we could send down, if the Bureau doesn't object," Smythe suggested. "It'll take a few more days but we can do that."

"No objections here," Goldberg replied. "Technically we have the lead on these terrorist attacks, but we're glad to have your help. As a practical matter, we're treating this as a joint investigation and besides, your people seem to have a knack for getting results," he added, looking directly at Reagan.

"My agents may not be known to the cartels, but the moment we ask for permission from the Mexican government to operate there, that information will be passed along very quickly," Smythe warned. "We'll eventually run into the same problem."

"Not if we don't tell the Mexican government" Reagan replied. "I've got some Spanish-speaking friends planning a vacation to Mexico, and they have an interest in this as well. If, that is, the Agency doesn't have any assets it can use."

"Not there we don't," Gallagher said.

"Your suggestion certainly has possibility," Goldberg told Reagan, glad that the issue was on the table. It would make what he was about to ask much easier. "I suppose you'll be going down as well. How's your Spanish?"

"It's good enough, I suppose," he shrugged. "It makes sense I should go, of course. The only reason I'm hesitating even a little is that I'm not exactly excited to be conducting an operation on foreign soil without some kind of cover," he explained.

"Well that's easy enough to fix," Smythe grinned. "In case you're missing the obvious, I want you on board. Officially, that is – no more pretense and unspoken understandings. I want you to come work for me at NCIS. Your sense of honor won't let you just sit by the sidelines and besides, we need you. No political bullshit and no bureaucracy – you have my word. I know the people you've worked for haven't always had your back, but I'm not like that. You'll always have my full support, Jack – I promise."

"If you go work for Francis, you'll still have my full support as well," Goldberg said. "But I have to put this out there – I'd like you to think about coming over to the FBI. I'll admit, we have a lot more bureaucracy than Francis' agency, but I can shield you from most of that." Goldberg *had* to make the offer, but he could already guess what Reagan was going to say.

"Thank you, Director – David. But I started this with NCIS and I'd like to finish it with them as well. It feels like a good fit, and at the very least I owe them a debt of loyalty for allowing me to participate in this investigation."

"I'm afraid you've got that the wrong way around, Jack. We're the ones in your debt," Smythe said, rising to shake the man's hand. "Welcome aboard. Keep the credentials I gave you – eventually we'll figure out exactly what to do with you, but for now, that's as good a position as any."

"Welcome to the team, Jack," Cannon said, standing to shake his hand as well. As much as he liked Reagan and respected the work he was doing, Cannon knew there would be a lot of growing pains as the two men adjusted to one another's different styles of doing things. All things being equal, though, his

Director had made a very good call. "I suppose that means you're staying too, Francis?"

"I am," he confirmed. As soon as this meeting was over, he would be calling the Secretary of the Navy to announce his new hire and his acceptance of the permanent position offered him as Director. "So, Miss Watson, are you looking forward to Mexico? You and Jack seem to have a natural cover to work with," he grinned. "If, that is, you're willing to go."

"I go where Jack goes," she replied with a smile, wondering how her Director had figured out her relationship with Jack.

"Good. In that case... Dave, how much longer to finalize his clearance?" Smythe asked.

"End of the week to cross all the 't's and dot all the 'i's for TS and better," Goldberg promised.

"In that case, Jack, why don't you and Miss Watson take the week to rest and recreate while we get things set up in El Paso. We'll keep in touch by phone, but I don't really see a need for you to come in every day while we churn things out."

"Works for me," Reagan smiled.

"Works for me too," Watson replied with a smile of her own. Five whole days with Jack, probably on a beach somewhere, sounded perfect.

"Now we just have to sit through some yelling and screaming from the good Secretary Jackson," Cannon laughed. "But after that, we need to get some drinks into you to celebrate properly."

Much to everyone's surprise, Moses Jackson was not the least bit hysterical. He was quite pleased that things had worked out so well. Despite the tragedy of the United Airlines 777, a major terrorist attack had been averted, and that was something he was already taking credit for. While the news had already reported that New Jersey had been an NCIS operation and the FBI had saved the day in Washington, Jackson was looking forward to setting the record straight on the Sunday morning talk shows. Yes, those agencies had been the ones in the field, but he had personally met with them earlier in the week and given them their instructions. He was America's hero for the actions taken by others, and that made him very happy indeed.

35

Celebratory drinks were offered, and celebratory drinks were had, in a quiet pub in Georgetown just a block away from Osman Mansuraev's favorite haunt. Over a dozen agents had driven in, most from the office, to congratulate their now official colleague on his success in New Jersey and properly welcome him to the team. Cannon was struck by the way Reagan described the events – to hear him tell it, you'd think he had been onboard the helicopter the whole time. That was one more thing to like about the guy – he wasn't self-aggrandizing in the least. He didn't care about accolades, only about getting the job done.

Amanda was by Jack's side the whole evening, and at first Cannon wasn't sure how to feel about that. He was slightly worried that the promising young agent would be distracted from her work by the burgeoning romance. But the more he thought about it, the more at ease he was with the idea. Her work was definitely sharper around Jack, and that was not something that could be attributed to her undercover stint with DEA. More than that, she seemed to be coming out of her shell and into her own. Reagan was a good influence on her, Cannon realized, and probably would prove to be a good teacher too. Besides, their relationship effectively meant that they would be on the clock 24 hours a day, and that thought occasioned a chuckle.

After excusing himself to make a call for some updated information on the case, Cannon made his way over to where Watson was standing, joking with Pembridge and Hollerman. "So where are you two kids off to?" he heard Hollerman ask.

"I don't know, really – I told Jack to surprise me," Watson replied. Her cheeks were flush with color, but not just from the drink, all three men thought. This was a woman clearly in love.

"Where *is* Jack?" Cannon asked.

"He wandered over to the kitchen a while ago," Pembridge said. "Why don't you go and drag him back here? We're not done grilling him yet, especially about his intentions for our Amanda," he laughed.

Cannon headed over to the kitchen, where he was surprised to find Reagan chatting with two busboys – in pretty fluent Spanish – about their favorite hang-outs in Ciudad Juarez. He was about to interrupt with a joke about Reagan ignoring the people who had turned out in his honor when he suddenly realized exactly what Jack was doing – Juarez was just across the border from El Paso. Cannon quickly turned and stumbled out of the kitchen, pretending he was drunk. He leaned against the wall in the narrow hallway and closed his eyes, suddenly a little dizzy. *That son of a bitch is working the case – at a party in his honor on a Saturday night while we're all out there drinking at the bar.* Cannon opened his eyes and shook his head, chuckling to himself. Whatever doubts he had still harbored about Jack Reagan were well and truly gone.

Anatoly Lavrov dropped his bag on his bed and went to check to make sure the air conditioner was working. It was well over 30C in Buenos Aires and his villa was sizzling. Satisfied that cool air was flowing through the vents, he stood by the window, looking out over the Rio de la Plata. For the first time in days, he felt safe; the ownership of this house was well-hidden behind multiple corporate shells, none traceable to him. Besides, if the Americans had been on to him, he would have been detained in Rio, or on arrival in Buenos Aires.

His Mansuraev legend was burned – of that, he was sure. Several of his men had been taken alive in Washington, and eventually they might be persuaded to provide his description. It was far from certain that they would talk, of course, and the current occupant of the White House was reluctant to extract such information by more aggressive means. Still, it would be too risky ever to use that name again, and in a few weeks his features would be sufficiently changed so as to render any physical description useless.

Over the previous few days, Lavrov had increasingly started viewing his operation as a success. One downed plane and several recovered mortars had been more than enough to send America into a panic. Commercial aviation had ground to a halt simply from fear – most passengers had immediately cancelled their reservations and expressed reluctance to ever fly again until the government did something to show it could protect them. Airline stocks had the floor yanked out from under them and by the time the markets closed on Friday, the ripple effect had sent the Dow plunging over 500 points.

It would be worse still in the coming week, with airlines speculated to begin laying off employees within days. That would have a carry-over effect into other industries, and analysts were already wondering how many years it would take to reverse the expected losses. The only companies that were expected to see an uptick in their share prices were automobile manufacturers. That was only natural, since if people could no longer fly, they would have to drive. Lavrov had a plan for that, too, but the time wasn't quite right to implement it. Yet.

Still, he couldn't help but wonder what had gone wrong. Clearly the Americans had known – his men at Sandy Hook had been killed without ever launching a missile, a fact repeatedly mentioned on the news. More than that, they had been killed by agents of NCIS, the very agency he had chosen to attack as a diversion. That couldn't be mere coincidence, Lavrov realized, but as much as he analyzed the problem, he couldn't begin to guess how they had known. The more he thought about it, the more it bothered him – and the only way he could stop thinking about it was with drink. He walked over to his well-provisioned liquor cabinet and opened a bottle of vodka, drinking straight from the bottle. In a few days he would have to sober up, he knew. But for now, the alcohol helped.

With so many flights cancelled, Jack and Amanda were happy that theirs was still scheduled to depart on time. She still had misgivings about their destination – Amanda had been to Miami for a conference some years back and had found it too loud and full of people the one night she went out exploring with her colleagues. At least this time she was going with Jack, and she figured the very worst case scenario would be that they never left their hotel room. That suited her just fine, she thought, squeezing his hand and flashing him a smile as they boarded the plane.

They had been upgraded to First Class, of course, just as soon as they had showed their credentials at check-in, and no sooner had they taken their seats than the pilot had walked back to shake their hands and thank them for their service. The Federal Air Marshal in 2B shook their hands as well, discreetly showing his identification. Formerly an MP stationed at Fort Bragg, he had watched the second amateur video to surface with great fascination. Though taken from a greater distance than the rappelling video, it showed three agents taking on the terrorists with the same sort of precision he had seen the Deltas practice so often. He had always thought NCIS were just glorified Shore Patrol – he had no idea they had shooters of that caliber. Woe be to any terrorist trying to take *this* flight, he thought, taking his seat and buckling in.

As soon as the flight reached cruising altitude, Amanda took her laptop out and started going through the call logs compiled by the FBI from the terrorists' phones. Jack, she saw, was chatting up the middle-aged Hispanic flight attendant working First Class. She remembered enough high school Spanish to understand he was asking what male Latino passengers were like – what they wore, how they acted, what they talked about. It took her a minute to realize what he was doing.

"My mind is slow today," she said, leaning in to him with a smile. "But I know what you're up to."

"Oh?" he replied, looking longingly at the flight attendant as she went to attend to another passenger.

"You turkey!" she laughed, elbowing him in his ribs.

"You know I only have eyes for you," Jack said, looking into her eyes and leaning in for a kiss.

"You better!"

"I absolutely do," he said, looking at her in a way that made her feel wanted as a woman. "Hmm. I wonder what the lavatory is like on this flight," he added with a wink.

"Probably unsanitary," she laughed. "Besides, too many people, Jack," she pointed out. Normally it was something she wouldn't even consider – but with him, anything was possible.

"Big deal," he said with a wry smile. "I bet if we showed our credentials, we'd even get a standing ovation." That made her laugh hard enough that she spilled her champagne into her lap.

"I'm all wet thanks to you!" She tried to sound stern but couldn't pull it off.

Jack leaned in to kiss her on the cheek. "That's the general idea," he whispered in her ear.

"Whatever am I going to do with you?" she asked no one in particular, leaning back in her seat with a grin.

"Director Smythe? Special Agent Cho, sir. I've been trying to reach Jack Reagan but keep getting his voicemail."

"I think he's in the air right now. What's going on?" Smythe was at home for a change, enjoying a quiet lunch with his wife, who surprisingly didn't mind that he was putting off retiring again.

"Something pretty hot, actually. I was just in a village about 35 klicks from base and talked to some people who recognized the photos of the Abdali family. They know Dawar by a different name, but are pretty sure it's him. They gave me the name of the town they think he's from. It's nowhere near here, so I'm not quite sure what to do."

"How solid is this?" Smythe asked.

"Pretty solid, sir. This family had relatives a few houses down from Dawar and met him once or twice, just to say hi to. They say he seemed to be somehow involved with the old government, the Taliban one, and that fits with what we know. What do you want me to do with this?"

Smythe thought a little before replying. "Did you leave a message for Jack?"

"Yes, sir."

"In that case, wait for him to call you back and see how he wants to proceed. I have a feeling he's probably going to ask some friends of his to pay that house a visit late one night."

"Will do, sir." Cho had seen the videos from New Jersey too, and what his Director said just clicked. "That was Jack and his friends in the parking lot at Newark, wasn't it?"

"No need to go spreading it around, but yeah. He works for us now – officially, I mean. Anything else I can do for you, Cho?"

"No sir, sorry to bother you at home," he replied, ending the connection. *Hot damn!* he thought, wondering if that meant Reagan would be putting together some kind of team now. If so, that was one team he'd kill to be on. Working with this guy, even if only over the phone, had turned into an adventure that he absolutely loved. With nothing else to do at the moment, Cho turned to his laptop, playing the two videos from the IKEA. Friends to pay a visit late one night could only mean special forces, and Cho stared at his screen, trying to figure out which one was Reagan and which ones were his friends.

It took a little over ten minutes and thirty replays of each video for Cho to realize the answer was staring him in the face. *You're slipping,* he told himself when it finally occurred to him that it didn't really matter which one Reagan was. All three had pretty much the same moves, at least from a distance. They moved cohesively, like a unit used to working together. And that meant... *Oh man, I* really *want to be on his team!* As fun as it was riding around with Marines, those guys were on a whole different level.

It didn't take much longer for Reagan to return his call and tell him pretty much what Smythe had predicted he would say. It would take a few days to arrange properly, but his "friends" would most certainly pay the house a visit. The only surprise – and a pleasant one at that – was that Reagan wanted him to ride along with his friends and participate in any intelligence gathering and interrogation that took place.

"How about after that?" Cho asked hopefully.

"It rather depends on what that mission turns up," Reagan replied as he held the taxi door open for Watson. "If you bag Muska, I'll probably want you to transport her back to DC. She's the key to breaking Eggerton." Eggerton was on a hunger strike, praying in Arabic when he wasn't pacing his cell cursing. "What does your gut tell you about tracking Kerimsolta's movements?" Reagan had come to trust Cho's instincts.

"He was a ghost in the night, Jack. Only way we're going to track his movements is if we get Abdali and he talks."

"How are your language skills?"

"I'm fluent in Mandarin, Spanish and Italian. Conversational in Arabic and French," Cho replied, sensing an opportunity.

"And you're good in the field," Reagan pointed out. "If you bag the Abdalis, come back to DC with them. I could use you. If not... let's play it by ear. I'll talk to our cousins up the river and see what they can do to track him. I'll probably still want you in Washington, if that's ok with you."

"Hey, whatever you need, I'm there," Cho promised, trying hard to hide his excitement. Barely a week earlier, he had been eager to return to his nice, comfortable apartment in Naples and his nice, comfortable routine duties. But damn if this wasn't so much more exciting!

The drive to the hotel was blissfully short, but there were just as many people out and about as Amanda had feared there would be. She preferred her vacations as quiet as possible, and besides, all she really wanted was to spend time alone with Jack. The room at the Ritz Carlton South Beach, at least, was quiet and secluded, even if it did overlook the pool. "I forgot to pack my bathing suit," she said as they looked out over the pool from the balcony, the beach a short distance to their left.

"That's ok," Jack said. "We can always go shopping."

"I'm not like any girl you know, Jack — I hate shopping," she laughed. "And we really don't need bathing suits for what I have in mind."

"Oh? What's that?" he asked, as expected.

"How about this, for starters," she said, wrapping her arms around his shoulders and kissing him passionately.

"Not bad for a start," he admitted before kissing her again, reaching down with his arms to give her rear a playful squeeze.

"Let's leave the show to them," she said, tilting her head towards some synchronized swimmers performing their routine in the pool. She took Jack's hand and led him back inside, pushing him playfully down on the bed before climbing up to straddle him. "Hell, Jack, you can't even wear a bathing suit like *that*," she said playfully, feeling how excited he was. "Whatever am I going to do with you?" she asked, unbuttoning his shirt and running her hands on his chest before leaning in to kiss him.

"I'm sure I can come up with some ideas," he said, removing her blouse and unclasping her bra.

"That's a very hard idea," she giggled, reaching down to undo his belt. "But that's ok," she added, kissing his chest, her lips moving lower. "Hard is just what I need." Hours later, they came up for air just long enough to order dinner from room service before putting the "Do Not Disturb" sign back on the door.

Jack opened his eyes slowly, finding a mass of hair on his face and Amanda draped across his chest, her arms and legs wrapped around him. He moved his fingertips slowly down her bare back, feeling her shudder gently in her sleep and press herself tighter against him. He thought himself blessed to have found such an amazing woman, but wondered what this extremely bright, witty, attractive – and very sensuous – young lady could possibly see in him. Everything with her felt so comfortable, yet so very exciting. Being together just felt *right*, more so than with anyone he had ever known. It didn't quite occur to him yet that she felt precisely the same way.

Her eyes opened slowly, as though to a dream, and she squeezed Jack tighter still. "Good morning, beautiful," he said, kissing her forehead softly.

"Good morning, handsome," she replied, smiling as she tilted her face up to kiss his lips.

"How did you sleep?"

"Like a dream," she replied. "In fact, I think I'm still dreaming. Maybe I should pinch myself to be sure I'm awake."

"I can do that," he promised, moving his fingertips to her exposed breast.

"Ouch!" she said playfully. "They're still a little sore from last night."

"Ok, I'll stop," he sighed.

"Don't you dare!" She held his hand firmly in place. "I rather like that."

"I wonder what else you like," he said, moving his hand slowly to her silky-smooth thigh.

"That, too," she replied softly, closing her eyes, her heart aflutter. She slowly moved her leg further up and felt her heart start to race as she kissed Jack, the intensity of passion growing. "Time for Round 11," she said after gently biting his lower lip. "Or is it 12? I lost count."

"Me too," he admitted, rolling her onto her back and lifting himself over her. "I guess that means we should start over," he grinned, kissing her neck in exactly the spot he knew excited her. He didn't stop there; his lips moved slowly down her body as she shuddered a little and moaned softly.

36

Their first meal out together was lunch at one of the many restaurants on Ocean Drive, where they sat outside under a light-green umbrella and watched the people saunter by. They both had Chilean sea bass, which was just flaky enough to be quite good, and then lingered over coffee, talking about anything and everything, trading jokes about what they saw out on the street. It was all very casual, and felt as natural as everything else they did together. Although Amanda generally disliked crowds and going out to busy places, she was seeing the world through Jack's eyes now, and she found herself excited by the whole experience.

Jack turned to chat to the couple sitting at the table next to them, who were lingering over coffee as well. He spoke in Spanish to the young couple from Venezuela, who were enjoying part of their honeymoon in Miami Beach before flying off to Los Angeles. Amanda joined in as well, using Spanish learned in high school and two semesters in college, but she was unable to keep up with some of the colloquial expressions Jack was dropping. His Spanish, she quickly noticed, was now almost entirely without accent. Within a day, native Spanish speakers would be asking him what country he was from, and a day after that, having changed his pronunciation of 'll's from a 'y' sound to a slight 'j' sound, people would ask where in Argentina he was from.

"What now?" Amanda asked after both couples had settled their bills and the honeymooners turned to walk south along Ocean Drive.

"How about we practice tailing them," Jack suggested.

"Won't be easy," she replied. "We've been up close and personal."

"That's the point," Jack grinned. "Why don't you take the lead and show me how it's done."

"I'm up for a challenge," she said, forming a grin of her own. She had excelled in this sort of thing in training. They followed the couple down, crossing over to the beach behind them and walking until they reached South Point Pier. They had stayed close enough to the Venezuelans to just about hear what they were saying at times, but had been discrete enough that their presence was not remarked upon when the couple turned around a few times, looking past them. "How was that, Jack?" she asked as they watched a massive cruise ship pass by, standing side by side, his arm draped around her shoulder as her arm wrapped his waist. She was pretty satisfied with the job they had done.

"Not *too* bad," Jack allowed. "Now tell me about the people behind us."

"Two Hispanic men, mid twenties," she said at once. "They've been behind us pretty much the whole way since the restaurant, about a hundred feet back."

"And?" he asked.

"And... what did I miss?" she asked, forming a little frown. Jack turned her around gently and hugged her from behind, pointing out something up the beach to their right.

"At your ten o'clock," he said softly in her ear. "Man in the blue shirt and sunglasses with the woman wearing a hat. They've been with us since just past Lummus Park. And at around your nine o'clock are two young ladies in bikinis who came on a little shortly after."

"Whoops. I missed them," she admitted. Jack felt her deflate a little in his arms and he turned her around to kiss her. "I guess I'm a little rusty," she offered. "What else?"

"Just this," he replied, holding up his phone and showing her a picture of herself looking rather focused and intense. "Try to relax a little and enjoy yourself," he suggested.

Her eyes went a little wide when she saw the picture – she hadn't even observed Jack take it. "Ok, I'm a lot rusty," she said, biting her lower lip. "But we have time to practice," she added.

She was always determined to excel at whatever she did, and she quickly realized that Jack was a teacher of note. She realized something else too, and now seemed like a good time to bring it up. "You were CIA, weren't you?" she asked, her hands pressed against his waist as she leaned against him.

"Once upon a time, yes," he replied with a sigh. He had not been looking forward to this particular conversation. "Why don't we walk up to the Fontainebleau and talk about it – they have great mudslides there and I think I'm going to need a drink."

"Sounds like a plan," she said cheerfully. She had never felt Jack this nervous, and quickly understood that he was probably anxious about what she would think of him. "But first, three things." She leaned in to kiss him. "First, what's a mudslide?"

"It's like a tasty chocolate shake with alcohol," Jack chuckled.

"Sounds good," she said with a chuckle of her own, leaning in to kiss him again. "Second, where's the Fontainebleau?"

"About four miles up the beach."

"*Four* miles? You weren't kidding when you said you liked to walk!" She leaned in to kiss him again. "Third, and most importantly, I want you to know that nothing – and I mean *absolutely nothing* you say will change in *any* way what I think about you or, more importantly, how I feel about you. I promise," she smiled, leaning in to kiss him yet again. "Now tell me the story of Jack Reagan," she ordered, squeezing his hand as they started to walk up the beach.

"Once upon a time, there was a young college student who met a very remarkable professor," he began, walking arm in arm with Amanda. His story took most of the walk to tell, and she listened attentively, occasionally squeezing his arm for reassurance. Nothing he said came as much of a surprise – not with what she'd come to know of him during the previous week.

The most remarkable thing was the matter-of-fact way in which he recounted everything, almost as if anyone else could do the things he had done. "So that's the story of Jack Reagan," he concluded as they stood on the beach in front of the Fontainebleau. "So... what do you think?"

She could see the worry still in his eyes, and lifted her hands up to hold his face, replying first with a soft kiss. "I think you are easily the most remarkable man I've ever met – and I've thought that even before knowing your story. I'm just sorry at how alone you must have felt, going through all of this. That's in the past, though. Now you have me, and I will always be there for you and support you. Whatever you've done – and come what may – you will always have me. *Always.*" She leaned in to kiss him again, this time even more passionately. The wind carried the sounds of the crashing surf and laughing children as she hugged him, feeling fiercely protective, resting her head on his shoulder. She kissed the side of his neck gently before softly whispering in his bad ear. "I'm head over heels in love with you, Jack Reagan."

The couple walked hand in hand across the sand and boardwalk to Coconut Willie's, ordering burgers to go with their mudslides. The drinks were every bit as delicious as advertised.

They quickly settled into a routine, starting their days lazily in bed, curled up together, with soft kisses that grew in intensity until any lingering inhibitions dissipated and the throes of passion overtook them. A mid-morning swim in the pool followed – both were avid and skilled swimmers, but Amanda was surprised at how long Jack could hold his breath underwater, especially after he started smoking after-dinner cigars purchased from any of the numerous young cigar girls skating their way around the restaurants on Ocean Drive. She didn't mind the cigars one bit, even finding them rather manly.

After their swim, they would walk up to the Fontainebleau, sometimes on the sand along the waves lapping at the shore, and sometimes along the boardwalk – but always hand in hand. Lunch followed, from the grill at Coconut Willie's, accompanied by a couple of mudslides before the walk back down to the Ritz Carlton, usually practicing tailing techniques and discrete photography along the way. A few hours in the afternoon were set aside for catching up with work, and they would sit side by side, reviewing every new development together by the desk. Eventually, work would be set aside and they would migrate to the bed – or the armchair, dresser, desktop, floor and, on one particularly adventurous afternoon, the balcony – for some 'frolic and detour,' as Jack had jokingly called it.

A quick shower – together, of course – would follow before they headed out in the evenings. They would walk along Lincoln Road or Ocean Drive, window-shopping and browsing through stores. As much as Amanda detested shopping, she secretly loved doing it with Jack. More than that, she loved each and every thing he picked out for her, especially the more colorful or daring outfits that stretched her more conservative tastes. She would try them on in front of a mirror with Jack standing next to her, and would always form a smile at their reflection – not so much happy with how she looked as she was happy with how they looked together.

Amanda, in turn, helped select some new outfits for Jack, aided by the shop girls in choosing the sort of clothing preferred by Latin American businessmen. Wearing those clothes, with his dark tan, eloquent Spanish and extensive knowledge of arts and antiquities, he could easily pass for an art dealer from Argentina – with her as the arm-candy he had picked up in Miami. It was a cover that needed no discussion or explanation; it came as naturally to them as everything else they did together.

Dinner would follow, at a restaurant randomly selected from among the many on Ocean Drive. They ate and laughed as people walked by in their evening finery, never running out of things to talk about. More than that, they soon found they were able to talk very easily without words; they knew one another so well – so intimately – that they could communicate with just a glance or a look, a skill reserved only for the luckiest of couples that had been together for ages. After dinner, they would linger over coffee and Jack's cigar, engaging others in conversation and improving their Spanish. Then they practiced trailing and surveilling random people, trading techniques and learning from one another, refining their skills in the process.

It was work, but it was also fun – Amanda and Jack loved what they were doing, almost as much as they loved that they were doing it together. They were partners in every sense of the word, but no more so than when they returned to their room. She yearned for his touch, as he yearned for hers. Whether softly and gently or harder and more vigorously, they always made love, collapsing in each other's arms, spent and satiated. They fell asleep intertwined together as one and woke the same way, always pressed together, a physical manifestation of the way they both felt. Neither one ever wanted to let the other go.

Outside of the perfect little world inhabited by Reagan and Watson, the investigation proceeded apace. The apartments that had been occupied by the terrorists were eventually all located, and while some leads did develop, none seemed to go anywhere. A few of the terrorists had been found in the files of Israel's Mossad, but all had been such small and insignificant players that none had so much as a partial biography, let alone a reliably accurate name. The most promising lead by far was Raul Ernesto Velazquez, and Special Agents Cannon and Monaghan were in El Paso, setting up discreet surveillance on his known associates. That was proving to be exceedingly difficult, in light of the very isolated neighborhoods they frequented and daily trips across the border.

In Afghanistan, a drone tasked to provide real-time imagery of the town suspected to be the Abdali family's home had confirmed their presence in a well-built and fairly modern two-story home to the rear of what passed for a cul-de-sac. A mission to extract them was in the works, and Special Agent Cho was exceedingly happy to be sitting in on the planning. At first, the men – he suspected they were Deltas – had been reluctant even to talk to him, his agency affiliation notwithstanding. Not even a phone call from Director Smythe seemed to do the trick, until, that is, he described Cho as Jack Reagan's personal representative. That had magically opened the doors previously closed to him, and not for the first time Cho wondered what kind of pull Jack had that his Director lacked.

Anatoly Lavrov opened his laptop and loaded the anonymizing program for his browser before accessing the White House calendar of events. The President, he was relieved to see, was still scheduled to fly out on holiday the next day, joining his family already enjoying the sandy beaches of Hawaii. The Dow may have dropped by over a thousand points and the American people may have been in a veritable panic following the previous week's terrorist attacks, but the President apparently loved his holidays as much as he loved golf. He had spoken on television – twice, in fact – over the course of the previous days, his empty words of reassurance ringing hollow to anyone but the most gullible of audiences.

A strong leader would have called for vengeance and retribution, vowing in the name of an Almighty God to track the terrorists to the ends of the earth if need be, before torturing and then executing them publicly for their crimes. A strong leader would have urged his people to brush off the attacks against their country and continue doing business as usual – continue engaging in commerce and the vast activities of social and economic enterprise that made America so uniquely powerful. A strong leader would have reminded his people that what makes America so great is the strength, resilience and enterprise of its people, and that this was a moment to rise to the occasion and not fall prey to cowardice and submit to the whims of those who would seek to destroy them.

But the President had said none of those things. He had promised to "seek justice" for the "crimes" committed, but called for restraint, tolerance and even understanding. He had urged people to remain "cautious and vigilant" in conducting their affairs, promising that the American people would overcome this "tragedy." In short, he came across as weak and ineffectual.

Not that anyone else could have done any better; Lavrov understood very well that the current politicians in high office were nothing like their predecessors, whose strength had proven to be so dangerous to his Rodina. The leaders of the twentieth century had been of a much higher caliber than those of today – quite simply, they had been made of sterner stuff. Compared to their powerful and sage leadership, the current batch of leaders were rank amateurs who failed to grasp how to govern effectively, even from strength. Whether in two years or two days, if his plan was successful, America would have a new leader, one who would be just as weak as the last.

The little girl sat on the floor of the lobby of the Ritz Carlton, bawling her eyes out, her high-pitched shrieks interspersed with mournful sobs and tearful wails. Her parents were besides themselves, trying to comfort her and coax her to her feet as the other people in the lobby looked on, some in anger and some in disgust. The hotel staff was huddled behind the desk, engaged in an animated talk with a lot of pointing in the direction of the family. No one seemed to know what to do, and everyone steered well clear of them. Everyone, that is, except for Amanda and Jack. They merely shared a look and, without a word, walked straight over.

"Hi there, sweetie," Amanda said, kneeling down next to the girl. "What's wrong?"

"I lost my Kevin," the girl replied between sobs.

"Kevin is a stuffed koala," her father explained to Jack, who was standing with the parents. "She travels everywhere with him." His accent was decidedly Australian.

"It's my fault," the mother added, clearly holding back tears. "We had him on the flight from Sydney, but then I must have dropped him when we rushed to make our flight in LA. She slept the whole of that flight – our little Maddie, that is – but when we landed here in Miami and she couldn't find him, she started crying and we haven't been able to get her to stop." The mother was on the verge of despair and barely holding it together, and her husband seemed unsure what to do.

"Excuse me for a minute," Jack said, squeezing Amanda's shoulder as he walked quickly to the store in the lobby. Less than two minutes later he returned, holding something behind his back. Amanda, he saw, had managed to calm the girl, but only a little. Maddie was fascinated by the beautiful woman in front of her, and was playing with Amanda's long hair between sobs. Jack knelt down next to her.

"My name is Jack, and this is my very good friend Max." He pulled a small stuffed bear from behind his back, watching the child's eyes widen and fix on the toy. "We're on holiday, too, but unfortunately we're going to be very, very busy. Can you do us a big favor?"

"What?" Maddie asked, her eyes never leaving the bear.

"Can you take Max with you and show him around? He's really a very sweet bear, and I think you two will have a lot of fun together."

Maddie hesitated only an instant before grabbing the bear and hugging it. "Ok," she said, her tears suddenly gone and her missing Kevin already a distant memory.

"And when you're done showing him Miami, why don't you take him back home with you?" Jack continued. "He loves to travel and really wants to see Australia. Do you think that would be ok?"

"Yes!" the girl replied brightly, with a very warm smile. "I can do that!"

As soon as Jack and Amanda rose to their feet, they were immediately hugged by the girl's parents. "I can't begin to thank you enough for your kindness," the father said, while the mother struggled to hold back tears as she added, "You were both sent by the angels."

Jack watched the family head off to the elevator; little Maddie was skipping along and talking to Max, telling him about all the exciting things they would be doing together. As he turned back to Amanda, he could see tears welling up in her eyes and was about to ask what was wrong when she threw her arms around him, hugging him so tight that he could barely breathe. She buried her face in his shoulder, and he could feel her trembling a little. The tears then started, and were not soon to stop.

"What's wrong, babe?" he asked softly, holding her and trying to comfort her by gently rubbing her back. Eventually the tears stopped, and then the trembling, and Amanda lifted her head, her eyes fixed on his shoulder.

"I've made you all wet," she remarked, almost in surprise.

"That's not a problem," he replied with a reassuring smile. "All that's important is that you're ok. What's wrong?" he asked again.

"Nothing is wrong," she said, finally looking into his eyes. "Nothing at all. I just realized something, and it just made me very emotional. You know what I realized? I could live a thousand lifetimes and never meet anyone who comes close to being as good a man as you are, Jack Reagan." She leaned in and kissed him softly, pulling away to reveal a coy smile. "Just so you know, I'm never letting you go."

Jack couldn't help but smile as he leaned in, his lips hovering just next to Amanda's. She had started to close her eyes, expecting to be kissed, but Jack waited. "Just so *you* know," he said when she opened her eyes to see why he hadn't kissed her yet, "I'm never letting you go, either." Then he kissed her, softly at first, and then more passionately as they held one another in the hotel lobby for all to see, neither of them caring a whit about the people around them.

37

The hardest part to engineer had been the explosive devices. The first limitation had been weight. Lavrov's initial tests suggested a maximum payload weight of exactly 1 lb., but after extensively studying the machines, he realized that he could trim down on some excess parts that were more decorative than functional and so increase the payload to 1.35 lbs. That *might* be enough, but he wanted more, and he had spent days online researching parts to see if he could remove any redundant features. It was all very frustrating because it seemed that with the exception of a couple of wires he could shorten and thereby save a few ounces, everything he had left on the machines was crucial for their operation.

Weeks passed and Lavrov had focused on other things, but always wondered about this problem in the back of his mind. The breakthrough occurred, fittingly enough, on one of his early scouting trips to Sandy Hook. The beachside hotel he stayed in, just before peak season, lacked the excitement he had hoped to find. There wasn't a single woman under 30 in the hotel, so he had stood on his balcony, studying the beach carefully through the telephoto lens of his camera for any promising candidates for some evening entertainment. That's when inspiration struck – the cameras on his machines were themselves redundant. They weren't needed at all for his purposes, since the whole thing could be made to work on GPS alone.

As soon as he returned to his farmhouse in the Shenandoah Valley, he had found that removing the camera and its associated wires and controls meant a savings of a little over a pound and a half. This brought his maximum payload weight to just around 3.1 lbs., and that was plenty. Better still, removing the camera had resulted in less power being drawn from the battery, which in turn meant that the devices could travel a greater distance. The problem with the weight limitation was thus elegantly resolved.

The second limitation was the placement of the explosive charge within each machine so as to maintain the perfect weight distribution. This, in turn, would be somewhat guided by the ignition device he would use – itself the third and most challenging limitation. This was the challenge he turned to first, and it took Lavrov well over a year to come up with a solution he could live with. Some things he could rule out immediately; a fuse ignition system, for instance, would be totally inappropriate for this application. Likewise, a radio control detonator would be inappropriate for two reasons. First, it was highly likely that the Americans would employ jammers to interrupt his frequency and second, his men would need line of sight of the target, and Lavrov had no doubt they would be quickly spotted and put down by snipers.

Electrical ignition systems were out as well, but an electro-mechanical system initially seemed promising. Lavrov had long used mercury switches to great effect, and he had made some attempts to use a similar system in these devices. The problems, however, were twofold: the switches would either trigger prematurely if the device was not delivered smoothly to the target, or it would not trigger at all if the delivery was *too* smooth. Lavrov spent a couple of weeks at his villa in Buenos Aires playing with different electro-mechanical igniters before giving up on that idea.

That, essentially, limited the ignition systems to either some kind of delay – whether chemical or a timer – or a an impact trigger. A simple timer delay would be the easiest thing in the world to use. After a few weeks of carefully recording his multiple trials, Lavrov could determine with precision exactly how long it would take for one of his devices to travel to its target. His excitement, however, was mitigated by the realization that his men would need to be at precise, predetermined positions to deliver the devices – and it would be nearly impossible for all his men to be in exactly the right place at exactly the right time. A timer delay would be very useful in future applications, but it wasn't the right fit for this one.

That left a contact ignition system, which would be highly difficult to fit into the devices without affecting weight distribution. More than that, Lavrov couldn't figure out how to choose the precise location at which the devices would make contact, which would mean fitting multiple igniters along the sides and on the bottom. Months passed before he found an uninterrupted stretch of time to figure out a design that would work best, but eventually his efforts came to fruition. He put together a design that incorporated enough contacts that an explosion was almost certain to result – but he still wasn't satisfied. The many contacts weighed enough that the explosive itself could weigh less than a pound, and that probably would not be enough.

And then something happened that changed everything, all thanks to Lavrov's libido. He picked up a young German stewardess at one of his haunts in Buenos Aires, and she had proven far more useful than just satisfying his appetite. She had shown him an app on her iPhone that tracked her location with great precision and plotted her movements on a map. If anything, Lavrov had been more excited by her phone than by her body, and no sooner had he left her hotel room than he was searching the internet for the weight of an iPhone. At just under 0.25 lbs., even with wires and the actual triggering mechanism, it was perfect. He could use two pounds of explosives on each device, he quickly figured, and the weight distribution would be ideal. More than that, he wouldn't have to worry about timers or contact systems. His ignition system would rely on GPS. The monstrous helicopter landed in the same place every time, and it would be very easy for Lavrov to calculate its coordinates.

It took just a few days for Lavrov to assemble a prototype device after searching the dark web for instructions on how to toy with an unlocked iPhone to actually trigger an action at a predetermined set of coordinates. He excitedly tested his prototype and was satisfied that it would trigger properly within a few feet of the programmed destination. A few feet here or there wouldn't matter much, not with 2 lbs. of explosives. All Lavrov had left to do was select his men, train them in what to do, and scout the target area for approximate locations from which to launch the devices. Upon further reflection, he decided that while most of his bombs would use the GPS ignition system, he would also use a few contact devices as well. It was very possible that none of his devices would even reach his target; this way, there would still be a few explosions to terrorize people in the vicinity.

The Secret Service was not without a good amount of anxiety at the President's upcoming trip to Hawaii. The M252 81 mm mortars recovered from Hains Point had been determined to be just within range of the White House, and the Stinger missiles from New Jersey had served as a scary reminder at just how vulnerable Air Force One and Marine One were, even with their sophisticated countermeasures. Worse still was the notice from JSOC that while all mortar systems were now accounted for, there were still several MANPADs in the wind. As a result, Secret Service personnel, aided by the FBI and the military, were deployed en masse within a five mile radius of Andrews AFB to assure a safe departure, and the base at which the President would be landing on Oahu would only be selected on final approach.

The Director of the Secret Service had requested that the President travel to Andrews by motorcade instead of by helicopter, but his boss, the Secretary of Homeland Security, had shot down that idea firmly and forcefully. The President could not be seen to alter his routine in response to the terrorist attacks of the previous week, Moses Jackson had said, not altogether unreasonably. What Jackson didn't say was that he thought the whole idea of someone directly attacking this President – outside the political arena – was simply ridiculous. Besides, the helicopter ride was far shorter and more convenient for him, too; he would be travelling with the President and National Security Adviser, both as a political statement and as a practical matter. Less time travelling meant more time for golf.

The Director was not entirely satisfied with Secretary Jackson's outright dismissal of his strong suggestion, but there was little he could do. He told the President's Head of Detail, Stan Walker, to raise the issue discreetly with the President, but Walker, too, was rebuffed. The Director did, however, find some support from the Colonel commanding Marine Helicopter Squadron One, and the Colonel agreed to use five additional VH-3D Sea Kings to swap positions with the President's identical helicopter in a shell game that would start just as soon as Marine One lifted off from the South Lawn of the White House.

The well-dressed and neatly-groomed young men loitered near their four SUVs and two sedans parked at intervals around Ellipse Road NW. They had been chosen largely for their ability to blend in and their history of steadiness under fire. The skills needed for this mission were minimal; all they had to do was remove the devices from their cases, place them on the ground, activate the remote control, flip a switch on each device, and then shut down the remote control. Once the connection between each drone and its respective remote was broken, the drones would follow a pre-programmed course to the GPS coordinates selected by Lavrov, at which time the GPS on each iPhone would trigger an explosion. There were a dozen drones in all – all of them commercially available and costing just under $1,500 apiece. Nine of them had GPS triggers and three were equipped with contact ignition systems.

The VH-3D Sea King had landed without incident in an area where snow had been thoroughly cleared from the South Lawn, and the stage was being set for the President's departure.

His luggage was brought aboard the aircraft – Secretary Jackson's bags and those of the National Security Advisor had already been delivered to Air Force One by car – and an erstwhile young Marine sergeant took his place by the helicopter, prepared to render honors as the President boarded the craft. The sergeant did his best not to shiver visibly in the single-digit temperatures, having seen the numerous network news cameras pointed in his direction.

The departure ceremony of Marine One had become so frequent and routine over the years that it had long since stopped being covered live by the networks. Today, however, would be different. It was the President's first flight since the terrorist attacks against aviation the previous week, and this was a newsworthy event. Every single cable and network news channel would air live footage, and many local stations around the country would interrupt their routine programming to show the departure. Television executives, many with friends in the aviation industry, knew that it was important for the people to see the President unafraid to fly.

About fifteen minutes after the luggage was loaded aboard the Sea King, the President was seen leaving the White House, walking with the National Security Advisor and Secretary of Homeland Security, both of whom were close friends and important political allies. Special Agent Walker was within arm's reach of his charge, somewhat more anxious than usual at this most routine of departures. Several other Secret Service agents walked with the men as well, looking for any potential threats but seeing none.

The reporters assembled on the lawn a safe distance away called out questions to the President, who merely grinned in reply and waved his hand. He felt no need to address these reporters – he had already said everything he had to say. Not that the reporters expected anything different, of course; this President was often called imperious, in large part because he avoided taking questions from the media. At first, the reporters

393

had been excited to see a lectern set up in front of them, thinking that perhaps this time would be different. But the lectern had only been set up for some junior official to remind the assembled press how safe Marine One and Air Force One were.

When they reached the helicopter, two Secret Service agents entered first, followed closely by the National Security Advisor and Secretary Jackson. The President stood behind with Agent Walker and one other agent, turning back to the reporters and waving his hand again, as much to say good riddance as goodbye. Even the normally tame reporters had been unusually critical of the Administration in the aftermath of the attacks; that the weapons used were American and British in origin had already leaked, and everyone wanted to know how they had fallen into the hands of terrorists.

As the President turned to board his helicopter, one of the many onlookers pressed against the fence to the south of the White House hit the "send" button next to a text message programmed to send to 18 recipients. The message said, quite simply, "Begin." In the parking spaces along Ellipsis Road, three men moved quickly to each of their vehicles – two would launch the drones quickly while the third would ready his weapon to defend against any government agent who detected the launch. In all six cases, the devices were unloaded and launched within seconds, quickly speeding to their destination. There were, in fact, numerous Secret Service agents in the area, but none had been suspicious of these men and all were looking in precisely the wrong direction at the time of launch. They also failed to notice that inside the vehicles, Kalashnikov rifles had been readied for action; once the explosives detonated, the men would rush the White House fence and engage any target they could find.

The President strapped himself in, joking with his friends as the command pilot started the powerful engines, the rotors slowly coming to life. Special Agent Walker, a short distance away, was still anxious. He would only relax more once the President was aboard Air Force One and cruising at altitude, far above the range of Stingers. He would feel even better when he saw the fighter jets take up formation abreast of the massive plane. Still, so far everything was going as routinely as ever, and Walker felt the rotors pick up speed, knowing from experience that it wouldn't be long before Marine One lifted off.

A spotter on the roof of the White House saw them first, just as they crossed above the fence at an altitude of about 75 feet. "Drones – Cobrastrike!" he called into his radio, repeating the codeword used for such an eventuality several times as he reached for his sniper rifle and brought it to bear. "Damn, those things are fast!" he remarked to the man crouching next to him, searching for targets. The Secret Service had a protocol for an attack by drone. The first line of defense involved turning on powerful radio jammers to block the control signals for the drones, which would in theory cause them to drop from the sky. Not so this time, as the drones were effectively pre-programmed and operating without controlled guidance. None of them fell from the sky.

The second line of defense came into play at the same time, with agents positioned on the South Lawn drawing their service weapons – and in several cases, submachine guns – in an attempt to shoot down the drones. At this they were more successful; nine of the things were shot out of the sky halfway to Marine One. But two of them had been equipped with contact devices and exploded upon impact with the ground, either killing or seriously injuring several agents and causing the group of reporters to drop in terror. Three of the drones kept flying, and the two agents on the lawn who had them in their sights could no longer risk a shot out of fear of hitting Marine One.

The most important line of defense involved the President's personal safety. Here, the command pilot and Agent Walker were in an instant quandary; in the event that Marine

One was at full power, the playbook called for the pilot to zoom to altitude as quickly as possible while deploying flares and chaff, and then rotate away at speed. But the aircraft had only built enough power to just take off, and the pilot knew that he couldn't get to altitude fast enough. He was barely a few feet off the ground when he called out to Walker to execute the second option in the playbook, which was far simpler: get the President off the helicopter and race him to safety as quickly as possible.

The pilot landed hard, jostling the passengers and causing the President and Walker to waste a precious few seconds as they both fumbled with their seatbelts, trying to get them off. The pilot, seeing the delay, made an instant decision to deploy flares anyway. He would never have the chance to realize the magnitude of his mistake. The snipers on the White House roof had engaged two of the remaining drones, and an agent had the last one lined up in his sights when the sudden and unexpected burst of flares blinded him. He jerked the trigger, missing badly, and in the second it took him to readjust his aim, it was too late to matter.

The reporters were all on the ground, unable to see what was going on, hearing only gunfire and explosions. But a brave cameraman for NBC News remained standing, focusing on the helicopter. Millions of people around the world saw the door open and two figures rush out, one white and one Black. They made it all of thirty feet when the first explosion occurred, mere inches to the south of the helicopter. An instant later the rotors were sheared off, flying through the air as the helicopter seemed to start toppling over onto its side, suddenly destabilized by the force of the blast wave. The two men rushing away were knocked off their feet, and just as one of them was starting to rise, they were enveloped by a massive fireball. The hard landing had caused one of the fuel shut-off switches to malfunction; the first explosion had ignited vapors streaming from the engines, resulting in a second, much larger explosion, as Marine One came to an ignominious end.

38

It was their last day on South Beach, and they decided to spend it on a pair of lounges on the sand, in the shade of a light blue umbrella that bore the name of their hotel. First, however, they needed to see if the ocean was as warm and inviting as it seemed. After tucking their phones under their towels, Amanda gave Jack a playful slap on his rear and took off for the water, unbuttoning the shirt she wore over her bikini and dropping it on the sand as she ran, laughing. Jack was hot on her tail, dropping his own shirt very nearly on top of hers; he almost caught her as she plunged into the ocean, but then she dove fully in, just beyond his reach.

She swam out about fifteen feet and turned, surprised that she didn't see him anywhere. Just as she was about to stand to get a better view, she felt herself being lifted out of the water and found herself suddenly in Jack's arms. She started to laugh – a very special kind of laugh that only seemed to come out for him. "I got you," he declared with a grin as she turned to wrap her arms around his neck.

"You most certainly do," Amanda replied, her playful pout just asking for a kiss, which was promptly delivered.

"A little salty," Jack said, humor in his eyes as he licked his lips. "Ok then, back into the pot you go!" He made as if to throw her back in, and she screamed.

"Don't you dare!" She was laughing again – she just couldn't help herself around him.

"I wouldn't dream of it," he replied, placing her gently on her feet. "You most certainly are not catch and release," he declared, his hands on her waist as she leaned in to kiss him again.

"Neither are you, Jack. Neither are you." She felt a little sad that they would be leaving so soon, catching an American Airlines flight late in the afternoon so they could be back in the office Friday morning for a round of briefings. Four nights hadn't been nearly enough, but then Amanda remembered that this was merely one holiday – the first of many in what she was sure beyond a shadow of a doubt would be a long life together.

He didn't need to say it – she already knew. She knew from his eyes and from the way he looked at her, from his every touch and caress. She knew from his voice and from his laugh, from the way he smiled at her, even when he thought she wasn't looking. She could feel it in his heart when they were together, and feel it in hers when they were apart. He didn't need to say it, but he did – after dinner the previous evening, just after their dessert was delivered. He told her he loved her, and she had struggled to contain the tears welling up in her eyes. Neither of them gave their love easily, but with one another, they had given it easily and fully as well.

Jack's phone rang first, its loud tone somewhat muted by the towel placed above it. The ringing paused, just long enough for a message to be left, and then it resumed. It fell silent again as another message was left, but when it started ringing a third time, it would not stop. It was joined seconds later by the secure phone he had tucked in his messenger bag, now sitting atop the lounge. Finally, Amanda's phone rang as well, joining in the cacophony of sound demanding immediate attention. Jack and Amanda were still too far away to hear all this, just as they were too far to hear the sirens in the distance, racing across a causeway on approach to their hotel. They were walking slowly out of the ocean, hand in hand, talking and laughing in a moment of perfect happiness, not yet knowing the full extent of the storm that lay ahead.

www.ingramcontent.com/pod-product-compliance
Lightning Source LLC
Chambersburg PA
CBHW060144260626
47160CB00001B/115